WARSHOT

GEORGE WALLACE
DON KEITH

Severn River
PUBLISHING

WARSHOT

Severn River Publishing
www.SevernRiverPublishing.com

This is a work of fiction. Names, characters, businesses, places, events and incidents are either the products of the author's imagination or used in a fictitious manner. Any resemblance to actual persons, living or dead, or actual events is purely coincidental.

ISBN: 978-1-64875-123-3 (Paperback)
ISBN: 979-8-50788-329-5 (Hardcover)

ALSO BY WALLACE AND KEITH

The Hunter Killer Series

Final Bearing

Dangerous Grounds

Cuban Deep

Fast Attack

Arabian Storm

Warshot

Silent Running

Hunter Killer

By George Wallace

Operation Golden Dawn

By Don Keith

In the Course of Duty

Final Patrol

War Beneath the Waves

Undersea Warrior

The Ship that Wouldn't Die

Never miss a new release! Sign up to receive exclusive updates from authors Wallace and Keith.

Wallace-Keith.com/Newsletter

Dedicated to all the men and women who go down to the sea in ships in defense of the American way.

PROLOGUE

The mineral-rich fumarole had formed over a million years before. The volcanic opening in the planet's crust was ten thousand meters below the ocean surface in what mankind would, much later, name the Tonga Trench. Of course, when it first burst forth, the trench was several hundred miles to the west and north of its twenty-first-century location. As land masses continued to adjust their positions in response to inexorable geo-forces, the Pacific Plate was shoved beneath the Tonga Plate, taking the trench and the fumarole along with it as it slowly moved to the east and south. Now it rested at the center of a triangle of palm-studded islands: American Samoa, the Tongan island of Niuatoputapu, and the tiny nation of Niue.

Situated on the Pacific Rim's notorious and volatile "Ring of Fire," the fumarole provided an inexhaustible supply of thermal energy. It heated seawater to almost a thousand degrees before shooting it up into the cold blackness of the ocean depths. But before that, the water was forced through layer upon layer of sulfite-bearing rock. The sulfites dissolved, forming a sulfuric acid mixture. That acid, under searing-hot high pressure, dissolved the surrounding rock as the water rose through the fissured crust, and it all emerged as a mineral soup. Black tubes slowly built as the super-heated, acidic water hit the very cold ocean waters and dropped its mineral load. Micron by micron, over the eons, the tubes grew higher and higher, forming into towering pipes.

The nutrient-laden deposits were rich enough that a complete ecology of strange inhabitants slowly formed and evolved amid the growing black forest. Mammoth tubeworms drew their energy from the heat and minerals, using chemosynthesis since there was no light for photosynthesis at this crushing depth. Blind shrimp and huge, ghostly yellow crabs fed off the tube worms before falling prey themselves to other deep-water predators that stalked the dark abyss.

But one unique feature of this forest of black mineral pipes was another byproduct, one that lay on the ocean floor. One that would have glittered brightly had any hint of light penetrated these depths. The corrosive sulfuric acid passed through a thick, deep-seated vein of gold on its trip from the earth's innards, slowly dissolving it away. Once the mixture emerged into the cold ocean water, the gold precipitated out as a fine dust. Slowly, over the millennia, the gold dust had built up to form a deep layer of lustrous, invaluable mud, lying loosely on the sea bottom, undiscovered and untouched by man.

Ψ

Dr. Rex Smith rested in a chaise lounge on the deck of his ship, enjoying, as best he could, a fine cigar. It was difficult, though, due to the troubles he and his ship were facing.

The research vessel, *Deep Ocean Explorer,* currently considered Pago Pago, the capital city of American Samoa, as home.

At least so long as Smith and his team of scientists were in the area exploring the geology of the Southern Hemisphere's deepest trench. The tropical town was, in reality, far too small to be called a city. But what there was of it had just dropped below the horizon as Smith's white-painted ship motored away, leaving a frothy wake in the flat-calm, azure sea.

Smith relished the relaxed, warm beauty of the moment, the power and majesty of his vessel, the smooth taste of the cigar. But he really could not fully enjoy any of it. He had himself an especially knotty problem that spoiled the moment for him. At the end of the week, he would jet back to California to meet with his expedition's sponsors, who had made their expectations quite clear. They anticipated that his months of expensive exploration would have by now delivered some very real results. So far, his team had come up with very little, meaning he would not be able to secure the funding that he needed to continue his research. His ship and her crew required operating capital and plenty of it.

The ungainly vessel could never be said to have beautiful lines, but as a deep-ocean workhorse, she was ideal. A converted drill rig supply vessel, broad-shouldered and heavy, she was originally constructed to deliver to the North Sea oil fields in any weather, a job she had done for the first twenty years of her life. But those very attributes made her equally ideal for Dr. Smith's purposes, even if her capabilities had not yet fulfilled the hopes of those who wrote the checks. If only he could report some discovery of value, whether it be scientific, economic, historical, or valuably shiny.

Just then, Smith's attention was drawn to a bustle of activity on *Deep Ocean Explorer*'s open afterdeck. Mitch O'Donnell, every bit the red-haired Irish roustabout, was flailing his arms wildly, clearly in a heated discussion with Sandy McDougal. From the sounds drifting up from the deck, it appeared the petite scientist was more than holding her own with the gruff Irishman. It seemed, from the snatches that Smith could catch, that McDougal wanted to get the *Sea Raptor* unmanned underwater vehicle (UUV) into the water immediately to start a survey run. O'Donnell was every bit as profanely adamant that the newly modified submarine was not yet ready, that it required at least another day of testing.

Rex Smith sighed deeply and pulled himself out of the chaise lounge. He figured he had better get down there and intervene before the two hotheads actually came to blows. One of them could end up in the drink, and Smith knew them well enough by now to not take any bets on which one it would be.

"When did being chief scientist morph into being the playground monitor?" he grumbled under his breath as he started that way.

Just as Smith grabbed the ladder, Bill Bix stepped around the starboard side of the superstructure. The *Deep Ocean Explorer*'s captain was making one of his rare trips away from the bridge while the ship was underway. That alone was enough to cause Smith to pause and see what was up. Bix glanced down at the two bickering crewmembers, shook his head, and chuckled.

"Kids still arguing about their toy, huh?" The captain turned to Smith, all the humor dropping from his voice. "Rex, you see the latest? Just came over SOPAC News that 'King Two-for-One' has gone and signed the Chinese deal. He all but gave them a navy base at Nuku'alofa and the rights to build an international airport on the island."

Bix was clearly exasperated. King Tofuwanga II was derisively known by the moniker "King Two-for-One" for his propensity to sell any and everything on the islands of Tonga —where he was the nation's leader—to finance his lavish lifestyle. King Tofuwanga had taken the historic graft and greed of his ancestors to an entirely new level, though, making deals with the Chinese for loans that were theoretically to be used to build a shipping terminal, factories, sumptuous new infrastructure projects, and even—from scratch—a Tongan international airline, to be owned, of course, by Tofuwanga's government. Now those debts were coming due, little had been built with the money, and with practically no revenue, the king had no hope of even coming close to repaying them. The joke was that his people could hear him squeal as the Chinese tightened the screws. The shipping terminal, which handled very little shipping, would now become a navy base. And the airport, which serviced precious few flights, would almost certainly become a welcome host for the Chinese People's Liberation Army Air Force. Tonga International Airlines? It still consisted of a single aircraft, whose only passenger was King Tofuwanga II when he wanted to visit Sydney for a few nights of entertainment in King's Cross, or Bangkok for a week of who-knew-what.

Bix slammed his fist against the rail, his Australian accent becoming thicker and more difficult to understand as he grew angrier.

"Don't we ever learn anything? Our fathers fought a long, hard war to stop the Japanese from cutting off Australia's lifeline to the US. Hell, I lost two uncles when the *Canberra* went down during the Battle of Savo Island. Not to mention all the good people of these islands whose fathers and mothers suffered so much back then and who will now catch the brunt of all this corruption. All while we allow some two-bit Tongan grifter to give it to the Chinese without so much as a g'day?"

Smith put his hand on the skipper's shoulder.

"Easy now, Bill. We don't find something interesting out there on this run, Hitler could take over Tonga and it wouldn't make any matter to us." The scientist took the stub of the cigar from his lips and flipped it over the side, into the deep green water. "Let me see if I can just keep those two down there from murdering each other and try to salvage this situation. Let the politicians worry about the politics."

Bix shook his head as he turned and walked away, back to his wheelhouse.

Ψ

Several of the seats in the Senate Select Committee on Intelligence secure hearing chamber, hidden deep under the Hart Senate Offices, were empty, indicating members did not see the need to show up. Other senators had their laptops open, checking the day's stock market update or poll results from back in their home states, clearly uninterested in the hearing about to be gaveled into session. Even though it was an open hearing, C-SPAN had not deemed this afternoon's testimony worthy of television coverage. Not even on their third network.

At the table opposite the senators' perch, behind a microphone and a printed name card, a stunningly beautiful Asian woman, maybe thirty-five years old, patiently waited. The name on the card was Li Min Zhou. When the chairman of the Senate Intelligence Committee finally opened the proceedings, only a few of the senators perked up and appeared even remotely interested in hearing the woman's remarks. And a couple of those openly leered at the striking witness.

"Miss Zhou, we appreciate you coming here today at the behest of the...who was it, Pat?" A staffer whispered to the chairman. "Oh, yes. The junior senator from Virginia."

Senator Thad Murson was quite openly called the "Senator of the Navy."

The chairman's voice was almost a caricature of a Southern drawl. "We have an important vote on the Senate floor staring us in the face, I'm afraid, ma'am. Some banking bill the Democrats just had to bring up today when they thought we weren't paying attention. We have a copy here of your statement, which we'll certainly consider, so we'd appreciate it if you'd make brief opening remarks and we'll...maybe...have a few questions afterward. Okay?"

Li Zhou cocked her head and considered the senator for a long moment. She finally spoke, her voice strong, her face resolute, her eyes afire.

"Mr. Chairman, thank you. In the time it took you to introduce me, thirty-two children were born in China. That is over 1,900 every hour, almost sixteen million people per year. Despite what you may believe, virtually none of them will ever experience even the most basic of human rights or freedoms. Those who believe modern communications, the internet, or cable news will serve to inform and liberate the Chinese people by showing them a better way are, at best, delusional. And the communist government of my native country has long been using money, ironically obtained through their own version of capitalism, to..."

The senior senator from the state of Michigan, a four-term Democrat, abruptly and loudly closed his briefcase, stood, and stomped out of the hearing room. The senator had once personally intervened in and helped secure a huge Chinese investment in a renewable energy consortium in his state. One that had long since become defunct. He had heard enough.

Another member of the committee, the seventy-seven-year-old, six-term Republican from Mississippi, was jarred awake by the sound of his colleague's briefcase slamming shut.

Li Zhou's jaw tightened as she tried to remain calm.

"My father died in Tiananmen Square in Beijing on June 4, 1989. That day—my fourth birthday—brought to a bloody end the final realistic effort to bring any semblance of a free and open society to my country. Meanwhile, China has continued its mission to not only maintain brutal control over its own people but to gain influence around the world through the use of what I call 'dollar diplomacy' and they call the 'Belt and Road Initiative,' building industrial parks in Ethiopia, airports in Chile, shipping terminals and super-highways on Tonga, shopping malls in Nigeria, all with money loaned to those governments—who are often riddled with corruption— with no hope of ever repaying their debts other than capitulating to..."

"Miss Zhou, I've just been informed..." the chairman interrupted. Another staffer whispered in his ear. "Just been informed that the vote on the Senate floor is imminent. Is this information you were wanting to share this afternoon contained in the files you have left for us?"

"Yes, Senator, but..."

"Then we will recall you for further testimony at a future date, and we do appreciate y'all coming before this body..."

Li Zhou again cocked her head.

"Senator, what I hope to share with you could be the most crucial testimony to ever come before this committee. The most important information regarding the future of not only the United States but the entire..."

"I'm sure it is, Miss Zhou. I'm sure it is. But if we don't get this banking bill shut down, we'll all be in deep trouble come election time, considerin' where most of us get our campaign funds these days. And you have no idea how much it costs, even for an incumbent to continue to serve his..."

With a bang of his gavel, the chairman closed the hearing.

Li Min Zhou sat there at the table, her lips still inches from the microphone, seething.

1

Yon Ba Deng greatly enjoyed the respite his commute offered him each morning. Once the three-car motorcade—a bodyguard in front, another behind, and his own Mercedes-Benz limousine sandwiched in the middle—left his sprawling home in the exclusive Jade Spring Hill section of Beijing, they passed through some of the most exclusive parts of the capital city. He could almost—but not quite—imagine a totally peaceful world existed beyond those gardens and ornamental gates. But then, he ultimately arrived at his ceremonial offices in the heavily guarded Zhongnanhai leadership compound, immediately adjacent to the Forbidden City. That would certainly nudge him back to reality.

This morning, Yon Ba Deng could smell the foliage from Jade Spring Hill's quiet, park- like setting, even inside his vehicle with the bulletproof windows rolled up. Soon the red leaves would burst forth with their autumn splendor, announcing yet another winter was on its way. He watched the walled estates, the homes of the country's ruling elite, as they passed, but they quickly gave way to the bustling Xicheng district with its many restaurants, clubs, and vibrant nightlife.

Beijing's contrasts were always exciting to him. The juxta-positions. The anachronisms. That was what made living in modern China so invigorating.

But not today. Yon Ba Deng's rising excitement came from an entirely different direction this late-summer morning. He had to consciously calm himself. For that, he relied on his Taoist training, willing his racing pulse to slow, sending his mind in search of inner calm. He smiled slightly as he watched his own reflection in the car window. Another juxta-position. The ancient Taoist precepts being employed as a tool to assist his bold grasp for power in modern-day China. The ancients would smile at the paradox that presented. But they would certainly appreciate how Yon found the yin and yang of the situation perfectly comfortable and quite a useful tool in his quest.

The motorcade had just swung onto Lianhuachi West Road when Yon's private cell phone buzzed, rudely inter-rupting his deep thoughts. The only people who had the number were his wife, who was back at home sleeping, his mistress, who was on holiday in Macau, and his administrative assistant, who never slept or went on holiday.

Yon checked the encryption setting on his phone and answered, "Yes, Bing Dou. This must be important for you to disturb the peace of my morning commute."

His assistant was Yale-educated and had the knack—and the audacity—to always respond to his boss in his typical, somewhat sardonic, but classically honorific style.

"Elder brother, the vice deputy's office has called twice already this morning to inquire about your schedule. What should be my response?"

Since he held the title of Assistant Vice Deputy to the Minister of National Defense for Naval Matters, Yon Ba Deng ostensibly worked for the vice deputy, Soo Be Xian. But in the convoluted tripartite labyrinth of Chinese governance, titles did not necessarily denote hierarchy. In his case, Yon carried a similar title in the Communist Party's Central Military Commission. Soo did not. That made them about equal in rank and power. However, neither official had so far tested the pecking order.

When the lion prowls near the tiger, both are wary.

"If Minister Soo's office should call again, tell them that I am en route to the ceremonial offices at Zhongnanhai," Yon answered Bing Dou's question. "I will meet with the minister there. We can then discuss our next steps."

Yon clicked off. But always the obsessive-compulsive, he checked the phone again to be certain they were disconnected.

Next steps, indeed. Steps long in preparation. Steps now ready for implementation.

He tapped the partition between him and his driver.

"Could we stop admiring the scenery and proceed to work? With some haste, please?"

Ψ

TJ Dillon took a sip from his cup of tea, but his interest was on the far wall of the room. Across the table from him, Professor Sun Shen clicked the remote control, changing the charts and images on a presentation playing out on the large-screen monitor that covered much of the room beyond the table. The two men were sitting in the professor's office in the expansive glass-and-brick Central Weather Bureau offices in downtown Taipei, Taiwan. Traffic bustled past on the nearby Gongyuan Road, but the sound was little more than a distant hum, no louder than the projector's fan.

The screen revealed a chart of the island of Taiwan and the

surrounding ocean in a colorful three-dimensional representation. A red dot appeared in the deep water, well to the east of the island. Then, as they watched, a series of concentric circles developed and radiated out from the dot.

"As you see, Mr. Dillon," the professor stated, "an earthquake happening in deep water sends a shockwave out that propagates at the speed of sound in water, roughly one and a half kilometers per second. Or in your American measurements, about a mile a second. Most of the damaging earthquakes we have suffered have had epicenters at one hundred to one hundred and fifty miles offshore. That gives us about a minute to a minute and a half before a tsunami would strike."

TJ Dillon shook his head and let out a low whistle. "Sure ain't much warnin', Perfessor," he drawled, doing his best imitation of a Texan accent. "Reckon that's enough time to make much difference?"

Professor Sun Shen offered a wry smile and took a sip of his own tea before responding.

"There might be enough warning to get some of the emergency procedures underway. To put the sea gates in place to help prevent some of the flooding. But the tsunami is not our biggest problem. The more serious issue is the earthquake propagation through the crust."

He clicked a button. Suddenly, the concentric circles developed and radiated out from the red dot at almost lightning speed.

"As you can see, the tremors pass through rock at over five times the speed at which they travel through water. Where we had nearly two minutes' notification for the tsunami, we only have about twenty seconds' warning of the earthquake's shock wave. That is especially problematic for a number of reasons. For example, it takes fifteen seconds for an emergency stop of the bullet train, the Gaotie High Speed Rail. Those trains have less than half a meter's clearance when they are in the tunnels. At three hundred kilometers per hour, with this much distance between the train and the concrete walls..." Sun held his hands twenty inches apart. "And with so little warning of a powerful earthquake, you can imagine the catastrophe."

Dillon shook his head. "Wow! What you want us to do, then?"

"Mr. Dillon, we think that your company's experience in planting deep water seismic sensors can give us the additional warning we need to possibly prevent such destruction and terrible loss of life." Professor Sun Shen searched through a high stack of papers on his desk, found the one he wanted, and pulled it out. "I would like for you to go talk to Ameri Wang. He runs a construction company out on Yong Chi Road called GroundMat. I think your two companies may be able to make this work for the benefit of all."

TJ Dillon took the offered slip of paper, shook the academic's hand, thanked him for the presentation and the tea, and headed out. Back on the street, he watched the hustle and bustle all around with interest as he waited for his car. Dillon was once again impressed with the work ethic and efficiency of the people of this country, despite the constant threat from China hanging like a black cloud over them. He could not imagine what it must be like to live and thrive in the shadow of a massive and powerful nation, one that constantly maintained that they would one day take a step across the Taiwan Strait and stake their final claim on the island.

Dillon pulled out his phone and quickly placed an overseas call. The conversation was short and terse.

"We're in," he reported, now with no hint of a West Texas twang. "You have the sensor mods ready?"

The voice at the other end replied curtly. "We'll be ready

in time. Just make certain you get the gig without risking blowing our cover."

"Easiest assignment you've given me in a long time, Boss," Dillon shot back.

He ended the call. Then, always a bit obsessive-compulsive, he double-checked to be sure he had cut the connection.

Dillon's car pulled to the curb and he hopped in.

Ψ

The sun was just rising to the east, peeking above the wavetops out beyond Molokai. A warm breeze from the west brought the sweet scent of tropical vegetation out over the deep blue waters of the Pacific. Colorful small boats played near the shoreline and the high-rises of Oahu to the north, while large merchant ships waited out in deep water for their turn to enter the Sand Island Terminal.

Brian Edwards, captain of the US Navy's nuclear-powered submarine *George Mason*, took it all in from his perch on top of the submarine's sail. It was a time for calm reverie and relaxation before the hectic activity of entering a new homeport for the first time. A rare opportunity to enjoy the beauty, the pure peace and quiet of a dawn at sea.

"Captain," Lieutenant Bill Wilson, the officer of the deck, called out. Always the interruption, Edwards thought. Always. "Messenger to the bridge with your coffee and the message traffic."

Edwards nodded and returned to watching the distant horizon. Such vigilance was part submariner caution, the need to know about everything in his immediate world, and part fascination with the broad, open expanse of water that surrounded his warship. But he also wanted to keep an eye on something else going on at the moment. He occasionally glanced down into the bridge cockpit where Bill Wilson was busily teaching Ensign Sam Walters the intricacies of driving a submarine while on the surface. Walters was the newest officer in the *George Mason* wardroom. Fresh out of SUBSCHOL and the NUCPOWER training pipeline, he had reported aboard just as they were leaving Norfolk for the trip to *George Mason*'s new homeport in Pearl Harbor, Hawaii.

The messenger with the coffee, Seaman Strutt, appeared at the top of the ladder. With the lookout and the two junior officers already in the cockpit in the sub's sail, there really was not room for him to come all the way up into the daylight. He had to be satisfied with seeing the pale blue sky looking up from their feet. Strutt handed up the aluminum message board and cup of coffee for Edwards before taking one last glance at a clear sky and breathing in a deep draw of fresh air. Then he disappeared back down the ladder.

Edwards was idly leafing through the admin traffic and sipping his coffee when the 7MC speaker blared, "Bridge, Conn, XO to the captain. We are in voice comms with Pearl Harbor Control. We are delayed an hour for on outbound carrier. Also, we will do a PERSTRAN at Papa Hotel. Commodore Glass will be riding into port with us."

Joe Glass had been Edwards's skipper on *Toledo* when Edwards was XO of that boat. Now Glass was Commodore of Submarine Squadron Seven, based at Pearl. That once again made Glass his boss. Edwards smiled. It would be good working for Joe Glass again. And it appeared the commodore was looking forward to taking a very short cruise on a submarine again.

But right now, they had an extra hour to kill while they waited for an aircraft carrier to exit the harbor. Free time while underway and on the surface was not to be squandered, even for something as enjoyable as sightseeing off Diamond Head.

"Mr. Wilson," Edwards called down to the pair in the cockpit. "Please call below and have the XO get Oscar ready for a swim. Then discuss man-overboard procedures with your eager trainee."

Wilson grinned. "Yes, sir. We've already discussed the Y-backing and racetrack maneuvers. I was just covering the Williamson turn now."

Edwards smiled as he watched the young lieutenant swinging his hands around, explaining to the even younger ensign the complicated maneuver for bringing the big submarine around one hundred and eighty degrees so that it steamed right back down the precise same track that it had just covered. That way, if they lost sight of Oscar, or did not know where Oscar fell overboard, they could retrace their steps across the vast ocean until Oscar appeared right off their bow. At least that was the theory.

Seaman Strutt appeared at the top of the ladder again. This time he handed Oscar up to the lookout, who, in turn, gave him to Edwards. Oscar was, in reality, a large plastic trash bag with a crudely drawn face and the letters "OSCAR" written in magic marker. The bag was weighted so that it would float upright and not go skittering across the wavetops, all to adequately simulate some unfortunate crewmember who might fall overboard.

Edwards threw the dummy off the sail. It bounced once on the main deck and then fell into the sea. Once sure it had splashed down, the lookout yelled, "Man overboard, port side!" and began pointing at the green trash bag bouncing along the submarine's side.

Ensign Walters grabbed the 7MC microphone and

shouted, "Man overboard, port side! Left full rudder! All stop. Stop the shaft." So far, so good.

As the rudder swung over, *George Mason*'s stern pushed away from where Oscar floated as the pump jet propulsor spun to a halt, lest the poor "man overboard" should abruptly and tragically end his days by getting run through a giant Cuisinart.

Oscar fell astern of the submarine as the 1MC blared, "Man overboard, port side. Man overboard party muster at the lockout trunk."

Chief Schmidt, the pilot, sitting at his station some twenty-five feet below the bridge, was reporting, "Passing heading two-seven-zero, my rudder is left full. No ordered course. Passing two-six-zero. No ordered course."

The sub began to sluggishly wallow in the waves as she slid to a halt. The 7MC blared, "Hold Oscar visually, bearing one-three-two, range three hundred yards." The reports were coming fast and furious. Edwards squatted down so that he could more easily coach the now flustered ensign.

"Mr. Walters, let the rest of the crew do their jobs. You just need to drive the boat. What do you think the pilot is telling you? Don't you think he needs a course to steer?"

"Oh. Uh...yes, sir."

"Well, then, let's get some speed on and drive around to pick up poor Oscar," Edwards suggested. "Why don't you come to ahead full. When the heading comes around to sixty degrees off your old course, shift your rudder and order the reciprocal course. With this boat's advance and transfer, that will bring us right back to where Oscar is impatiently treading water. Got it?"

Walters nodded that he understood. Edwards was not entirely sure that was the case.

"All ahead full." Walters's voice wavered slightly as he

ordered the bell. The young officer was obviously working out his next order in his mind.

"Coming to ahead full," Chief Schmidt's voice boomed over the speaker. "Passing two-four-zero. No ordered course."

"Lost sight of Oscar," the lookout yelled. "I can't see him anymore."

The wheels were turning in the ensign's head as he quickly tried to do the mental calculations and give commands before they skated right past their "man" in distress. He had been on a course of three-one-zero when Oscar fell overboard. Skipper said to shift the rudder when they had swung sixty degrees, but that was two-five-zero, and they had already missed that. Better do something now, before it got even worse.

"Shift your rudder to right full," Walters ordered. "Steady, uh...uh. Steady one-three-zero."

Edwards nodded and encouraged the trainee. "Good. You swung past, but you can fix that. Just finetune it when you steady up. The navigator can help you with that when we come around."

"Oscar bears one-one-four, range seven hundred," the speaker blared. "Losing visual intermittently in the wave troughs."

The sub's executive officer in the control room below could still see the dummy using the photonics mast. But probably not for much longer. Oscar would soon disappear in the swelling waves.

The *George Mason* picked up speed as the propulsor bit into the waves. She swung around in response to the right full rudder. White water shot high up on the submarine's sail before washing back over the main deck.

"Lost Oscar visually," the XO reported. "Plotted bearing one-three-zero, range one thousand." Old Oscar was in real danger of becoming chum.

The wind coming off the island was picking up. Whitecaps now crowned the wavetops.

"Oscar estimated position bears one-two-two, range one-one-hundred," came another update.

"Steady course one-three-zero, making ahead full," Chief Schmidt reported.

"Bridge, Navigator, hold you one hundred yards to the right of track." LCDR Jim Shupert, *George Mason*'s navigator, was plotting their track on the sub's electronic navigation system, the ECDIS. "Recommend you steer one-two-two to regain track."

Edwards leaned forward and quietly spoke to Walters. "See what Nav is doing? He's easing you over to the old track so you get on line before you get to where we think Oscar is waiting for us."

"Oscar estimated position bears one-two-five, range nine hundred."

"We don't want to go flying past our guy at a full bell," Edwards whispered into Walters's ear. "And you need to get the man-overboard party topside. At a full bell, you would certainly get the COB wet."

Walters nodded and ordered, "Ahead one-third."

The large bow wave dropped to little more than a ripple climbing up the sub's rounded nose. The main deck was now high out of the water and would soon be dry.

"Bridge, XO, man-overboard party is mustered. Recommend sending the man-overboard party topside."

Walters looked questioningly at Edwards, who nodded. The ensign ordered, "Control, Bridge, open the lockout trunk upper hatch. Have the man-overboard party lay topside."

"Bridge, XO, regained Oscar visual. Bearing one-one-nine, range seven hundred, ten degrees off the port bow."

The lookout swung his binoculars in that direction. "I see

him!" the young seaman shouted, pointing toward the floating trash bag as it was lifted up on a wavetop.

"Probably a good time to rig out the outboard," Edwards coached, "and come to all stop."

The outboard was a small electric-driven outboard motor that could be lowered from the after ballast tanks and then trained to push the stern around when the sub was moving at slow speed.

"All stop," Walters ordered, this time with a bit more confidence. "Lower the outboard."

The submarine's propulsor quit driving the boat through the water as the throttle valves on the main turbines shut. The big boat glided forward under its massive momentum. Back in number-five ballast tank, the outboard slipped down out of its housing and into the boat's slipstream.

"Answering all stop," Chief Schmidt reported. "Outboard is deployed, trained to zero-zero-zero relative."

Oscar was now clearly visible, only a hundred yards ahead and just off the port bow, and so far, none the worse for wear.

"Give her a few seconds of back-one-third to stop her," Edwards suggested, "and then come to all stop."

"Back one-third," Walters ordered, applying the "brakes." *George Mason* shuddered mildly as the backing bell forced the big boat to slow its forward movement through the water. Just before the boat came to a halt, he ordered, "All stop."

Oscar floated serenely a mere ten yards off *George Mason*'s port beam.

"Mr. Walters, get Oscar back aboard," Edwards directed. "Now that we've saved the guy's life, we need to get moving toward Papa Hotel. The commodore's waiting for us over there and he's a busy man."

Edwards moved down into the cockpit and, in a voice that only Ensign Walters could hear, said, "Nicely done for your first one. Now, the key is to just pretend like you had complete control and knew exactly what was happening all the time." The skipper smiled. "My watchword is 'it's always better to be lucky than good.'"

With that bit of advice, Edwards disappeared down the ladder.

2

The gray ship sailed serenely through a spectacular early-morning twilight. A gentle breeze played across the vessel's bridge, bringing a faint earthy smell that mingled with the familiar tang of saltwater. Only her large battle ensign, snapping briskly in the breeze, belied the tranquility of the scene.

The USS *Tarbox*, the Navy's newest fast frigate—so new that her paint still smelled fresh—cut smoothly through the gentle swell. The bow wave curved up almost to where her hull number, 72, was painted on her bow. Her SPY-6(V)3 radar searched out to find every contact for hundreds of miles around the warship, but Commander Malcom Fritz, *Tarbox*'s skipper, was much more concerned about one particular return. That one marked the bit of land just appearing on the horizon off his ship's port bow. He could barely make out the low-lying island from his perch on the port bridge wing.

Only a few months ago, North Danger Reef had been a conglomeration of coral and rock, just barely emerging from the warm waters of the South China Sea. Marking a point at the northernmost end of the Spratly Islands, the reef had earned its name honestly, sending many an unsuspecting ship to its doom. These days, though, North Danger Reef appeared on the electronic charts under a new name. Dong Doa Island was the newest bit of Chinese-government-claimed sovereignty in these waters. Even if some of the islands hereabouts had barely enough dry "territory" to erect a flagpole and flag.

The *Tarbox*'s orders were to challenge that sovereignty claim. She was to steam boldly past the newly claimed real estate, conducting what were termed FONOPS—or Freedom of Navigation Operations—figuratively thumbing their noses at the Chinese government's assertion of ownership.

But something else had changed besides the island's name. A new airfield and missile launchers now fit on what had become a man-made spit of sand barely large enough to hold the improvements. China made no attempt to hide their purpose. They were meant to reinforce China's claim that all of the South China Sea was within her territorial waters. And beyond that, the Middle Kingdom could and would deny any nation the right to traverse that water. Violently if need be.

Dong Doa Island was merely the newest in a chain of airfields and anchorages that the People's Liberation Army Navy had constructed, ranging from the Spratlys in the south through the Parcels, and right on up to Hainan, the island province that marked China's southernmost point. Lately, the PLAN had been making noises about extending their claims all the way to the Riau Archipelago. That would effectively close off the southern entrance to the South China Sea while the Chinese continued to rattle their swords about claims to the Dongsha Islands at the northern end, chillingly near Taiwan. PLAN warships had been spotted frequently circling both areas from a menacingly close distance. The Indonesians did not say very much about incursions into the Riaus, but the Taiwanese complained loudly to anyone who would listen every time the PLAN sailed too close to Dongsha.

The heightened tensions were only one of the reasons Commander Fritz was concerned about these FONOPS. The other was because his crew was every bit as new and untested as his ship. They had completed their work-up training and left Pearl Harbor only two weeks prior. A quick couple of days in Guam had relieved the tedium of a long ocean transit, but the crew was distracted, anticipating arriving in Singapore. It would be *Tarbox*'s first ever foreign liberty port. The tales that the couple of old salts aboard had been sharing about the delights to be found in the tropical city had everyone anxious to speed across the intervening distance. And that was exactly what they had been doing until just before sunrise.

That was when some desk jockey back in the Pentagon noticed that North Danger Reef was barely off the ship's track. Maybe they should make a quick detour, knock, and say "Hi" to their Chinese friends in the area.

Commander Fritz barely had enough time to break out Seventh Fleet's FONOPS instructions, scan them, and hold a hurried discussion with his XO and ops officer. None of them had any experience with FONOPS, but thankfully, it looked simple enough. All they had to do was veer slightly off their original course, steam through the disputed waters with their flag flying, then resume the trek toward shore leave. Should they be challenged, they were to respond that they were peacefully exercising their right to pass through these waters under international law. And then, of course, they would have to write a report detailing their transit of the disputed area and everything that transpired. All sounded simple and easy. Besides, how many other ships had conducted FONOPS without serious incident?

"Captain." The officer of the deck stuck his head out to the pilothouse. "We are being challenged on the bridge-to-bridge circuit, channel sixteen."

Fritz frowned as he stepped inside the pilothouse so that he could hear the radio speaker.

"American warship, this is Dong Doa Control. You have entered restricted waters. You will secure all electronic emissions and leave Chinese waters immediately." The voice was harsh and seemed to brook no discussion.

Fritz snorted as he grabbed the microphone. "This is the USS *Tarbox*. Please be advised that we are engaged in freedom of navigation of these waters as is our right under international law. We do not recognize Chinese claims that these are territorial waters."

"*Tarbox*, I repeat, you will immediately secure all electronic emissions and change course to leave our waters or you will be engaged." Immediately after the voice stopped, static burst from the speaker.

"Captain, Combat," the tactical action officer reported over the tactical circuit. "We are being jammed on all frequencies. All radars are down. I think we detected an aircraft launch just before we lost the SPY-6. The X-band precision tracking radar locked on for just a second."

"Locked onto what?" Fritz asked. The X-band was an anti-air fire control radar programmed to automatically lock onto threat profile airborne targets. It had detected something that fit a threat profile. If the system was in automatic mode, anti-air missiles would already be outbound. But this was peace time. The Chinese may fly something close by, but it was all for show.

Right on cue, a Shenyang J-16 strike fighter came in low and fast. Fritz shook his head. Obviously, these guys had ratcheted up their show of force a notch or two.

But then, the first burst of fire from the aircraft's GSh-30-1 thirty-millimeter cannon tore through the frigate's bridge and shredded the comms masts. A YJ-12 anti-ship missile

impacted, penetrating deep into *Tarbox*'s interior before deto-
nating in the vessel's CIC just seconds after the fighter roared
directly overhead.

In fifteen seconds, the proud warship was reduced to a
burning, defenseless hulk.

A salvage tug was already steaming out of Dong Doa's tiny
harbor, headed directly toward the burning ship. It would take
just over an hour to rescue the survivors, extinguish the fires,
and put what was left of the *Tarbox* under tow, headed back to
the tiny outpost in the South China Sea.

Meanwhile, thousands of miles away, people were already
trying to figure out why the Navy's newest warship and her
crew had seemingly vanished from the face of the earth.

Ψ

The MQ-4 Triton orbited at sixty thousand feet, far too
high to be seen by the frequent Tokyo-to-Singapore airline
flights passing twenty thousand feet below the gray-and-white
unmanned spy plane. From this high perch, Triton flight PE
Six-Zero sent a steady stream of data back to its "pilot" and
sensor operator, senso, who were sitting in a cinderblock
building at Naval Air Station Jacksonville, Florida. PE Six-
Zero's pilot, Lieutenant Cindy "Stick" Sidirourgos, had not
actually seen her bird up close in more than six months. Her
squadron, VUP-19, was homeported at NAS JAX, only a couple
of blocks from the main runways. Their six Tritons, however,
flew out of Anderson Air Force Base, high on a bluff in the
northeast corner of Guam, over eight thousand miles away in
the Mariana Islands.

Most of the considerable data that Six-Zero sent back from
its package of state-of the-art sensors held little interest to
Cindy Sidirourgos. She was only considering the information

from the drone that she needed to know to be able to fly the bird. All that appeared on the four large flat-panels that fronted her "cockpit." The rest of the bits and bytes went to the senso and then were shunted off to the numerous organizations and three-letter government agencies that really cared about what was going on in the contentious waters of the far western Pacific.

The flight up from Guam had taken almost three hours. Then, as ordered, Sidirourgos put her bird into a long elliptical search orbit. After a few quick button pushes, confident the craft was obeying her commands, she stood to stretch. The bird—she secretly and affectionately called it "Polly"—would now fly itself for a while. She shivered in the blast of cold air conditioning designed to keep the electronics cool, ignoring the humans and their comfort, then threw her leather flight jacket over the green flight coveralls she routinely wore when she was "flying a mission." Sidirourgos then stepped across the hall to the tiny pantry for a cup of coffee and a donut.

Flying these ocean surveillance missions was hard, boring work, collecting valuable data, and she was responsible for the well-being of a very expensive hunk of machinery. Four hours in the cockpit, then four hours off, followed by four more hours flying, all to complete the twelve-hour watch. Four days on, then four days off.

Sidirourgos selected a plain glazed donut, not one of the jelly-filled ones she preferred. Just one more day to go, and then it was beach time. Four days of fun in the sun with her boyfriend on the sugary sands of Seagrove Beach, one of the Florida Panhandle's best. She could hardly wait. But she had been watching her figure lately, better to fit into her new bikini.

Just then, the red light hanging outside the cockpit door flashed and the buzzer blasted. Something was happening to her bird. Sidirourgos quickly put down her coffee cup—no open liquids allowed in the cockpit, a cup of coffee spilled in the wrong place would be a bad day for a lot of people—and stuffed the rest of the donut in her mouth as she hurried back.

The chat link with Seventh Fleet was flashing red as she plopped down in her seat, still chewing.

"Mission PE-60, Seventh Fleet Ops," the text on the screen read. "Emergency re-target your mission. Establish patrol area vicinity one-two-dot-five north, one-one-four-dot-eight east. Conduct all-sensor search. Target of interest USS *Tarbox*. Last contact eight hours, vicinity Spratly Islands. Highest priority. Report contact with *Tarbox* Op Immediate."

She frowned, shook her head, and quickly re-read the message. In her six years in the Navy, Cindy Sidirourgos had never seen a communication like this one. Quickly acknowledging the text, she grabbed the joystick and swung the big bird around to its new course. Then she pushed the throttles to the firewall. After punching the ordered coordinates into the nav system, she learned that she had an hour's flying time before she began this new and seemingly urgent mission.

Time to finish that coffee and maybe indulge in a second donut. No way it could show up on her thighs or hips in just one day, right?

Ψ

As the unmanned MQ-4 spy plane reached the northern end of its new search area, the senso, AWP-1 Flint Allerman, set up the systems for an all-sensor search of the cluttered ocean area far below. To the east and south was a vast area of rock, shoals, and tiny islands. Thousands of fishing boats littered his sensor screens. Just to the west were the main shipping channels through the South China Sea, perhaps the most heavily trafficked sea lane on the planet. Locating a lone frigate in all this clutter was not going to be easy.

Then, as Allerman watched intently, the image on the screen abruptly turned to fuzz. And there was nothing being reported by any of the bird's sensors. Even the optical and IR circuits were suddenly out. Something very powerful and very close was actively jamming his bird, something the senso had never seen before. Not even during his extensive training.

Allerman was just keying his mike to call Sidirourgos when her voice blared over his speaker.

"Senso? Pilot. I've lost contact with our bird. What are you seeing?"

Ψ

Eight thousand miles away from where the two stared at their suddenly blank screens, the shattered remains of "Polly," PE Six-Zero, fluttered down, eventually plunging into the sea far below. Meanwhile, the pilot of the Shenyang J-16 fighter was busy on his radio, proudly reporting that his mission had been successfully completed and that he was now returning to base on the speck of land once called North Danger Reef.

Ψ

TJ Dillon braced himself against a stout sea breeze as he stood outside Eluanbi Lighthouse, at the far southern end of Taiwan, overlooking the South China Sea to his right, the Philippine Sea to his left, and a narrow, rocky beach almost a thousand feet below. Down there was a flurry of activity. A couple of bright yellow dozers were pushing piles of sand around. Barges and tenders were making regular shuttle runs between the spit of land and a bright red ship that rode at anchor half a mile offshore.

Dillon did not need his powerful binoculars to read the six-foot-tall white letters along the ship's high side, spelling out "GLOBAL MARINE." He could also easily read the ship's name, CS *Sovereign,* in smaller black letters toward her stern. Dillon's employers had hired the British cable company, an affiliate of British Telecom, to do some critical cable laying. In the process, they used a fictitious but legally valid corporation to execute the contract and deliver the deposit for the job. In truth, British Telecom had not deemed it necessary to investigate the transaction very deeply once the check cleared. Besides, they had done business with this particular "company" before, and all had gone well. So, there was nothing that could tie back this job to Dillon's actual employer. One of those three-letter US government agencies.

As Dillon watched—now through his binoculars—a heavy black line draped over the ship's stern and disappeared below the waves. A pair of tugs laboriously pulled a large barge loaded with heavy equipment toward the beach in a straight line from the cable-laying ship. A heavy crane hung out over the barge's broad stern with cables and power lines disappearing from it into the water. The last few thousand yards to the beach were where a submarine fiber-optic cable was most vulnerable. Anchors, fishing trawls, just about anything somebody dragged along the shallow bottom could snag on and break them. For this reason, the barge was guiding a remotely operated trencher as it buried the cable on the bottom and right up to the water's edge under ten feet of sand, stone, and bottom muck.

As Dillon watched the process play out far below, his encrypted cell phone buzzed.

"TJ, how's it going?" Dillon immediately recognized the

voice of Rear Admiral Jon Ward. Now this was a most unexpected call. "Looks like we are getting good data from the north string as well as the ones on the east coast. The data extraction seems to be working quite well."

Ward was cryptically referring to the technology hidden in the sensors now tapping off raw hydrophone data at the shore terminal and re-routing it back to the US for intense analysis. And the technology was doing its job while not allowing the Taiwanese engineers any opportunity to detect hacking on their seismic monitoring system. They were listening for the first rumblings of earthquakes and resulting tsunamis. But thanks to fiber-optics and the wonders of the internet, the spooks back in Norfolk were studying the same data, looking instead for Chinese submarines.

"Jon, guess I shouldn't be surprised that you are read in on this particular little operation," Dillon answered. "After all, you're now the Navy's top spook."

Jon Ward was a former submariner who had been kicked upstairs. Way upstairs. He now ran Naval Intelligence from his office at the Pentagon in Washington, D.C., after the retirement of its longtime head, Tom Donnegan.

"Yeah, and after all the times we've worked together, your boss was happy to help us with this little plan," Ward responded with a chuckle. It still amazed Ward how often other agencies, purportedly defending the country against the same foes, could not seem to be able to cooperate. "But look, since you are really over there vacationing on my nickel, I figure you have another day or so in Eluanbi to wrap things up, so why don't you enjoy a couple of days in Taipei? You gotta have dinner at Din Tai Fung on Xinyi Road. Michelin Star and the xiaolongbao are out of this world. Easy walk from the Grand Hyatt."

"Admiral, thank you for the suggestion," Dillon replied.

"You know my previous visits to the area were considerably more stressful. And the best meals we had were MREs. Far as I know, Michelin hasn't rated those things."

Dillon was a retired Navy SEAL, called back into service doing covert and dangerous duty on behalf of the aforementioned three-letter government agency.

"Delicious, I know. But at the time, you were probably glad to get them, right?"

"Always. They were meals and they were ready to eat. Thanks, Admiral, and I'll let you know if I see anything out of whack over here."

"Likewise, TJ. Be careful, though. You never know. You just never know."

Ψ

Jonathan Ward sat back in his big office chair. He was still getting acclimated to being a flag officer, having an office in the Pentagon, a desk half the size of an aircraft carrier, a chair with electronic adjustments for height, tilt, and back resistance. Nothing like these digs in all those submarines he had ridden for most of his military career. And he had already developed even more respect for what Tom Donnegan, his predecessor and godfather, had been forced to contend with. Papa Tom was retired now, obsessing over his orchids and watching his beloved submarines going into and out of Pearl Harbor from his lanai, high up on Aiea Heights in Pearl City, Hawaii. And that meant Jon Ward now had the unenviable task of wading through yet another stack of reports that somebody somewhere who outranked him believed needed reading.

Most were important, frightening, but ultimately boring. This latest one, though, Ward did not like. No, not at all. The reports out of Southeast Asia—and particularly the South China Sea—had been especially worrisome for quite a while now. The Chinese had upped their belligerent stance considerably with a lot of talk about the Middle Kingdom returning to its rightful place among the world's nations, to fully revert to center stage after what they termed the "Century of Humiliation." Ward well knew that the Chinese Communist Party viewed the Middle Kingdom's rightful place was to be the world's dominant power economically, but more. Right now, it was clear that they were looking to a military effort to convince the rest of the planet of that fact.

The *Tarbox*'s mysterious disappearance and the loss of the drone Triton flight PE Six-Zero certainly added to the angst that the Navy's new top spook was feeling. Was this only the initial steps in a deadly escalation? Were the Chinese looking for some kind of rash retaliation, some overreaction, so they could claim to be in the right and that the United States was the imperialistic aggressor at their doorstep? Jon Ward needed some answers and he needed them now.

He jumped up and stepped to his office door. "Get me General Willoughby on the phone. He's over at the Australian Embassy," he told his aide. "Then get me COMSUBPAC. I need a couple of subs and I need them quick."

Ψ

Yon Ba Deng smiled broadly as he read the message traffic. Those haughty Americans had fallen into his trap, just as he knew they would. Flying the "stars and stripes" as they openly flaunted international law and sailed into Chinese waters to show their muscle and thumb their noses. And using one of their weapon radars was proof that they were hostile.

Then, just as he also knew they would, they flew one of

their spy planes over to see where their missing ship might be. The only regret was that they had used one of their new remotely controlled, unmanned contraptions. Otherwise, even more dead Americans would be littering the bottom of the South China Sea, paying the price for violating Chinese air space.

The phone on his desk buzzed.

"Ni xiang yao shenme?" he called out to his assistant, Bing Dou, in the outer room.

"It is your brother calling," the aide announced. The telephone continued to buzz. "He wants to speak with you."

Even having a brother was an extreme rarity in modern China. Although the one-child policy had been relaxed over a decade ago, it would be many more years before family dynasties again became common in the country. Except at the very highest levels, of course. The privileged and the favored had always remained exempt from the Party's political excesses. And a good thing that was. It assured a steady supply of the best and brightest. And those most loyal to the Party.

Yon Ba Deng punched a button on his phone. "Didi, ni hao ma?"

"I am fine, elder brother," Yon Hun Glo replied. "I have just returned to Yulin from a patrol down to the Riau Archipelago. I suddenly learn that I have jumped from senior captain and commander of a submarine to vice admiral. And that I now command the PLAN Submarine Force. Elder brother, is this your doing?"

Yon Ba Deng chuckled. "I may have had some small part in bringing your talents to the attention of the Party decision makers. As Confucius teaches, 'No one can find fault with what his parents and brothers have to say about him.' And I am sure you recall that Sun Tzu told us, 'The strength of the nation derives from the strength of the family.' We, together, will now contribute much to the strength of our nation."

Yon Ba Deng had the remarkable ability to instantly quote from memory the most appropriate phrase from *The Art of War* by Sun Tzu, regardless of the situation or context. Just then, Bing Dou stuck his head through the massive doors to the outer office.

"Excuse my interruption," the assistant murmured. "Soo Be Xian is here and demands to see you immediately. He does not appear to be calm."

Ah, yet another occurrence fully anticipated by Yon Ba Deng. The Vice Deputy to the Minister of National Defense stormed through the door without waiting any longer, shouldering Bing Dou aside. The short, portly bureaucrat, clearly agitated, waved a document in his hand. Then he slammed it down on the desk and, ignoring the fact that Ba Deng still had the telephone to his ear, yelled, "What is the meaning of this? I never authorized using force against the Americans! Are you trying to usurp my authority?"

Yon Ba Deng said a quick goodbye-and-good-luck to his brother, then gently returned the phone to its cradle. He glanced at the report and smiled.

"Worthy Vice Deputy Minister," he answered, lingering slightly on the "vice" title to give it just the proper amount of emphasis to make his point. "The Party Central Military Commission approved those actions. You must recall that I hold office there, too. If the Party chose not to inform a government official, it is the Party's way, and I, for one, do not question the Party's decisions."

He smiled—proud he had mentioned the word "Party" multiple times—as he politely picked up and handed the offending document back to Soo Be Xian.

"But I..."

"And I might suggest that you take a similar stance. I find that questioning the Party is not profitable. Perhaps in the future, we should work together more closely to avoid these unfortunate misunderstandings. I do not know how the Party might react if they believed you and I were not pulling together to accomplish the Party's ultimate goals."

Soo Be Xian closed his eyes, fought to control his breathing, then muttered that perhaps Yon Ba Deng was correct. He nodded, backing his way to the door, then turned and left the office much less dramatically than he had entered it.

As the outer office door closed, Bing Dou frowned, raised an eyebrow, and glanced at his master questioningly.

Yon Ba Deng smiled and rubbed his chin.

"Sun Tzu said something else. 'We are to build our opponents a golden bridge across which to retreat.' Of course, I just gave the vice deputy minister a golden bridge that will not only allow him to retreat, it will ultimately lead him to his defeat."

Ψ

The New China News, the CCP's official mouthpiece, broke the news on its nightly Asian round-up. In a short, low-key piece, the news anchor, with a full-color map of the South China Sea as a backdrop, stated that an American warship had entered Chinese territorial waters near a scientific and military base on Dong Doa Island. When challenged about their illegal act, the American ship had initiated hostilities by opening fire on the island's Coast Guard base.

The backdrop zoomed in to show the Spratly Islands with a large red star marking the location of Dong Doa.

Though only a very small garrison with limited defensive weaponry, the Chinese had bravely and rightfully defended themselves against this unprovoked attack. The American vessel, identified as the USS *Tarbox*, was defeated and nearly sunk. After the crew surrendered and pleaded for mercy, the ship had been quickly stabilized and salvaged by the efficient, well-trained crew of the People's Liberation Army Navy tug *Nan-Tuo Pennant 185* and towed to safety in Dong Doa harbor. The surviving crew were being held there until they could be tried for their crimes before the People's Court.

The screen shifted to show the aggressor ship's burnt and battered gray hull, the number—72—just visible through smoke-blackened paint.

The news anchor shifted to a story about a state visit from the president of Azerbaijan, including an official trip to a cellular telephone manufacturing plant and a tour of a new robotic soybean-processing facility.

Ψ

Stanley Smitherman, the president of the United States, sat behind the Resolute Desk, his elbows resting on its glossy oak surface, idly chewing on a huge bite of beef jerky. Two of his cabinet members awaited his questions. Secretary of State Sandra Dosetti and Secretary of Defense Harold Osterman were the only other people in the Oval Office at the moment. Each sat, as if at attention, in relatively new straight-back chairs, directly across the ancient desk from the president. They had both watched carefully to be sure he had not switched on his recording device.

The late-afternoon sun cast a warm, golden glow through the thick bulletproof windows behind Smitherman. The effect, however, belied the tense mood permeating the big room.

"Okay, what do we do about this *Tarbox* fiasco?"

Smitherman finally asked, his thick Texas drawl almost as pronounced as the *Saturday Night Live* characterizations of him. "Sandy, what in hell do those experts of yours say?"

Sandra Dosetti, a major player in her political party, hailed from the northeast corridors of power and academia. She had unofficially been dubbed by some in the media as the "Secretary of State for Wall Street." She hesitated for a moment before answering, a trait often mimicked by members of her staff. Behind her back, of course. Then she cleared her throat and spoke.

"Well, Mr. President, our ambassador in Beijing advises me that the Chinese military is now on heightened alert. And our China desk warns that everything they are seeing points to an unprecedented belligerency from both the government and the Party. They are recommending we deal with this with a very delicate touch diplomatically so as not to play into whatever scheme they are carrying out. They believe overreacting would be a costly mistake."

"Scheme?" The president was biting off another big piece of jerky.

Ever the astute politician, Secretary Dosetti ignored the question, referring to a sheet of paper on her lap. "Our polling is showing a very mixed voter response to media reports about tensions with China and our administration. Sixteen percent favor a show of military strength. Forty-two percent want to go to the United Nations for a resolution. Almost forty percent of the respondents were undecided. The rest is statistical noise."

"Soccer moms." Smitherman snorted. "That's the ones where we're lagging. Where do the damn soccer moms fall? I figger that's always the best road sign on which way to turn."

"Mr. President," Dosetti replied. "I am afraid I don't have an answer for you there. That particular demographic made up most of the undecided sample."

"Well, that sure as hell ain't much help," President Smitherman grunted. He turned to the Secretary of Defense. "Help me here, Harold. What does the military make of all this struttin' and spittin'?"

Harold Osterman, newly confirmed as Secretary of Defense, represented the West Coast power structure in the Smitherman regime, specifically Silicon Valley and Hollywood. He was still finding his way around the labyrinthine corridors of the Pentagon.

"Mr. President, the Joint Chiefs are doing their usual little noncommittal routine, but the best I can tell, they don't think we are in a position to go head-to-head against the Chinese right now. Especially way out there. Our supply chains are very vulnerable. We depend on Chinese sources for many vital materials, not the least of which are high-performance computer chips and the primary ingredients for solar panels, which your administration is pushing very hard."

Smitherman muttered a decided, "Harrumph," in response to Secretary Osterman's last statement.

The SECDEF ignored him and continued. "Military intelligence informs us that they would expect a strong military response to any action we take, claiming they are only defending their historic territories in the South China Sea. You know they've put a flag on every rock, reef, and turtle in that ungodly pool of water. You saw that silly twelve-segment, dotted-line map they just released. It shows them claiming everything from just off Vietnam all the way around the South China and Philippine Seas to northeast of Taiwan. Including Taiwan. Any miscalculated armed response and things could easily spiral into something very damaging. Maybe even World War III, and the Joint Chiefs have no assurance that we would win such a conflict."

President Smitherman leaned way back in his leather desk chair and clutched his hands behind his head.

"Well, that kinda decides things, then, don't it? We hem and haw for a bit, and just let everything play out with the talking heads on the news channels doing all our fussing for us. Make a fire-and-brimstone speech in the UN that nobody will notice. We'll keep everybody on alert over there, just in case the Chinese get stupid about it. But this *Tarbox* thing will have all died down and been forgotten long before the primaries start in the early states. Then we can tell 'em how tough we've been and how we kept the peace. Right?"

Both secretaries nodded their agreement and simultaneously said, "Yes, Mr. President."

"Oh, and Harold. Have your folks get with my folks and get the names and numbers of the wives and mothers of the boys we lost out there on that ship. Once the media knows, I'll give 'em all a call and let 'em know how deeply sorry we are for their sacrifice. All right?"

"Girls, too, sir," Secretary Dosetti interjected.

"What?"

"Girls. Two young female sailors were lost in the incident."

"Yeah. Well. Of course. Thank you."

3

Soo Be Xian was in a full rage by the time he returned to his offices at CMC Headquarters in the First of August Building. The long car ride through thick, tedious traffic from central Beijing had not helped diminish his anger. It only served to remind him that Yon Ba Deng had benefit of a palatial office at Zhongnanhai in the Forbidden City. But he, Yon Ba Deng's superior, was relegated to little more than a closet at the Ministry of National Defense on the outskirts of western Beijing, far from the seat of power.

Soo Be Xian stormed into his office suite, slamming the door behind him. Bien Sung, his general factotum, was waiting, wringing his hands. "General Xiang is on the video conference line already. It is past time for your meeting with the Southern Theatre of Operation staff."

Soo Be Xian waved him off as he stepped into his inner office. He plopped down in the red leather armchair at the head of the heavy mahogany conference table. The far wall was covered with a large-screen display. Colonel General Xiang's florid face nearly filled the screen. The three-star general was one of the most senior officers in the People's

Liberation Army. He commanded the Southern Theatre of Operations and the three complete armies stationed there. With these forces, General Xiang was responsible for protecting China's southern border as well as projecting the government's will toward the south.

Xiang's chief of staff, Major General Shun, was just visible in the background, looking over his boss's shoulder. Soo well knew that Shun was the iron fist and real brains on this team. Shun would be his most dangerous enemy or his greatest ally, depending on where his allegiance would ultimately lie. And Soo knew that Shun's greatest loyalty, above all else, lay with the People's Liberation Army.

Soo began the meeting. "General Xiang, General Shun, it is good to see you again and I apologize for my tardiness. Traffic in this city is impossible. Now, I have read your reports detailing the conditions of your forces. I must say I am most concerned with the lack of coordination that the PLAN appears to be giving your One-Twenty-Fourth Amphibious Division. It concerns me that our brothers in the PLAN seem to harbor some disrespect for your Land Forces."

Soo could see General Shun visibly bristle at this. He had taken the baited hook.

"But that is only part of the problem our Navy friends have caused," the vice deputy minister went on. "It seems that some in the higher reaches want to kick the Americans some more." He held up the same report that he had waved in Yon Ba Deng's face. "I am sure that you have seen this action report about the latest so-called FONOP by the Americans and the PLAN's dangerous response." He slapped the paper onto his table. "This presents us with two problems. First and most obvious, the Americans will once again have cause to bluster and pontificate on the subject of the 'freedom of the seas.' We must be fully prepared to provide a strong response to them should their rhetoric escalate beyond the verbal. The second problem is that all this sea-going schoolyard pushing and shoving will inevitably cause the Party to move even more resources to the PLAN. They are clearly committing assets and influence in the direction of the navy at great costs to our army."

Soo took a deep breath and watched both men's responses. Xiang and Shun, as expected, were angry and agitated. But both remained silent, waiting for Soo to go on.

"However, I believe we can successfully resolve both problems with one bold stroke. It is really quite simple. We will move the crisis so it becomes a land-based one. One where only the PLAN is in a position to respond. General, you will move several brigades of the Fourteenth Army from Kunming down to the Vietnam border across from Lao Cai. At the same time, deploy the Forty-First Army brigades from Liuzhou down to the border at Lang Son. You will not be subtle in making these moves. Create much dust and noise. We will let the world think that we are replaying the 1979 incursion. But I do not want you to do anything other than make abundant noise and dust. Do you understand?"

He looked carefully at the two generals. Xiang, as expected, gravely nodded. And also as anticipated, Shun was unable to hide a sly grin.

Soo signaled and the screen went blank. He rose, stretched, and smiled. Bien Sung entered the office with a cup of tea on a tray.

"Did it go well, Minister?"

"Indeed. Very well," Soo told him, almost gleefully. "We will teach that peacock, Yon Ba Deng, who really understands the quotations of Sun Tzu. Remember, Master Tzu also said 'Engage people with what they expect; it is what they are able to discern and confirms their projections. It settles them into predictable patterns of response, occupying their minds while you wait for the extraordinary moment — that which they cannot anticipate.' We will soon see if he is familiar with this quote."

Ψ

Joe Glass stood back and watched all the activity that surrounded him, yet he took no part in it. This was an entirely new position for him. He was in the back corner of the USS *George Mason*'s control room. All of the high technology and the highly trained team were working like a well-tuned race car engine. But Glass was all too aware that they were not his team. At least not directly. Nobody turned to him with a question or report. Those were all directed to Brian Edwards, the skipper of this boat, who was standing next to him. Glass's only role was to observe and evaluate.

"We're at the launch point, Skipper," LCDR Jim Shupert, *George Mason*'s navigator, called out. "Range Control reports that the range is clear, COMEX in two minutes. Launch helo is outbound."

Glass glanced at the electronic navigation chart. Only the Navy would saddle it with a name like "Electronic Chart and Navigation Display System," ECDIS for short. The chart showed that they were located about ten miles west of Kauai and equidistant from Niihau to the south, almost in the center of an area marked off as the Barking Sands Tactical Underwater Range. The BARSTUR range was in deep water, safely far enough away from shipping channels, but close enough to the island to heavily instrument the bottom of the sea so as to accurately track submarines and surface ships operating there.

Glass glanced up at the large-panel command display in

the center of the control room set to show the photonics mast view. The deep-blue Pacific water melted into the brilliant blue Hawaiian sky. A haze-gray CH-53 helicopter suddenly cut across the scene, bright orange torpedo dangling on a long cable below the big bird. As they watched, the chopper transitioned into a hover and the torpedo dropped away.

Almost immediately, STi Joshua Hannon, the on-watch sonar operator, called out, "Torpedo in the water, best bearing zero-six-five." Within a couple of seconds, he called out, "Classified YU-9, Chinese submarine launched torpedo. Zero bearing rate. Best bearing, zero-six-five. Best range five-five-hundred yards."

Brian Edwards nodded and turned to LCDR Aston Jennings. "Weps, launch the CRAW from the port dihedral."

Jennings swiped through a couple of screens on the BYG-1 Payload Control System and made a selection. Almost immediately, Josh Hannon called out, "Detection of launch from the port dihedral." The sonarman paused for a second and then reported, "CRAW did not transition to SCEPS power. Loss of contact on the CRAW."

The CRAW, or Compact Rapid Attack Weapon, was a small, lightweight, very fast torpedo designed for close-in fights where range was not important but speed was. The torpedo was only about six inches in diameter and weighed nearly one hundred pounds. It was propelled by a sophisticated SCEPS engine that got its energy by dousing a block of lithium with a sodium hexafluoride bath. The resulting heat from that highly exothermic reaction was used to create steam from water to drive a turbine. The chemical concoction was very volatile, so the evasion-device launcher shoved the CRAW well away from the submarine before the SCEPS engine started, or "transitioned to SCEPS power."

"Weps, launch the CRAW from the starboard dihedral," Edwards ordered.

As Jennings manipulated the Payload Control System, Hannon called out, "Torpedo bearing zero-six-five, range four-two-hundred yards."

Joe Glass did not need a computer to figure out that the dummy torpedo was coming directly at them at better than sixty-five knots. Even if it was an exercise fish, it had the mass of a full-size pickup truck. It would certainly give them a headache if it hit.

Aston Jennings called out, "Starboard CRAW launched."

Hannon followed with, "CRAW launched, transitioned to SCEPS power. Best bearing zero-one-six, drawing right."

Edwards and Glass watched the sonar tracks on the command display. The route for the torpedo was a dead straight line pointing right at them. The CRAW's track slewed across the screen as it converged on the torpedo's bearing.

Hannon called out, "Torpedo and CRAW on the same bearing, zero-six-five, range two-one-hundred yards."

Just as the sonarman completed his report, a loud explosion shook the *George Mason*. The sonar screen blossomed in a burst on the bearing to the torpedo and then all contacts disappeared completely.

Glass turned to Edwards and smiled.

"I'd say that was a whole lot easier than some of the torpedoes we've run away from together, Skipper. I think I like this 'CRAW fish.' We just need to make it a bit more reliable."

Edwards nodded, pleased his former shipmate and skipper—now big boss—was pleased. And especially happy this test had gone reasonably well. Still, would the day come when the lives of his crew and his submarine depended on this newly developed technology?

Maybe. Maybe not. But he knew he had to assume it would.

Ψ

The research vessel *Deep Ocean Explorer* bobbed easily in the calm, ink-black sea. The stars put on a brilliant display of light, stretching broad swaths of twinkling points from horizon to horizon and making deck lighting superfluous.

Dr. Rex Smith leaned on the ship's rail and stared into the night sky, deep in thought. How many more nights would he be able to enjoy this view? How many more days could his team continue their research before the fat cats back on the mainland finally pulled the plug? His rushed trip to Los Angeles had been a limited success. The shareholders were not happy with his report on the status of their research. Investors are rarely complacent with vague promises of future finds. This was particularly true of the group who had decided to back his efforts. After some fancy footwork with interpreting the data and not a little old-fashioned groveling, Smith had convinced them to put forward enough funds to support another month. But he knew without a doubt that any return visit to this nearly dry well would be a waste of time.

Now there was only time for this one last sweep through the area. Fortunately, the bottom of the Tonga Trench was always pitch black, so it did not matter if it was day or night up here on the surface.

Mitch O'Donnell swung open the hatch and stuck his head out. "Doc, we need you in Mission Control. The *Sea Raptor* is acting up again."

O'Donnell pulled back to make room for Smith to charge through the hatch and down the ladder to the next deck. The ladder opened into a brightly lit room that stretched the width of the deckhouse and nearly the length of the structure. The large space was filled with workstations and computers. Flat-panel displays hung from every available surface. The space hummed with activity.

Four of the technicians huddled around Dr. Sandy McDougal's station, locked into an intense but quiet conversation. It was of immediate concern to Dr. Smith that the factory technician for their very expensive UUV appeared to be frantically defending his equipment.

As Smith stepped over to McDougal's workstation, they all fell quiet and looked up at the chief scientist.

"Sandy, what is so concerning that you sent Mitch to fetch me?" Smith asked, glancing at the face of each member of the group.

"Just like that Irishman to gloat!" the fiery research scientist shot back. "Not often he gets the chance to say, 'I told you so.'"

"Maybe so," Smith snapped back. "But what's our problem?"

McDougal blinked hard. "That damn *Sea Raptor* is acting up again. Not responding to orders and the data link on the acoustic modem is sending up garbage. Two of her primary jobs and she's determined not to satisfactorily do either."

The *Sea Raptor*, an autonomous underwater vehicle, was on a research mission to the very bottom of the Tonga Trench. At a depth of over six miles, the vehicle communicated by using an acoustic modem. A cable that worked at that depth and of that length was out of the question. And acoustic communications had proven tenuous at best.

"Now, just a cotton-pickin' minute," the tech rep responded as he jumped in to protect his company's reputation. "You're asking the system to navigate along an unknown sea bottom and to report real-time data back over an acoustic data path that takes over eight seconds to make the trip each way. It just ain't reasonable."

Smith held up his hand for silence. "Sandy, we can't afford to lose the *Sea Raptor*. Give it the emergency recall signal. And keep sending that signal until you get a response."

With that order, Rex Smith knew that he had just signed the death warrant for this research venture. And very probably for his career.

Ψ

The sun was low, about to dip below the shallow rise of Garden Island and the broad Indian Ocean that stretched out like a sparkling plain to the west. Vehicles and people bustled about Her Majesty's Australian Navy Station Stirling, winding up another busy day at Australia's largest and busiest submarine base. But all was quiet at the moment down by the submarine jetty. The only people moving about were groups of sailors topside on the lone boat tied up alongside and a few other sailors standing by the bollards on the jetty. A curl of diesel smoke rose from the submarine's sail and was quickly dispersed in the warm breeze.

The only evidence that anything was out of the ordinary was the platoon of heavily armed Special Air Service operators cordoning off access to the jetty. For those in the know, it was obvious that something serious was happening if these elite Special Forces soldiers were being detailed to guard duty on a submarine pier.

As the sun was finally obscured by the western horizon, the submarine HMAS *Audacious* cast off her lines and motored out into the broad bay that separated Garden Island from Kwinana Beach on the mainland. The *Audacious* was Australia's newest Shortfin Barracuda submarine, a diesel derivative of the French *Barracuda*-class nuclear attack submarine. Equipped with a fuel-cell air-independent power system and all of the most modern electronics, the Australian sub was even quieter than her French nuclear cousin. And every bit as deadly. The only things she lacked were the speed and endurance afforded by a nuclear power plant.

Standing on his sub's bridge and watching his crew maneuver the big diesel boat, Commander Geoffrey Smythe reviewed his orders in the last of the day's light. Essentially, go north, up into the South China Sea, blunder about a bit, and do his best to see what the Chinese were up to. All seemed relatively simple and routine, but the preparations had been anything but mundane. Only a week had passed since he had been summoned to Naval Headquarters in Canberra, where Commander, Australian Fleet himself, delivered Smythe his instructions. From there it had been a mad rush to get *Audacious* fully ready for a deployment on very short notice, almost a month before she was scheduled to complete overhaul and return to service.

The lights of Freemantle were just blinking on as the submarine sailed past, then turned to the northwest, out into the open Indian Ocean. The officer of the deck reported the course change and crossing the one-hundred-fathom curve.

Smythe nodded to the other men on the bridge and headed below. As he passed through the hatch, he ordered the OOD to dive the sub. It was time to wring the boat out and make sure the dockworkers had done their jobs without leaving any unintentional surprises. Smythe had been in service to his country and commanding a submarine long enough to know something was up. Something serious. His crew and his vessel would have to be ready for anything.

Ψ

The USS *Boise*, SSN 764, was an anomaly. Although she was an older Improved *Los Angeles*-class submarine, commissioned in 1992, she actually had considerably less time submerged and fewer miles steamed than several of the *Virginia*-class submarines built to replace her and her sisters. The incongruity came about as the result of a foul-up in scheduling shipyard maintenance. That snafu had caused her to sit alongside the pier for five years, unable to dive or even get underway. That was followed by another five years stuck in a shipyard, undergoing a complete overhaul. Almost ten full years tied up while her sisters were out steaming on the open ocean.

Now, at long last, the *Boise* was free to ply the seven seas again, almost as new old-stock. As something of a reward, maybe, the sub was moved from the East Coast to Submarine Squadron Fifteen in Guam. As one of the four boats home-ported in that most forward US submarine base, the *Boise* was part of what was termed a quick reaction submarine response force, or more commonly, "the tip of the spear."

It had been less than a week since RADM Jon Ward put down the phone after speaking with COMSUBPAC, and now the *Boise* was clearing the breakwater off Apra Harbor and heading due west with orders to get down to the Spratlys and find out what the hell was going on out there.

Not nearly as exciting as the action typically portrayed in submarine movies, but everyone aboard *Boise* knew that snooping around, listening, watching without being detected, were things submarines did very well. And though she had been virtually forgotten for most of a decade, the sub's crew were ready to get out there and go to work.

4

Yon Hun Glo stepped off the big blue-gray aircraft onto the hot tarmac. He stretched, trying to work the kinks out of his aching back. The interminable flight from the Yulin Naval Base on Hainan to Tonga had consumed more than ten hours of his busy life. Despite the Xi'an Y-20 being a very large aircraft and the most modern of its type currently being flown by the Chinese Air Force, it was still primarily a military transport. It had offered none of the creature comforts found on a commercial airliner. Even Yon Hun Glo's shiny, new three-stars could not change that.

The heat and humidity were Yon Hun Glo's first impression of the tropical island of Tonga. Fua'amotu International Airport, the kingdom's major air facility, was surrounded by subsistence farms on the southern side of Tongatapu, the main island. At just twenty-one degrees south of the equator, the flat farmland broiled in the unrelenting sun.

A three-car motorcade pulled onto the tarmac from behind the ramshackle single-story building that served as the airport's terminal. Two big, black, bug-spattered SUVs and a

Mercedes limo, flying the red-and-white Tongan flag, came to a stop in front of the Chinese aircraft.

The driver jumped out of the limo and opened the rear door. A rotund, dark-skinned man emerged. He was dressed in traditional Tongan garb, a finely woven ta'ovala loukeha worn over a sarong-like tupenu that matched his tailored linen jacket. Though hardly dressed for the mid-day heat, this man was no doubt in charge. This was King Tofuwanga II.

The monarch smiled broadly as he ambled over to where Yon Hun Glo stood at the foot of the aircraft's ladder, trying to find shade beneath the plane's wing.

"Welcome to Tonga," the king called out. "I trust you had a smooth flight, Admiral."

The two men shook hands and Tofuwanga shepherded Yon Hun Glo back to his limo.

"Come out of the sun, my friend. We have air conditioning inside the car. Very refreshing. We will ride in comfort back to the palace. We have a wonderful island banquet prepared for you and then we will have much progress to discuss. But first, I want to take you up to Mua. That is where you will see evidence of how your country is helping my country build a deep-water terminal. It is a bit of a detour but well worth the trip."

Yon Hun Glo smiled. Determining, in person, the progress in completing the terminal was the real reason for this long trip. China had proffered large loans to King Tofuwanga out of the Belt and Roads Initiative for the specific purpose of constructing the terminal and greatly expanding the "international" airport. Yon Hun Glo had already determined that there was no progress to see there. He could just make out through the weeds a row of survey stakes suggesting the new runway's location, and that was the only activity put toward building anything there.

The man was not to be trusted. The admiral was well aware of the king's derisive moniker, "King Two-for-One," bestowed by many of his subjects. China had loaned this potentate several billion pa'anga, the local currency. And the Chinese government had constantly made clear they expected the funds to be spent on the sea terminal and airport expansion, and to eventually be repaid, in full. So far, King Tofuwanga did not seem to be delivering on his promises.

That, of course, was no surprise at all.

The convoy swung out from the airport and onto the main road. It appeared to be little more than crushed coral instead of concrete or asphalt, but it was reasonably smooth. A sudden rainstorm blew in from the east as they charged down the narrow two-lane road, which remained devoid of traffic. It was as if the road had been cleared for the transit of the king, his special guest, and their motorcade. Nothing but small farm fields on either side of the road were visible through the downpour.

Then, after traveling only about six kilometers, the convoy swung off onto a wide, paved road. The rain squall blew past, revealing a broad turquoise lagoon spread out on their left. Ahead lay a small village.

"We are almost there, Admiral," King Tofuwanga said, pointing to a turn-off with a large, impressive sign that read, "Future Home of Tonga International Shipping and Cruise Ship Terminal." They turned off onto another crushed-coral roadway. A chain link gate barred the way, but one of the uniformed guards in the lead SUV hopped out and swung it open.

They drove on, into a huge, vacant, weed-infested lot. Except for a lone, rusty backhoe parked on a tilt in a ditch, there was no sign of any construction activity.

"As you can see, Admiral," the king offered, "we have

accomplished much and will soon begin laying foundations and raising the walls of this magnificent facility you and your country's generosity have made possible."

Yon Hun Glo looked over at King Tofuwanga with a cold stare.

"What is this? I fully expected to see the terminal construction well underway. We have given you billions of pa'anga to erect a shipping terminal. You have had adequate time and all the resources required. Please tell me that you have at least dredged the channel into the harbor and turning basin."

The Tongan king shifted uncomfortably under the admiral's glare.

"You must understand that there are many hurdles," he explained. "We must clear many administrative and planning gates before construction can actually commence. These are ancient grounds with many religious restrictions that must be dealt with carefully. Plus, the people are demanding that they share in the prosperity from the construction, though few are qualified, of course. Soon now, though, we will be able to start, beginning with the required dredging, of course. As soon as we negotiate a work share for my people and explain the necessity for the project to the elders, we will be able to renegotiate a new completion timeframe that..."

When he interrupted, Yon Hun Glo's voice was flat, dripping with menace.

"You are the ruler of this godforsaken little rock. You did not seem to require permission when you signed the agreement and accepted our money. Nor were any elders consulted. There will be no renegotiation. Two heavy-duty dredges left Quanzhou last week. They will arrive in ten days. A battalion of construction engineers will begin to arrive tomorrow. You will, of course, make certain they have adequate lodging and food for the term of their stay."

King Tofuwanga sputtered, protesting, "You are violating Tongan sovereignty. You have no right..."

Yon Hun Glo interrupted. "You lost your right to protest when you accepted our money. You will cooperate and enjoy the fruits of our benefice or we will replace you with one of your cousins who, we are assured, will be more than glad to move into the palace. Do I make myself clear?"

King Tofuwanga looked sick. He nodded meekly and slumped in his seat.

"Now, take me back to the airport," the Chinese admiral ordered. "I see no reason for any further discussions. The airplane will have been unloaded by now." The Tongan monarch looked at him questioningly. "I brought a communications center to set up at the airport. And a company of Marines to guard it."

The short drive back to Fua'amotu International Airport was made in complete silence. There was no handshake, no farewell, when Yon Hun Glo departed the coolness of the limo, strutted across the tarmac, and climbed up into the waiting transport.

As the Xi'an Y-20 climbed out and pointed its nose to the west, Yon Hun Glo was already calling his brother in Beijing.

"Elder brother, it is precisely as we expected. That foolish king has squandered every last one of the loans we have given him. No construction has begun. Even with much blasting, it will require more than a month before we have a harbor deep enough and wide enough for a squadron of submarines, let alone for large warships. I suggest we immediately reinforce our marine garrison to full strength just in case the king or someone else back there decides to make a foolish stand. Or some busybody ventures to come to his miserable assistance."

Ψ

The bright orange UUV swung from the crane that reached out over the *Deep Ocean Explorer*'s stern. Dr. Rex Smith watched as the crane slowly came around and deftly lowered the UUV onto its cradle. Sandy McDougal, Mitch O'Donnell, and the factory tech rep for the underwater exploration vehicle pounced on the UUV as if it were so much prey.

Minutes later, O'Donnell stepped over to Smith.

"Doc, you ain't gonna believe this. Looks like our little friend bounced into the bottom and ripped out the lower acoustic transponder."

"Yeah, so tell me why you're smiling," Smith replied.

Mitch O'Donnell opened his hand to show him something. His palm was filled with glittering yellow metal.

"Because the cavity where the transponder came from was filled with this! Gold! Sandy is downloading the mission data now. We'll know exactly where the UUV found this stuff in a minute."

Realization washed over the researcher's face, leaving him so dizzy he had to reach for a handrail to steady himself.

Ψ

Li Min Zhou was clearly just as comfortable in the office of the Chief of Naval Intelligence in the Pentagon as she would have been in her own unassuming office in Taiwan's Military Intelligence Bureau in Taipei. As unafraid as she might have been in a firefight on a night mission into hostile territory. Even as comfortable as she had been in front of the inattentive Senate committee the previous week. But thankfully, at least one of those senators had been listening to what she had been trying to tell them.

"Admiral, I hope you will relay to Senator Murson how much I appreciate his setting up this meeting with you," she said. "And I know you will find it is worth your time and attention."

"Thad is one of the good guys," Jon Ward told her. "He understands better than most what we are trying to do down here. Now, what can I help you with?"

She looked him straight in the eyes when she answered. No-nonsense lady, Ward thought. But he instinctively checked the antique ship's clock on the wall anyway. His schedule was full, overbooked.

"You are doubtless aware of many of my previous activities, Admiral. You know I hold the rank of senior field officer in the Taiwanese Marines. That I am an expert in demolition, all weaponry, and hand-to-hand combat. That I have combat experience in actions that made the news and far more skirmishes that never will. Officially, they never happened, but be assured our team won most of them, and I was fortunate enough to survive all of them so far. You may not know, however, of my activities on behalf of the Taiwanese National Security Bureau as an operative embedded high in the intelligence infrastructure of the so-called People's Republic of China."

She did not miss the slightest of tics near Ward's right eye. "Or maybe you do. Then you might also know I spent some time at the behest of the Chinese Ministry of State Security in North Korea, learning all I could, theoretically for China but also for the benefit of Taiwan and your own CIA."

Ward smiled.

"That, I concede, I did not know," he responded. "But Colonel Zhou, I was already duly impressed with your credentials. And with the intelligence you have previously and so generously shared with us. You have benefited the cause of freedom and peace in many invaluable ways. In all honesty, as much as I appreciate Senator Murson, your file..." Ward pointed to a thick folder on his desk. "...your resume is the reason I agreed to meet with you today. As you can imagine, we are quite busy. So, what brings you to the Pentagon today?"

"Desperation."

"Excuse me?"

"Because of my previous work, and because I still have people I can trust in high places within the Chinese Communist Party as well as the government in Beijing, I believe I have a unique understanding of and insight into the dynamics of what is going on there now. Crucial moves and developments with frightening ramifications are taking place. Conflict within the Party and the military. Infighting that will result in actions that will violently destabilize the rest of the world. Steps that are being taken and initiatives being set in motion even as we sit here discussing my resume and enjoying your nice view of the Potomac River."

Li Zhou leaned forward, a grim expression on her face. "But you see, I am having great difficulty convincing anyone within your government or mine of the dangerous nature of these developments. A series of events I have been warning about for years now. They will have consequences for your navy, your government, as well as mine, and very soon. And the rest of the world, too. I know what these moves will be, the reasons for them, and who is making them. And I know what will happen if..."

The phone on Jon Ward's desk suddenly buzzed loudly.

"Admiral, pardon the interruption, but General Bond is on line two," his assistant said. "And you have the ten o'clock with the under-secretary at his place. It's a twenty-minute walk."

Zhou looked hard at Ward, her eyes piercing. Then she whispered, "Dong Doa. South China Sea."

Though spoken quietly, the effect of the words on Jon Ward was profound.

"Tell the general I will call him later. And reschedule all my appointments." A brief pause, then he added, "For the balance of the day."

Ψ

Joe Glass walked the few steps from his office in the historic Building 661 to COMSUBPAC's headquarters.

Glass did not take for granted the submarine history that infused every inch of SUBBASE Pearl Harbor. From his office on the second deck in Building 661, his predecessor many times removed had witnessed the unbelievable destruction of 7 December, 1941. And other squadron commanders in the long line had sent the fleet boats out to perform their mighty role in winning World War II. Then others had dispatched their submarines out of the base on Oahu to Cold War missions that were still classified today. It was a proud legacy, one that now rested heavily on Joe Glass's broad shoulders.

He glanced up at the Submarine Escape Tower. It actually had not been used for escape training in many years and was now a historic landmark with a meeting room at the very top that offered some of the best views of Pearl Harbor. Glass crossed Morton Street, yet another reminder of the place's legacy. The byway was named for Dudley "Mush" Morton, the legendary skipper of the World War II boat USS *Wahoo*, who helped rewrite the book on how to use subs to defeat a fanatical enemy. Glass hopped up the stairs to COMSUBPAC's offices. The cement bunker of a building was every bit as historic as Glass's Building 661. And even more secretive.

The commodore was immediately ushered into COMSUBPAC's second-floor corner office. Again, even more history. The old wooden desk at the far end of the spacious room was the same one that Vice Admiral Charles Lockwood had sat behind as he ordered his submarine crews off to sink more than half the Japanese shipping sent to the bottom in the war. But to also incur the highest casualty rate of any branch of the military in the war.

The current COMSUBPAC, Rear Admiral Barney Fritz, rose from behind the desk and came around to shake hands with Glass.

"Joe, glad you could come over so quick." He waved toward a seat at the conference table. An orderly had already placed cups and a pot of coffee there. The SUBPAC Chief of Staff, Captain Rich Moore, filled three cups and then sat down across from Glass.

Joe took a sip. "Ah, Admiral, you serve the best cup of coffee on the island."

Fritz chuckled as he plopped down at the head of the table.

"Joe, you know damn well it's just Waialua Coffee. You can buy it in the commissary." His face turned serious as he shoved a sheaf of papers across the oak table to Glass. "Okay, I got a job for you. Rich thinks I'm sending you on a South Sea Island vacation, but I'm sending you down to American Samoa for some big doings. You are to set up an advance base for your squadron in Pago Pago."

Rich Moore picked up the thread. "That gives us an alternative to Guam and a bigger presence in the South Pacific. PACOM thinks we need to do something to counter all the Chinese moves down there. It'll make the islanders feel better that we are there to protect our sea lanes to Australia and New Zealand. Plus, we have some new reasons to think they do, indeed, need some protecting these days."

Admiral Fritz set down his cup and leaned forward.

"We're going to be testing a brand-new idea for forward basing. The idea is to use the *Chesty Puller*, one of those expeditionary sea-base ships, as a stand-in for a sub tender. It won't be able to give you everything a tender can but should be able to fix most things. Plus, it won't advertise the presence of subs over there. And by the way, you're going to have to share your new home with the battalion of Marines and squadron of Marine rotary types that COMPACFLT is sending for local security. The heavy brass up at Camp Smith seem to think they'll need some firepower down there."

Fritz took a breath and reached back to grab a file from a stack piled up on his desk. He checked the cover sheet and slid it over to Glass.

"Joe, I'm detailing a couple of ORCA UUVs from UUVRON ONE to you. You can operate them out of there, too. Some of this is still in the planning stages as we learn more...as you learn more...but I'm thinking of shuttle-running your boats out of Pago Pago. You can work out the details with Ops."

The ORCA unmanned submarines were a brand-new toy, bigger and more impressively equipped than any previous robot vessel. While not officially part of the fleet yet, they were obviously now available for this particular task.

Joe Glass took another sip of his coffee. He did not even taste it this time. He idly scratched his chin. His instincts were screaming.

"Admiral, my radar screen is lit up like a son of a bitch. Can you tell me what's going on out there?"

"If I knew more, I'd tell you. That's one of the benefits of your new job, you know. You get all the info. Like drinking from a fire hose sometimes. One thing I do know is that your old friend Jon Ward smells something rotten. You already know it's China, but this time...well...it ain't all for propaganda and bluster. Especially after what they did to *Tarbox*..."

"Enough said."

"You have plenty of reading to do there. But if it makes you feel any better, I have the same bad feeling in my gut about all this. Something's up. And you, of all people, know that usually means submarines are best placed to do a lot of the heavy lifting."

Glass downed the last of the java and stood.

"We got it."

Ψ

It was near the end of another very interesting day on the *Deep Ocean Explorer* research vessel. A balmy tropical breeze blew across the deck, but nobody on the ship was topside to enjoy the weather or the brilliant sunset.

Instead, they were all huddled around a bank of monitors down in Mission Control, raptly watching as Dr. Sandy McDougal played back the tapes from *Sea Raptor*'s last mission.

"Wow! I've never seen such a well-developed field of fumaroles!" McDougal exclaimed. "Some of them are almost two hundred feet tall. Truly amazing at this depth, too. This is way deeper than we would normally expect such massive and well-formed deposits."

Mitch O'Donnell interrupted the scientist's pondering. "Yes, Doc. Impressive. But look at the gold! There must be literally tons of it down there! There's enough to make us all gazillionaires!"

Rex Smith stood off to the side, frowning. "I hate to dash your enthusiasm, but there are a couple of issues here. Other than the question of ownership and who has a legitimate claim on this find, the gold is six miles below the surface of the ocean. I am not aware of any technology capable of mining anything that deep."

Smith allowed the team a few more minutes to gawk at the tapes and ponder his concerns. It was time to get back to work. The researcher turned to Bill Bix, *Deep Ocean Explorer*'s captain.

"Bill, we need to get parts to fix the *Sea Raptor*. Make best speed to Pago Pago. Hopefully, we can get the parts flown in from Sydney in the next week or so."

But everyone else in the room was fixated on the small mound of pure gold dust Mitch O'Donnell had placed strategically in the middle of a chart table.

Ψ

Commander Chet Allison stepped back from the Type 18 periscope and glanced around *Boise*'s control room. It appeared the battle-stations ship control team and fire control party were on-station. Allison stepped back up to the eyepiece again. Best to give everyone a few minutes to get settled in and ready to go.

The view outside was boringly nondescript. No visual contacts, either on the surface or in the air. The only object in his periscope view was a faint gray-and-green line on the far eastern horizon. That would be Dong Doa Island. Only a few months ago, the spot had been known as North Danger Reef. In reality, it consisted of only a very few square feet of dry land, even at low tide. Then the Chinese began hauling in dirt, rocks, and tons of cement. They had turned the reef into a bustling navy base, complete with a deep-water harbor and an airfield capable of handling high-performance combat aircraft. Allison's intel brief had been frustratingly sparse on several key points, but the most concerning one to him was what kind of search sensors might be in place to protect China's newest base.

Allison grabbed the 21MC microphone and pushed the button. "ESM, Conn, report all ESM contacts."

The reply came almost immediately.

"Conn, ESM, currently hold three contacts. Echo One equates to a Chinese Type Three-oh-five Alpha phased array air defense radar. Echo Two equates to a RES-1 Chinese air and coastal defense radar. Echo Three equates to a REL-6 Bravo air surveillance radar. Currently hold no emitters equated as a threat."

At least the Chinese did not appear to be expecting underwater guests. Just the typical search radars were up and scanning.

"Ship is manned for battle stations," Master Chief Dan "Hoss" Blocker called over his shoulder. Blocker was the chief of the boat and battle-stations diving officer.

"Thanks, COB," Allison answered as he lowered number two scope and turned to the battle-stations fire control party assembled in the control room. The group of young faces looked up at him expectantly as he explained what they were going to try.

"This is going to be just like we have walked through and practiced a thousand times," Allison told them. "We are going to stay at periscope depth and slip in nice and close to the harbor mouth. We'll grab whatever pictures we can. Satellite imagery shows the *Tarbox* tied up at the wharf directly across from the harbor entrance, but we need confirmation from this angle. If we can positively verify that it is the *Tarbox*, we will move back out to launch range, and then we will launch the MRUUV that's loaded in tube one and send it into the harbor. Weps, make sure the harbor mission is loaded on the UUV."

The Mission Reconfigurable Unmanned Underwater Vehicle (MRUUV) was an unmanned underwater vehicle about the size and shape of a torpedo. It had been specifically designed to be launched and retrieved from a submarine's torpedo tube. As the name implied, it was very versatile, easily converted from one mission to another.

Looking around the room, the skipper reviewed the safety precautions they had practiced.

"This bottom shoals up fast. Running aground would be a bad thing. We will set yellow sounding at ninety feet, red sounding at seventy-five feet. At a yellow sounding, immediately turn one-hundred-eighty degrees with a full rudder. Red sounding, immediately back down until all way is off. Then back out and turn using the outboard. Secure fathometer will be run continuously. Fathometer Watch, keep your eyes open. Let's not put a dent in our nice boat."

The sonar tech standing by the BQN-17 Secure Fathometer chimed in, "Yes, sir!"

Commander Allison quickly reviewed the rest of what they expected to accomplish, concluding with, "If we suspect that the Chinese have detected us, we will turn toward deep water and open the area as fast as covertly possible. If we are fired on, we will counterfire if possible and open the area. Make tube one ready in all respects for UUV launch. Make tube two ready in all respects for the self-defense weapon. Tube four will be the backup self-defense weapon. Any questions?" There were none. "Helm, right full rudder, steady course one-two-five, make turns for four knots," Allison ordered.

The big boat swung around to the harbor-entrance course and slowed to four knots. At that speed, it would be almost an hour before the boat was close enough to get good photographs. However, the slow speed meant that the periscope did not leave a telltale feather, or water plume, behind it as they approached.

"Raising number two scope," Allison called out as he swung the red lifting ring. The shiny silver tube rose from the scope well as the skipper slapped down the training handles and peered through the eyepiece.

"Bearing to the harbor entrance left tower, bearing mark," he called out.

The navigator read out the result. "Bearing one-two-seven. Recommend steer course one-two-three. Looks like we are being set to the south."

"Steer course one-two-three," Allison ordered. "Lowering number two scope. Next observation in five minutes. Nav, keep the timer."

Allison stepped away from the scope as it slid back into its housing.

The team repeated the process multiple times as the *Boise* slowly slipped toward the harbor mouth. Each time they raised the scope, they were a few yards closer, until finally Commander Allison could clearly see the shattered hulk of the *Tarbox* firmly tied to the wharf just inside the breakwater. Chinese workers dressed in blue coveralls scurried all over the wreckage like ants picking at a carcass, some stabilizing the ship, others stripping it for intelligence purposes.

As he watched, Allison had to grip the training handles and bite his tongue to keep from ordering the launch of something far more deadly than a UUV.

"Verify that *Tarbox* is tied to the wharf," he finally said with a grunt of disgust.

"Confirm identity," the navigator replied. "We have it on video."

Allison lowered the periscope. "Okay, let's back out and

launch the UUV. Left full rudder, steady course three-one-five. Make normal one-third turns. Sounding?"

"Sounding one-nine-two feet," the fathometer watch quickly replied.

"Dive, make your depth nine-zero feet."

"Make my depth nine-zero feet," Hoss Blocker answered as the boat slid a little deeper.

Thirty minutes later found them three nautical miles away from the island and back up, hovering at periscope depth. Dong Doa Island was once again a low green line on the southeastern horizon. The sons of bitches had even gone to the effort to do some landscaping.

"MRUUV launch checklist complete," Weps reported. "All checks are satisfactory."

"Ship launch parameters verified," the executive officer reported. "Ship is ready to launch the MRUUV."

"Launch MRUUV, tube one," Allison ordered.

The weapons officer punched a couple of buttons on the launch control panel. Down in the torpedo room, the MRUUV quietly came to life and obediently swam out of the tube into warm seawater. The unmanned underwater vehicle stabilized on its ordered course and briefly came shallow, using its antennas to check communications with the orbiting comms satellite and obtain a precise GPS fix. Then, as its program ordered, the vehicle dropped to thirty feet off the bottom and swam toward Dong Doa Island. At four knots, it took forty-five minutes for the small submersible to center up on the harbor mouth and then to swim on in.

The MRUUV made its way directly beneath the wrecked *Tarbox* and planted a couple of sensors on the harbor bottom. It then released a pair of sensors that floated up and magnetically attached themselves to the ship. Each sensor was attached to the submersible with a hair-thin fiber-optic line.

With its sensor deployment complete, the MRUUV swam back out of the harbor and turned to the north, just enough to get outside the shipping channel. There it settled on the bottom and promptly deployed a buoy antenna that floated up, stopping just below the surface. The antenna popped above the water just long enough—mere seconds—to exchange digital packets of data, reporting in before dropping back down.

Commander Allison received the deployment report as it was relayed by a satellite in geosynchronous orbit back down to his sub.

"Looks like our job here is done. Nav, plot us a course out of here so we can call home and brag to the boss."

5

Phuc Ngyuan and his family had been netting a living from these same waters for hundreds of years. Ten generations of ancestors had called the Vietnamese village of Tam Thanh on Long Hai Island home. The South China Sea's bounty had fed and housed them in reasonable and comparative comfort and security for most of that time, even paying for the steel fishing boat Phuc used to earn his income. Even though the vessel was now old and rusty, the *Mau do Rong* had reliably transported Phuc out to the same fishing grounds that his family had harvested for centuries, usually accompanied by the few other Tam Thanh families who earned their livelihood the same way.

It was too grand a description to call the boats venturing out of Tam Thanh's tiny, protected harbor a fleet. The dozen or so ragtag vessels huddled together for mutual support as they plied the fishing grounds more than two hundred miles out in the South China Sea. Phuc and his fellow fishermen knew little of international law or sovereignty claims and cared even less. They only knew that their fathers had instructed them on how to avoid the hidden reefs and interpret threatening weather as they filled their nets. And they had taught them to pray at the village shrine for a safe return home.

However, the last three times they had ventured to their traditional grounds, the Chinese fishing fleet had arrived ahead of them. Hundreds of boats filling the sea from horizon to horizon, pulling in nets filled with catch. Then, when Phuc and his fellows had started to lay their own nets, the big, white Chinese Coast Guard ships had rushed in and roughly brushed them aside. They had not caught enough fish to cover the cost of their fuel.

As he finished some much-needed net mending, Phuc Ngyuan considered the possibility that the Chinese would be out there again on this trip and wondered what to do if they again chased him and the others away from where they earned their livelihood. He was so deep in his worries that he hardly noticed the approaching small skiff until it pulled up alongside the *Mau do Rong*. Phuc was far too poor to pay to tie up his boat at the pier. It was anchored in a recess afforded by the piled-stone breakwater. Anyone had to want to see him specifically in order to venture out to this anchorage.

Phuc immediately recognized the Vietnam Coast Guard lieutenant who leapt from the boat over to the *Mau do Rong*, leaving his own boat's engine idling. Lieutenant Bo Tranh commanded the small, local Coast Guard facility on Long Hai. He rarely ventured out of his air-conditioned office in Long Hai City on the other side of the island, but all the fishermen knew him well. He occasionally felt the need to show his authority by enforcing arcane rules or harassing boat owners for no other reason than that he could.

"Ngyuan," Bo Tranh said, with no greeting. "I have come to inform you that the fishing fleet sails at sunset. You will have your little boat fueled and ready. We will escort you to your destination and we do not have time to wait for stragglers."

Tranh did not wait for a reply or challenge. He leapt back aboard his own craft and motored toward the next fishing boat.

Phuc sat there, net in his lap, with a quizzical look on his face. Was the Coast Guard suddenly taking an interest in the plight of the island's fishermen? And if so, why?

Then he shrugged, pulled out a cigarette, and lit it, then took a deep draw and went ahead mending his net. He could not afford to lose a single fish.

Ψ

Phuc counted two dozen boats in the group as they motored out past the breakwater. The sun had just disappeared, dropping behind the island, as two Vietnam Coast Guard patrol boats made slow circles around them, herding the fishermen into a loosely formed gaggle before making certain they steamed to the east. The patrol boats were Cold War-era Soviet torpedo boats gifted to the Vietnamese, primarily because it was cheaper than scuttling them. The torpedoes and other weapons had first been stripped off them. The only offensive punch that remained was a twenty-three-millimeter machine cannon on the bow of each vessel.

Dawn found the ragtag group riding the swell on the western edge of their traditional fishing grounds. Phuc strapped the ship's wheel in position and went to the stern, starting the backbreaking effort of deploying his nets. He was still curious about why the patrol boats had felt the need to accompany them out here, but now his mind turned to more practical thoughts. Maybe, if the catch was good this trip, if the Chinese had not already caught every single fish in the South China Sea, then he might be able to buy that used hydraulic winch on sale back along the pier in Tam

Thanh. What would it be like to allow the machine to do the heavy lifting while he enjoyed a smoke and looked on? But for now, he would still be required to do it the old, manual way. Like his father. And a long line of fathers before him.

Then he could see on the distant horizon that the Chinese fishing fleet was still there, filling the sea. Phuc could only imagine the devastation this vast armada was causing to any potential harvest. Another few days of such intense fishing and there would be nothing left for him and his family. Nothing at all.

Phuc was busy spending out his nets and did not notice when one of the white Chinese Coast Guard ships charged in their direction, an angry wave rising high on its bow. When Phuc did spot the belligerent vessel, he assumed she would steam around for a while, like a blustering bull, threatening them. She may even try to shoulder some of the Vietnamese boats aside. But this time, there was little need for worry. Surely not even the Chinese would want to pick a fight with the Vietnamese Coast Guard ships.

The sea was large enough for everyone. At least for this trip.

Just to make sure the Chinese were aware of them, the Vietnamese Coast Guard boats charged forward, clearly intending to protect their little flock. But then, Phuc saw the big gun on the Chinese ship's bow turn ominously toward one of the patrol boats. It spat once, then a second time. He watched, stunned, as the Vietnamese boat exploded. What remained burst into flames. Two more shots and the other Vietnamese patrol boat was a smoking hulk.

Phuc Ngyuan stood there, still clutching the nets of his father and grandfather, and watched in stunned disbelief as the white cutter worked its way slowly through the tiny Vietnamese fishing fleet. The ship's machine cannons ripped into the small, defenseless fishing boats, leaving them sinking.

Phuc Ngyuan's last image was the cutter's high bow towering over him, just before it cut the *Mau do Rong* in half.

Ψ

"Damn! Damn them to hell!" Commander Geoffrey Smythe cursed. "Did we get all that on video?" he asked no one in particular. But no answer was required. He already knew that the submarine's computers were storing every byte of what had just occurred up there for later replay and analysis.

HMAS *Audacious* was barely a thousand yards from the destruction wrought by the Chinese Coast Guard cutter. The Australian submarine's low-profile photonics mast was poking up just above the wavetops, raking in all the visual and electronic data that was available for it to gobble up. The gunfire and explosions recorded on the sonar "tapes" gave the audible counterpoint to the anguished scene captured by the video.

Smythe beat his fist against the control panel in frustration. There was nothing he could do to come to the aid of those poor bastards up there. The crews of the Vietnam patrol boats or the poor fishermen being brutally and mercilessly attacked above him, apparently with no provocation. There had been only one short radio transmission from the Chinese, likely a warning, as was typical. And a short reply from the Vietnamese Coast Guard ship. Certainly a "go to hell." Then the sudden and brutal assault.

Nothing Smythe and his crew could do. Nothing but slink off and report what they had just witnessed.

He took one more look through the periscope. Smoke, wreckage, bodies in the water. And beyond, the Chinese fishermen pulled in nets teeming with fish, their silvery scales winking in the light from the early-morning sun.

Ψ

The two stories hit the news services at almost the same time. The submarine video was grainy, but the story was obvious. The Australian Broadcasting Service led the story, but the world press immediately picked it up. The European press services, of course, soft pedaled the angle, charging that the Chinese Coast Guard had "allegedly" fired on "apparently defenseless" Vietnamese fishermen, even as the video clearly depicted the blazing devastation. Vietnam News, the country's official journalistic organ, was not nearly so benign. The editor demanded an immediate response from the United Nations and protection under the Association of Southeast Asian Nations Treaty. The story, of course, did not appear in the New China News feed. The Vietnamese government requested American military aid, including fifth-generation fighter aircraft and advanced anti-ship missiles. The Vietnam Navy's own "fleet" of a half-dozen *Kilo*-class submarines quietly got underway and disappeared from view.

Wheels were turning. A long-standing conflict over fishing grounds had just escalated to one with international implications.

Ψ

The other news story, one about a mountain of gold lying six miles beneath the Pacific, discovered by a scientific research vessel, also grabbed world-wide attention. It, however, played front and center on the New China News feed.

Within hours of hearing the news, King Tofuwanga II claimed an Exclusive Economic Zone out to two hundred nautical miles around Tonga, which just happened to cover the reported location of the golden mountain.

The United States, on behalf of American Samoa, and New Zealand, representing Niue in foreign affairs, immediately rejected the Tongan claims. Diplomatic missives regarding claims on the gold find flew around the globe at the speed of light, soon eclipsing in number and vitriol those concerning the massacre of the Vietnamese fishermen in the South China Sea.

Meanwhile, Yon Ba Deng, the Assistant Vice Deputy to the Minister of National Defense for Naval Matters, watched the controversy from his plush offices in the Forbidden City in Beijing with growing interest.

And no little excitement.

Ψ

The hotline around the Association of Southeast Asian Nations was abuzz. The Chinese Coast Guard openly attacking an unarmed Vietnamese fishing fleet in waters that Vietnam had claimed as theirs for centuries was causing a great deal of angst in all of the capital cities. But the leaders of ASEAN were, after all, practical people. They had lived their entire lives under the shadow of the Chinese tiger. After some clamoring for retribution or UN intervention, cooler heads prevailed. The lives of a handful of poor fishermen were not worth goading that particular stalking tiger. A major war would not serve the interests of anyone in the region. Who knew if the fishermen, with their rudimentary navigational gear, might have actually strayed too close to Chinese waters in their quest for full nets? Most unfortunate.

And the decision seemed to be the correct one. Within three days, any follow-up story run by major newspapers around the world—in every instance the story distributed by the Associated Press—was a mere four-sentence mention in their single-column "International" wrap-ups. Fox News, CNN, and the BBC failed to mention the incident at all.

6

The dark sea was bathwater warm. The only way that Navy SEAL Lieutenant Commander Jim Ward could even see the inside of the Shallow Water Combat Submersible was from the warm glow given off by the computer control panel. This was Ward's first adventure piloting the SWCS on an actual operational mission. With capacity for only six people and their gear, there was no room inside the mini-submarine for the luxury of a dedicated pilot or navigator. Everyone onboard was necessarily a shooter, a fully trained and qualified SEAL.

The world of the SEAL Delivery Vehicle teams was a new one for Jim Ward. Despite having seen more than his share of new technology—and old-fashioned kinds of engagement with bad guys as well—he had not yet ventured into the shadowy world of mini-subs and their surreptitious littoral missions. At least until now, when he got the chance to serve as executive officer of SDV Team ONE, based in Pearl Harbor.

He had discussed the opportunity with his dad, who just happened to be Admiral Jon Ward, now head of Naval Intelligence at the Pentagon. After giving him renewed grief for not following in his footsteps, and those of his grandfather, driving submarines for the Navy, the elder Ward told him he thought it was a fine idea.

"I knew you would come around and become a bubble-head before it was over," Jon Ward had told him. "Even if it is a toy sewer pipe you'll be skippering. Submarining is in your blood, Jimbo."

The younger Ward had spent several weeks at Coronado in California, learning how to operate the new SWCS. He assumed he would have more time to perfect his abilities. Now, though, it was time to prove that he had paid attention in class.

The process so far had been very easy, beginning with launching the craft out of the dry-deck shelter on the back of the USS *Hawaii* in deep water twenty-five miles to the northeast of where they now made their way through relatively shallow water. Unlike the older Swimmer Delivery Vehicles, the entire launch sequence for the SWCs was automated. Then, very little to do but watch the auto-pilot as they plodded without deviation on a course to the south and west. Sit back and try to relax in the dark, cramped space as the little electric sub cruised just a few feet below the wavetops. At a max speed of six knots, the outbound trip would take just over four hours for them to reach their target spot.

Then the navigation trace confirmed that Ward and his small team of SEALs had arrived at their destination, the southeast end of the North Luconia Shoals. The mass of coral heads and reefs sat about sixty miles off the Sarawak coast of the big island of Borneo. Like most every geographical feature of the region, these coral structures were the object of disputes, with primary claim being that they were part of the territory of the Spratly Islands. But none of this was of interest to Jim Ward and his mini-sub crammed with scuba-breathing SEALs.

Seahorse Breakers lay only a few hundred yards dead ahead. The reef was named not for the seahorses that swam these waters but for an English opium clipper of that name that had met its deadly fate on the coral heads almost two hundred years ago. The reef stretched across an eight-mile arc of ocean from the northwest to the southeast. Its entire length lay in perilous wait, solid but not necessarily visible, in perfect position to tear the bottom out of the vessel of any unwary mariner. At its highest point, the reef was covered by no more than six feet of seawater.

The SWCS's bottom profiler showed precisely the sandy ocean floor that the hydrographers had predicted. Ward inched the vessel upward until it cruised only a couple of feet below the surface, then reached over and toggled a switch. From somewhere just behind his seat, he could hear a low hum as the sensor mast outside hinged up. His computer screen shifted displays, now showing a video picture not of the bottom but of the calm, dark ocean surface above them. The high-definition, multi-spectral video camera sitting at the very top of the folding sensor mast panned around, revealing an empty sea. The sun was just rising, low on the eastern horizon.

No sign of one of the stray Chinese ships that Ward knew were anchored off Aitken Reef, twenty miles to the north. Those ships were the reason Ward and his team were out here in the South China Sea, late on a moonless night. The cargo of sensors they were here to plant covertly would give the brass hats back in Pearl a set of hidden eyes and ears on what the Chinese were doing.

Ward stole a glance over at his co-pilot/navigator's control panel. Ensign Tad Riley, the newest member of the team, fresh out of SWCV pilot's school and SEAL Qualification Training, sat staring tensely at his monitor, as if he were waiting for the next level of a video game to appear. The screen was still set to the inertial navigation display.

"Tad! Wake up!" Ward told him over the vehicle communications system. "You're fixated on the screen. Sensor mast is up. You need to get a quick GPS fix and check ESM. We need to know if we have any unfriendlies close by. Then see if we have any message traffic."

Ward could faintly sense the young SEAL shaking his head, coming back to the here-and-now. Then he could see the monitor flicker to different screens as Riley quickly danced through the displays.

"Skipper, picking up an RM-1290 nav radar and an MR-36A surface search radar. Best bearing three-four-seven. Signal strength is pretty high. Best bet it's a Chinese Type Fifty-Four ALPHA. And he's within twenty miles." Riley rattled off his report. Then, his voice quavering just a bit, he added, "Ain't supposed to be any warships down here. Intel was we'd see only a couple of research types."

Ward smiled. He remembered his first contact with someone who might want to shoot at him.

"He's not likely to know we're anywhere in the neighborhood. Let's just get our job done and get our asses back to the ship for some hot chow."

Ward cut power to the SWCS's screw and allowed the small craft to settle slowly onto the bottom. The boat ride was over for now. Time to go to work.

The team slid back the steel canopies that covered them, switched to their SCUBA air tanks, and swam out of the SWCS. Jason Hall and Tony Garcia, two longtime members of Ward's team, each grabbed a sensor package and swam away, headed up the reef to the north. Bill Ross and Sean Horton, only slightly less veteran to the team, flippered off to the south. Ward and Riley got busy connecting up the comms and control module for the main device they were delivering.

Ward was just finishing burying the module out of sight beneath a convenient coral head when Hall called him over the comms link.

"Skipper, think you'd better see this." The miniature acoustic communication system made Hall's normally deep, gravelly voice sound tinny, but it allowed the divers to communicate clearly out to a couple of hundred yards. Optionally, they could shift to text messaging and go even further.

Ward kicked over to where Hall was hovering over something located on the bottom, half covered with sand. The dull-gray metal tube was about six feet long and a foot in diameter. But there was no marine growth on it. Whatever it was, it had not been down there very long.

Ward dropped closer to the bottom and closely inspected the tube. The fiber-optic line coming out of the tube was almost invisible. Ward followed it for a couple of hundred yards until it ended in an anchored buoy that floated, tethered, just below the surface. He could just make out a dozen or so other fiber-optic lines heading out in various directions from the anchor.

A light flicked on for the SEAL. This was a sensor net, very similar to the one he and his team were in the process of planting. Besides the United States, only one other country had the technology to do this. Now the question became what were the Chinese looking for, and, even more importantly, had Ward and his guys already been detected?

Ward grabbed the buoy and its anchor, snapped the thin fiber-optic cables, and headed back toward the SWCS. As he passed Jason Hall and Tony Garcia, he ordered the pair to take the mystery sensor back to their mini-sub. Some geeks in some labs would love getting a look at this thing.

Without the purloined sensor and buoy, Ward could now swim hurriedly back to the SWCS and get ready to drive as far away from this spot as he could. He climbed into the pilot's seat and quickly scanned the gauges. Tad Riley was a half-second behind him, sliding down into the co-pilot/navigator seat.

As Ward powered up the craft, the rest of the team piled in.

"Please raise your seatbacks and tray tables. We hope you enjoy the flight."

The men grumbled, as much over the accommodations as their leader's joke. It was a tight fit, even without now carrying the Chinese sensor and comms node. Ward ignored the grousing as he deftly lifted the sub off the bottom and headed upward, toward the surface.

"Tad, get a message off to *Hawaii*. Tell them that we found a bottom-mounted Chinese sensor network out here in the same area where we were placing our own sensors. Let 'em know we're heading back to home base ASAP."

Ward saw it as soon as the sensor mast cleared the water. The Chicom helicopter. And it was coming in out of the north, low and fast. The bird was headed straight at them, too, and it was already too damn close!

"Skipper, that's a sixty-R," Riley called out. "It's one of ours."

"Nope. Not likely. That's one of the new Z-20 ASW birds. Almost for sure off that Chinese destroyer we were hearing." Ward was already lowering the sensor mast and angling the boat back toward the bottom again. "I'm betting he's here to find out what happened to his sensor system. He finds us, he'll put two and two together. And he ain't gonna be happy."

Even with a couple feet of water separating them from the sunshine, they still felt and heard the Chinese helicopter flying directly overhead. Ward moved the boat even lower, trying to snuggle up against the bottom, but the depth gauge only read ten feet. That meant only about four feet of water separated them from a very angry Chinese ASW helicopter. The trick would be to stay as deep as possible without kicking up a telltale cloud of sand and silt from the big screw that drove their submersible.

Riley nudged Ward.

"Skipper, I'm picking up heavy screws on the sonar, off to the north. SNR is going up."

Ward grunted. That would be their buddy, the Chinese destroyer. The neighborhood was suddenly getting very crowded with people who would not be at all hospitable to Ward and his SEALs. Best to slink out as quietly and unobtrusively as possible, let the chopper chase sharks and the destroyer dodge coral outcroppings.

"It makes sense," Ward said, mostly to himself. "That Z-20 can't do anything to us except hold us down. She doesn't carry much in the way of ordnance. But the destroyer...we need to get really, really lost before that tin can shows up."

That's when the first grenade exploded in the water nearby. The concussion rocked the SWCS and had each man's ears ringing. Jim Ward had a momentary flashback to another mission. He had endured a near-death experience in the Bahamas when a Russian spy tried to concussively end his days with hand grenades exploding while Ward was underwater. Lucky to be alive. Even luckier to still be able to be a SEAL after that.

But at the moment, Jim Ward did not feel so lucky.

Then a second and third grenade boomed, even closer. The helicopter pilot had likely concluded that he could do more than simply hold the SEALs down until the surface warship got to the scene. A well-placed grenade might just send this interloper to the bottom forever.

A fourth grenade, this one extremely close to the SEALs. The mini-sub rocked sickeningly. Ward wrestled the control to keep her headed downward.

Enough of this! he thought.

"Break out the weapons, guys," he ordered. "We're gonna have to shoot it out with that bastard before he gets lucky with one of those firecrackers. We'll surface. Concentrate fire on the cockpit. If we can take out the pilot..."

Ward reached down beside his seat to feel for his own SCAR-17 assault rifle. With the other hand, he angled the sub toward the surface again. He felt more than saw the team slide back the steel canopies above them.

Just then, another grenade exploded, certainly only yards away.

"This son of a bitch is giving me one hell of a headache," Ward muttered just as the boat broke the surface into brilliant sunshine. Even as he set the controls to run on the surface, he heard the crack of outgoing rifle fire from the four SEALs behind him. He ripped off his diving mask and then stood with his SCAR-17, ready to contribute to the fusillade.

The Z-20 was only fifty yards astern. Maybe a hundred feet in the air, if that. Little wonder he was coming so close with his cherry bombs. As Ward put his laser site on the cockpit, he could already see several bullet holes pocking the plexiglass. His guys were good. He added his own firepower in the form of aimed, three-shot bursts.

The helicopter pilot had obviously been surprised by the sudden emergence of a mini-sub full of angry SEALs. And that they had come out of hiding, trying to shoot him from the sky. He pulled back on the collective, trying to gain altitude and distance. As the bird pitched up and away, a side hatch slid open and a pintle-mounted, 12.7mm machine gun swung out, a viper ready to strike. The first burst splashed a stream across the water in front of the SEALs. Ward felt the boat lurch as a couple of slugs pierced through the boat's bow dome.

Ward immediately switched his aim over to the hatch and emptied his magazine into the hole. The gunner fell out, dangling from his safety harness, already dead.

Then, as the helicopter continued its upward pitch, frantically trying to escape the hail of bullets from the six SEALs, it assumed an impossibly steep angle, defying the laws of aerodynamics.

Suddenly, the bird lost its grip on the air and slid backward, falling, crashing into the water tail first. Its rotor continued to spin, splashing, flailing in desperation like a drowning swimmer, flames and debris shooting off in every direction as the helicopter exploded. Then it settled deeper into the sea, the gentle waves covering most of the smoking hulk.

It was a few moments before anyone in the mini-sub said anything. They stood there as the SWCS bobbed gently in the waves, then bobbed even higher when the swells from the chopper's impact reached them. It was Tony Garcia who finally piped up.

"Skipper, we don't want to be late for chow. Supposed to be pizza night and I don't want the anchovy ones to be gone."

Ψ

It always seemed to be rush hour in Taipei. If traffic was a measure of the success of the nation's economy, Taiwan was on a roll. But at 2230 on a weeknight?

TJ Dillon stepped out of the Tonghua Night Market. Linjiang Street was jammed with traffic, as usual. He looked up and down the busy thoroughfare in front of the restaurant. No sign of his car and driver.

Admiral Ward's dining recommendations had turned out to be superb so far. He touched his belly. The cho dofu had been delicious, if aromatic. It wasn't called "stinky tofu" for nothing.

He really needed to stay in shape, just in case his employer required him to do something more strenuous than read reports and peruse data and keep track of the newly planted submarine sensors out there in the Philippine and South China Seas. Which, by the way, had so far shown little more than whale farts.

Now, where was Bo, his affable and helpful driver? Too helpful, sometimes. Bo kept telling Dillon he would be honored to take him to those places where he could sample every one of his nation's pleasures. Emphasis always on "every." Even when TJ assured him there was a Mrs. Dillon back in the USA, in St. Petersburg, Florida, and that he had chosen to remain true to her and his son, TJ Jr., regardless of the intensity of the temptation.

"Okay, but if you ever want, ours is a very open society. You can only imagine," Bo would insist, with a sly grin and a quick wink to emphasize the possibilities.

Bo had texted, not three minutes ago, that he was circling the block and would pick him up right here. So, where was he? There was actually work to do on his laptop back in his hotel room.

TJ leaned out, trying to catch a glimpse of the maroon Mercedes. Not exactly the least ostentatious choice for wheels while he was here. Not for someone specifically trying not to be noticed.

Exactly what a rich American executive would arrange, Jon Ward had assured him.

Whack!

Something solid and quick sent TJ Dillon sprawling painfully, tumbling backward almost to the building that housed the restaurant. His head hit the cement sidewalk hard. His first thought was that he had been struck by a car. But then, as he struggled for breath, he heard the unmistakable cracks of gunshots—from two different directions—the screech of tires, a loud, heavy crash as something—an automobile, maybe—slammed into something else immovable.

Then, more sharp gunshots. A barrage of them. A ricochet. Shouts of fear. Or pain?

He tried to get to his feet, to spot an alleyway, a trash barrel, anything for cover. Dillon had been in enough shootouts to know when he was in the middle of one. All he could do was roll into the skinny alcove that led into the restaurant's foyer. He tried to make himself as small and invisible as he could.

He smelled garlic. Garlic and gun smoke. Then gasoline.

"Master Chief Dillon! Master Chief Dillon?"

Someone—a female voice—was calling his name. At least a name to which he had not answered in more than a decade. He dared a quick look around the corner of the alcove.

A beautiful Asian woman, in a business suit but assuming a perfect fighting shooting stance, her pistol pointed not toward him but at something happening in the street. He glanced that way. A car, on its side against the median barrier, flames already lapping at the engine compartment. A single shooter stretched half out of the driver's side, motionless, draped across the door, pistol still in his hand, considerable blood dripping off the barrel of his gun onto the pavement.

"Sorry for the body block, but...you okay?"

He finally found the strength to stand, but things around him continued to swirl.

"I think so."

Traffic was snarled. A few curious drivers were climbing out to see what was going on. Smoke billowed from the overturned vehicle. The waver of a distant siren.

"There was another one in the car. Before he wakes up, how about you come with me?"

"My driver was going to be..."

"He won't be coming."

She motioned for him to follow her. They stepped quickly to the end of the block and turned left, up the next street. The maroon Mercedes sat there, half on the curb, its front fender against a crooked light pole. Bo was at the wheel, eyes open, a bullet hole in the middle of his forehead.

TJ Dillon knew not to even slow down. Nor to doubt the woman. If she had wanted to kill him, she'd had her chance. He dutifully followed her as she quickly jaywalked across the street to a parking garage entrance.

"You obviously know my name. I must have missed yours."

"I am Li Min Zhou. Admiral Ward told you I would be in contact, right?"

Yes, he had. But not necessarily in the middle of a raging gun battle on a Taipei boulevard. Someone who could fill him in on some things that might impact what he was doing there. Some things to be on the lookout for and why they might matter.

Li touched the key fob and lights flashed on a Honda Accord backed into a spot not far away. She motioned for him to get into the passenger seat. Only then did she stick the pistol into the handbag she had been carrying on her shoulder.

"Bed bugs."

"Excuse me?"

"If anyone asks why you switched hotels, tell them there were bed bugs."

"I'm switching hotels?"

She turned and looked at him as she cranked the engine.

"We have already moved your things." She pulled out of the parking spot with a screech. "Look, they were not after you. They were after me. But they knew before you did that I was going to contact you as you left the restaurant. And you would have been killed in the crossfire, just in case. So far, as far as I know, they suspect that I was merely trying to get close to an American businessman who was working in Taipei. That I wanted to see if I could learn about anything else that might be going on. Like they smell a rat and it might be a cover for other types of espionage."

TJ Dillon rubbed his forehead with his thumb. He was now dizzier than before, but not from the body blow or the hard landing on the sidewalk.

She steered the Honda to the attendant's stand, waved at the woman inside—who had already opened the gate for them—and pulled out into the street, turning away from the wrecked Mercedes, the dead driver, and all the mayhem on the main road in front of the restaurant.

"I don't understand."

Two police cars rushed past them, lights flashing and sirens shrieking, headed the other way.

"Of course not. It's complicated. Let's just say that they know a lot more than they should. Not all. Not nearly all. Just enough to be suspicious, which is concerning but not a show-stopper. And to get you, me, and your driver killed. But let's get as far from here as we can while they are still just one out of three. And then I'll explain it. If I can." She turned and gave him an absolutely dazzling smile. "It's complicated."

He looked at her sideways and braced himself for the on-two-wheels, tire-squealing turn she was in the process of making.

"Bed bugs, huh?"

That dazzling smile again.

"Occupational hazard."

❧

7

Vice Admiral Yon Hun Glo awoke from a fitful nap and glanced out the window as his plane banked, coming around to the approach course to Sanya Phoenix International Airport. The city and its powdery sand beaches stretched out along Hainan Island's southern coast. This tropical isle was one of China's most popular vacation destinations. High-rise hotels and condominiums lined the beachfront while luxurious vacation homes dotted the hillsides up and away from the beaches.

But Yon Hun Glo had not rushed down here from PLAN Naval Headquarters in Beijing to enjoy some fun in the sun. Far from it. By this time tomorrow, he fully expected to be several hundred miles out to sea.

The staff car, a black Mercedes limo, met the admiral at the VIP gate and immediately sped away, headed out onto China National Highway 225, the Guo Doa. Traffic was thick, slow-moving. Even so, the usually impatient Yon Hun Glo sat back and reviewed the secure emails on his tablet as the limo inched down Jiefang Road into Sanya. Finally, traffic thinned a bit and they made better speed once they cleared the center of the city and were on Yuyu Road toward Yulin. By the time they pulled to a stop at the pier, Yon Hun Glo had managed to wade through most of the detritus that seemed to pile up in his virtual in-basket. For a fleeting instant he longed for the days when all he needed to do to escape the cloying bureaucracy was to lower the periscope and take his submarine deep. Now, with the responsibility as Commander of the PLAN Submarine Force, he was at the mercy of every minor Party gofer anxious to make points. There was no escape.

The Admiral's Barge, resplendent with polished brass and gleaming teak, made short work of crossing Yulin Harbor from the pier to the vast and growing naval base on the far shore. The harbor was crowded with warships, ferries, and cruise liners, either heading out or returning from the deep, blue South China Sea.

A UAZ personnel carrier was waiting at the pier to whisk Yon Hun Glo past the surface-ship piers, filled with destroyers and frigates, all busily getting ready for sea. There was frenzied activity everywhere. Next, the gigantic carrier pier served as a temporary home to two of the PLAN's massive aircraft carriers.

The admiral smiled and snorted as he watched the hustle and bustle all around him. His brother had quoted Sun Tzu—as usual—as they had discussed the plan for the mission he was now on. The great military strategist had said, "All warfare is based on deception. There is no place where espionage is not used. Offer the enemy bait to lure him."

As Yon Hun Glo gazed out over the vast beehive of activity, he saw the massive deception at work. The American spy satellites would closely watch the surface fleet arm for war. It was all a massive sleight of hand, a diversion to keep them busy while he did something else entirely. A Shakespeare quote came to his mind: "Sound and fury, signifying nothing."

The personnel carrier hurried further down the coast road, passing still more piers, warehouses, and maintenance buildings. Then, it suddenly made a sharp left turn into the entrance of a mammoth man-made cavern. The granite had been hewn out to offer an accessway that was fully twenty meters from the surface of the water to the top. It was easily thirty meters across the water, plus another ten meters on either side to form a very wide entrance road.

The admiral had to blink a few times as his eyes adjusted to the change from the brilliant tropical sun outside to the much less glaring artificial illumination inside the giant cavern. Then, he caught his breath as he saw, nestled up against the nearside wharf, his old boat, the *Wushiwu*. And beyond, three sister submarines. Across the dark water, on the far-side wharf, a pair of Type-93A modified *Shang*-class nuclear attack submarines sat motionless. His brother, Yon Ba Deng, had strongly suggested that they use these nuclear-powered boats for this mission. It had required considerable persuasion to convince the Assistant Vice Deputy to the Minister of National Defense for Naval Matters—and technically Yon Hun Glo's boss—that stealth was far more important than speed for this mission. Besides, as capable as they were, the *Shang*s would be no match for the American *Virginia*-class boats in the unlikely possibility they encountered such an adversary out there.

And there was a much more interesting use for the nuclear-powered boats. They could perform a far more sinister diversion. And the key to his and his brother's bold plan was diversion.

The personnel carrier came to a halt at the foot of the

Wushiwu's gangway. Yon Hun Glo was surprised to feel such a strong wave of nostalgia as he walked toward the brow of his old boat. Once a submariner, always a submariner. Now, even as her new captain, Liu Zhang, and the boat's political officer, Yu Feng, waited at the boat's end of the short brow, Yon Hun Glo hesitated for a moment, watching his former command bob easily in the light swell from a passing vessel.

Yon made a quick inspection. The *Wushiwu*'s mooring lines were crisply faked out in neat figure eights. Line handlers stood stiffly at the ready at each mooring line, awaiting the command to cast off. The shore power cables dangled limply from a crane, while the ship's diesels already grumbled deeply, announcing they, too, were prepared to depart.

The admiral—always on command—could not suppress a tight smile. "His" boat was ready to get underway, precisely as he had ordered.

Yon Hun Glo finally crossed the brow and boarded the *Wushiwu*. He bowed, greeting Captain Liu and Political Officer Yu, both of whom knew precisely what was running through the admiral's mind as he stepped aboard. Then he dropped down the hatch into the boat, skimmed down the ladder with the practiced submariner's style, immediately passed through the control room—noticing that the same swirl of smells still circulated throughout the vessel—and then climbed the well-worn ladder to the bridge. He was a little surprised—but very pleased—to see that *Wushiwu* had already backed from the pier and out into the channel, and she was now heading toward the cavern's mouth.

The other three boats were in various stages of following *Wushiwu* out to sea as soon as she led the way. As with all PLAN submarines, they were officially known only by their pennant numbers, Pennant Numbers Eighteen, Nineteen, and Twenty, respectively. However, sailors being sailors, and inevitably a superstitious lot even in today's PLAN, they knew their boats as the *Shiba,* the *Shijiu,* and the *Ershi.*

The trio of *Yuan*-class submarines dutifully followed the leader out to open water in a line, like ducks behind their mother. Then, they all turned south before diving and disappearing from sight.

Ψ

The KH-12 Advanced Keyhole satellite passed two hundred and fifty miles above southern China. The bird's advanced multi-spectral cameras continuously photographed a swath of almost a thousand miles wide and streamed the data up to a geosynchronous communications satellite orbiting at twenty-three thousand miles out over the central Pacific. From there it was downlinked to the National Geospatial Intelligence Agency, located in Fort Belvoir, Virginia.

The images, each with a resolution good enough to read a license plate number, were automatically reviewed by some very advanced artificial intelligence algorithms running on some of the world's most advanced super-computers.

Fifteen minutes after the four *Yuan* submarines emerged from the cave on Hainan Island, the phone rang in Jon Ward's office in the Pentagon.

Ψ

The *George Mason* had this stretch of the Philippine Sea all to itself. In one of the most heavily traveled shipping lanes in the world, that was an exceedingly rare event. The submarine's officers knew it was time to make the most of the opportunity. LCDR Jackson Biddle, the executive officer, and LCDR Billy Jonas, the engineer, both stood as their commanding officer, Brian Edwards, stepped into the wardroom. The chief of the boat, Dennis Oshley, and three other chiefs—all nukes— were sitting at the other end of the wardroom table. They stood as well.

When Edwards took his seat at the head of the table, they all plopped down.

"Okay, Eng," Edwards started. "We can spend the next couple of hours playing around out here in all this empty ocean. The Nav says we are at the front end of our patrol box already, so we have a couple of hours before PIM catches up with us. You got your trainees all ready to show their stuff?"

Billy Jonas was a product of the University of Nebraska NROTC program and the Navy Nuclear Power Training pipeline. He had reported aboard the *George Mason* only a few days before they left Pearl Harbor on this WESTPAC deployment. At just five foot seven and a few pounds overweight, he was already known to the crew as "Fireplug."

"They've finished the check-outs and prac facs for these drills," Jonas answered. He flashed an evil grin. "Whether they really are ready or not, we'll soon find out. ET3 Maddox is the reactor operator trainee. I've got four trainees in the engine room. MM1 Nelson is the engineering watch supervisor trainee, and Ensign Walters is the engineering officer of the watch under instruction."

As Edwards nodded his approval, Jackson Biddle chimed in. "Skipper, I've got ST1 Hannon as copilot U/I and Lieutenant jg Pawley as officer of the deck U/I. If you can observe Mr. Pawley, the COB can observe Hannon."

Edwards nodded and the discussion shifted to what havoc they were about to wreak on the trainees. They also ran through the safety precautions to make sure nothing got out of hand. Despite the common belief, there was very little down-time on a submarine at sea. Continual training helped ensure every man and woman knew what to do while on watch, and especially if something went haywire. These drills were as close as they could get to train for the real thing, because for most of them, once they started, they pretty much were the real thing. Thirty minutes after the start of the meeting, they all filed out and took their stations.

Edwards walked into the control room. Ray Pawley was huddled with Ashton Jennings, the WEPs, and the on-watch officer of the deck. They were closely studying a screen that told them all the immediate actions that should be taken for a reactor scram. That was the term for an emergency shutdown of a nuclear reactor by dropping all the control rods to squelch the fission reaction.

Joshua Hannon sat in the co-pilot's seat. Chief Schmidt sat in the pilot's seat beside him. The atmosphere in *George Mason*'s control room was tense, expectant.

"Mr. Pawley, you think you have a handle on this?" Edwards asked as he stepped up to the command console. He flipped through the sonar displays as he waited for the young officer's answer. Good. Nothing on the screens. No contacts out as far as *George Mason*'s supremely sensitive sensors and high-tech processing algorithms could reach.

"Yes...yes, sir," Pawley answered, stuttering nervously, a thin trickle of sweat running down the side of his face.

"Reactor scram!" the announcing system suddenly blared throughout the boat. "Conn, maneuvering, reactor scram, answering all stop. No apparent cause."

"Pilot, make your depth one-five-zero feet," Pawley coolly ordered, but then, "Left full ridder...uh...I mean rudder. Steady course south. Rig ship for reduced electrical."

The big boat was already angling upward as the pilot used

what remaining speed he had to get shallow and maneuver the ship around to the ordered course.

Joshua Hannon grabbed the IMC microphone and announced, "Reactor scram, rig ship for reduced electrical, casualty assistance team lay aft." He then flipped a couple of switches that secured most of the ventilation fans and other electrical equipment that were, at least temporarily, unnecessary. That included the toaster and coffee pots in the galley and almost all of the ventilation and air conditioning systems. The control room suddenly got quiet—no one noticed the noise of the constantly blowing ventilation fans until they were no longer there—and the temperature had already begun to rise.

"Sonar, clearing baffles to the left. Report all contacts," Pawley called out to the sonar operators. They sat over on the starboard side of the control room and could hear the OOD U/I just fine without using the communications system. They would be looking for any quiet contact that may have snuck up on them in the sub's baffles, the area directly behind the boat where hull-mounted sonar units were unable to hear anything.

"Conn, maneuvering, rigged for delayed scram. Request 'prepare to snorkel,'" came the report over the engineering announcing circuit. The nukes had not immediately found and fixed the cause of the reactor scram. But they had secured all unnecessary steam loads so that the residual reactor steam and heat would be available for emergency propulsion. They had also lined up the engine room systems to be ready to rapidly come back online when the reactor was "fixed."

Everyone on board the submarine knew one thing for damn certain. This might be a drill for training purposes, but when the control rods back there in the nuclear reactor hit the bottom, it was no longer just a drill. The reactor was really shut down. It would not be making power again until they had successfully completed all the procedures to safely and rapidly restart it. It was analogous to the pilot of a fighter plane turning off his jet engine to go through procedures for a flameout. It might be for training, but if he did not get power back quickly, very bad things would really happen.

"Pilot, make your depth six-two feet," Pawley ordered.

Chief Schmidt reached over to his flat-panel display and keyed in six-two feet as the ordered depth. The big sub started to angle up, but their forward speed had dropped to near zero. It just was not moving fast enough to get up to periscope depth. Ray Pawley recognized that he had a choice to make: use some of the remaining residual reactor heat to turn the propulsor, or shift propulsion to the emergency propulsion motor and use the battery to move the sub. Or he could hover up, using high pressure air to blow water out of the trim tanks.

But Pawley also recognized he did not have a great deal of time to study the situation.

"Co-pilot, hover up to six-two feet and prepare to snorkel," he ordered confidently.

"Hover up to six-two feet and prepare to snorkel, aye," Joshua Hannon answered, reaching toward a button on his flat-panel display. Chief Schmidt reached over and swatted Hannon's hand away. Shaking his head, the experienced pilot pointed to the correct switches to line the trim system up so they would automatically blow water overboard. That would bring them up to periscope depth. Sure enough, the big boat started to move vertically upward.

Ashton Jennings leaned over to Ray Pawley and quietly asked, "You suppose you might want to be able to see out when you get up to PD? Might be helpful, just in case some-body's up there."

Pawley nodded. "Co-pilot, raise number two scope."

The low-profile photonics mast (LPPM) slid up, but the only picture on the large screen command display was a uniform blue. Gradually, though, the blue shade became paler, until finally the video cameras cleared the sea surface. It was a clear, sunny day in the Philippine Sea. And a quick 360-degree scan verified that no unexpected company was up there to greet them.

"No close contacts," Ray Pawley called out. "Commence snorkeling."

"Snorkeling" was exactly what it sounded like. A pipe deployed up to the surface to take in fresh air while allowing smoke from the diesel generator to be ejected from the boat.

"Commence snorkeling, aye," Hannon answered. "Snorkel mast coming up." The big covered pipe appeared on the command display. Seconds later, Hannon announced, "The ship is snorkeling. The diesel is ready for full loading."

Air began to move in the control room again as the big Caterpillar diesel down in lower level sucked in great gobs of fresh sea air and pushed diesel exhaust smoke back overboard.

"Conn, maneuvering. The diesel is not assuming electrical loads. The diesel breaker will not shut. Engineer recommends securing from the drill," the engineering announcing circuit boomed. There was a problem, and it was a real one, not part of the drill. The generator was not able to provide the power needed. It was time for the first team to fix the problem with the diesel.

Edwards grabbed the 1MC microphone and ordered, "Secure from scram drill for training. Secure snorkeling. Conduct a fast recovery start-up."

Ten minutes later, the reactor plant was back up online, supplying steam to the turbines and main engines. The sub was back down at three hundred feet, again heading west. The electricians had found a blown fuse in the diesel breaker-closing circuit and replaced it. The drill had gone well and had even uncovered a problem that would have been serious had they been engaging the enemy. Or if they had actually experienced a reactor scram.

Meanwhile, the *George Mason* had received orders. They were to proceed to Subic Bay in the Philippines for a liberty call in four days.

Nice prize for a—mostly—successful drill.

Ψ

Two hours after the *Yuan* submarines disappeared beneath the waves, the two Type 93A nuclear submarines at Hainan completed their load-out. The last bus to pull up to the pier disgorged two platoons of black-uniformed Jiaolong Assault Team special operators. The highly trained and supremely fit Marines efficiently moved their mounds of equipment onto the submarines. A pier crane lifted each of their assault boats and swung them over to where they could be manhandled into each submarine's dry-deck shelter. The shelter, like a giant wart on the sleek nuclear submarine's back, had a large clamshell at its aft end that swung open to allow easy access to the shelter's cavernous interior. There was plenty of room in each shelter to store a pair of assault boats and all of the team's heavy weapons.

An hour after the Jiaolong Team arrived, the clamshells slammed shut on the shelters. The last special operator scurried across the brow as it was being lifted away. The two submarines moved out into the center of the channel and slipped out of the cave mouth. The sun was setting over Hainan Island as they steamed out into open water.

An hour later, the two dived at almost the same point

where the *Yuan*s had submerged that morning. But these two subs steered a course to the northeast. At a cruising speed of thirty kilometers per hour, they would be off the coast of Taiwan and ready to execute their mission in thirty-six hours.

An hour after they submerged, the Naval Ocean Processing Facility (NOPF) Whidbey Island was reporting their first hits on a suspected Chinese nuclear submarine in the South China Sea. The new seismic array lying on the ocean bottom on the south side of Taiwan—supposedly only there to detect earthquakes and potential tsunamis—was doing its optional job. NOPF's high-speed computers churned away on the mass of acoustic data, separating the extraneous noise from the contacts of interest, and then applying advanced algorithms to identify the submarines and figure out what they were up to.

Fifteen minutes after the first alert warning, a message flashed on Rear Admiral Jon Ward's classified computer. An hour later the first of a rotation of P-8 ASW aircraft was wheels up from Anderson Air Force Base on the island of Guam in the Marianas.

The USNS *Impeccable,* with her twin TL-29 towed arrays streaming over a mile behind the ship, was conducting a routine patrol in the East China Sea, just north of Okinawa. The ship spun around and headed south, but it would take a while before it could be of help. At its ponderous speed of four knots, it would be five days before the ship would be in a position to do any good in this search.

Ψ

The USS *Boise* cruised at periscope depth three miles off the coast of Prattle Island, on the western edge of the Paracel Archipelago, the cluster of reefs and islets at the northern end of the South China Sea. Being almost equidistant between Vietnam and China, the islands were claimed by both countries, but China currently possessed them. And they had wasted no time getting several of them heavily fortified.

That included Prattle Island. Though little more than a pile of sand and coral, Prattle now boasted a deep-water protected harbor and an airfield capable of handling heavy bombers. This was all protected with batteries of surface-to-air and surface-to-surface missiles, besides the menacing natural reefs that encircled almost all the island.

The *Boise* had spent the better part of a week cruising back and forth, steaming as close as they could safely and covertly, gathering all the electronic and communications signals that they could vacuum out of the ether. Being close but hidden allowed the submarine to gather intelligence when the other side had no suspicions that they were being monitored. And the submarine could stay on station for a very long time.

The downside was that it was excruciatingly boring work. As the navigator so eloquently described it, "So far all we've done is watch seagulls fornicate."

"Conn, Radio, request captain come to radio."

The sudden voice of the 21MC announcement disturbed the quiet in the control room. Commander Chet Allison ducked out the back door of the compartment, dodged around the ring-laser gyro binnacles, and stepped into the radio room.

The radioman of the watch was already extending to him a paper printout as he stepped inside the small room. The skipper scanned the document, then promptly spun on his heel and headed to the control room.

After a quick glance at the electronic navigation chart display, he ordered, "Officer of the Deck, come to course three-two-zero. Make your depth one-five-zero feet. Come to ahead standard. When we get to deep water, come to six hundred feet and a full bell."

Turning to the chief of the watch, the skipper continued, "Send the messenger to find the XO and the navigator. Looks like a couple of CHICOM nukes are out of the barn. We are being vectored to find them."

8

The little wolf pack of Chinese PLAN submarines —or *lang qun*, as Yon Hun Glo had dubbed them—steered a precise course of one-three-zero for exactly two hundred kilometers. Yon Hun Glo's planners at naval headquarters back in Beijing had calculated that a two-hundred-kilometer diversion was the distance necessary to distract the Americans in that direction. At a signal from the *Wushiwu*, the *lang qun* swung around to a course of zero-seven-zero. That headed them toward the Luzon Strait, eleven hundred kilometers off their bows.

The admiral calculated that it would take the better part of six days steaming at their current ten-kilometer-per-hour speed. The slow pace was frustrating, especially to a man accustomed to going where he needed to be at all good speed. But the admiral knew that if they tried to go any faster, they would have to use their batteries to supplement their air-independent propulsion systems. The AIP simply did not have the capacity to push the boats at any more than a patrol speed. And, of course, using their batteries meant that the boats would have to snorkel frequently. Every time they ran their diesels, they were just inviting the Americans to come find them. Stealth was far more important than speed, typically, and especially on this particular mission. It was essential that they arrive in Tonga before the Americans had any idea that the Chinese Navy—and more importantly, four of their submarines—was swimming about anywhere in the South Pacific. Or noticed they were taking extraordinary steps to remain undetected.

Admiral Yon Hun Glo glanced up from the chart he was studying to see Captain Liu and Political Officer Yu walk into the control room, almost as if in lock-step marching formation. The two men seemed to always be together, shadows of each other. So far, he had never seen one without the other. He could only be thankful that he had left command of a submarine before a political officer had been assigned to his boat, there at his elbow to always consider the Communist Party aspect of any action the boat's captain might desire to undertake. Nowadays, almost every ship in the PLAN had such a political officer.

Just then, he felt the boat angle upward and watched as the *Wushiwu* proceeded up to periscope depth. He frowned, then glanced over questioningly to where Captain Liu stood.

The officer answered the admiral's unasked question. "It is time to copy communications. The operations order specifies copying communications every eight hours."

The admiral glanced at his watch. Indeed, it had been precisely eight hours since they dove beneath the surface after departing Yulin. He sensed that this pair of officers were *apparatchiks*, blindly devoted to the Communist Party and totally incapable of independent thought. He was not surprised but reminded himself that he would have to take that into account going forward.

The trip to periscope depth and copying the broadcast proceeded without event. But then, as Admiral Yon Hun Glo read through the intelligence summary, he noted one message that immediately raised the hairs on the back of his neck. Navy Intelligence was reporting that an American submarine was scheduled for a port call in Subic Bay, Philippines, due to arrive sometime within the next four to eight days. The analysts gave the report a very high probability based on the reliability of the sources cited within the Philippines.

Yon Hun Glo smiled to himself as he read the information and credit given to the very spy network that he and his brother maintained in the Pacific island nation. Filipino civilian dock workers at the base. A stock clerk for a supplier. Deckhands on harbor tugs. Hotel clerks, taxi drivers, dollar-to-peso currency-exchange spots, anyone who might be alerted to expect an uptick in business. Even bar maids at the many joints that ringed the sprawling Subic Bay Freeport Zone—as the former US Naval Base was now known—just as they inevitably did at any port anywhere in the world. They all seemed to know the comings and goings of ships, aircraft, troops, and other assets, all before anyone else, and with impressive accuracy. They were also happy to accept a nice payment for information that proved to be correct and useful, even if they had no idea about the source of such extra income. Many of them unabashedly trafficked info to all sides if there was money to be made.

The admiral keyed the navigation display screen to shift to a scale that showed all of the South China Sea and beyond, out into the Philippine Sea between Luzon and the Marianas. Fiddling with the controls, he back plotted several possible tracks for the American submarine and immediately saw the very real possibility that its route might well pass right by where he was leading his little *lang qun*. That would be disastrous. The Americans were good. They were also relentless. Though they would have no reason to suspect that four

Chinese submarines were transiting in the vicinity, and despite the PLAN boats' stealth, there was a real chance they would be detected. That must not occur.

After staring at the electronic chart for a long time, Yon Hun Glo remembered yet another one of the interminable Sun Tzu sayings that his brother was always quoting: "Be where your enemy is not."

But how could he tell for certain where that was? How far off plan did he dare redirect their course?

Then he saw a way. The shortest, least detectable, least expected route was right through the Philippines. Head south, down into the Sulu Sea, instead of north through the Luzon Strait. Then proceed through the Celebes Sea. He was well aware most of such a track would be within Philippine territorial waters. Going through there while submerged would be an act of war. But to hell with Philippine sovereignty. Such political territorial nonsense only mattered if he was caught. And nobody was going to catch his *lang qun.*

"Captain Liu, come to course south and steer for the Mindoro Strait," Yon Hun Glo ordered. "Signal the *lang qun* to follow you."

The political officer, Yu, snapped around to face him.

"Admiral, with all respect, we cannot simply make course changes on our own like this. We must discuss this in the context of broader Party objectives and potential ramifications. Then, when we have an approved plan, we would need to ..."

Admiral Yon Hun Glo glared at the upstart and held up a hand, palm out.

"Political Officer Yu, there was no 'we' in my order. Nor was there any room for opinion or discussion. Take this as your one warning. If you dare to question any of my orders in the future, you will learn about 'broader Party objectives' in a very hard and painful way. Do you understand?"

The diminutive officer seemed to shrink to an even smaller stature under the flag officer's tirade. He could only nod meekly that he understood, then slink off toward his stateroom.

"Now, Captain Liu, carry out my orders. Make best course for the Sulu Sea and then through to the Celebes Sea."

For an instant, Yon Hun Glo actually hoped the submarine captain would question his orders, too. Then he could unleash the full wrath and power of his exalted position in the People's Liberation Army Navy.

No such opportunity. The naval officer was well indoctrinated into doing what he was ordered to do by a superior without question. He promptly gave the orders to assume the new course. If there was an issue, it would be between the admiral and the political officer. And, as the Americans would say in their western movies, "Let the chips fall where they may."

Ψ

HMAS *Audacious* was exactly where Commander Geoffrey Smythe wanted to be, doing a barrier search fifty miles to the west of the Paracel Islands. The Chinese wolf pack would surely turn south after clearing the shallow water around Hainan and head down the South China Sea. The Australian submarine was perfectly positioned to detect them and then fall into trail behind them to try to learn what they were up to.

Smythe knew that the Type 2076 sonar with which *Audacious* was equipped was far superior to the *Yuan's* sensors. He also knew that his boat was quieter than anything the Chinese had afloat. It would not exactly be easy since he was outnumbered, but he also figured that four-on-one was about even odds.

The first leg, from west to east, had come up cold. It was time to turn around and do an east-to-west leg.

"Watch Officer, come left and steady on course two-seven-zero," he ordered.

The big diesel submarine had just begun its turn when Sonar reported, "Possible contact on the 2065 towed array just before the turn. Best ambiguous bearings zero-three-zero and one-five-zero."

Smythe smiled broadly as he grabbed the microphone. "Sonar, classification on the contact?"

"Captain, we didn't hold it long enough before the array went unstable. No classification."

The smile was gone. Smythe jammed the microphone back in its holder. Damn bad luck! Now there was nothing to do but finish the turn and pray that the contact would be regained. If not, then he could chase to the northeast, or maybe the southeast, to try to regain it. And it might not even be the Chinese boats. He could be chasing some amorous whale. There simply was not enough information to make any kind of intelligent decision.

The wait was interminable. Ten minutes after coming to the new course, Sonar finally reported that the array was stable and they were commencing a search.

An hour passed before Smythe admitted to himself that whatever they thought they had heard before the turn was now long gone. Even if it was really anything at all.

Ψ

"Do you know what a fumarole is?"

TJ Dillon had not a clue. "Some kind of sushi?"

Li Min Zhou smiled and took a sip of her tea. It was three a.m. local time in Taipei. Dillon and Zhou were the only customers in the McDonald's, a block down the street from the Grand Hyatt in the city's Xinyi District. An elderly employee slowly mopped the floor at the far side of the dining area. There were relatively few cars on the normally busy Songshou Road outside.

"Don't feel bad. I had to Google it." She gave him a brief description.

Dillon winced and shook his head. "Okay, I know we're killing time until your guy gets here with my stuff, but why do we care about a pile of undersea mud?"

"Apparently, or at least according to some well-founded rumors, while Mother Earth was puking up all that sludge, she brought up a treasure trove of gold and left it there, on the bottom of the sea, for the taking. Assuming you have a means to go down that deep and scoop it up. That, we believe, is one of several reasons for a sudden and eager push within the Chinese government and military to extend their Belt and Roads Initiative down into the South Pacific. And into Tonga in particular. Not much else there unless you are working on a suntan."

Li Min took another sip and glanced up at Dillon.

"Some higher-ups in the military know about the gold and would like to get a bunch of it for themselves. That meshes nicely with the desires of some others—in the Party and out—who have no idea about any gold mud. They simply want to restore the Middle Kingdom to what they see as its rightful place, at the center of the world. But they will not question such a favorable turn of events for their cause."

The Chinese operative was getting more and more agitated as she continued her tirade.

"Then there is the third faction, the ones who have gotten

filthy rich with their odd amalgam of communism and capitalism and would like to keep things tense, all right, but definitely do not want to push the US or other economies so far that they and their fat bank accounts get hurt in the rebound. They've prevented hostilities so far, but, as you know, that has begun to change, and this group is outnumbered, outranked, and will soon find themselves on the outside."

TJ Dillon sat, open-mouthed, staring at the beautiful spy with the stunning eyes. Then he shook his head again, trying to take it all in.

"Okay, most of that I know. At least the three factions. And a few guys who blur the lines. The part about the gold down there at the bottom of the ocean...I can see how that might tip things toward a new quadrant." He finally took a sip of his coffee, not even noticing it was cold.

"Something was bound to," Li Min Zhou went on. "The military doesn't trust the Communist Party. The Party doesn't trust the military. The quasi-capitalists don't trust anyone but wouldn't dare challenge anybody so long as they are taking over the world one iPhone or kid's toy or American savings-and-loan at a time. Then, of course, there is enough corruption everywhere and at all levels that an explosion is inevitable. As big as they are, as many tentacles as these bastards have in governments all over, and assuming they don't blow up the planet in the process, the global economy will be a disaster when it all hits the fan. And guess what that does to the value of that gold mud down there on the sea floor. If it even exists."

She sat back and looked at the ceiling. For the first time in the six hours he had known her, TJ Dillon could detect signs of fatigue on her face. Fatigue and sincere worry.

"May I ask you a question?" he queried. She gave the slightest of nods and closed her eyes. "There are...what?...a billion-and-a-half people in China. Why are so few of them like you? Why has there not been a revolution?"

She leaned forward, resting her arms on the table, and looked TJ Dillon squarely in the eyes. It appeared she had been waiting a long while for someone to finally ask her this question. And waiting just as impatiently to answer it.

"There are plenty more like me, but they do not dare. They have a roof, four walls, at least enough food to survive, and some kind of job. And they have their children, or as many as the government allows. They have been convinced since childhood that the country is ungovernable any other way, that there would only be chaos if the collective—the people—do not submit to the will of all. The alternative is to be governed by rich capitalists who prey on the people to build wealth and grab power. As they are told that it is in the USA, of course. Plus, if they do not submit to the will of the masses, their children will be taken away, their homes stolen, their jobs eliminated. All those bad things will happen for the good of all the people and, by the way, Mother China."

Zhou slumped down, as if the speech had claimed all her strength. Then she cocked her head, regained eye contact, and went on, quietly.

"When I was a little girl, the first song I learned was 'I Compare the Communist Party to My Mother.'" She quietly sang in Mandarin a few lines of what sounded like a sweet, peaceful lullaby. Dillon, fluent in the language, understood every word.

"Jesus. How old were you?"

"Four. Four years old. We stood at our desks every day in school...like your kindergarten in the West...and recited, 'Father is dear, Mother is dear, but none compare to the dearest Party.' From the earliest age, we constantly heard that the Party would take care of us, that we had all we needed and could be happy, and all we had to do was remain loyal to the Party."

She slumped down once more, leaning back on the bench seat, as if the words had worn her out.

"So, what changed you? Why did you turn on your own country? That had to be difficult..."

"I was lucky. I had skills they needed. Mathematics, digital communications, computer technology. I got to go to school in the US. Cal Tech. That was when I learned the real story. Logic convinced me that what I had been told all my life was wrong. Why was it necessary to lie so much if the Party really was the best hope for China? Did you know more than one hundred million people were murdered by the Party during the decades of Chinese communism? One hundred million good, honest, hard-working people who believed there was no better choice of government. I vowed I would make it my life's work to do what I could do to bring positive chaos to my country and the people there who would prosper if free. Chaos. The good chaos of democracy and a free society."

"I can't even imagine," Dillon responded when she finally stopped. The former SEAL suddenly tensed, his hand inches from the gun inside his suit coat. "So, who do you like in the World Cup?"

Zhou was savvy enough to not react at all, not to Dillon's tension, not to the sudden change of subject. A young man was quickly approaching them from the rear entrance of the restaurant.

"At ease. One of my guys," she said. "Hey, thanks for letting me blow off steam."

"Glad to listen."

"You have the data on the thumb drive for Ward. We'll have more details on what all the new activity out there is about shortly, who exactly is involved, and we'll know what to do. I hope. Looks to me, though, that all the factions are lining up and ready to make a move like right now. That, as you know as well as anybody, means somebody's going to get hurt in the melee."

The young man had stopped a respectful distance away, over near the soda dispenser with its scores of competing flavors of pop.

"Chan has your stuff," she told Dillon. "I assume you can upload the data on the drive. Just like checking your Gmail account, right?"

"I got it. Thank you again for saving my ass tonight. Maybe we can create some chaos. First the bad kind. Then the good kind, like what you've been trying to bring about," Dillon said, with all the sincerity he could muster.

"I don't think we have a choice, TJ. The whole planet is depending on us."

9

Lt. Bill Wilson stepped over to the Electronic Chart Display and Information System console (ECDIS) to check the *George Mason*'s position. As the mid-watch officer of the deck, his job was to make sure everything was ready to surface at first light. They would be just outside the twelve-mile limit off the entrance to Subic Bay, on the western coast of the Philippine island of Luzon.

He could feel his watch-section's eager anticipation, more than ready to pull into the most storied liberty port in all of Asia. Subic Bay and Olongapo City might have lost some of their allure from the heyday of when they housed the largest US military installation in the world, when the massive US Naval base graced those shores. All of that was gone now. But the stories of liberty in Subic Bay continued to reverberate around the fleet. And since the location still served as a replenishment port for US vessels, submarine sailors had the opportunity to blow off steam there after being submerged for months at a time.

"Sonar Supervisor," Wilson ordered, "take station to stow the TB-29 towed array."

ST1 Josh Hannon, standing watch as sonar supervisor, stood behind the narrowband operator. Frowning, he held up his hand. "Officer of the Deck, give me a couple of seconds. We're analyzing a new contact."

"Okay, but we need to have the array stowed in time to surface at first light," Wilson responded, rolling his eyes. What now? "Skipper ain't gonna like it if we hold up a perfectly good liberty port because sonar was busy analyzing snapping shrimp."

Hannon looked up. He was still frowning.

"Mr. Wilson, I suspect you had better call the skipper. I'm thinking our Subic liberty may be delayed for just a little bit."

"What are you rambling on about?"

"Well, those snapping shrimp just got classified as a submerged submarine. The eleven-hertz lines equate to a Chinese *Yuan*-class," Hannon reported. "Recommend you call the skipper and station the section tracking party while we get a leg on this guy. Sooner we find out what it is, sooner we can be wettin' our whistles on Magsaysay Boulevard."

Two minutes later, Brian Edwards walked into the control room, still wiping sleep out of his eyes but carrying his coffee mug. The section tracking party was just starting to gather information, working to identify this unexpected guest.

"What do you have, Mr. Wilson?" Edwards busily scanned the command display as the young OOD related what he knew for certain.

"Captain, on course south, making twelve knots. We have an eleven-hertz line on the TB-29. That equates to a Chinese *Yuan*-class submarine. Ambiguous bearings are three-one-zero, designate Sierra Four-Five, and zero-five-zero, designate Sierra Four-Six."

The TB-29A was a mile-long line of highly sensitive

hydrophones that were being towed along behind the *George Mason*. Since it was a single long line of phones, any sonar contact showed as being somewhere in a three-dimensional conical "bearing" around the array. The conical "bearing" was formed by the time delays in the beamformer. What this effectively meant was that any new sonar contact arrived as two contacts—now designated as Sierra Forty-Five and Sierra Forty-Six—on either side of the array and at equal, ambiguous angles. The only way to determine which of the two was the real one was to maneuver the sub to a new course and regain it. The side where the contact reappeared from the same direction was the true bearing line.

Edwards nodded, chewing his lower lip. He could see everything Wilson was telling him on the passive narrow-band display. "Okay, what are you planning to do?" he asked.

"Skipper, I'm thinking that if I come left to a course of something like one-two-zero, I can resolve ambiguity and still stay close to the navigator's track. If we're wrong, if it's not a Chinese boat, we could still get to the surfacing point, maybe an hour late."

Edwards shook his head. He stepped back to the ECDIS table. "First off, let's look at priorities. Finding and tracking a *Yuan* has a higher priority than a liberty call. The boss would not be happy if we were drinking San Miguel in Olongapo while the Chinese had a sub on the loose out in the South China Sea."

Lieutenant Wilson nodded as Edwards went on. "Now, look at the geography of this. If our new best friend was on bearing zero-five-zero, he is either really close to us or he is snuggled up to the Philippine coast and we went blowing right past him last night." He pointed at the chart display. "But, if he is really out at three-one-zero, he would probably be in the deep water somewhere to the west of Scarborough Shoal. Higher probability is that he is out that way. Let's come around to two-seven-zero to resolve ambiguity."

Jackson Biddle, his hair still wet from the shower, joined the group huddled around the ECDIS.

"So, we caught a fish, did we?" the XO asked as he looked carefully at the sonar displays. After flipping through several screens, he scratched his chin. "You know something, Skipper? The signature looks an awful lot like that *Yuan* we played with in the Arabian Sea a couple of years ago. What was that boat's name? The *Wushiwu*, wasn't it? One trigger-happy bastard."

Edwards nodded. "Sure looks like it, XO. Not one either of us is likely to forget. How about you draft a message to Subgroup Seven that we have contact while I supervise getting up to periscope depth. Better tell the boss that we have a friend out here. And we can grab the latest intel while we're up. Maybe there'll be a clue about this guy there."

Edwards turned to Bill Wilson and ordered, "Mr. Wilson, clear baffles to the right and come to periscope depth for comms. Come up on course two-seven-zero."

"Pilot, right full rudder, steady course two-seven-zero," Lt. Wilson ordered. "Make your depth one-five-zero feet."

The big boat swung around smoothly and came shallow, all the while searching for any close sonar contacts that could be a hazard.

Ten minutes later, the *George Mason* was back down at depth. Subgroup Seven, operating out of a nondescript building in Yokosuka, Japan, was now aware that the *George Mason* was playing footsie with a suspected Chinese submarine and probably would not make her port visit to Subic. The intel crowd would certainly be scurrying around, trying to find where the Chinese boat had come from and, more importantly, deduce where he was going. The operations team would be working out the complicated dance to make sure that the *George Mason* had enough water assigned to her so that she could maneuver without worrying about running into any friendly submarines. Literally.

In the crowded waters of the South China Sea, especially given how many of the littoral nations now operated diesel electric submarines lately, this had become a very real and complicated problem.

Underwater blind man's bluff with a ten-thousand-ton submarine would not be a fun game to play.

Ψ

Joe Glass had spent most of his long flight reading through a great stack of thick, boring reports that his chief of staff had dumped into the empty seat between them. Glass was beginning to understand that the old expression was absolutely true. The Navy really did sail on a sea of paperwork. It never seemed to end. At least the five-hour Omni International charter flight from Honolulu to American Samoa had provided a great opportunity to catch up.

The cabin steward's warning that they were descending into Pago Pago International Airport caught Commodore Glass in mid-red-pencil mode, editing new instructions for conducting a monitor watch. Hardly compelling reading. He shifted his interest to look out the window.

Pago Pago Harbor, encircled by small villages, came into view. Glass spotted the *Lewis B. Puller* anchored out in the middle of the harbor. The Military Sealift Command expeditionary mobile base ship—better known as the *Chesty Puller* after her famous Marine namesake—would be his new home for the near-term. He could also make out the black form of one of his submarines nestled up alongside the much larger ship. That would be the *Cheyenne*, newly arrived in port for a brief mid-deployment maintenance period.

Glass glanced around the cabin. The planeload of submarine sailors, shipyard workers, and technical experts would soon be busy, helping transform the sleepy harbor at Pago Pago into a bustling submarine maintenance and repair facility. Marrying up the expertise that his team represented with the pre-positioned equipment on the *Chesty Puller* would allow them to fix just about anything on a submarine short of something requiring a drydock. This saved almost two weeks of steaming each way for any boat operating in Southeast Asian waters.

The big 767 slapped down on Pago Pago's main runway and taxied over to an out-of-the-way corner of the apron. Glass could see a pair of C-17 Globemaster airplanes being unloaded directly to a pair of CH-53K heavy-lift helicopters. He smiled. That was certainly one of the benefits of using the *Chesty Puller*. She came with her own heliport.

"Proper preparation prevents poor performance," Glass muttered under his breath as he slid from his seat and pulled his sea bag from the overhead rack.

"Sir?" a sailor in the aisle in front of him asked.

"Oh, nothing. Just something a former skipper of mine used to tell us."

Ψ

Vice Deputy to the Minister of National Defense Soo Be Xian sat at his desk and watched the large monitor hanging on the far wall of his office. In split-screen on the other end of the video conference were Colonel General Xiang, Commanding General of Southern Theatre of Operation, and his Chief of Staff, Major General Shun. General Shun had just spent the last fifteen minutes explaining the tactical positioning of the three brigades from Fourteenth Army in the heavily forested highlands overlooking Lao Cai on the Red River in the far southernmost reaches of China. His elaborate maps and animation clearly showed how the mounted infantry units and armor brigades could be driving into Vietnam within an hour of receiving such operational orders.

Shun shifted the map to the east, down to where the border was depicting a decided bend into Vietnam to form the Muc Nam Quan border crossing. The bulge on the map, barely two miles wide and roughly four miles long, moved the border from the ancient Ming Dynasty Friendship Pass further into what had once been eight square miles of Vietnamese territory. This seemingly minor result of the 1979 Sino-Vietnamese War still rankled Vietnamese pride, even after all these years.

"We have moved the One-Twenty-Third Infantry Division to the Daxiang Reservoir area," Shun was explaining, waving his laser pointer to an area on the map only a few miles north of the disputed border crossing. "The Fifteenth Armored Brigade and the One-Twenty-First Motorized Infantry Brigade are both encamped in the hills just east of Youyizhen." He waved the pointer to an area a little further south.

Soo Be Xian nodded, understanding. The two generals had done exactly what he had ordered. However, the Vietnamese reaction so far had been much more measured than he had expected. They had only moved a few more companies of border guards north. Even the Coast Guard attack on the fishing fleet had only resulted in a minor diplomatic clamor and a Vietnamese request for still more arms from the US. He apparently needed more provocation if he was going to goad them into some action that he could turn right around and claim as a preemptive attack by the Vietnamese. A reaction in response to their unprovoked assault on the Middle Kingdom's sovereignty.

"General Xiang, I want you to move a battalion of main battle tanks right up on the border at the Muc Nam Quan border crossing. I want them so close to the border that if a mosquito flies out of the gun barrel, it will be in Vietnam. Am I clear?"

General Shun smiled. He, too, was disappointed their activities so far had not resulted in the opportunity for his forces to demonstrate their might in defense of China.

"Honored Vice Deputy, the Twenty-Second Tank Battalion is a Rapid Reaction Unit. It is equipped with the latest Type 99B main battle tanks. They can be lined up at the border crossing in two hours."

The screen showed an animated video sequence of a dozen tanks charging ominously down the Nan You Gao Su Road toward the border crossing.

Clearly impressed, Soo Be Xian smiled.

"Excellent! Make it happen now. And I have something a little more lethal that I want you to put in motion. From that Special Operations Brigade that you have in Guangzhou, I want you to move the best platoon of covert operators down to Fangcheng. From there, make arrangements for the team to do a covert insertion across the border into Vietnam. There is a Texhong facility just outside Quang Dien that must be destroyed. The extraction can be noisy. In fact, very noisy would be better for our purposes."

General Shun nodded grimly. An attack on the well-known yarn company's factory at the industrial park was required. It was not his role to question why. But the slight grin that crept onto his face assured that he was pleased to do his commander's bidding.

"Honored Vice Deputy, I have the best covert operations team in the PLA. And, for once, they will not be nearly so covert."

10

Yon Hun Glo watched carefully as the quartermaster plotted the latest GPS position on the submarine's electronic chart. When he was completely satisfied that the sailor had accurately plotted *Wushiwu's* position, the admiral ignored all the technology available to him and used his thumb and index finger to walk off the distance to the Mindoro Strait. He really wanted to make the transit through the narrow strait between the islands of Busuanga and Mindoro under the cover of darkness. That way there would be much less chance of being detected in that narrow and heavily traveled stretch of water.

Yon Hun Glo did the familiar time/distance/speed calculation in his head. They needed to make four hundred and seventy kilometers. At their current twelve-knot speed, they would arrive in the straits in the middle of the afternoon. Not acceptable.

"Comrade Captain Liu Zhang," the admiral said, glancing up at the submarine's captain. The admiral no longer made any effort to avoid sounding condescending when he spoke to the commanding officer. "Please signal the *lang qun* to come left to course one-four-seven and slow to ten kilometers per hour." Yon Hun Glo stopped, watching the toady little officer constantly nodding as he wrote down every single word. "And then you change course and slow accordingly. Do you understand my orders, Captain?"

Liu Zhang nodded even more vigorously as he stepped over to the submarine's underwater communications system. He first referred to his notes, lips moving as he ticked off each step.

Only then did he begin to send his message out to the rest of the trailing Chinese submarines.

Ψ

"Detecting underwater comms from Sierra Four-Five," Josh Hannon called out, a hint of pent-up excitement in his voice. "Fifteen-point-four kilohertz. Equates to a Chinese Wolfdog encrypted acoustic comms."

Jackson Biddle jumped across the *George Mason*'s control room to look over Hannon's shoulder at his display. "Are you sure?"

"XO, I really gotta cure you of jumpin' on my screen every time I report something," Hannon complained, only half joking. "You can see the same thing on the command display and it's a whole lot easier for me to do my job without you breathing down my neck."

Biddle, mumbling something about sonar techs and their love of taking showers, stepped back over to the command display. There, Billy Jonas was already trying to make sense of the tactical picture of what Hannon had just observed.

"XO, this doesn't add up very well at all," Jonas admitted. "Their Wolfdog system is supposed to be very narrow-beamed, highly directional, and very short range. Primarily for one sub to briefly communicate with another or with a single vessel on the surface. This guy's basically broadcasting. So, who is our Chinese friend trying to talk to? And where is whoever that might be?"

"Eng, I have the same questions," Biddle told him. "We've been tracking him putzing along due south for the last several hours. He's been staying real quiet, like he doesn't want to get his ass found out here. Now, all of a sudden, he has gotten real talkative. What gives?"

Just as Jonas was about to reply, Josh Hannon called out an update that was even more puzzling.

"Possible contact zig based on bearing rate. Zig toward. Increasing bearing rate."

Jonas immediately punched up the display for the narrow-band passive towed array. He cocked his head, now even more perplexed.

"I'm not seeing any change in received frequency. How sure are you that you're seeing a contact zig?"

"Went from a right-point-zero-five-degree per minute to a left-point-one. Pretty definite change in speed across the line of sight. He had to have zigged," Hannon explained.

"Well, he sure didn't change his speed in the line of sight," Jonas shot back. "Solid eleven-point-one hertz. No change."

Jackson Biddle, listening to the exchange, tapped his chin with a forefinger.

"Boys, a wise old submariner once told me that there are only two truths in passive ASW, bearing and received frequency. Everything else is a guess. If our two truths are telling us different stories, there is something we don't yet understand. And we absolutely need to, correct? Now, what are we overlooking? And do I need to remind you that this is not a drill? We are tailing a Chinese submarine in a highly inappropriate portion of the ocean."

As the three were trying to sort out the problem, the

passive search operator suddenly called out, "I have a second eleven-point-five-hertz contact. Two degrees to the right of Sierra Four-Five. Designate...Sierra Four-Seven. Classified submerged *Yuan*-class submarine."

The three men looked at each other.

"Well, that probably solves the riddle of who Sierra Four-Five was jabbering with," the exec said. "This thing just got twice as interesting, I'd say. But it still doesn't resolve our zig riddle."

Ensign Sam Walters was sitting at the fire control panel.

"XO, I might have an answer," he volunteered. "If I put an anchor on the solution where Hannon called a zig, then slew the solution course to match the bearings, then slow the solution to five knots to keep the speed in the line-of-sight constant, I get a solution that matches both the bearing rate and the frequency. I reckon he slowed when he turned."

Biddle nodded. It made sense. But now he had two Chinese subs out here to worry about. Two boats where they should not necessarily be, doing maneuvers that indicated they had some purpose in these waters rather than simply passing through. And even more worrisome, two submarines that might take violent issue with *George Mason* and her crew spying on them. One thing was certain. His orders from COMSUBGROUP SEVEN were to trail the *Yuan* and not lose contact. He meant to use every technology that his submarine possessed and every trick that he knew to make sure the Chinese subs didn't slip away.

He turned to Jonas. "Eng, stay on this course for now. Don't close either of the contacts within twenty-thousand yards. Last thing we want is for these two guys to know we are in the vicinity. I'm going to go wake the skipper and give him the good news."

Just as Biddle headed out of control toward the CO's stateroom, Josh Hannon called out some even more interesting news.

"New contact! Sierra Four-Eight, bearing two-one-two, just to the left of Sierra Four-Seven, another eleven-point-five line." A moment's pause. "Classified Chinese *Yuan*-class submerged submarine."

"Damn, this swimming pool is suddenly getting very crowded," Biddle muttered.

Then he hurried to let the CO know they were no longer shadowing a single PLAN submarine. It had turned into a wolf pack.

Ψ

The brilliant sunshine effectively blinded Jim Ward as his head emerged from the USS *Hawaii*'s personnel access hatch. The noontime tropical sun hung high over Singapore. The waters of Changi Bay twinkled with a thousand diamonds. Even the young SEAL-team commander's Oakley sunglasses did not really help. Too many days spent in the "fluorescent sunshine," as his dad, the former sub skipper, used to call the lighting inside a submarine.

Ward's team had been assigned to ride the *Hawaii* for another month, but with the SWCS shot up there was no reason for them to stay onboard. So, the submarine had pulled into Singapore to unload its SEAL team passengers. Now their first chore was to lug all their gear topside and pile it onto the pier. Then they would need to catch a ride to the airport where a flight was supposed to be ready to haul them back home.

Jim Ward, his heavy pack strapped to his shoulders bending him over at the waist, was just stepping off the brow onto the wharf when someone stepped between him and the broiling sun.

"Need a hand, sailor?"

The voice startled Jim Ward. Somebody very familiar. Then he realized who it was as he slid out of his pack and stood up straight.

"Dad! What in the world are you doing here?"

Rear Admiral Jon Ward smiled broadly, enveloped his son in a tight bear hug, and pounded him on his back.

"Pretty much the same thing you're doing, son. Enjoying the tropical sunshine. Doing some sightseeing." He pulled back and looked his boy in the face. "And you are a sight for sore eyes, Commander. Even if I have to fly halfway around the world at taxpayer expense to get a look at you."

"Speaking of flying, Dad, you being a flag officer and all, reckon you could arrange us a ride over to the air terminal? We got a plane over there that's supposed to be waiting for us. I'm due for a month's leave and I can't wait to get home and have some of Mom's cooking."

Jon Ward cleared his throat, frowned, and looked around the area where they stood. The rest of the SEALs were still on the submarine's deck about to cross the brow to the wharf, carrying loads of gear to add to the steadily growing pile. Nobody else was nearby.

"About that, Jim. We need to talk. Let's step over here out of the way for a minute. Maybe find some shade."

Jim knew his dad well enough to understand that he had just switched from father role to head-of-naval-intelligence role. The two men stepped out of the way of the heavily loaded, hard-working team as they brushed by them.

"You men don't mind if I borrow this pack mule for a minute, do you?" Jon Ward asked.

"He's just gettin' in the way anyhow, sir," one of the SEALs replied. "He's all yours."

The two men found a narrow sliver of shelter from the sun behind an idle forklift and a stack of shipping crates, well out of earshot.

"Son, I'm afraid Mom's cooking is going to have to wait for a bit," the admiral said, a solemn look on his face. This conversation was decidedly serious now. "Much as I enjoy the opportunity to meet you at the pier, this is a business call, not a personal one."

"I assumed so."

"I have a couple of things to discuss. First off, the intel weenies have been deconstructing that sensor you brought back. First cut, it looks like some kind of acoustic monitoring system. We think the Chinese are making preps to set up one of their 'we dare you to stop us' bases on the North Luconia Shoals. We've given the Indonesians a heads-up."

The elder Ward took a breath and wiped perspiration from his forehead with a handkerchief. He noticed his son had hardly broken a sweat. "Now, the part that really affects your leave plans. A very reliable intel source tipped us to some possible Chinese activity. If it's what she thinks it is..."

"She?"

"Gender is not important right now. If it is what she thinks is behind the activity, we need to be in a position to observe."

"And by 'observe,' I assume you mean 'and possibly engage.'"

Jon Ward grinned, nodded, then got serious again, glancing around the pier. Still no one within hearing distance.

"You're getting ahead of me. Another tendency you inherited from your mom. Here's all I can tell you right now. You'll get details at the briefing in an hour. It seems the Chinese are really working hard to piss off the Vietnamese. Troops right up against the border, strike fighters flying attack profiles before banking hard, right at the border. And shooting up anything Vietnamese that blunders into waters that they claim. They just wiped out a bunch of fishermen a couple of weeks ago."

Jim Ward nodded somberly. "Nothing new in any of that. What do you need us for? Worth giving up Mom's pork chops and applesauce?"

"Two things. First, the Chinese are being especially blatant about all of this. It is almost as if they are waiting for a satellite pass to initiate action. I'm surprised they aren't calling up CNN and asking for a camera crew to be on hand. But the big reason? Our Vietnamese friends have asked for our help. We sent in a very special team to set up a covert signal intercept station near their border with China. They are there to give the Vietnamese early warning of any imminent Chinese attack. We have actually gotten quite good at intercepting both their comms and data links. Plus, with their carefully orchestrated command and control philosophy, they have no choice but to be quite talkative. An intercept station close to the border is capable of giving us fifteen minutes to half an hour of a heads-up. More than enough time."

The admiral took a breath and once again glanced around before continuing. Jim Ward's SEAL team had gone back aboard the *Hawaii* and were now bringing over the last of the equipment that had been heaped in a mound near the sub's hatch. The men were in a good mood, joking with each other, ready to head for home.

"The Chinese may have gotten wind of our having ears there. Noisy and belligerent as they have been, we don't think having us there fits into their plan. Our source says that they are sending a special ops team, and I don't think they are just making a social call. We can't let them find our team. Or, worse, capture anything or anyone. Especially that close to their border. You know they'll claim we violated their sovereignty. They're really good at doing that lately."

"Okay, Dad," Jim said. "Can you give me a quick preview of the briefing, then?"

Jon Ward closed his eyes and took a deep breath. This was one of the situations to which he had not yet grown accustomed. Parents of SEALs or other special military units typically had no idea where their sons or daughters were, what they were doing, what risks they might be undertaking at any given moment. Certainly not before and usually not afterward, either. He did not have such a blessing of ignorance. Most of the time, he knew exactly what his boy was doing, where he was, and the kind of danger he was facing. More often than not, he was the one giving him the orders.

The admiral answered, "We need you and your merry band of miscreants to high-tail it up there to answer the door when they come calling. Let's hope they don't. But our source has not steered us wrong yet."

Jim looked perplexed. "Why aren't the Vietnamese providing the security? It is their country, after all."

"Well, the fact is not everyone in Vietnam knows that we are there, and we would kind of like to keep it that way. Some of them would not approve. We are using an industrial park, a *khu cong nghiep,* as the Vietnamese call it, just outside Quang Dien, for our listening post. It's a Texhong fabric mill that normally has a slew of CONEX boxes stacked in its lot. A few extras don't raise any eyebrows. Far as we know, not even the workers know we are there. But it looks like somebody is aware now. I've got a flight laid on for you up to Haiphong. You will be met there."

Jon Ward stopped and dropped his head, almost as if he was suddenly exhausted. Jim touched his dad's shoulder.

Anyone watching the exchange would have assumed this had been a typical but emotional father-and-son visit.

"When you gonna quit worrying about me, Dad? I'm not borrowing the car to go to the prom for the first time."

The elder Ward looked up with a quick grin.

"I'll quit worrying when your mom does. And you know when that'll be?" The young SEAL shrugged. "When a red man with horns and a pointed tail comes running up screaming, 'It froze over! It froze over!'"

The two men hugged again and then stepped back out into the blistering heat of the Singaporean sun.

11

"Skipper, on this course, our Chinese friends are making directly for the Mindoro Straits." Jackson Biddle looked up from the Projected Track display on the ECDIS aboard the submarine *George Mason*. "If our solution is worth the electrons we spent solving it, they will be in Philippine territorial waters in about half an hour." The XO's report contained an obvious unasked question: What the hell are we going to do, Skipper?

Brian Edwards nodded as he gazed at the electronic display. The yellow generated solution track crossed the bright red territorial waters boundary into the open waters of the Sulu Sea. Operating a submerged submarine in someone's territorial waters without permission was considered an act of war by international law. It certainly appeared that the Chinese wolf pack meant to do just that, counting on not being seen while they did. But Edwards and his boat were about to do the very same thing while tailing the PLAN boats.

The *George Mason*'s CO knew that he had some decisions to make and not a lot of time to make them. And there was a good possibility that whatever he did would be wrong.

Should he follow the Chinese into the Sulu Sea and risk a major international incident with an allied country that had been a bit prickly lately? Or should he peel off at the boundary line to call home? If he precisely followed his instructions to shadow the Chinese boats and got caught, he knew that he would not be able to hide behind his orders. COs were expected to know and follow international law. On the other hand, if he peeled off and called home, the Chinese would almost certainly be long gone by the time anyone got back to him. And COs were expected to complete their missions, if at all possible.

Edwards stepped back and rubbed his chin, deep in thought. His mind was telling him to be cautious, pull off track, and call home to request instructions. His gut was screaming that this bunch was up to no good and he was the only one in position to stop them.

What should he do? What would his old skipper, Joe Glass, do in this situation?

"Well, XO," Edwards said with a crooked grin. "There are two old submarine sayings that cover this situation."

Biddle looked at him quizzically. In their time together, he had never seen Brian Edwards resort to riddles.

"Okay."

"Yep," Edwards went on. "'No balls, no blue chips.' And, 'What's the use of being a submarine if you can't hide from everybody every once in a while.'"

Biddle looked even more confused.

"XO, here's what we'll do. We'll get up ahead of our friends and pull off to the side a little. As they march through the door into Philippine waters, we'll call home and tell them what is happening and that we intend to remain in trail as long as we hold contact. We'll ask them to please clear with the Philippine government. The next comms period will be in twelve hours. By the time they get everything sorted out, we'll be well on our way to figuring out what our Chinese friends are up to."

Biddle smiled as he caught on. "You really think it will take Group Seven twelve hours to figure out what we should do?"

Edwards looked at his XO and, with considerable seriousness, said, "XO, I expect you to scrupulously follow the chain of command and copy every addee that was on our tasking order. There were enough four-star brass and three-letter government agencies on that list that it will be the second Tuesday of next week before they all figure out and agree on what to do. Now, you get in to radio and draft up the message while I get us off track and up to periscope depth."

Ψ

Joe Glass was still finding his way around his new temporary digs in Pago Pago Harbor. One thing he found quickly was that the *Chesty Puller* was immense, much larger than any submarine tender he had ever been on. At over seven hundred and sixty feet long and displacing over eighty thousand tons, it was nearly twice the size of submarine tenders that Glass had pulled up alongside. And the helo deck on the roof took some getting used to.

Normally assigned as a forward base for Marine units, the massive Expeditionary Mobile Base, or ESB, was now pulling double duty. She was substituting for a submarine tender while standing by, just in case the Marines needed her somewhere to help them kick in a few doors. But now her mission deck was full of CONEX boxes converted to shops and offices. The place hummed with early morning activity as Glass strode across the deck, careful not to trip over the thick power cables and hydraulic lines that snaked everywhere.

"Skipper! Hey, Skipper!"

The voice sounded familiar.

Glass turned to see LCDR Walt Smith emerging from one of the CONEX boxes that had been converted into a machine shop. Smith had been Glass's engineer from his days commanding the USS *Toledo*. And one of the best he ever had the pleasure of knowing.

"Eng! Great to see you," Glass cried out. "What are you doing in this tropical paradise?"

"Well, Skipper...I mean, Commodore," Smith answered, shaking his hand. "But it's XO now. I just relieved as XO on the *Cheyenne*."

Their conversation was interrupted by the whistle blowing for morning colors. Both submariners stood at attention and saluted as the National Ensign was raised and "The Star-Spangled Banner" played over the ship's loudspeaker. At the "carry on" signal, the pair snapped their arms down and resumed their chat, taking little notice that they had just participated in a tradition as old as the Naval Service.

"XO, huh? Well, congratulations!" Glass told him. "*Cheyenne* has one lucky CO to have you as his exec. That is, if he can convince you to do XO things and stay out of the engine room."

Walt Smith laughed at that. "Is this a case of the pot calling the kettle black? I seem to recall you always wanting to play engineer back on *Toledo* every time something needed to get fixed."

It was Glass's turn to chuckle. "Yep. It's a temptation to want to relive your best tour. I'm just trying to give you some sage advice. I didn't say that I necessarily followed it myself."

Smith pursed his lips and deftly changed the subject.

"I would ask if you had time for a cup of something black and bitter, but I suspect you're not down here for the weather."

"Good deduction, Eng. Uh, XO. Raincheck, though?"

"Deal."

Ψ

Lieutenant Commander Billy Jonas stepped into *George Mason*'s Control, his hands full of file folders and loose papers. It was time for him to relieve LCDR Jim Shupert, the Nav, as officer of the deck. Although it was just after midnight, local time, and moonless dark up on the surface, there was no way to tell the time of day down here except for a glance at a clock. One of the benefits of submarining. Same LED sunshine twenty-four hours a day.

Billy Jonas liked to stand the midwatch, the least preferred of the watches. It was usually the curse of the most junior qualified officer on board. But Jonas had figured out that the midwatches were an especially quiet time because everybody's first team was resting. Even their Chinese wolf pack had been remarkably quiet and consistent, just steaming a straight course punching holes in the waters of the Sulu Sea. Here was his chance to catch up on the grinding load of paperwork that was the engineer's challenge. Tonight's task was reviewing and checking the Reactor Quarterly Data Report, his report card back to Naval Reactors Headquarters, assuring them that *George Mason*'s nuclear-powered tea kettle was performing up to snuff.

"'Bout time you showed up, rack hound," Jim Shupert kidded as the two looked over the tactical situation plot on the ECDIS. "I've been smelling whatever Cookie's been baking for the last hour. My stomach's growling like a cement mixer."

"Hate to disappoint, Nav," Jonas replied, "but it's beanie-weenies again. Whatever Cookie is baking, it must be for breakfast. Nothing good for mid-rats. So, what're our Chinese friends up to by now?"

Shupert waved his hand at the track history printed out on the tactical display.

"Pretty much the same-ol', same-ol. They've been on a course of one-six-zero, speed a little under five knots all watch. Steaming in line, a few thousand yards apart. I've been staying out here at twenty to twenty-five thousand yards off their starboard beam, holding good contact on the thin line array."

Stepping over to the command console, Shupert punched up the sonar displays and grunted.

"What you got?"

"A lot of contacts out ahead of us," he replied, pointing out a series of traces on the broadband waterfall. "Sonar thinks they are mostly a fishing fleet, but it's a pretty crowded fishbowl in this part of the world. Trying to sort out the contacts is going to get really interesting if our Chinese friends get mixed up in that gaggle."

Jonas chuckled dryly. "Wouldn't be fun if it wasn't a challenge. Anything else going to pique my interest? Or keep me from getting work done?" He still held the armful of paperwork.

"Well, Eng, glad you asked." Jim Shupert grabbed the CO's Night Orders and handed them to Jonas. "Skipper and the XO both want to be awakened at zero-two-thirty. We're scheduled to copy comms at zero-three-hundred. I suspect they both want to see what CTF-74 is going to say about us paddling into Philippine territorial waters without a permission slip."

"Well, at least the first couple of hours should be quiet. Maybe I can still get some paperwork done." The engineer plopped down his stack of files on the top of the command console. "I relieve you as officer of the deck."

Jonas settled back in the OOD's chair and was quickly

deep into the complexities of the Quarterly Data Report. The normal watch-standing routine hummed around him as everyone in Control settled in. The pilot and co-pilot maintained course and speed while the sonar operators detected and tracked the fishing boats and freighters plodding above them across the crowded surface of the Sulu Sea. The roving watches kept the control room watchstanders well stocked with coffee.

Almost two hours passed before the routine was abruptly disturbed.

"Possible contact zig, Master One, the lead Chinese sub," STi Hannon, one of the sonar operators, suddenly called out. "There's a drop in bearing rate, drop in received frequency. He's slowed."

A few seconds later, Hannon added new information. "Possible contact zig, Master Two," and then, "Possible contact zig, Master Three. They have all slowed." He chuckled. "It's like watching synchronized swimming. And just about as exciting."

Jonas dropped his file folder onto the desk and punched up the sonar displays on his console. Sure enough, there were the three traces, still shadowing each other but now tracking off from the expected solutions.

"What are you seeing?" Jonas called over to Hannon.

"Not sure yet, sir," the sonarman replied. "It's getting real confused. They are merging into that fishing fleet. Pretty much under them now. Keeping them sorted out is going to be a challenge."

"Okay. I'll hold course and speed until we get this figured out."

"Get what figured out?" Brian Edwards strode into the control room with a cup of coffee in his hand and a quizzical look on his face. "We have a problem, Eng?"

"The Chinese have just zigged, Skipper," Jonas reported. "All on cue. Not sure yet what they're doing, except heading through a fishing fleet just to mess with Hannon over there."

"Picking up loud transients on the bearing to Master One," Josh Hannon piped up. "Sounds like he just started snorkeling. Loss of the eleven hertz tonal on Master One. New broadband contact on the bearing to Master One on the conformal array. Also, on the wide-aperture array. Range two-five-thousand yards. Equates to Master One."

Hannon had barely finished shooting out his report on Master One when the broadband sonar again blossomed. He immediately updated the captain and his OOD.

"Master Two has commenced snorkeling, loss of eleven hertz tonal, gained broadband on the conformal array and WAA. Range two-three-thousand yards. Master Three commenced snorkeling, range two-nine-thousand yards."

The Chinese submarines had slowed and came close enough to the surface to extend a pipe up into dry air. Edwards shook his head and looked at the situation on the tactical display.

"Looks like they're using the fishing fleet to mask their diesel noise while they charge batteries and run toward the Mindanao Sea. Smart move."

Captain," ST1 Hannon called out. "New sonar contact on the conformal array. Classified snorkeling submarine, bearing one-nine-three. Now hold on the WAA, range three-one-thousand yards."

Edwards jerked his head up from staring at the tactical display, looking puzzled once more.

"You sure?"

"Yes, sir. Same signature as the others. This is a fourth *Yuan*," Hannon answered. A fourth Chinese submarine, just like the other three they had been tailing.

Jackson Biddle, the XO, joined Edwards at the display. "Looks like our new friend is about two thousand yards astern of Master Three." In his best C.W. McCall twang, Biddle added, "Looks like we got ourselves a convoy."

Edwards glanced over at the master clock. It read eighteen-fifty-three zulu time or zero-two-fifty-three local time. "XO, you keep an eye on our convoy. Eng, let's get up to periscope depth so we can call home. We need to tell them about our party crasher. And I want to see how hard they're going to slap my hand for venturing into Philippine waters."

The *George Mason* slid smoothly up from the depths to stick its low-profile photonics mast into the clear dark skies. Despite all of the sonar contacts currently popping up all over their displays, for all they could see from the periscope, they were alone on a quiet tropical sea. There were only a couple of masthead lights barely visible, low down on the eastern horizon. Almost certainly fishing boats.

Within seconds, the 21MC speaker blared, "Captain, Radio, receiving a 'Personal For' from CTF Seven-Four addressed to you. Patching it to the command console."

Edwards punched up his personal message account on the command console and entered his password. The screen quickly shifted to a message from Rear Admiral Dan Jorgensson, Commander Submarine Group Seven and Commander Task Force Seventy-Four. Most importantly, he was Brian Edwards's boss. The message was curt.

BT:

Personal For: Commanding Officer George Mason

    1. *Acknowledge your contact report message 0718Zulu.*

> *Higher authority directs that you maintain passive trail on contacts until relieved.*

2. *You are to exercise every precaution to ensure that you are not to be detected by any forces while you are in Philippine waters.*

3. *If detected, you are to make every effort to ensure that you are not identified as a US warship.*

4. *Use of force is authorized for self-defense in accordance with the current rules of engagement.*

5. *You are to minimize your time in Philippine territorial waters.*

6. *You will maintain a six-hour comms cycle until further notice.*

7. *We will discuss your actions taken to date upon your return to port.*

CTF 74 Actual sends.
BT:

Edwards whistled under his breath. Then he told Jackson Biddle, "Don't think the boss is in a good mood right now. Sounds like maybe the heavy brass in Pearl, or maybe in DC, disturbed his golf game. Anyway, we have sent them everything we have on our Chinese friends. Let's get back down and work our way out in front of them a bit so maybe then he can't hide with all the fishing boats."

12

The night was wardroom-coffee black. Treetop-level clouds hid even the stars and the slightest sliver of a moon. Through his night vision goggles, Jim Ward could easily see the Texhong fabric mill as a green glow, half a mile away over the sandy, bramble-pocked beach dunes. A narrow, barely paved roadway snaked across the dunes, past where the young SEAL-team commander lay hunkered down, and on to a rickety pier that jutted out into the shallow, brackish waters of the bay. A cloyingly humid tropical breeze brought the stench of mud flats and rotting vegetation. It did nothing, though, to dissipate the humming cloud of mosquitoes that circled Ward's face.

The goggles also allowed him to just make out Jason Hall in his hiding spot across the road. The big, black SEAL had set up his emplacement at the top of one of the sand dunes. That provided him a shooting lane that covered the southern approaches to the old ferry pier as well as the low marshes to the west. Elevation was an advantage. But it left him a bit more exposed, too.

The rest of Ward's team were hidden around the perimeter

of the Texhong facility. That allowed them the opportunity for as much warning and protection as his meager six-man team could provide. Unfortunately, the intel source had only provided the expected target and the approximate timing of the impending attack. Not the threat vector. That meant the SEALs would be forced to cover all three hundred and sixty degrees around the sprawling plant. That also meant the range of his tiny inter-squad radio was being tested to the max. He could just hear Tad Riley at the far northwest corner. Bill Ross, dug in on the northeast corner, and Sean Horton, over on the southwest corner, were significantly closer and easier to talk with, without the digital artifacting on their audio.

The tactical situation was certainly not ideal. Only he and Hall were in positions to easily support each other. Any one of the others would have to be on his own until someone could scurry over to help out.

Ward was hedging his bets. The logical attack vector would be from the sea, then over the ferry pier or across the nearby beach. The attackers would not expect opposition or think they needed the cover of the nearby woods. That was why he and Hall were dug in where they were, waiting, watching.

What they lacked in numbers the SEALs certainly made up for in firepower. Ward again checked his Mark 48 machine gun. Still locked and loaded. His M79 grenade launcher, with half a dozen forty-millimeter grenades, lay ready beside the machine gun. His MK4A1 carbine that he kept strapped across his chest was set, too. Ward settled back and scanned the dark horizon.

"Skipper!" The whisper in Ward's earbuds sounded like raspy thunder, jolting him alert. "Couple of dark boats coming in from the south, real quiet like." It was Jason Hall reporting.

"Just coming around Hon Mieu Island now. I'd say there are at least a half dozen shooters on each boat."

Ward nodded, as if Hall could actually see him. Two boats. A dozen men. He and his guys were only outnumbered a little better than two-to-one.

"Roger, Jase. Heads-up, everyone. Keep your eyes open for anybody trying to slip in the back door while we're watching the front. Remember the plan. When I give the word, everyone fall back to the CONEX box."

Ward counted the mike clicks as each SEAL acknowledged that he had heard him. Five clicks. Good.

Now Ward could just make out the low, wicked shapes of the two boats against the dark water. It took him a second, but then he recognized the profile.

"Jase," he whispered into his throat mike. "You need to get your eyes checked. Those are Chinese Type 928 assault boats. And those bastards got a real stinger on their bows. We'll need to shoot and scoot on this one."

One mike click.

Ward watched as the two blackened Chinese assault boats silently slid across the calm waters toward the ferry landing. Now he could see that at least a couple of dozen shooters were crowded topside. The odds just went badly askew for him and his team.

The SEAL could also see that each boat's bow-mounted 12.7 mm machine gun was manned and ready. For an assault team with no reason to expect any resistance, these guys were not taking any chances.

Ward now knew one other thing their intel had not told them. They were facing a team of China's Sea Dragons, an elite special forces group within the PLAN Marines. But it made sense. They were the only ones with the reach and training to pull this raid off. And do enough damage to attract the world's attention.

"Jase, they're Sea Dragons. We need to tackle them before they get ashore. Wait until they dock and then let's blitz 'em with a couple of grenades."

Another single click of Hall's microphone. Hall had once been an All-American linebacker for the Alabama Crimson Tide. He understood the football metaphors as well as the value of stuffing a play with a well-timed and unexpected defensive move.

Ward continued to build his plan even as he spoke.

"Then...then let's scoot back to Doug's hole. I don't think it would be healthy sticking around here once we kick the hornet's nest."

Ward could now barely hear the burbling diesel engines as the boats slid to a smooth stop alongside the pier. Then he watched as a few of the black-uniformed marines jumped to the shore and took defensive positions while crewmembers efficiently tied the boats up to the pier. This was a well-trained team performing a choreographed, well-practiced tactic.

It would be a difficult shot, almost three hundred yards from where Ward now stood, the M79 Thumper grenade launcher at his shoulder. The weapon was not the newest of its type, but it was the easiest to carry and use. And the 40 mm grenade could do some damage if he got it close enough.

He sighted carefully, allowed for the slight crosswind, and squeezed the trigger. The launcher's deep, roaring thump split the quiet night, almost simultaneously with Jason Hall's similar shot. Ward did not hesitate. He broke the gun's action, slammed another grenade in the chamber, and fired again. At eighty meters a second, he had just over three seconds to get the next grenade in the air before the first one landed.

Ward was grabbing his machine gun when his and Hall's

first rounds hit. In the brilliant explosive flash, he could see that one round had hit the wheelhouse on the lead assault boat and the second one exploded on the pier.

The heavy machine guns on the two boats' bows opened up immediately, spraying the sand around him with deadly fire. Ward slid out the backside of his firing pit on his belly. Small arms fire buzzed and snapped all around him.

"Come on, Jase," he called out. "Time to get scarce."

Ward heard a painful grunt, then, "Son of a bitch! Skipper, I'm hit."

He turned. Jason Hall was slumped down on the ground. Ward, in a crouch, raced across the narrow roadway and quickly scooped up the big SEAL, throwing him across his shoulders. Ward balanced the load but he was sure that his knees would buckle under the weight. But then he managed to stumble forward, headed for a better hole in the ground with the plant's tech center building the interim destination, and Horton's position just beyond.

He could hear his fellow SEAL's labored breathing in his ear.

"Stay with me, Jase," he implored. "Stay with me, big guy." Sweat filled his eyes, obscuring his vision. He could feel his heart pounding. Surely the Chinese could hear his gasping breath. He felt like his legs were incapable of taking another step. Still, he plowed on.

The tech center did not seem to be getting any closer. It was nothing more than a hazy blur, off in the distance, tantalizing him.

Then Ward was sure that he could hear the footsteps and shouts of the Chinese chasing after him. He veered off the edge of the road and into the dunes. The going was much tougher and slower, the sand bogging him down. But being off the roadway at least made him and his load a harder target for the Sea Dragons.

"Stay with me, Jase. Almost there," Ward grunted, as he staggered and slid down the backside of a dune. He rearranged Hall on his shoulders, took a deep breath, and pushed his way up the next dune.

Somehow, he finally reached the chain link fence that circled the tech center. Now, from here, it was only a hundred yards to Sean Horton. Bullets spattered around him, whistling past or ricocheting off the fence. Ward dove to the ground and whipped his MK4 around.

If he was going down, he would go down fighting. And be damned if he let them do any more damage to his buddy.

Ward forced himself to be deliberate. Do not fire randomly, he told himself. Make it count.

He caught one black ghost in his sights and squeezed off a couple of rounds. The shadow flailed awkwardly backward. Then Ward moved his aim to another. He, too, fell.

But it was only a matter of time now. He had been lucky on the first two. Numbers were on the side of the Chinese.

He caught sight of another Sea Dragon crossing a bit of open ground, moving to flank him on the right. He launched two rounds toward the specter. No way to know if he got him or not.

Ward tugged Jason Hall back into a low, bush-covered hollow next to the fence. Then he lay in front of him, facing the road, protecting the fallen SEAL.

"So, Dad, I guess this is where it's going to happen," he said out loud. "Up against a chain link fence under a bush in some forgotten corner of Vietnam. Plenty of other guys have likely been..."

Ward stopped, snorted, and slammed another magazine into his MK4.

But just then, he heard the unmistakable sawing rip of an MK48 machine gun, surprisingly close and off to his right. Then there was the whump of an MK79 grenade launcher, also somewhere to his right. Yet another MK48 joined the chorus just before the grenade exploded on the backside of the dune directly in front of where he and Hall lay against the fence.

"Jase, hang on," Ward grunted. "Looks like the cavalry just showed up."

Ward continued to watch the road and the trees along each side. Nothing. The return fire from the Chinese was becoming more sporadic, seemingly more distant. Another grenade exploded, but this time it was further down the road.

The Sea Dragons were falling back.

Then Ward heard the distinctive *whup-whup-whup* of an approaching "Huey" helicopter. The green bird feathered out and touched down in a small clearing only a hundred yards or so down the dirt road. It carried the insignia of the Vietnam People's Navy. A dozen Vietnamese Marines leapt from the helicopter and charged off in the direction of the retreating Sea Dragons. At the same time, a Russian-made Mil Mi-24 Hind gunship roared overhead from the west. It sprayed the area where Ward knew the pier and assault boats were located, cutting loose with its chin-mounted 23 mm machine cannon. The chopper also peppered the retreating Sea Dragons with its 12.7 mm door gun.

Within minutes the battle was over. The assault boats had been reduced to burning hulks. The Vietnamese Marines were rounding up the few surviving Sea Dragons scattered around the sand dunes.

Meanwhile, Jim Ward was busy tending to Jason Hall's wounds, ignoring the lingering action around him. From the corner of his eye, he could see his guys regrouping, still on alert. But then, a Vietnamese officer separated from the rest of his Marines, spoke briefly with the SEALs, then walked over to where Ward kneeled over his team member.

"I am Lieutenant Duc Tran Trou," the officer said. He spoke English with very little accent. "Is one of you Lieutenant Ward?"

Jim Ward stood and said, "I'm Ward. I have a badly wounded man here. He needs medical aid fast."

Trou extended his hand and started to speak. But suddenly, Jim Ward collapsed, face down in the sand.

Tad Riley rushed past the Vietnamese officer and was immediately at Ward's side. He rolled the SEAL officer onto his back. His hand came away bloody.

"Skipper's hit!" he cried out as he tore away Ward's body armor. His shirt had wicked up a startling amount of blood. Riley reached into his armor kit and grabbed the medical bag, then slapped a wad of bandage over the wound, holding pressure to try to stop the bleeding.

"We need to get him out quick!" he yelled.

Duc Tran Trou frantically signaled two of his men. They placed Ward on a stretcher and followed two other Marines already carrying Hall toward the Huey.

Once the wounded men, the rest of the SEALs, and Lieutenant Trou had climbed aboard the bird, it revved up for lift-off. Then, it disappeared into the moonless sky, as if none of them had ever been there.

13

Yon Ba Deng, China's Assistant Vice Deputy to the Minister of National Defense for Naval Matters, struggled to maintain his composure. He growled to himself, mostly under his breath, "The noble-minded are calm and steady. Little people are forever fussing and fretting." Over and over, he muttered the mantra as he fought for inner peace.

Bing Dou, his trusted assistant, finally asked him, "Elder brother, what are you saying? What is disturbing you so greatly?"

Yon Ba Deng shook his head and forced a wry smile.

"It is an old Confucian quote I use to attempt to reach inner peace. Soo Be Xian is playing some clumsy game down on the Vietnam border. That incompetent old man is so jealous of my Party ties that he is trying to start a war. And all just to thwart me."

Bing Dou nodded as he listened. He and his boss had long been planning their move out into the South Pacific as a means to enhance Yon Ba Deng's status within the Party. Successfully extending his country's territorial waters would ultimately elevate him to the highest echelon. The carefully choreographed plan was well under way and its intricacies required clockwork timing. At this point, even the slightest deviation could throw the whole scheme into disarray. And now, when he needed him the most, Yon Hun Glo, his younger brother and strong right arm in the PLAN, was out of communications, riding a squadron of his submarines, making way for Tonga.

"What should we do, then?" Bing Dou inquired. "If Soo Be Xian is successful with starting a border war, the Central Committee, the Politburo, and the Secretariat will all be putting every effort into that. They will have no time or attention for us and our gains."

"Remember what Sun Tzu said," Yon Ba Deng answered. "'Victory comes from finding opportunities in problems.' Our worthy Vice Deputy Minister for National Defense has presented us with a problem. Now, it is up to us to find the opportunity that it hides from us."

Deng idly scratched his right ear as he stood. He slowly paced around his large office until stopping at the window that overlooked a quiet park and the Beijing Archives Building across the way. But he was not admiring the view. His mind was racing through the possibilities. He turned on a heel and smiled at his assistant.

"Bing Dou, once again Master Sun Tzu has provided us with the answer. As he said, 'The quality of decision is like the well-timed swoop of a falcon which enables it to strike and destroy its victim.'" Yon Ba Deng's eyes glowed with an inner fire. Such an expression would once have sent chills through Bing Dou. Now, he had grown accustomed to his master's intense emotions. "Call our compatriots over in the Air Force. It is now time to swoop. Have them shuttle our marines and transport planes to...what is the name of that airport in Tonga?"

Bing Dou quickly consulted the tablet on his desk. "Fua'amotu, elder brother."

"No, no, that is the airport on the main island. What is the little one to the north?"

"You mean Vava'u," Bing Dou answered, again after checking the data on the tablet.

"Yes, Vava'u. That is the one. The one that is very near to that other island. What was its name?"

"That would be Niue." Bing Dou had no need to consult the data on the screen for this answer. "It purports to be an independent country, but really, they are a protectorate of New Zealand," the assistant offered. "It is only about four hundred kilometers from Vava'u and about the same distance to the Tonga Trench. You remember that is where those scientists claim they found the gold."

"Fine. Fine," Yon Ba Deng responded. "That part I certainly recall. Let us just get the parts moving. The more quickly we grab the gold, the sooner we crush that loon, Soo Be Xian."

Ψ

Commander Chet Allison stretched his aching back and groaned. Far too many hours pacing *Boise*'s hard steel decks were taking their toll on his spine. Over a week of trailing the two Chinese nuclear submarines had been physically taxing but ultimately very boring. The pair were noisy enough that they were not particularly challenging to trail as they meandered over what felt like the entire ocean. So noisy they hardly offered a decent training opportunity for his guys.

Then there was the aimless nature of their trek. There seemed to be no rhyme or reason to their antics as they steamed about with no particular destination in mind. And now here they were, pretty much right back where they had started, a couple of hundred miles east-southeast of Hainan Island.

Allison scratched the several days' growth of stubble on his chin. His poopie suit was causing him to itch in strategic places and he could not really remember the last time he had showered. Or slept. The submarine skipper was of the opinion that his team on *Boise* was still too new and inexperienced to be unsupervised for any length of time, so he was required to keep a close eye on them. Especially as they tailed the Chinese boats. As a result, he had remained in the control room almost continuously, trying to catch cat naps as he sat on the low stool on the port side of the periscope stand. That was exactly what he was attempting to do when one of the crew spoke up with something new.

"Possible contact zig, Master Two-One and Two-Two." The fire control coordinator was hunched over a screen reading bearing rates on the two ambling contacts. "Shift in bearing rate from left-point-four to right-one-point-one." Allison was now fully awake. After a few seconds, the fire control coordinator called out, "Confirmed zig Master Two-One, set anchor range one-eight-thousand yards. Confirmed contact zig Master Two-Two, set anchor range one-six-thousand yards."

More idle rambling, or were they finally going someplace?

"Conn, Sonar," the 21MC speaker blasted. Allison recognized the voice of his leading sonarman, Chief John Vincent. Vincent was the one man in the crew that Allison felt had the experience to allow his skipper to totally rely on him. "Master Two-One and Two-Two bearings are merging with new broadband noise source bearing three-four-six. Captain, I don't know what the source is, but it's blanking out most everything over a ten-degree sector. It's nasty. We'll lose these two for sure unless we maneuver."

Allison quickly glanced at the plot and calculated his next move. He measured off the distances with his fingers. There was no way to move far enough to keep from losing these two before they merged with this new noise source and disappeared. The only maneuver was to dash out around it and hope he caught them when they came out the other side. If they came out the other side. He measured the distances, again using his fingers.

"Officer of the Deck, come to course north and ahead full."

"Come to ahead full and course north, aye," the OOD, Lieutenant Juan Esteban, echoed.

Just then, *Boise*'s executive officer, Lieutenant Commander Henrietta Foster, walked into the control room and quickly stepped back to the plot table where Allison stood. She glanced down at the plot and studied it for a few seconds, then glanced sideways at the skipper.

"Well, I think I know what your noise source is," she said. "There was a Notice to Mariners message on the last broadcast. It said that some Chinese oil firm was working on their Panyu gas wells a couple of hundred miles southeast of Hong Kong. You're listening to the sound of somebody setting up a deep-water drill rig."

Allison shook his head. It was incomprehensible that they had received a NOTAMS hours ago and it still had not been plotted on the submarine's ECDIS charts. And what was really bothersome was that this particular risk was only a few miles away from their position. They could easily have run right smack into whatever it was without ever knowing.

Allison, face flushed, looked around the control room. The navigator, Lieutenant Jeremy Chastain, was doing his best to melt back into the radar repeater.

"Nav, what the holy hell is going on?" Allison growled. "Did you not see the NOTAMS?"

"It...I...it was on list for today," Chastain stammered.

"It takes thirty seconds to download and check," Allison shot back. "That NOTAMS has been onboard for twelve hours. Nav, that is simply not acceptable. Get the damn NOTAM plotted and evaluated immediately. Then, if it's not too much trouble, plot a twenty-mile safety circle around it. And get your Leading Nav ET up here. You two better sort out your navigation division's priorities."

"Conn, Sonar. Captain, we have lost Master Two-One and Two-Two. They are both masked by the noise source."

Allison nodded to no one in particular as he tapped the tabletop with a finger. Then he turned to the OOD.

"Officer of the Deck, stay outside the safety circle and come around to here." He pointed to a location to the north and east of the blaring drill rig. "We'll catch those two as they come around the other side."

The XO moved over to where she could talk with Allison without being overheard.

"Skipper. Suggest you take a deep breath and count to ten," she whispered. "Nav screwed up, but you know you shouldn't tear his head off out here in front of the crew." She glanced around the compartment. Everybody was busy, out of earshot. "Look, why don't you go lie down and get a couple of hours sleep? I'll stay out here and keep an eye on things while we re-position. Then I'll give you a call when we regain contact."

Chet Allison closed his eyes and willed his breathing back to normal. His XO was right, of course. She usually was. Henrietta Foster was one of the first women to rise to such a high position in submarines. One of the first African Americans, too. She would have her own boat before long, and deservedly so. That would check a bunch of boxes in support of diversity in the Silent Service. And nobody deserved that signal honor more than she did.

"You're right, XO," Allison said wearily.

Foster all but shoved the exhausted captain out of the control room and in the direction of his stateroom.

"And while you're at it, take a shower. You positively stink."

That was another reason Henrietta Foster would make a fine sub skipper. She called it the way she saw it.

Ψ

Six hours later, Chet Allison emerged from his stateroom, hair still wet and glistening from the shower. He walked back to the chart table where Foster stood. Gauging from her expression, she was still apparently studying the same problem.

"Thanks, XO," he told her. "I needed that. You regain our Chinese friends yet?"

Foster shook her head. "Not a squeak. I don't understand it. Those two made more racket than a fleet of garbage trucks. If they come out of that noise anywhere within thirty thousand yards, we should have them again."

"Well, much as I hate to, let's go report lost contact. Tell the boss they got away. One thing I've learned is that bad news is nothing like fine wine. It does not improve with age."

The trip to periscope depth was uneventful. They confirmed that they had this piece of the South China Sea all to themselves. Or at least as far as surface contacts were concerned.

The lost contact report was sent. Almost immediately, the reply came back.

"Contacts of interest bear three-five-zero from you, range sixty miles. Apparent course one-one-zero, speed twelve."

"Now how the hell do they know that?" Foster asked, reading the cryptic report again.

Allison, lips pursed and a frown on his face, was already playing with the ECDIS tactical display.

"Looks like they turned pretty much due north while they were invisible to us, almost as if they knew they were being tailed. Then they sprinted up toward those gas fields off the Pearl River. Now they're heading straight toward Dongsha Island. Let's get over there in front of them."

Foster shook her head, still reading the message as if it held a clue.

"I still don't understand. Where did that information come from? It sure ain't SURTASS. The latest TACSIT still has them putzing toward us on the far side of Taiwan."

SURTASS was the Surveillance Towed-Array Sensor System, a global network of ships using passive sonar to keep track of submarines.

Chet Allison smiled and nodded slightly.

"Obviously, somebody out here has a pretty good set of ears located somewhere in this particular pond."

"They saved our asses, whoever they are," Foster noted.

"One other thing," Allison said with a grim expression. "If they know precisely where those two Chinese boats are, they know exactly where we are, too."

Ψ

Joe Glass's IMMARSAT phone jangled alive. The commander of Submarine Squadron Seven grabbed it.

"Joe Glass," he spoke into the receiver.

There was just a hint of static, then Jon Ward's voice boomed out of the speaker.

"Joe, I'm sending you a link to a presentation that your

next-door neighbor over Tonga way just made to the United Nations Security Council." The head of Naval Intelligence was not sharing idle podcast recommendations with Glass. Whatever the presentation revealed, it would not be good news. "Listen to what King Tofuwanga has to say and give me a call back. I think we need to make some plans."

Glass hung up the suddenly dead circuit. As if on cue, his computer screen blinked and Jon Ward's email popped up. Sure enough, there was the link Ward had promised, a news feed from the United Nations.

When he clicked on the link, a video began to play. King Tofuwanga, dressed in a finely-tailored suit instead of his usual traditional Tongan garb, sat at a table with several microphones arrayed before him. The United Nations logo hung from pale blue curtains behind him. They formed an impressive backdrop for the portly monarch, making him appear almost legitimate.

Joe Glass could only appreciate the irony. This man was the titular head of a tiny island nation that even the diplomats in the room would have trouble locating on an unlabeled map. Even fewer knew anything about its long history, the recent struggles by some of its people—sometimes violently —to move toward a more democratic form of government, or this well-dressed ruler's efforts to delay such nonsense. At any rate, the diplomats and media would typically not bother to appear for an address by such a minor player on the world political stage. But, from what Glass could see, the room was packed.

The camera slowly panned to reveal that all the seats at the kidney-shaped table were filled as well. The name plates identified the various countries whose representatives were currently sitting on the body's Security Council. The Chinese ambassador to the UN sat on King Tofuwanga's right-hand side. He was smiling and nodding slightly as the Tongan strongman began to speak.

After a few polite perfunctory remarks, Tofuwanga quickly got to the reason why he had bothered to travel all the way to New York City to appear in person before the Security Council. The man's typical strong Tongan lilt was gone. Instead, he spoke with a pronounced English public-school accent. That was a vestige of his youth, spent in posh British private schools. Or at least until the stories of booze, sex, and drugs became so prevalent in the British tabloids that his father, King Tofuwanga the First, called him home to begin to prepare in a different way for his own regal term. Nowadays, the ruler conveniently switched to the English accent when he wanted to appear to Westerners to be well-educated and more convincingly king-like.

"Tonga is a small, beautiful, but poor nation," he began. "As with many of our sister nations in the South Pacific, western colonialism has taken its toll over the centuries. But we are an ancient, proud people, one with a long sea-going tradition. Our warriors have traveled the Pacific for thousands of years to sustain and protect our people. The waters that surround the small bits of land that make up our homeland have traditionally been our domain for hundreds of years. From Niuatoputapu in the north to 'Eua in the south, from Neiafu in the east to Esia in the west, Tonga has considered the sea to be our domain and depended on it to feed our people. Now the warm, blue waters that wash our shores have brought us a great gift. As is our ancient and long-recognized right, we are making the world aware that the Tongan people, and I, Tofuwanga, their king, have declared sovereignty over this traditional sea that continues to sustain our lives and domain."

The screen shifted to a map of Oceania, the 169 islands

that made up the Tongan kingdom clearly labeled amid all the blue of the South Pacific. But those specks of land were surrounded by a thick, bright-red boundary line at a distance of five hundred kilometers from the islands. The ocean waters between the northernmost Tongan island and Samoa to the north were divided neatly in half. So was the sea between Tonga and Fiji to the west. But to the east and south, the newly claimed boundary stretched far out across the open waters, encompassing all of the seas over the Tongan Trench.

Joe Glass snorted and shook his head. Of course it did. The new line of claimed territory included the spot where that huge mound of gold had been located by the research ship.

"These are our historic waters," Tofuwanga continued, dropping the tone of his voice to a new level of authority. "To these we once again emphasize our long-held and historic claim even as we see more threats and intrusion by European and North American powers—as well as nations in our own region—for their own strategic and invalid purposes. Today, we call upon all the world to recognize the ancient rights of our poor and weak nation. We urge the world to honor our sovereignty and territorial integrity. Henceforth, no ship—and particularly no warship—may enter our sovereign waters without our prior permission. And we call upon the United Nations to defend our rights against any who would challenge them."

Tofuwanga paused, allowing his words to echo throughout the chamber and to be translated for those on the Council and in attendance in the galleries. Then he turned toward the Chinese ambassador, who was still smiling, still nodding.

"Our dear and long-time friends, the People's Republic of China, have become the first of the world's peace-loving nations to formally renew their recognition of and respect for our rights," the Tongan monarch continued. "By promise and treaty, they have pledged to come to our aid to assist us in defending those rights as well as the seas on which our very existence so totally depends. Any threat against or incursion into the territories of the people of Tonga will be considered a threat against the People's Republic of China."

The monarch smiled broadly, again looking toward the Chinese ambassador, who merely continued to smile and bob his head. The room was silent for a few seconds as the Council, as well as the media, took in the astounding news.

A mouse had just roared like a lion!

Then, as a gavel pounded and media members shouted questions, those sitting on the Council clamored for attention, for the right to question such a blatant power grab. Not to mention such an unabashed annexation of what by all rights were international waters.

Glass clicked off the screen. Jon Ward had been correct. This political fiasco, although revealed on the other side of the world, was indeed going to likely play out in Glass's backyard. After all, the Tongan Islands were only two hundred miles across the deep blue waters from where he now sat, in American Samoa.

He and some other folks would have to quickly decide what to do about it. Tonga certainly had some very powerful and dangerous friends. And exactly what part would the deep-sea treasure play in this thing. Power or wealth. Either one often caused men to do bad things. With both at stake, who knew to what lengths these people would go?

Glass pushed back from his desk. Ever since his days as Jon Ward's XO, he found it helped him to think if he could just get up and walk around. That was sometimes difficult to do on a submarine, but it always got the blood flowing, and that allowed him to better consider his options. He walked out of his cabin on the big tender and slid down a couple of ladders, to where he could step out onto the *Chesty Puller*'s enormous main deck.

It was a beautiful, peaceful day. The brilliant Polynesian sunshine left the sky a bright, cloudless blue. A warm breeze wafted across the harbor, carrying sweet scents from the surrounding jungle out over the broad harbor and serene azure waters.

Then he noticed a large, white vessel motoring across the harbor, making for the Port of Pago Pago main dock. Glass watched as the big, beamy ship passed nearby. Hard to tell from her lines what the ship was designed for, but she clearly was not a cargo vessel or one of those deep-water tuna factories that called the StarKist cannery home. He had been so deep in his thoughts about the Tongan mess that he had neglected to grab his binoculars when he left his office. He typically did, just in case there was something interesting to see from the tender's high deck. Some of the sailors claimed a clear day offered views of sunbathers around the outdoor pools at the beach resorts but Glass had not yet had time to confirm it.

But then, as the white ship steamed past, Glass could make out the letters painted across her stern. *Deep Ocean Explorer*. So, this was the very ship that originated all the fuss when she located that golden hoard on the bottom of the Tongan Trench. He made a mental note to go over and meet with the ship's master. And maybe determine if he had any idea the storm he and his vessel had caused.

But then Joe Glass's attention was torn away from the *Deep Ocean Explorer* as he sighted another vessel rounding Tafagamanu Point at the mouth to Pago Pago Harbor. Glass did not need his binoculars to see what this ship was. The tall, gray, composite masts towering above the rocky outcropping were the first indications that this was a very large ship entering the harbor. And the gray color was a telltale sign that it was a Navy vessel.

Slowly and majestically, the ship rounded the point and steamed directly toward the inner harbor and to where Glass stood on the *Chesty Puller*. He could just make out the hull number—27—painted on her bow. It was the USS *Portland* (LPD-27), a *San Antonio*-class amphibious transport dock. And she was showing up at the dance just in time. Glass knew that the ship had over seven hundred Marines aboard. That might be useful in light of the video he had just watched. But, more importantly, in *Portland*'s well deck were the two ORCA Extra Large UUVs that Jon Ward had promised him. Those long-range, long-endurance, unmanned submarines would be a vital tool for keeping tabs on what was happening in what was turning into a very busy neighborhood.

Joe Glass had jobs for both ORCAs. And, he knew, for some of those old-fashioned underwater vehicles, too.

The ones with living, breathing human beings aboard.

He headed back toward his office. Enough sight-seeing. He owed Jon Ward a return call.

14

"I don't understand. Where the hell are they?" LCDR Aston Jennings was paging through the sonar displays on the *George Mason*'s command console. "If they stayed on the course they were supposed to, they should be here by now."

There was no sign of the Chinese diesel submarines they were tasked with trailing. The ones *George Mason* had risked an international pissing match to keep an eye on. The four *Yuan*-class AIP boats had maneuvered themselves right into a fleet of Philippine fishing boats, no doubt to hide while they snorkeled long enough to recharge their batteries. As soon as the *Yuan*s had shifted over from AIP propulsion to their diesel engines, the eleven-hertz tonal had disappeared. But even then, the broadband diesel noise had been easy to track.

That is until they got in amongst all the fishermen. Then there were dozens of diesels, all pretty much sounding alike. With no way to track their prey in the midst of all that noisy mess, Brian Edwards had decided to run around it. The intent had been to catch the Chinese when they came out the other side of the fishing fleet, continuing on to wherever they were going.

It all appeared to be a good plan. Just someone forgot to tell the Chinese. Or maybe somebody had told them and they decided to follow a different and far less obvious plan. Regardless, the *George Mason* had been making slow circles in a barrier search in the passage between Cagayan and Negros Islands. Not a hint of a scent on either the TB-29 thin-line array or the hull arrays. Lots of surface traffic—fishermen, coastal freighters, even the occasional cruise ship and ferry— but nary a sign of the missing *Yuan*s. They had effectively vanished.

Jackson Biddle, *George Mason*'s executive officer, stood looking over the tactical display on the ECDIS with a puzzled expression. He measured the distance from where they had lost the *Yuan*s to where they now sat helplessly, listening to the frustrating clatter. It was just a bit over seventy nautical miles and pretty much straight down the track that the Chinese submarine group had been steaming when the tail went off kilter.

"Well," Biddle drawled, "the laws of physics tell us that if they ain't here, they are somewhere else."

Jennings, who was quite proud of his master's degree in nuclear physics from MIT, shot back, "XO, there you go applying that old Newtonian physics solution to what is clearly a quantum physics problem. Quantum physics tells us that they are simultaneously nowhere else and everywhere else. We just need to figure out where Schrodinger left the cat."

Several nearby crewmembers looked at each other, frowning and shrugging. They were accustomed to the esoteric arguments between Biddle and Jennings but, as usual, decidedly in the dark about what the hell they were talking about.

Biddle chuckled dryly. "Well, we have a couple of hours

before we have to call home. If we don't find your cat before then, that particular chat will not be a fun one."

He drew a circle around the last location they held the Chinese with a radius of how far they could likely have steamed in the last couple of hours.

"Using my antiquated and outdated physics approach, they could be anywhere in this circle. We thought they were heading to the Surigao Straits, then out into the Philippine Sea." He moved the cursor to the west and, lips pursed, thought for a short moment. "But what if they are really heading south, toward the Celebes Sea. From there, they could head further south into eastern Indonesia or make a turn out toward the South Pacific."

Biddle drew an X a few miles to the west and a little south of Cagayan. "No point in sitting here idling. Let's get our butts over there as fast as we can. Maybe we can see if our friends slid between there and Palawan. Come to course two-four-zero, ahead full."

The *George Mason* jumped ahead and raced across the Sulu Sea. Biddle and Jennings, soon joined by Brian Edwards, their skipper, watched the clock's inexorable movement toward their next communications window and the accounting they would need to make for the failure of their mission. For his part, the captain of the boat agreed with the idea of searching more aggressively to the west.

Skirting to the south of tiny Cagayan Island, an atoll almost in the center of the Sulu Sea, the submarine slowed to search speed a few miles to the west. From here, they could cover the western portion of the circle that Jackson Biddle had drawn.

Edwards, Biddle, and Jennings clustered around the command console, staring at the sonar display, willing a submarine contact to suddenly appear. But there was nothing that could be classified as a submarine. Only plenty of fishing boats, their blips on the display like a sky full of stars winking in defiance at them from all directions. The sonar team was doing their best to sort it all out, but STI Joshua Hannon could only shake his head when Edwards shot a questioning look his way. Nothing.

Jackson Biddle pointed at the clock. "Skipper, hate to say it, but it's time to talk to the boss. Ship is rigged for a broadside."

Edwards blinked hard and nodded. They had delayed the inevitable as long as they possibly could. They were already as late in the communications window as possible. Now he had to tell the boss that they had failed. Barging into Philippine territorial waters had come up with nothing except egg on his face. And a bunch of nagging questions about where the flotilla of Chinese boats was heading and why.

"Officer of the Deck, come to periscope depth for communications," Edwards finally ordered, the reluctance heavy in his voice.

"Captain!" STI Hannon suddenly called out. "Detecting eleven hertz tonal on the TB-29. Reciprocal bearings zero-three-one and one-four-nine. I think we have regained our *Yuan*s."

"Hannon, first port call, your beers are on me," Jackson Biddle promised the sonar technician.

"That's cutting it way too close," Edwards growled. "The SOBs must have been hiding between Cagayan and Calusa, just in case somebody was tailing them. No way they know we're that somebody. Lesson learned. In case we didn't know it already, these guys are sneaky and good." He allowed himself a long sigh of relief. "Okay, now we have something worth telling the boss. Let's do it before Hannon decides we've spotted a pod of migrating whales with digestive problems."

Ψ

President Stan Smitherman impatiently waved the briefer to hurry through his slide deck. The president had an important golf outing scheduled with a pair of key benefactors. He was looking forward to some time on the links, but more importantly, this pair was promising to donate fifty million dollars to his campaign. With money like that on the line, they needed his full attention. And all this economic crap had long since given him a massive headache.

Secretary of State Sandra Dosetti leaned over and whispered, "Mr. President, you really should listen to this next part. It is extremely important."

Smitherman snorted. "Get on with it, then. But know I am in one hell of a hurry."

The briefer shifted over to a discussion of current gold prices. Smitherman squirmed in his seat and thumbed impatiently through the briefing notebook, looking for the end. Dosetti knew the signs well. The presenter had maybe thirty seconds before the President of the United States exploded and tossed him out of the conference room.

"Mister President, recent gold finds in the deep waters of the Pacific, if the projected volume proves out, could severely and negatively impact the price of gold," the briefer droned on, flashing up a series of graphs. "It is located in international waters, and economical recovery of the gold is very problematic, but if someone should decide it's worth it, go get it, and dump it on the market too quickly, the projected tonnage could affect the underpinnings of our economic model. We are already seeing some impacts on the gold mining stock futures market."

"What the hell is he saying?" Smitherman shouted to no one in particular. Nor did he really expect an answer. "Look, don't give me fancy-pants State Department bullshit. Give it to me in plain English. And, by the way, what the hell is this about 'tonnage?' I have sense enough to know that gold is always priced by the ounce."

"Now, Stan, calm down and listen for once," Dosetti coolly told her boss. "It's all pretty plain. There's a shit-ton of gold down there, enough that if we can figure out how to get it to the surface, the law of supply and demand will pull the rug out from under gold prices. That would tank the world economy like nothing else in history has done. But, on the positive side, no one seems to be taking a lot of interest yet in chasing this motherlode. That is, except for the two-bit potentate of Tonga. He is trying to claim everything as his, but there is no way on God's green earth that he can recover any of the stuff. He would need a real sugar daddy to do this thing."

Smitherman's face reddened for a moment, then he nodded a couple of times. "Okay, how do we get on top of this? Or, better still, how do we leverage it to our advantage?"

"We already have a small naval presence in American Samoa. Those sailors can protect our claims there," Dosetti answered. "And we already have a company working on a method to mine the stash and do so at a carefully controlled level."

"Carefully controlled level?"

Dosetti grinned. "Yes, controlled at a level that doesn't affect the market, but fills our coffers up quite nicely. I think that we will have plenty of funds to support your re-election. And you wouldn't even have to pretend you know how to play golf."

Ψ

Jim Ward blinked awake. The bright lights were blinding.

It took the young SEAL-team leader a few seconds to realize where he was. Or at least what kind of room he was in. The helicopter flight down to Hanoi and then the next hop to Singapore on some kind of smaller fixed-wing aircraft was mostly a blur. Now he could tell that he was in an antiseptically white hospital room with a couple of nurses hovering over him.

But the first voice he heard was a familiar gruff male one.

"Son, you really need to learn to keep your head down."

"Dad?"

Jon Ward stepped over to the bedside, into Jim's range of vision. "You know your mother is losing her patience with these late-night calls about hospital visits. She..."

"How's Jase?" Jim interrupted.

"He's still in the ICU. Look, it's been touch and go for him, but he's finally turned the corner." Jon put his hand on his boy's shoulder. "You know you saved his life out there. No doubt about it."

Jim smiled through dry, cracked lips.

"Where am I anyway?"

"We flew both of you down to Singapore," the elder Ward explained. "You're in Changi General Hospital. Doctors told me that you lost a lot of blood, but that the bullet passed clean without hitting anything you need to keep functioning. Your left side's going to be sore for quite a while. Don't plan on any triathlons in the near future."

Jim tried to sit up, only to grunt in pain. His dad and one of the nurses helped him up while the other nurse plumped the pillow behind his head. Out the window, he could see a palm tree swaying in a gentle breeze.

"How long?"

"Before your next Ironman?"

"Before I can get back to work with my guys?"

"Doctors are saying that if you behave yourself and follow orders, you should be out of here and ready to fly home in a week or so. I have already told them that you are not good at either behaving or following doctors' orders. The nursing staff is authorized to use extreme measures to ensure your compliance. Understood, tough guy?"

The younger Ward nodded sheepishly. Just his luck, having a father who not only out-ranked him by quite a lot but also knew his son's every thought.

Sometimes before he even thought it.

"Now, there are several rough-looking SEALs hanging around outside your room who really want to talk with you."

Ψ

The flight of four blue-gray Shaanxi Y-9 turboprop transport aircraft slowly circled the jungle-shrouded island as they noisily descended. One hundred fully-combat-armed PLAN Marines sat in the cargo bay of each plane, rocking with the motion, trying their best to hang on to their lunches as the planes bounced around in the hot, turbulent air.

A low, rainy mist hid the tops of the craggy volcanic mountains that formed the island's twisting, curvy spine. The heights threatened to grab any flyer who might be unwary while attempting to descend into such thick clouds.

Finally, the airfield, hard on the island's north shore, broke into view. Honiara International Airport and its single six-thousand-foot runway was barely long enough to land the heavily loaded Chinese aircraft.

In many ways, not much had changed since the airfield was named Henderson Field and was the site of one of the most violent battles of World War II. Guadalcanal was far more peaceful these days, but it was still a backwater with little value except as a hopping-off place for air traffic bound for somewhere else. And that was exactly the intention of the Chinese Air Force.

Once on the rough concrete, the planes pulled off the runway onto a little used apron that led to an area beside a pair of dilapidated Quonset Hut hangars. The buildings appeared to have been left over from the Henderson Field days. One still had a weather-beaten sign wired in place above a doorway that might have once had that name inscribed on it. Grass and weeds were making significant inroads on the cracked and broken tarmac. Vegetation was slowly reclaiming a couple of wrecked, rusting airframes that appeared to have been shoved to the side and forgotten for three-quarters of a century. Indeed, this entire corner of the airfield looked as if it had been shoved aside and forgotten.

It was soon obvious that someone was expecting them, though. The transport pilots were still spooling down their engines when two fuel trucks emerged from one of the hangars.

Meanwhile, inside the first plane, the mission commander was already on the radio, back to headquarters on Hainan Island. He reported that the ten-hour flight was complete, that re-fueling was already underway, and that they would be standing by for orders on what was necessary to complete their mission.

The PLAN Marines climbed out of the stuffy cargo holds to stretch their cramped muscles. The heat and humidity were stifling. Just drawing a breath in the cloying air took real energy. The Marine officers set about having their troops set up a temporary camp. Their orders said that they might be required to stay for a week or more but must be ready to take off in under an hour when word came. That meant the camp would lack any of the comforts of an established base.

Several of the more enterprising non-commissioned officers, the NCOs, slipped off and headed down the Kokum Highway in search of a few cold beers. None of them likely were aware that they were walking on the same ground that another nation's Marines had once fought and died for, all to wrest it from Imperial Japan.

Or the fact that the same war and the bravery of those American Marines had freed China from conquest.

Ψ

The presenter at the front of the conference room rattled on and on, mostly reading the contents of each slide being projected onto the big pull-down screen behind him. Yon Ba Deng, Assistant Vice Deputy to the Minister of National Defense for Naval Matters, struggled to stifle a yawn. He dared not close his eyes or he might well have drifted off to sleep. He needed to at least pretend to be interested in the minutia of correct political training for PLAN officers.

These interminable meetings were becoming more and more taxing on his limited patience. But he knew that the Party structure performed much like a beehive. He could learn from watching the drones at work. Despite little individual accomplishment, if enough dedicated, indoctrinated worker bees were applied to attempt to accomplish a task, it would eventually be completed. These lesser committees under the auspices of the Politburo were populated with just such dedicated drones. Deng knew the value of keeping a finger on them as they provided the pulse of the hive. And each of these drones reported back to someone higher up in the Politburo structure. Painful as it could be, he needed to maintain the appearance of an apparatchik, a loyal functionary of the Party.

Yon Ba Deng glanced over toward the heavy oak door

entrance to this drab conference room. As if by Deng's will, Bing Dou, his obsequious aide, opened the door and stepped inside. The little man literally tiptoed around the conference table, bent down, and whispered in his boss's ear.

"Elder brother, it is confirmed that our marines have landed safely in Guadalcanal. The four planes with our tanks are still in flight but due there within two hours. By first daylight tomorrow morning, they will be ready to carry out the next-stage orders from you."

Yon Ba Deng's expression remained impassive as he gave a short nod. Then he could not avoid a quick smile flitting across his face. His complex scheme was finally coming together. Now, all he needed was for his brother and his flotilla of submarines to arrive in Tonga.

The intricate trap was poised, ready to be sprung. And nobody even suspected what was about to happen.

Ψ

Joe Glass stepped onto the gently pitching deck of the captain's gig. The coxswain, neatly dressed in whites, snapped a salute just as Glass's foot hit the deck. As Glass returned the salute, he noted out of the corner of his eye that his SUBRON SEVEN broad pennant was broken on the forestaff. Such formality was still difficult for a former sub captain to get accustomed to.

Glass stood in the boat's cockpit as the gig glided across Pago Pago's inner harbor. A cooling breeze rippled the turquoise water. Palm trees and bright flowers lined the distant shoreline. It was nice to enjoy the beautiful tropical afternoon and play tourist for a few brief minutes, not having to think about the boiling tension that had brought him out here to paradise in the first place.

The one-mile jaunt over to the Port of Pago Pago Main Dock did not take nearly long enough for Glass. Before he knew it, the coxswain brought the gig smoothly alongside a Jacob's ladder that hung down from the high, white side of the *Deep Ocean Explorer*. Glass leapt over to the ladder and climbed up to the research ship's main deck.

Two men waited there to greet him as he stepped onboard. Both were casually dressed in shorts and T-shirts. The older and shorter of the two smiled as he stuck out his hand. His grip was firm and brief.

"Welcome aboard the *Deep Ocean Explorer*, Commodore. I'm Rex Smith, the chief scientist onboard. I try to give this motley crew some modicum of adult leadership." He nodded toward the other man. "This is Captain Bill Bix. He points the bow in the right direction and gets us where we need to be."

"Thanks, gentlemen," Glass responded. "It's a beautiful vessel. I've heard much about the work you do and I salute you."

Smith thanked him with a smile and a nod and then ushered the little group from the broad, open main deck, past the orange UUV strapped securely to it, and forward to the deck house. The three entered a nicely appointed office space and took seats around a small conference table covered with empty coffee cups, charts, and a pile of papers.

"I'm glad you could come over and visit us today," Smith began. "Bill and I have been discussing King Two-for-One's little speech before the Security Council. You are, of course, aware that his...well, I guess you call it a 'land grab' since 'sea grab' doesn't sound quite right."

Smith waved toward a chart and continued. "Anyway, whatever you call it, he is claiming that he and his little kingdom own all of this area, and that coincidentally includes the spot where we found the gold field. Pretty obvious bit of timely annexation. Our lawyers are already working on filing a lawsuit and we are in conversation with the US Department of State. But what I really need most is some protection for my ship and my people when we go back out there to continue our research."

Joe Glass picked up a large-scale chart that mapped the water between where they were located at the moment, in American Samoa, and over to Tonga to the southwest. He pointed to the territorial boundaries clearly marked on the chart.

"Doctor Smith, as far as I am concerned, and as far as my boss is concerned, these have always been, currently are, and forever will be international waters, not under the control of any country. The *Deep Ocean Explorer* is an American flagged vessel. If you sail out here..." Glass stabbed with his index finger the point on the chart where the research vessel had found the spewing gold. "...and if someone tries to stop you or interferes in your operations in any way, we are obligated to defend you and your rights. You can be assured we will do just that. And do so effectively and enthusiastically." Glass sat back in his chair. "But I wouldn't worry too much if I were you. King Tofuwanga doesn't have any navy to speak of. Just a few marines. Certainly, there is no army other than ceremonial. And even if the Chinese say they are backing him, the nearest Chinese base is over five thousand miles away."

The compartment was quiet for a long moment. All three men gazed out across the open waters of the tranquil bay. Smith finally turned back to his guest.

"I am so sorry, sir. May I offer you coffee? A cup of tea?"

"No, Dr. Smith. Thank you very much. I rarely turn down coffee, but I do need to get back to some boring meeting or the other. I do wish you had not shared news of your find out there, though. It certainly has caused some issues."

Smith nodded his understanding.

"Understand we are obligated to tell our donors and supporters of anything of interest," the scientist said. "And manage their expectations. They have to understand the limited possibilities for ever recovering enough of that gold to even make it worthwhile to attempt to get it. I'm afraid many others are not at all aware of that very big issue. But obviously someone in our group let the word get out."

"Yes, and I know they did not anticipate how such news might play into the rather complicated political stuff that is going on now, partly as a result of your discovery. But be assured we will do all we can to protect you, your ship, and your work."

"Allow me to thank you for your assurances," Smith replied. "That makes me, and I'm sure all our crew, feel much better as we prepare to return to the area. We have much work to do, including understanding the science behind geo-physical actions that created that mound of precious metal out there."

Joe Glass shook the hands of the two men, thanked them again for the work they did to better help mankind understand the planet's least explored territory, the oceans. Then he quickly headed back to his boat.

The submariner was not at all sure the scientist and the boat's captain believed what Glass had just told them. And he did not blame them one bit.

One thing was solid, though. The US Navy would do all it could to protect the vessel. But Glass well knew that might turn out to be a much bigger job than he had led the scientist to believe.

Ψ

The old and much used Boeing 737 taxied up to the terminal at Vava'u Airport's tiny single-story terminal building. The airplane, a secondhand gift from the People's Republic of China, was painted in the red and white livery of Tonga International Airlines. Of course, it was TIA's only jet, and the aircraft had only ever served one passenger.

The ground crew shoved the air-stairs up against the aircraft as the passenger door swung open. King Tofuwanga emerged from the interior and paused for a moment at the head of the stairs to allow his eyes to adjust to the brilliant sunlight.

No cheering throng of loyal subjects greeted the monarch. Only a few disinterested ground mechanics milled about.

All just as well, the king mused. He was here at this place, after all, to greet and then send his armed forces off on a vital mission. Secrecy and discretion were of some importance in such a matter.

An ancient jeep, probably left over from some long-forgotten cooperation treaty with this or that western country, wheezed up to the foot of the stairs and stopped amid a cloud of blue-black smoke. King Tofuwanga came down the steps, ignoring the salute of the jeep's driver, who had jumped out to greet his king, and then carefully slid into the rear passenger seat, trying to avoid soiling his field marshal's uniform on the grease and oil that festooned the vehicle's side. Once he was seated, the jeep shot off toward the airfield's back gate, leaving a trail of the blue-black smoke across the tarmac.

The ten-kilometer drive down Tiu Road ended at the piers in Neiafu, Vava'u's principal village. The entirety of the Tonga Maritime Force, consisting of three Australian-built patrol boats and a Vietnam War-vintage landing craft, were tied up at the village pier. The entire Royal Tongan Marines—all three companies of them—milled about on the adjacent street.

When the jeep screeched to a halt at the pier, King Tofuwanga stood, prepared to address his troops. When they saw their king, the troops began to congregate around his vehicle, but still mostly managed to stay back in the shade of the nearby fish-cleaning sheds.

"Warriors of Tonga," the king called out, his voice lost in the shrieks and calls of the seabirds congregating around the refuse from the sheds. Only then did the driver remember to turn on and hand to Tofuwanga a bullhorn. The monarch cleared his throat and started again. "Warriors of Tonga. Today you venture forth to right an historic wrong. As you are aware, the island of Niue and our brothers and sisters were wrongfully separated from us many years ago by the colonial powers of the West. Ultimately, they and the sovereign territory were given to one of the colonialists' own, New Zealand, to protect. The white man calls this a 'free association.' But our Niue brothers and sisters are still not free. They still remain reluctant subjects of the English queen."

"Warriors of Tonga," he ranted on. "Our ancestors settled Niue in times before white man's written history. Our legends speak of crossing the Deep Waters. The people of Niue are of our clan. We must return them to Tonga and finally please our common ancestors and honor the sacred mutual heritage of our people." The king pointed to the waiting boats alongside the pier. "Go! Go, and with your bravery, restore pride and honor to all our people!"

The Marines gave a desultory cheer. Then, urged on by their officers, managed something a bit more enthusiastic. Finally, they formed up and marched toward the waiting craft.

Within a few minutes, the three patrol boats and the lone

landing craft cast off and steamed away, down the winding channel, heading out for the open water.

King Tofuwanga stood and watched until they had eased away from the pier. Only then did he sit and direct the driver to take him back to the airport and his waiting jet.

Ψ

Yon Ba Deng frowned as he read the message a second time. Then he slammed his fist brutally on his desk.

"That pompous, fat fool!" he yelled. "He is going to ruin everything! Does not the idiot understand how delicate the timing is?"

Bing Dou had delivered the message and, having read it beforehand, prudently stepped back a safe distance. Experience had dictated that when bad news was revealed to the Assistant Vice Deputy to the Minister of National Defense for Naval Matters, it was best to put some distance between himself and his chief.

"Elder brother," Bing Dou said, employing his most placating voice. "It may not be so damaging as it might first appear. King Tofuwanga's troops have at least a thirty-hour journey ahead of them. Their only landing craft is an LCM, what the Americans call a 'Mike boat.' It will be a struggle for them to make a speed of fifteen kilometers per hour. And it is five hundred kilometers across open water. I believe we have adequate time to take corrective measures."

Yon Ba Deng nodded and calmed noticeably.

"You are right, of course, younger brother. We must remain calm and prudently adjust our plan."

Bing Dou smiled and stood just a bit taller. This was the first time that Yon Ba Deng had ever used the honorific of "younger brother" toward him. Clearly, he had finally earned a hard-won place of respect. Respect and trust.

"I will remind you of what Master Sun Tzu said," Bing Dou offered. "'Victory comes from finding opportunities in problems.' It will take six hours for our Marines to land on Niue once they are commanded to do so. They can take off from Guadalcanal tomorrow afternoon. Then they will land on Niue in darkness." Bing Dou paused to gauge his boss's reaction so far. He appeared to be listening with great interest. The minion pressed on. "And Master Sun Tzu also told us, 'Conflict is darkness and light, danger and opportunity, stability and change, strength and weakness, the drive to move forward, the force that restrains it. All conflicts contain the seeds of creation and destruction.'"

Yon Ba Deng smiled ever so slightly. The man rarely smiled. And often when he did, it foretold dire actions.

"So now the servant quotes to the master? But there is insight in what you are telling me. Perhaps a better quote would be, 'If, in the midst of difficulties, we are always ready to seize an advantage, we may extricate ourselves from misfortune.'"

Yon Ba Deng stood so suddenly it startled Bing Dou. He retreated another step. But his master maintained his half smile. "Arrange for the Marines to attack tomorrow at sunset." The vice deputy strode over to the office window, still contemplating something. "However, the primary weakness in the plan is now our submarines. The most recent report had my brother just entering the Celebes Sea. At that rate, he will not arrive on time, considering these changes. Contact him and order his force to make best possible speed."

Bing Dou bowed slightly and replied, "The orders are already drafted, elder brother."

15

Vice Admiral Yon Hun Glo read the message a second time. Again, he could only shake his head. It still did not make a lot of sense to the submariner. The admiral, according to orders, had been leading his *lang qun*—his wolf pack of four submarines—in a stealthy transit, first through the Sulu Sea and now across the Celebes Sea. The only way that his AIP-powered boats could make the long voyage to Tonga without the risk of being detected by every sub-hunting nation in the Western Pacific—including, of course, the USA—was to do it with the near silent air-independent propulsion systems. At a maximum speed of ten kilometers per hour, they would require a month for the transit. Clearly, his older brother did not realize how large the Pacific Ocean was and how long it took to cross without alerting the entire world of what was occurring.

Yon Hun Glo turned to Captain Liu Zhang, the commander of the submarine *Wushiwu*, the boat in whose control room they now stood.

"Captain, you will now signal the others to come to a speed of ahead flank. Steer course zero-nine-zero and head straight for the Philippine Sea. Once we are again in international waters, we will make a surface transit at flank until we are east of Fiji."

The diminutive commanding officer frowned as he considered the charts. He carefully measured off the distance and consulted with his report of fuel status.

"Admiral, with all respect, this is a distance of seventy-five hundred kilometers. We will be critically low on fuel when we reach Tonga. It would be much better to use our most fuel-efficient transit speed." The captain did some quick calculations. "We would arrive a day later, but not nearly so seriously low on fuel. We would have practically no tactical usefulness since we..."

Liu looked up and saw Yon Hun Glo shaking his head with a wry smile. Maybe Liu Zhang was not a complete idiot, even if he was a Party sycophant. But in this case, common sense did not matter. The admiral's orders were to arrive as soon as physically possible. And that was precisely what they would do.

"Captain Liu, I have my orders. Now you have yours. You will carry them out."

Yon Hun Glo turned on a heel and headed toward his stateroom. He had only just sat down with a cup of tea when he felt the pronounced nudge as the submarine surged forward.

Ψ

The Chinese admiral was not the only one who noticed the dramatic increase in transit speed of each boat in the wolf pack.

"Possible contact zig, Master One," Ensign Sam Walters called out. "Bearing rate increased to right-two-point-three."

Bill Wilson, *George Mason*'s on-watch officer of the deck, was just flipping to the fire control solution when Sonar called out an update.

"Increase in received frequency, all four contacts of interest. Unless they turned straight toward us, they gotta be making twenty knots!"

Wilson watched the fire control solution. With an increasing right-bearing rate, they certainly were not coming straight at the *George Mason*. The only possible answer was that the Chinese wolf pack had kicked in the afterburners and were now hightailing it out of Dodge for some unknown reason. And the Chinese apparently did not care who might hear their sudden skedaddle.

"Mister Wilson," Chief Schmidt, the pilot, spoke up. "I think you should tell the XO. He is the command duty officer right now."

"Tell the XO what?" LCDR Jackson Biddle asked as he strolled into the control room, still licking the sticky-bun syrup from his fingers. "Something going on I need to know about?"

"XO, the wolf pack just zigged. Looks like they are steadying up on course zero-nine-zero, speed twenty."

Biddle whistled softly.

"Either they want to drag race, or they are suddenly in one hell of a real hurry to get somewhere."

Ψ

Joe Glass heard the knock at his stateroom door. At his grunted acknowledgement, a tall, fit Marine lieutenant colonel opened the door and stepped inside. He stood at attention as he announced, "Lieutenant Colonel Stanton Readly reporting, sir."

Glass stood and stepped around his desk toward the door, extending his hand.

"Colonel Readly, glad to have you and your Marines aboard." He waved toward the sideboard that held a coffee pot. "Grab yourself a cup of coffee and have a seat. I'm assuming the rest of them are right behind you."

As Lt. Col. Readly poured himself a cup, stirred cream into his coffee, and pulled out a chair at the conference table, he reported, "Yes, sir. I believe Captain Jones and Commander Weiss stopped in on the way to say hello to Captain Wooten. Apparently, Captain Jones and Captain Wooten are old shipmates."

Glass grabbed his coffee cup—no cream or sugar—and moved toward the conference table just as the other officers arrived. After greetings all around, and cups of coffee poured for all, the group sat down to business.

"As Senior Officer Present Afloat, USINDOPACOM has made me responsible for the security of the local area," Glass told them as he opened the meeting. "If you have been keeping up with the news lately, you will already know that things are getting interesting, and from a lot of different directions. The announcement of the gold find at the bottom of the Tonga Trench has certainly focused some attention on this particular tropical paradise. The attack on our frigate and King Tofuwanga's little performance at the UN has heightened security concerns. So has recent intel we're getting from some well-placed sources within PLAN. This thing is a veritable stew of intrigue, apparently. The gold is only one element, pun intended. So is the recent ramp-up in the Chinese pressing their territorial claims by violent means. We've had very curious reports from some of our submarines that are keeping tabs on several Chinese boats. But our sources tell us that there is also some considerable in-fighting and intrigue within the Chinese military, with some high-placed individuals jock-eying for power. They are apparently willing to push us close to war to achieve their goals. Besides, it appears their goals are not all the same."

Glass took a sip of his coffee. All eyes were on him. It occurred to him yet again how far he was now from the ward-room of a submarine. "But our job is simply to watch and react to whatever all that James Bond stuff might end up being. I called us all together to see exactly what we have to play with and to set up a little planning on how we respond. Should it come to that."

Looking around the table, Glass was pleased to see each officer nodding, listening. He went on. "For Naval assets, it looks like we have the *Cheyenne*. The sub should be completed with her maintenance and ready for underway in a couple of days. I'm thinking that the *Puller* is best kept here in Pago Pago and used as a command center."

Captain Wooten offered his agreement. "That's what she's designed for. If we try to use her as a warship, she is only going to get in the way."

"Once we get the ORCAs off-loaded and underway, we can use the *Portland* to show the flag when she is underway," Glass went on.

Both Jones and Weiss started to speak, then Weiss nodded for Captain Jones to go ahead.

"We have a problem with that," Jones reported. "ORCA TWO is down hard. Parts are being shipped in from the States, but even at best, it will take a couple of weeks to get it fixed. You don't get parts for those submersibles at the local yacht marina. Until then, our well-deck is out of action, too. On the bright side, ORCA ONE is ready to go."

Glass frowned.

"Not the best timing. That puts a crimp in our style. Let's

go ahead and get ORCA ONE out on mission. I want to keep constant eyes on the area that King Tofuwanga claims is his new backyard. We all know there is a reason for his choice of neighborhood. Can we do that?"

CDR Weiss answered, "No problem. As soon as we complete fueling and load the mission package, we can be underway. Say eight hours."

Well, at least one thing is going our way, Glass thought. He turned next to the Marine.

"Colonel, it looks like you are our boots on the ground if we need them. Where are you going to be useful?"

Lt. Col. Readly sat up straight. "Captain, I have a Marine Special Purpose Force detached from the Fifteenth Marine Expeditionary Unit. I have three hundred and twenty shooters. The MSPF is qualified Special Operations Capable. You get us where you need us and tell us what you want done. We'll get it done."

Glass did not doubt it. Not for a second. Not from the set of the Marine officer's jaw.

Ψ

The USS *Boise* slowly turned in a big arc to the east. Her skipper, Chet Allison, his eye pressed to the periscope eyepiece, watched disbelievingly as the unexpected scene unfolded. Two Chinese SSNs were broached on the surface, just visible against the night sky, barely three thousand yards away. A full moon added illumination to the scene so that *Boise*'s skipper could just make out the activity topside as the two submarines launched several small craft, probably inflatable boats.

As many times as he had shadowed Chinese submarines in his career, this was the first time he had actually seen one live and in color and on the sea surface. Just then, a new element was introduced into the unfolding event.

"Conn, ESM. Detecting an SPS Fifty-Five surface search radar. Just lit off. No threat to us. Probability of detection for the surfaced submarines, very high."

Someone else was in the vicinity, also watching the Chinese boats. However, they were using radar to do so.

Lieutenant Juan Esteban, the battle-stations officer of the deck, keyed the 21MC, responding, "Conn, aye."

So, who else was out there? Allison spun the scope around until he was looking at Dongsha Island. There was a *Kee Lung*-class Taiwanese destroyer anchored there. He shifted the scope to twenty-four power. Sure enough, he could make out the "bed-springs" radar antenna on the former USS *Kidd*-class DDG. It was slowly rotating.

"Conn, Sonar, hearing what sounds like gas turbines lighting off and anchor chain noises, bearing zero-one-three." Chief John Vincent's voice was calm and assured.

"Sonar, Captain. I hold a *Kee Lung*-class destroyer on that bearing. Sounds like he is getting underway."

"That sounds right," Vincent answered. It appeared the Taiwanese navy was not going to allow the Chinese to steam into their territorial waters, surface, and launch some rubber boats. At least not without some kind of perfunctory challenge. Now Allison had a front-row seat to this little stare-down that appeared to be on the verge of taking place.

The skipper swung the scope back to see what was happening with the SSNs. He was just in time to see the men topside scurrying toward hatches. It was either time for them to go, or they, too, were aware of the Taiwanese destroyer heading their way.

The small boats the subs had put into the water were lost

in the darkness. Seconds later, both SSNs slid smoothly below the surface with barely a ripple.

"Conn, ESM, detecting SPG-Sixty gun-control radar. Equates to a *Kee Lung*-class destroyer. It's in target acquisition mode."

The destroyer was in the process of homing in on the proposed targets, the final step before shooting. Or at least trying to convince the PLAN vessels that they were about to do just that if they did not go away.

Allison spun the scope back toward the destroyer in time to see it charging boldly out into the open water. Just then, a brilliant orange-red flame shot from the barrel of the vessel's forward five-inch gun. Three more shots followed in rapid succession.

This was no bluff. They were trying to sink the two interlopers!

The AN/WLY-1 Acoustic Threat Intercept System on *Boise* began ominously chiming. Simultaneously, Sonar reported, "Receiving three-point-five kilo-hertz active sonar. SQS-Fifty-Three. Signal strength forty-five. Probability of detection eighty percent."

Allison nodded. The situation was getting very serious very quickly. The destroyer had stormed out of its anchorage looking for submarines and was already shooting. The Fifty-Three sonar system they were employing was a really good high-power active sonar. There was a damn good chance it would be able to detect all three of the submarines swimming around in Taiwanese waters, the two Chinese boats and the *Boise*. But great as it was, it could not sort out the good guys from the bad.

"Captain," the XO, Henrietta Foster, jumped in. "Recommend we go active to tell the destroyer who we are."

Allison did not hesitate. He was already thinking the same thing.

"Sonar, go active on the BQQ-Ten. Max power omni mode."

The BQQ-10 sonar transmitted on the same frequency as the SQS-53. They were very similar systems, actually designed and built by the same people. The sonar operators on the destroyer should easily be able to identify that one contact they were seeing was a US submarine.

Of course, the two Chinese SSNs would also know now that *Boise* was an uninvited guest at their little party. Allison would have loved to see the looks on the Chinese skippers' faces when *Boise*'s BQQ-10 popped up.

There was, of course, a chance their reaction might be drastic. Time to get the gun cocked, just in case.

"Make tubes one and two ready in all respects. Assign tube one to Master One, tube two to Master Two." Now it would only take a few seconds to put two torpedoes in the water if they needed to, one aimed at each of the Chinese submarines.

"Conn, Sonar. Three active returns. Master One, bearing three-four-four, range three-five-hundred yards. Master Two, bearing three-five-one, range four-two-hundred yards. Sierra One-Seven, the Taiwan DDG, bearing zero-one-six, range six-five-hundred yards."

It was a regular South China Sea regatta!

Allison spun the scope around again. Time for one final look and then they would get out of town. He did not want to be in the middle of an Old West gunfight.

The skipper was just in time to see two ASROC missiles leap from the forward launch rails of the destroyer. Brilliant white flames arched across the night sky.

"Torpedo in the water!" The pitch of Vincent's voice had

gone up a notch or two. "Hold two...wait...hold four torpedoes in the water."

"Snapshot tube one Master One. Tube two Master Two," Allison called out. He reached up and spun the red ring to lower the scope.

The captain hardly had time to consider what had just happened. Torpedoes had been launched at them with the intent of blowing them up and sending them to the bottom. He was about to launch weapons at the two submarines attacking him, occupied by fellow living, breathing submariners.

Foster checked the fire control solutions and calmly said, "Solution ready, both weapons."

"Ship ready," Esteban confirmed.

"Two torpedoes bearing three-four-five. No bearing drift." Chief Vincent's voice was tight with tension over the 21MC. "The other two have a right bearing drift. They are heading for the destroyer."

The Chinese SSNs were shooting at everything they could see or hear.

Allison looked over at the weapons control panel just as the weapons officer yelled, "Weapons ready."

"Shoot tubes one and two," Allison ordered. He felt a sudden shudder as the impulse ram forced high-pressure water around the stern of each two-ton ADCAP torpedo and flushed them out of the tubes into the sea.

"Normal launch, both tubes," the weapons officer reported, as calmly as if this were just another drill and they had launched water slugs or exercise torpedoes.

Turning to the chief of the watch, Allison ordered, "Launch the EMATT, launch a pair of evasion devices. Wait fifteen seconds and launch two more evasion devices."

The EMATT, or Expendable Mobile ASW Training Target,

was designed to simulate a submarine while training operators. However, since the device sounded and behaved just like
a real submarine, it made a good decoy. Hopefully good
enough to fool the two oncoming weapons zooming toward
Boise.

"Hold both weapons running normally," Chief Vincent
reported. "Inbound weapons still bear three-four-five and
three-four-three."

With the counterattack launched, it was time to get out of
town. Allison ordered, "Ahead flank. Make your depth three
hundred feet. Steady course zero-eight-zero."

Foster had moved back to the ECDIS display. "Skipper,
recommend stay on this course for thirty seconds, then come
left to zero-six-five. And depth four hundred feet."

Boise jumped ahead and angled downward.

"Incoming weapons still bear three-four-three and three-
four-five. Loud splashes bearing three-four-zero. Sounds like
multiple Mark Forty-Six torpedoes on that bearing."

The Taiwanese destroyer had added to the fusillade aimed
at the two Chinese boats. Allison mumbled to no one in
particular, "That would be the ASROCs. At least the destroyer
shot at the right guys." He looked quickly at the ECDIS that
Foster was watching. Allison could tell that she was guiding
him behind Dongsha Atoll, staying as close to the coral mountain as possible.

Good tactic. Maybe it would be enough to keep them alive
if the evasion devices failed.

The XO held up her hand and then signaled.

"Come left, steer course zero-six-five, come to four
hundred feet," Allison ordered.

"Loud explosion on the bearing to Sierra One-Seven,"
Chief Vincent called out. It appeared that at least that
part of the Chinese subs' attack was successful. *Boise's*

task remained to be sure that the other part would not be.

"Loss of contact on the incoming weapons. Blocked by the countermeasures," Vincent reported. Maybe the Chinese torpedoes would go for the countermeasures. Or maybe they would be lured off by the EMATT.

"Detect, first weapon!" Weps yelled. "Detect! Weapon shifted to acquisition." The bloodhound from *Boise*'s tube one was on the scent.

"Loss of wire continuity, tube one," Weps reported. The fine cable that connected the torpedo to the submarine had snapped. Allison knew that their maneuvering could have broken the wire. Or maybe it had found the enemy and blown them up already. With a speed of sound in water of fifteen hundred yards per second, it would be over six seconds before they would know if that was the case.

"Re-acquired both incoming weapons. First weapon bears three-two-six. Looks like it is tracking the EMATT." Chief Vincent's voice carried pure relief. It appeared that the little electronic device was going to sacrifice itself to save the *Boise*.

"Loss of wire continuity, tube two," Weps reported. The reports were coming so fast Allison had a hard time absorbing them all.

"Second weapon bears three-four-three. Still closing." Damn! No relief on this one. One of the Chinese torpedoes was still doggedly on their trail.

"Launch two evasion devices," Allison ordered. "Then wait ten seconds and launch two more."

As he gave the commands, the skipper glanced at the ECDIS display. It showed that they were just rounding the corner of Dongsha Atoll. But not by much. How accurate was this little electronic wonder? Accurate enough to bet the lives of every member of the crew?

"Multiple explosions on the bearings of Master One and Master Two."

Well, Vincent was reporting that something was happening back where it all started. No telling what, but those two SSNs were definitely in the middle of it.

"Range gating on incoming weapon," Vincent yelled. He really did not need to use the 21MC. The fear in his voice rolled right through the door from Sonar.

Allison rolled the dice in his head.

"Come to course north. Make your depth one hundred feet."

According to ECDIS, they would just skirt the reefs on the east side of the atoll. That is, if the charts were accurate. And if they were where they believed they were.

The big sub angled over as it swung around to the new course.

"Incoming weapon still range gating," Chief Vincent reported. "Now bearing two-seven-seven."

Allison looked at the plot. If the weapon was where they thought it was and if they were where they thought they were, the remaining torpedo was taking a straight-line course directly at them. That would take it right over the shallow reef at the south end of the atoll.

Allison and the crew had done all they could. Now, their lives depended on billions of coral polyps and calcium carbonate standing in the path of that deadly weapon hurtling their way.

A tremendous explosion rocked the *Boise*. Lights flashed off, then back on again.

Chet Allison tried to grab hold of something but was knocked to the deck, banging his head brutally on something hard and unmoving. The last thing he heard was a 1MC announcement—"Flooding, flooding in the engine room!"—echoing, growing fainter, until it was lost in a dull roar.

Then, darkness.

Ψ

Chet Allison seemed to be groping his way through a long tunnel toward an incredibly bright white light. His legs felt like they were mired in molasses, but there was a voice. A voice urging him to stop struggling.

"Easy, Skipper. Just lie still." It was Henrietta Foster. "You got a pretty nasty bump on your head. Doc just gave you an injection for pain."

Allison opened his eyes and tried to focus. He was still in the conn. His XO was cradling his head and wiping the blood away from a gash behind his right ear.

"The... the boat?" he stammered.

"*Boise* is okay," Foster answered. "Looks like that last torpedo hit the coral just aft of us. That still gave us enough of a jolt to cause some flooding through the stern tube. We're bobbing on the surface right now, inspecting damages."

"And..."

"Crew is good. Few bumps and bruises, like you. Damage reports coming in. Port turbine generator breaker popped open. Re-shut okay. Steam leak on the evaporator, isolated now. Sonar reports loss of the TB-34 towed array. No signal and no continuity. All in all, looks like we were pretty lucky."

Allison tried to shake his head, but it hurt like mortal hell. "We wouldn't have been so lucky if you hadn't thought of sneaking behind the atoll, XO. Good thinking. You saved our butts. We know anything about the rest of the players?"

Foster answered, "Heavy fighting on the island. Must have been assault troops on those rubber boats the Chinese were launching. It appears the *Kee Lung* was sunk. And both of the Chinese subs. There's no way to tell who hit what in all that mess. But folks died. Lots of folks."

Allison nodded, grimaced with the pain even that small amount of movement caused, then held his head as a wave of nausea rolled over him. He relaxed and sucked in a deep breath, which seemed to help.

"Just as well. I imagine there will be a lot of finger pointing from all points of the compass." He felt himself drifting back into the darkness. "Good job, XO. Relay that to the crew, too. Something tells me we have steamed right square into the middle of a massive shit storm."

"You may have gotten a good crack on the noggin, Skipper," Foster told him, "but your navigation instincts are impeccable."

16

Soo Be Xian was absolutely ecstatic. Finally, here was the chance to put his over-reaching rival, Yon Ba Deng, and his upstart submariner brother in their proper place. That would preferably be a place of disgrace, far from the corridors of power. Apparently, the Assistant Vice Deputy to the Minister of National Defense for Naval Matters had lost control of his own navy. And certainly, his brother's submarine force. How else to explain a pair of rogue submarines trying to start a war with Taiwan? And possibly, by extension, with the rest of the world.

Soo Be Xian rubbed his chin as he relished the situation. Yes, it was unfortunate that his country would be seen as the aggressor against Taiwan over such a bit of worthless flotsam, a little coral atoll of no real value. Still, assuming it did not kick off another world war, was there something he could personally gain from this situation? Maybe a way to remove Yon Ba Deng from the Party position that the blowhard so liked to flaunt. Perhaps he could even wrangle himself a path to reach a Party position?

But, how to proceed? What should his strategy be? Soo Be

Xian doodled on a scrap of paper as he pondered the possibilities. There were two possible approaches in which to deal with the current ugly situation.

They could always order a hasty retreat, abandoning the Jiaolong Assault Team special operators still fighting against superior forces on the atoll. After the media had moved on to their next click-bait and ratings, tensions would quickly de-escalate. Yes, there would be a significant loss of face, not to mention the loss of some good and loyal soldiers, but that would be fleeting. Soon, those who complained the loudest—with the exception of the pretenders in Taiwan itself—would be coming around again, wanting to complete trade deals, accept investment capital, and bask in the glow of China's growth and prosperity. But, at least in the interim, China would be seen as a paper tiger, cowed by a tiny break-away part of the homeland.

The other option was far more visceral and much more likely to save face. They could decide to be the big tiger in the jungle. Shove aside the Taiwanese and, after all these years of threats and bluster, take back at least this small island that was rightfully Chinese territory in the first place. If Taiwan—or anyone else—still believed that such a clump of coral was worth an all-out war, then so be it. China was ready and had plenty of cannon fodder to use to make its claim stick.

Plus—and it was a big plus—the PLAN could still claim, and with considerable evidence, that a Taiwanese warship had brutally attacked Chinese vessels conducting basic operations in territorial waters. Taiwan started it. China was merely protecting the assets and brave patriots of its navy, ambushed for no apparent reason.

"Bien Sung!" Soo Be Xian suddenly yelled.

His general factotum peeked through the narrowly opened door.

"You called, Minister?"

"Yes. Yes, I did. I want you to contact the Party Secretary's staff at once. It is time for the Politburo to discuss the Dongsha matter. Then get Colonel General Xiang on a secure video call. We have some actions that must be set in motion. And we must do it quickly."

Ψ

Yon Ba Deng furiously massaged his temples, as if that might make his crushing headache disappear. He struggled to remain calm. Equilibrium was the key. He must maintain a level balance if he was to avoid allowing anger and frustration to replace clear thinking. As the ancient master Laozi taught, he would have to get back in harmony with the *tao*, with "the way."

Yon Ba Deng sat upright and forced a calm smile. The *Tianshi*, the Celestial Masters, pointed the way to the *wu wei*, a state of perfect knowledge, of perfect efficaciousness, of perfect economy of energy. Now, more than ever before, he needed to center his thoughts and find the way.

As his breathing stabilized, Yon Ba Deng idly caressed his ancient copy of the *Taishang Ganying Pian—Treatise on the Response of the Tao*—drawing calming comfort from the yellowing xuan paper with its faintly musty smell and smooth rice-paper texture.

But then the high-level Communist Party functionary lost control of his emotions once again when he glanced at the message on his computer screen. His quest for calm was immediately shattered. Yesterday it had been that pompous, fat pig of a monarch, King Tofuwanga, trying his very best to start a shooting war in the South Pacific, and just to grab all the gold long before Yon Ba Deng was ready to claim it and parse it out properly.

Now, though, new details on the screen sent his blood pressure soaring. A couple of submarine captains, sent on a simple diversionary mission, instructed to shoot up some out-of-the-way Taiwanese guard compound, had decided, apparently on their own, to launch an invasion. To make matters far worse, for some reason, they had attacked and sunk a Taiwanese destroyer in the process. The intelligence report said that heavy fighting continued on the little island. And now, the Taiwanese Air Force was flying combat sorties over it. And the worst of it? It was all over CNN and Times International.

Stubborn submarine captains often acted independently. But once these two were back in port, Yon Ba Deng would meet them at the dock to personally end their careers and their freedom.

"Excuse me, elder brother," Bing Dou said as he stuck his head through the door. "South Sea Fleet Headquarters now reports that both of the submarines involved in the Dongsha Island affair have missed their second communications cycle. They are presuming that both submarines are lost. Likely at the hand of the destroyer before it was sunk. Searches are being launched."

Yon Ba Deng slammed his fist onto his desk, any semblance of calm and balance now gone. The Celestial Masters had never been required to deal with such incompetent fools. Or to face the inevitable second-guessing from the Party.

Set up a diversion. That was all those idiots were supposed to do. Now it appeared they and their crews had died while effectively starting a major shooting war. Maybe even the one the West and the traitors on Taiwan had expected China to launch since 1949. And, if things went badly—as they certainly would—then the blame would surely fall on him.

Yon Ba Deng looked around the room, again attempting to draw comfort and inspiration from the ancient artifacts he had carefully assembled over the years, artifacts from when China was truly the Middle Kingdom, the center of the world. Before the Century of Shame that had been brought about by the uncivilized Westerners and their exploitation. Surely there was something in the artifacts from which he could draw on the wisdom of the ancients. A bit of guidance to how he should work toward rectifying the wrongs of the last century and return China to her rightful place as the leader of the world.

And, of course, elevate him to his deserved position along with it.

But even the ancients' eternal wisdom was failing him when applied to this immediate crisis. Another note appeared with an ominous ding on the computer screen: The Party Committee for Internal Security was calling an emergency session, almost certainly at the behest of that toady, Soo Be Xian. The only agenda item to discuss was the Dongsha fiasco.

Yon Ba Deng needed a strategy more than ever. And it would have to be bulletproof.

Ψ

The long and bumpy open-water voyage was mercifully almost over. Two days and nights being bounced around onboard the open LCM or doing little more than lying around topside on the three patrol boats had left most of the Tongan Marines irritable, tired, and battered. Many hung onto the railings, wrung dry by repeated bouts of seasickness. That was the primary reason the high limestone bluffs of Niue that loomed on the eastern horizon were a welcome sight when they popped up from the waves, a dark splotch against the gray-pink glow of the rising sun.

The tiny Tongan armada had actually arrived off the coral island in the middle of the night, but navigating the narrow opening through the reef that surrounded Niue was too hazardous to attempt in the moonless darkness. The Tongans, though anxious to get the operation underway, wisely decided to wait a few hours for the rising sun.

Finally, when the sun was a bare glimmer on the horizon, the elements of the Tongan Navy threaded through the hole in the crashing surf, into the calm turquoise waters awaiting them inside the sheltering reef. The closest thing that Niue had to a harbor was the capital village of Alofi. It had no piers and only one small beach that the LCM landing craft could use, the only logical access for an invasion force. Everywhere else, the waves lapped up against a cliff that rose several meters above the water's surface.

The LCM boldly drove up onto the beach and dropped its bow door so that the troops could loudly rush ashore. They were greeted by a couple of curious fishermen heading out for the morning catch and a pair of energetic Japanese tourists completing their early run.

The first company of invading troops charged down the Coast Road and then onto Tapeu-Porritt Road, the crushed coral track that led to the airport. Meanwhile, the LCM made runs out and back, shuttling the rest of the troops from the patrol boats, anchored just offshore, back to the beach.

Niue had no defense force and only a couple of constables to keep the peace. By the time the last of the Tongan marines were on dry land, the airport and the telephone exchange next door, the only real links to the outside world, were officially in the hands of the invaders. Not a shot had been fired, except the accidental discharge of one constable's Webley pistol when he was being relieved of it. The only injury in that incident had been to a cell phone charging station that happened to be in the line of fire.

Then, several squads of marines headed out to commandeer pickup trucks. Their purpose was more to sightsee and scrounge food and alcohol from the beachside cafes than to consolidate their victory.

Ψ

The sun had just plunged below the western horizon when the first blue-gray Chinese Shaanxi Y-9 turboprop transport aircraft touched down on Niue at Hanan International Airport, without benefit of assistance from the island's air traffic controllers. Built in the early seventies to service a twice-weekly flight to Auckland, New Zealand, the tiny facility was not designed to handle the massive four-engine transports. Certainly not eight of them at once. The apron and short taxiway were quickly cluttered with parked aircraft. The last two to touch down were forced to find a resting spot on the runway itself.

Over four hundred Chinese Marines were disgorged from four of the big birds. Six ZBD-3 tracked airborne fighting vehicles and a pair of FB-6C anti-aircraft vehicles rumbled down the ramps from several of the aircraft as the Marines lugged their gear off the aircraft and toward a large open field alongside the terminal and behind the telephone exchange. The ZBD-3s left a thick fog of acrid, black diesel smoke as they traversed Tapue-Porret Road, in the direction of Alofi.

The Chinese Marines quickly and efficiently established a command center in the terminal building and a defense perimeter surrounding the airport, ignoring the questions and protestations of the few airport officials they encountered. All this was observed with much amusement by the Tongan Marines, who enjoyed their purloined cold beers while watching sleepily from their resting places under a nearby grove of palm trees.

The sun was little more than a suggestion on the eastern horizon when the now-empty transport planes revved up, got airborne, and headed west. Toward Fua'amotu International Airport on Tonga, there to await whatever orders they might receive next.

Ψ

Chet Allison leaned against the BPS-15 radar set in the after part of control on the submarine *Boise*. It seemed like he and his second-in-command, Henrietta Foster, had been standing back here for most of the day, trying to get a handle on what might happen next after the shoot-'em-up and close call they had just been through. That included formulating answers to the seemingly endless "Immediate Attention, or the world as we know it will cease to exist" inquiries they were being peppered with, emanating from every possible layer of the chain of command. And many sources well outside that chain. Some of which Allison and Foster had never even heard of before.

Carefully and diplomatically, they were now telling each and every functionary that they had already provided any morsel of information they had, every minor detail of the events they had just endured. That constant pressure and endless questioning as well as the gallons of coffee he had consumed had long since left Allison with a raging headache and a shaky stomach. Of course, some of that could also be attributed to the really hard bump on his admittedly hard head.

Boise was at periscope depth at the moment, slowly circling a few miles south of Dongsha Island. "Slowly" being the operative word. They were now using the submarine's secondary propulsion motor. The SPM was a little outboard motor that could be lowered out of an after-ballast tank and used like a slightly more powerful version of a trolling motor on a bass boat. More powerful but still barely able to move the big, heavy vessel at a speed of little more than about two knots. But it was their only propulsion until the engineers repaired the shaft seal leakage caused by the close-aboard explosion of the Chinese torpedo.

Lieutenant Commander Tim Anson, *Boise*'s engineer, opened the after door and barged into the compartment, almost knocking Foster over as he did so. Everything that Anson did was full steam ahead. It was the engineer's philosophy that any obstacle in his path was easier to go through than around.

"Oops! Sorry, XO. Didn't see you there," the big bear of a man told Foster. "Skipper, I have an update for you."

"What's the status, Eng?"

"Well, the shaft seals are kaput," Anson shot out in his usual rapid-fire manner. "My guess is that the carbon got cracked from the pressure surge when that torpedo hit the reef so close to us. The guys have been working hard and managed to snug up the emergency flax packing. So far, it seems to be working fine. I don't recommend any speeds above ten knots or diving below two hundred feet or we could be on the inflatable boot. You know what that means."

Before Allison could respond, Foster chimed in.

"Eng, I hear what you're saying, but I believe the NAVSEA Tech Manual specifies a depth limit of three hundred feet and speed of twelve knots if you establish a leak-off rate of at least ten drops a second with the flax packing. And you would also need to station a watch to adjust it."

Anson pondered the XO's words for a long moment. He had seen it before. Henrietta Foster had the uncanny ability to memorize even the most arcane facts. If she saw it, she had it stored somewhere in her brain and could find and recite it in a second. And often did so if it served her purpose.

"Well, yes, ma'am," Anson finally answered. "I did refer to the Tech Manual. I was just applying a safety factor to the tolerances. Believe me, I don't want to go all the way home at two knots on the SPM."

"Skipper," the leading radioman interrupted, passing Allison the red, top-secret message board. "You're going to want to read the top message."

Allison flipped open the board and read the short message. Then he read it again.

"XO, get the Nav up here to plot this out. Eng, get propulsion shifted back to the mains. We'll use your safety-factor limits right now. But be ready to go to the NAVSEA limits if we have to. The ones in the Tech Manual."

Foster shot Allison a questioning glance.

"We are to stay here on an 'Indications and Warning' mission until we get relieved by an Aussie diesel boat," Allison told her. "Then, we are to make best speed back to Pearl Harbor."

"Indications and Warning" meant they were to continue observing all they could see and provide near real-time actionable information. Allison had worked long enough with Henrietta Foster to know exactly what that look on her face meant.

Any actionable information they might deliver to the

powers that be could possibly be the impetus for full-blown war.

Ψ

Jim Ward was at his wits' end. Stir-crazy. Cooped up in a private room at Changi General Hospital in Singapore. Lying around simply was not the young SEAL-team commander's style. One more soccer game or cooking show on the TV set in the far corner of the room, one more scorched glob of some kind of meat with a tasteless gray sauce, and he would be forced to extricate himself from this place by any means necessary. He needed to be up and moving around, but every time he tried to get out of bed, the pain would come rushing back at the wound site in his side and he would collapse back into his state of utter uselessness. Then, inevitably, within seconds of him disobeying his bed-rest command, an officious nurse/prison guard, quite properly dressed in a white uniform and pronounced scowl, would rush in, attempt to make him reasonably comfortable, and scold him roundly.

Ward had vowed to locate and disarm the "patient confined to bed" alarm.

He assumed his next dosage of not-so-gentle scolding and over-cooked scrambled eggs was arriving when the door swung open and interrupted his internal griping. Instead, though, a stunningly gorgeous young woman walked into his room after knocking. He was about to reluctantly tell her she must have found the wrong patient when he noticed a some-how-familiar man with her. Then he recognized the guy.

TJ Dillon.

"Dillon!" Ward shouted. "Last time I saw your sorry tail, you were in South America heading downriver as fast as you could paddle that canoe chasing after some low-life son of a bitch."

The CIA agent nodded and grinned.

"Bingo! It won't surprise you to know your old man told me the same thing not so long ago. And in almost those very same words."

"And now, here you are, in a hospital room in Singapore. I'd say you took the wrong exit off I-10."

Ward smiled at the beautiful Asian lady with him. The room grew considerably brighter when she tossed back one of her own.

"TJ, for a southern boy, you are certainly lacking in manners. You haven't introduced me to your friend." Ward extended a hand. "I'm Jim Ward and am in no way associated with this dude here."

"Pleased to meet you, Commander. I'm Li Min Zhou," she answered, again smiling as she shook his hand with a surprisingly firm grip. "You certainly resemble your father, Jim. And you are both very direct. But I have to say I find you a bit more charming."

"You have me pegged, ma'am," Ward shot back.

"You got time to chat a few minutes," Dillon interrupted.

"Well, there is a show coming on TV in a minute about how to properly prepare pepper crab..." the SEAL jokingly began.

But Dillon was no longer grinning. Neither was his lovely friend. This visit had just become a business meeting.

17

Yon Ba Deng nodded curtly as the guards saluted him and swung open the heavy oaken doors for his passage. He stepped into the small but ornate conference room. As nothing more than a rather junior Party official, his assigned seat was one of the uncomfortable, straight-backed chairs that lined the walls.

Each time Yon was in this place, each time he sat in one of the straight-backed chairs, he imagined himself instead claiming a seat at the big, solid table. No, not just at the table but at the head of the table.

Soon, soon, he told himself. And the occurrences over the next few minutes might determine just how soon that would be.

As befit a junior official, he had arrived at the meeting ahead of the Politburo members. Even so, all of the other seats around the wall were already filled, each man sitting as if at attention, with no conversation or pleasantries between them. Yon Ba Deng had just sat down in the lone remaining open seat when the doors at the other end of the room swung open again. Twenty-three senior Chinese leaders paraded in, single file. Last to enter was Tan Yong. He was attending this particular meeting as the Head of the Party Committee for Internal Security, though everyone present was quite familiar with his other titles. He was also Communist Party General Secretary and President of the People's Republic of China. Most of the world knew him for the latter role.

Tan Yong took his place at the head of the large conference table and signaled for the doors to be shut. Then he took his time opening a chilled bottle of sparkling water on the table before him and pouring himself a glass half full. He took a sip and appeared to approve.

Finally, the president turned and glared directly at Yon Ba Deng for a full ten seconds before speaking. It was a well-known tactic, designed to throw his underlings off kilter.

"As we all are well aware, some hostilities are occurring on Pratas Island. What our misdirected brothers from Taiwan insist on calling Dongsha Island. It would appear that these hostilities might be the result of some unauthorized actions from members of our Navy. In light of these developments and their potential ramifications, we will now hear the report from the Assistant Vice Deputy to the Minister of National Defense for Naval Matters."

Yon Ba Deng swallowed hard. He stood and faced the group. What he said in the next few minutes, how he said it, and the Committee's reaction to both would determine whether he was on a trajectory to the highest levels of leadership or immediately on a painful trip to a dark prison cell and, sooner or later, termination. That is if he was fortunate enough to make it out of the meeting alive. There had been many rumors of bodies being carried out of this very room only to be unceremoniously dumped alongside the freeway.

The assistant vice deputy stood tall and launched into his explanation.

"*Tongzhui*, comrades, and thank you for the opportunity to relay the information we have gathered to this point. I will tell you that reports are still being received concerning this matter. What is confirmed so far is that two of our submarines were dispatched by South Fleet Command to transport a Jiaolong Team for a deployment aimed to conduct a simple and routine armed surveillance of Pratas Island, just as we have done for decades. As you are all well aware, Pratas Atoll is the legitimate territory of the People's Republic but remains illegally and belligerently occupied by the rebels on Taiwan, and that includes a garrison of armed troops."

Yon attempted to gauge the reaction thus far from the faces of everyone in the room. No indication. Each remained stoic, expressionless. He went on, choosing every word carefully, just as he had rehearsed at length before the mirror in his office.

"A Taiwanese destroyer was lying in ambush, waiting for the arrival of the submarines. Despite our vessels being in our own territorial waters, the warship attacked without provocation while our submarines were surfaced for the purpose of launching the surveillance teams. The submarines correctly and bravely defended themselves and China's sovereignty. In the process, the aggressor ship was sunk."

Perhaps a flicker of pride on the president's face. Heartened, Yon went on.

"I regret to inform you that neither of the submarines has reported in. They have now missed several communications windows, which does not bode well. We must presume that either they are lost or they have been too badly damaged to communicate."

Tan Yong held up a hand, interrupting Yon Ba Deng's narrative.

"You say the destroyer was lying in ambush. That would

mean they had prior knowledge that our submarines would be in the area. That would imply that we have a security breach, that somehow the Taiwanese were informed of this mission in advance, including information that our vessels would be on the surface and vulnerable. Do you believe this to be the case, Assistant Vice Director?"

Yon Ba Deng hesitated. This was precisely the inference that he wanted every man in the room to draw. Especially the president. And it was vital that everyone on the committee would make that logic leap on his own. Having the president help them do so was even more than he could have hoped.

"We cannot discount that possibility," Yon answered. "Only a very small group knew of this particular mission. It was a rapid tasking out of the Southern Theatre of Operations. Even my own staff was unaware of the details of the operation. I will, of course, order an investigation immediately, and we will learn if there has been a betrayal in the Southern Theatre."

There. He had just pulled the pin and thrown the hand grenade under Soo Be Xian's insular little club of pet generals. Let them deal with the carnage when things inevitably blew up around them.

Tan Yong again held up his hand.

"Thank you, but I believe we will deal with such matters from within this committee. I anticipate you and your staff will be otherwise occupied in the near term. For example, as to the continued fighting on Pratas Island, what does the Navy recommend?"

Yon Ba Deng had to concentrate hard to avoid smiling. This was going better than he had dared anticipate. He had suspected that the Party Committee for Internal Security might possibly insist on doing his dirty work for him. Clearly, that would now be the case. That meant that Soo Be Xian would soon be a toothless tiger and Yon would not have needed to risk anything to accomplish that goal. This also offered the perfect chance to use the same committee to keep his own necessary diversion in play, even if the submarines had botched things so badly for him.

Looking directly at Tan Yong, Yon Ba Deng answered, "General Secretary, the unwarranted and unprovoked attack on our submarines by the Taiwanese is either a potential disaster or a potential opportunity. We have two options. We can turn our backs on our brave Marines and suffer the loss of face before the world should we kowtow to the Taiwanese. Or we can give an immediate and overwhelming response to them. One that sends an unmistakable message to the world. Pratas Island has but a small garrison. It is situated nearer to Hong Kong than it is to Taiwan. In point of fact, the atoll is of no real value to Taiwan. Despite the inevitable diplomatic bluster from them and their allies, they will not risk an existential war to keep control of it. The People's Liberation Army Navy recommends that immediate air and naval support be dispatched to rescue our beleaguered warriors, attempt to learn the fate of our brave submariners, and reclaim our rightful territory."

For the first time in memory, Yon Ba Deng watched as every person in the room looked to the president to assess his reaction to such a bold plan. It all hinged now on Tan Yong.

The president remained stone-faced for a moment, as if he had heard nothing that had been proposed. Then, he smiled. There was no attempt to conceal his approval.

"Yon Ba Deng, how quickly can these forces be deployed?"

Yon felt dizzy. Still, he forced himself to remain calm, to not allow his glee to be obvious, to respond forcefully and confidently.

"With your order, the first aircraft from Shek Kong Airfield can be airborne in less than an hour from this moment.

Destroyers and patrol craft can depart Nyong Shuen Chau Naval Base within two hours. We can have overwhelming force around and over the island before the sun rises. They will be capable of quickly and effectively executing the plan."

Tan Yong nodded.

"Let it be so." He raised a hand and pointed directly at Yon Ba Deng. "But I must impress upon you, do not start a war with your little games or you will quickly learn how dry and desolate the Gobi is."

With that, the president waved Yon Ba Deng from the room and signaled to the others that the meeting was now completed. But he remained seated until the room was cleared and the doors had once again been closed by the guards.

Only then, as he was rising, did Tan Yong speak quietly to his aide.

"That one bears even closer scrutiny. He is not to be trusted."

The aide nodded. "Should I have him arrested?"

"No, no. He has potential. We will make use of his talents, his ambitions, and his connections so long as they serve our purposes. But the bear must always watch the young tiger. The other one, Soo Be Xian, the one our friend here has so neatly stabbed in the back. Him, we will need to punish. Find or invent some corruption—I doubt you will need to be very creative or look far—and let the Guoanbu discover the evidence."

The Guoanbu, the Ministry of State Security, would certainly know what to do with such information. And the ministry's results were often permanent.

Ψ

Captain Joe Glass stood on the catwalk high above the well

deck of the USS *Portland*. Alongside him, Captain Mort Jones, *Portland*'s CO, and Commander Steve Weiss, CO of the ORCA team, leaned against the rail, observing the activity below them.

Waves gently lapped up on the inclined well deck as two teams of sailors in small rigid-hulled inflatable boats—RHIBs—alternately pushed and pulled the large, black, ungainly ORCA ONE submersible from the ship's shadowy interior. It slowly backed out of the flooded-down well deck and into a patch of early afternoon sunlight.

The three officers watched as the unmanned submarine, now unleashed, turned and headed out toward the harbor mouth, dutifully falling in behind the outbound RV *Deep Ocean Explorer*. As it disappeared from view, Commander Weiss broke the silence.

"That's about the end of the show from here, gentlemen. I suggest we go up to CIC and take a look at the mission plan."

By the time they had climbed up to the *Portland*'s Combat Information Center, ORCA ONE had already cleared the harbor mouth and slipped below the waves. The darkened CIC looked very much like a video gamer's dream setup. It was illuminated with dozens of flat-panel displays hanging around workstations, each festooned with joysticks and Xbox-like controllers.

Weiss guided the two captains to a large flat-panel display that hung from an outboard bulkhead. The screen showed a chart of the island as well as the ORCA's outbound track. Weiss picked up a remote control and hit one of the buttons. The display shifted to a small-scale chart of a sizeable area of ocean, stretching from Tuvalu to the northwest to the Cook Islands to the southeast. He pressed another button and a track appeared on the chart.

"Since we only have the one ORCA right now, she's going to

have to do multiple missions." He looked toward Glass. "Commodore, you gave us a maritime surveillance mission around the Tonga Trench and a mission to plant remote sensors around the Tongan main islands. That's a lot of real estate to cover and this girl is not real fast, I'm afraid. She can do eight knots if she really needs to, but four is a more economical transit speed. I figure we'll tell her to make one pass around the trench and then head off to the islands. It'll take better than a week to put all the sensors in place and confirm that they're operating. Then we will be back to a full-time surveillance on the *Deep*."

Glass nodded. "That's just what we asked for, Steve. I know that you didn't bring your full team. How many people will be manning this control station? And do you need any augmentation?"

Weiss chuckled.

"Thanks, sir. But you remember that 'U' in UUV? That stands for 'unmanned.' And these babies are just that. She will go on out there and do her thing with little to no supervision. She will call home if she finds anything. Other than that, we just sit back and wait."

Ψ

Tim Anson walked a slow circle as he swept *Boise's* periscope around, looking at the horizon. "Dancing with the fat lady" was what submariners called it, and had since the days of the World War II diesel-electric boats. The slow shuffle as they swung the periscope around, looking at the outside world through a tiny soda straw.

Then, suddenly, something very fast flew past. A jet. A jet so low that Anson involuntarily ducked. Then, just as suddenly, three more aircraft flashed by, down low on the deck, likely roaring toward Dongsha Island. Anson caught just the barest glimpse of a red star on a wing as the planes screamed off into the distance. He could also see a heavy load of ordnance slung underneath those wings. Someone on Dongsha was about to get quite the fireworks display.

Anson was reaching for the 1MC mike to call the skipper to the conn when the 21MC speaker blared.

"Conn, ESM, receiving multiple pulse-doppler radar emitters. Probable fire control. Not a threat, but signal strength high."

Anson grabbed the 21MC mike instead.

"Conn, ESM, aye. Just saw a flight of Chinese jets close aboard. Can you classify the emitters?"

"ESM, aye. Classifying now."

They really needed to determine who was probing around up there.

"What you got, Eng?"

Anson turned to find himself facing the skipper.

"Flight of Chinese jets down low heading toward the island. Looked like they were heading in for a low-level attack. And ESM is reporting a bunch of radar emitters."

Commander Chet Allison grabbed the periscope.

"Let me take a look-see," he said as he trained the Type 18 periscope toward the distant island. "Dive, come up a couple of feet. I want to get a better look."

The diving officer smoothly brought the boat up two feet. With the added height of the scope above the wavetops, Allison could now make out the island on the horizon. And the view was disturbing.

Smoke hung heavy above the atoll. Bright yellow and orange flashes erupted frequently, like heat lightning. Planes flitted in and out of view. It was impossible to tell who was who, though. There were only fleeting images as the metal birds rained down death on the tiny island.

"Conn, ESM. That high-signal-strength emitter equates to a Type 1473H pulse-doppler fire control radar carried on a Chinese Chengdu J-10 naval attack jet. Also detecting GD-53 X-band pulse doppler radars, carried on Taiwanese IDF F-CK-1 attack jets. And APG-83 scalable agile beam radars carried on F-16 E/F fighters. Sounds like we have an air war happening up there."

"Eng, acknowledge that. Then get the XO up here."

Anson nodded and keyed the 21 MC mike.

"ESM, Conn, aye." Anson then grabbed the 1MC microphone. "XO to the conn." Any announcement on the 1MC system would carry throughout the boat. No matter where the XO was, she would hear the summons and come as quickly as she could.

Anson had barely replaced the mike in the holder when the XO charged through the after control room door.

"What's up?"

Allison pulled away from the scope for a second. "XO, looks like the Chinese and Taiwan have a major air battle going on over this hunk of coral. Go to radio and work with the ESM watch to sort out the players. Once we see who all has shown up for this party, get a status report off to CTF-74 as quick as you can."

Henrietta Foster disappeared back through the door toward the radio room.

Allison peered into the periscope lens again, just as a fighter jet swooped low and seemed to be racing right at them. He caught just enough of a glimpse to recognize the distinctive F-16 air scoop before the plane suddenly pulled into a vertical climb. The pilot frantically popped flares as fast as he could. Something was chasing him.

Then Allison saw a missile racing along behind the plane, unerringly arrowing upward toward the fleeing jet. And catching it. The jet disappeared in a brutal, blinding explosion. But then an ejection seat burst forth from the smoke. And an orange parachute canopy blossom above it. The pilot had somehow lived through that hellish blast. Or at least long enough to eject.

"Mark this bearing!" Allison called out.

"Bearing zero-four-seven," Anson sang out.

"Mark the chart at a range of five thousand yards." Allison kept the scope trained on the pilot's parachute as it gently descended toward the water. "Nav, do we have good water over there?"

Was there sufficiently deep water below them so they could dive if need be?

"Yes, sir. Depth sixty fathoms there. Shoals up quick a mile beyond that area, though."

"Okay. Ahead two-thirds, steer zero-four-seven," Allison ordered. "I just saw a Taiwanese jet get taken out and the pilot ejected. Let's go see if we can get that guy out of the water."

"You think that's a good idea?" Anson replied, frowning. "There's a bunch of mad people up there flinging around a lot of ordnance. Wouldn't want us to get caught in the crossfire."

"Eng, I don't see anyone else around here to pick him up." Allison swung the scope around. "Long swim to the beach and he may be hurt. Plus, he can surely tell us what the hell is going on out there." Allison suddenly stopped swinging the scope. He raised the elevation with his left hand as he shifted to high power with his right. "Damn. There's another chute coming down. Mark this bearing."

Anson checked and called out, "Bearing zero-nine-two."

"Range, call it six thousand. Nav, mark the spot. It's a white chute this time. I didn't see the plane."

"Plotted, Skipper. Good water in that direction." It was Jeremy Chastain, the navigator, with confirmation.

Allison glanced at the navigation plot on the ECDIS display. At this speed, it would take them fifteen minutes to get to the first pilot. The second one was a couple of miles beyond the first one. They should be able to grab them both.

"Chief of the Watch, on the 1MC, Chief of the Boat and man overboard party muster at the forward escape trunk."

"Skipper," Tim Anson said. "Maneuvering is reporting a lot of shaft vibration. They have increased leak-off to a gallon a minute to keep the flax packing cool. Recommend slowing to one-third."

Not a good time for a problem to crop up.

"Ahead one-third," Allison reluctantly ordered. "Do they have any idea the cause of the vibration?"

"Nothing yet," Anson reported. "They're investigating."

"Eng, have the Nav relieve you as OOD and get aft. See if you can find out what's going on and get back to me quick."

The engineer disappeared out the control room door just as the XO came in through it.

"Skipper, we just got another one of those weird messages," Foster told him. "Somebody...our guardian angel?...just let us know that we are making a hell of a lot of noise. They say it sounds like it could be shaft related, maybe a dinged screw."

Allison shook his head. Whoever was out there sure had some good ears. Neither Allison nor Foster had any idea who it could be. Well, at least it appeared they were on the right side. And that bit of knowledge the mysterious friend had shared correlated with the shaft vibration. If the close-call torpedo explosion had damaged the screw, then increased revolutions would cause more vibration. And plenty of noise. It appeared the rest of their time at sea would be very slow.

"Captain," the chief of the watch announced, "COB reports the man-overboard party is mustered at the escape trunk. Request permission to break rig for dive and open the lower hatch."

The chief of the boat was reporting that men were waiting to go up a passageway and through a hatch that would put them on the submarine's deck, ready to rescue the downed pilot.

"Skipper, hold the orange parachute visually," Lieutenant Chastain chimed in. "Thousand yards dead ahead."

In rapid fire, Allison ordered, "Chief of the Watch, open the lower escape trunk hatch and send men into the trunk. Open the lower bridge trunk hatch and enter the trunk. All stop. Rig out the outboard and shift to remote."

"See the pilot," Chastain reported. "Five hundred yards ahead. Just off the port bow."

"Chief of the Watch, thirty second blow on all main ballast tanks."

The diving officer called out, "Depth five-eight feet, coming up. Five-five feet. Five-zero feet. Four-five feet." Then, finally, "Depth is three-six feet and holding."

Their deck was out of the water and safe for the rescue party to open the hatch and climb out. Or as safe as it could be with war raging in the distance.

Allison scurried up the vertical ladder to the bridge. A phone talker closely followed him up. As the captain reached the upper hatch, he ordered, "To the chief of the watch, opening the upper bridge hatch. To the COB, open the upper escape trunk hatch and send men topside."

Allison spun the hatch handwheel and then pulled the latch handle. The hatch popped open, dumping enough seawater on the submarine's CO to get him thoroughly wet.

An occupational hazard. The bridge area smelled of saltwater and the sea faintly fishy, but also of wet iron.

He clambered up into the cockpit and rolled the lock to drop one of the clamshell covers, then stuck his head out into warm, late-afternoon sunshine. The downed pilot was only a hundred yards away, almost dead ahead, but *Boise* had already slowed to where she was dead-in-the-water, rolling in the gentle sea swell. Allison could tell that the pilot was floating face up, but did not seem to be aware that somebody was attempting to rescue him. He was almost certainly unconscious. Maybe worse.

The skipper looked back to see men emerging from the open hatch on the main deck. The COB was the first man topside, quickly followed by a pair of rescue swimmers and the corpsman.

"Ahead one-third," Allison ordered. He waited until he could just feel the boat move ahead, then ordered, "All stop!"

Such stop-and-go maneuvering was a delicate operation. Submarines had no brakes. *Boise* smoothly slid to a stop with the pilot a mere twenty feet off the beam. The man was still floating face up, his life vest inflated. The two rescue swimmers quickly hauled him back to the boat and then the team lowered him down the hatch, which swung shut as the last man headed down.

"Nav, best course to the other guy?"

"Captain, plot holds the second pilot bearing one-five-five, two miles. Do not hold him visually."

Allison did not like this. Two miles away when the best speed they could do was four knots. Thirty more minutes on the surface. Every additional minute increased the chances of their being shot at.

He pushed up the clamshell and locked it before dropping through the upper hatch. He shut and dogged it, then slid past the phone talker and down the ladder into the control room. Foster met him at the bottom, ready to give him an update. But Allison held up his hand for her to wait a second. Seeing a "straight board"—all indicator lights showing green, which meant all hatches were closed and it was safe to dive—he ordered, "Diving Officer, submerge the ship to six-zero feet. Nav, head for the other downed pilot. Okay, XO, what do we have?"

"The pilot is unconscious. Doc is moving him to the wardroom to see what his problems are. His flight suit has a Taiwanese flag on it. And we have orders to immediately clear the area and make best covert speed to Guam. And our weird, all-seeing, all-knowing friend says that we sound like a trash can full of rocks rolling downhill anytime we run above four knots."

"Any word on that Aussie who's supposed to relieve us?"

"CTF-74 says that he is still two days away. We are not—and they repeated, we are not—to stick around until the Aussie shows up. If I had to guess, I'd say things have gotten really janky in our part of the world all of a sudden."

"Well, let's find the other guy and then we'll get the hell out of this garden spot."

"You sure you want to do that? Boss was pretty adamant about us blowing this pop stand. I don't think us sticking around to offer rides to some fighter pilots was what he meant."

"XO, I'll tell you the same thing I told the Eng. If we don't pick this guy up, there's no one else out here to do it. At our current top speed, a few minutes spent pulling someone out of the drink is not going to affect our ETA to Guam."

"Yes, sir," Foster answered. "Then let's get over and get this guy aboard before someone up there objects."

The short cruise over to the second site was uneventful.

They found him floating a few yards away from the remnants of his parachute. They surfaced and repeated the process that had worked for the first pilot. Chet Allison brought the *Boise* to a halt only a few yards away and a short swim for the rescuers to reach the pilot. The sun was sinking below the western horizon and it was getting difficult to see, though, as the swimmers brought the man back to the sub.

"Skipper, planes inbound!" the phone talker yelled. "Nav sees them on the scope."

Allison dropped down from the bridge and slammed the upper hatch closed. He yelled, "Get everybody below decks and the hatch shut!"

Just as he slid down the ladder, he could feel the blast of jet engines close aboard.

"Diving Officer, dive the ship to six-two feet!" he ordered as he dropped down the ladder into the control room.

"But...but...I don't have a straight board," the flustered man responded. "The escape trunk hatch..."

"Open the vents," Allison ordered.

The chief of the watch reached up to flip the switches that opened the main ballast tank vents. The boat immediately started to go down, the deck tilting noticeably.

"By the time the decks are underwater, the hatch will be shut. If we wait for a straight board, we'll still be on the surface when those guys swing back around, and they will probably be shooting when they do."

"Depth three-eight feet," the diving officer sang out. "Answering ahead one-third."

Allison grabbed the periscope and swung it around in the direction the jets were going when they passed over while *Boise* was still mostly on the surface. The skipper watched as the two fighters made a wide sweeping turn and headed right back, directly toward the submarine. The aircraft were down on the deck and they were coming fast.

"Depth four-zero feet. Full dive on the planes. Still open on the upper escape trunk hatch."

The two jets had moved to the left and right to put a little more space between them. Allison was no jet jockey, but this appeared to him to be a firing pass. He looked aft through the scope and said, as calmly as he could muster, "Deck's awash." Then, "Deck's under."

"Depth four-four feet. Intermediate indications on the escape trunk hatch."

"Flooding, flooding in the mess decks," the 4MC Emergency Announcing System blared. "Flooding from the forward escape trunk!"

Allison watched in fascination through the scope as he saw twinkling lights from the nose of each jet. It took him only a second to realize that they were shooting. At him and *Boise*.

"Shut indication on the forward escape trunk hatch," the chief of the watch reported, the relief in his voice evident. Obviously, he did not realize the influx of seawater was not their most immediate problem.

"The flooding has stopped," the 4MC blared.

"Depth four-eight feet."

Allison, still looking through the scope, caught a glimpse of a string of waterspouts heading right for him. Then they could all hear and feel a heavy explosion from somewhere up in the sail above them.

"Depth five-five feet."

It took Allison a second to realize what had happened. They had been hit. The explosion was from the gunfire. Everything in the control room appeared to be normal. There were no incoming reports of damage. Judging by the sound and the jolt, they almost certainly had damage in the sail.

There was no way to investigate right now, though. Just pray they remained watertight.

"Depth six-two feet and holding."

Allison lowered the periscope as the XO and COB walked into the control room. Both were completely soaked.

"Skipper, we took a lot of water into the AMR bilge," the COB told him. "I expect the drain pump is taking care of that. The equipment in the AMR got pretty wet, but we're wiping stuff down now. It's going to take a while to get things cleaned up and shipshape again."

"Thanks, COB. Good work. And tell the crew, too," the skipper responded. "Now, you two go get some dry clothes. XO, find out how our guests are doing and see what Doc needs. I'm going to stay here until we have safely cleared datum."

"I don't think the COB and I will need our Saturday night baths," Foster said. "Will do, Skipper."

Allison turned to Chastain. "Officer of the Deck, make your depth one-five-zero feet, steer course zero-nine-zero. Limit your speed to three knots. We'll just pretend like we are a boomer on patrol for the rest of this run. Like they say, 'We'll hide with pride.'"

The OOD chuckled. But it was more from relief than from his skipper's weak attempt at submarine humor.

18

Lieutenant Bill Wilson checked the BQQ-10 sonar display on the *George Mason*. All four of the Chinese submarines they continued to shadow, designated as Master One through Master Four, continued to paint brilliant pictures on the broadband waterfall display, just as they had so helpfully done since emerging from the clutter of the fishing fleet. Wilson flipped the console over to see the target motion analysis display. Course one-two-zero, speed twenty knots. Absolutely nothing had changed with the four subs in the past week. This had all the promise of being yet another boring watch for the young submarine officer acting as the OOD.

Wilson's instructions were to keep the Chinese vessels at a range of twelve to twenty thousand yards and to not lose contact. As if that were a problem. The big excitement for the watch so far had been when he had to slow and come to periscope depth for routine communications.

The lieutenant stepped over to the port side of the control room where Sonar Technician First Class Josh Hannon had his team busily searching the immediate waters for any other contacts. Wilson watched the men do their work for a bit and then let out a long sigh.

"This is really getting boring," the OOD complained. "It would be nice if something, anything, would happen and break the monotony."

The sonar supe looked up and frowned.

"Respectfully, you should bite your tongue, sir," Hannon told him. "Boring is a very good thing on submarines. Exciting is downright dangerous."

Wilson could not suppress a grin. That was one of the things he liked about serving on submarines. Sailors were not afraid to express their feelings to officers if they felt they were saying or doing something wrong. Typically, the sailor was right. The informality went back at least to World War II when most submarine skippers informed their crews that they would leave their rank on the dock. Nobody should challenge authority, but every man could feel free to respectfully offer his opinion.

Just then the broadband operator called out, "Loss of broadband contact, Master Four. Looks like he just shut down." Then, a moment later, "Loss of broadband, Master Three. Loss of Broadband Masters Two and One. They all shut down. No contacts on broadband."

"Shift to the TB-29," Wilson directed.

"Mister Wilson, you'll have to slow to do that," Hannon suggested. "A flank bell is above the TB-29's self-noise speed. Recommend that you come broad so you don't overrun these guys, too. If they shut down, they aren't running all-out anymore. You can bet they are going to be really cautious after a long, fast transit like that."

A red-faced Lieutenant Wilson ordered, "Pilot, ahead two-thirds. Right full rudder, steady course two-three-zero."

As the boat swung around to the new course, ST1 Hannon

busied himself with lining up the TB-29 thin-line towed array to do a narrow-band search. He was soon muttering distract-edly to himself.

"Sonar Supe, what's the problem?" Bill Wilson asked.

"Damned thin-line," the exasperated sonarman answered. "We haven't used it for the last week since we've been going way too fast." He forcefully punched a couple of buttons. "Now we need it and it's on the fritz."

"Yes, we do need it," Wilson said. "You think you can get it back online?"

"Not sure yet, but not hopeful," Hannon answered. "Looks like an open in the acoustic path. I sent one of the guys back to check the towed array receiver board. If it ain't the TAR board, we'll have an out-of-commission twenty-nine. Better tell the skipper."

"Tell the skipper what?" Brian Edwards asked as he stepped into the control room.

Bill Wilson answered, "The Chinese wolf pack shut down their diesels and probably slowed. We lost them on broad-band. I slowed and came broad to use the thin-line, but we are having problems bringing it up."

Edwards nodded. "All the right actions, OOD. Except maybe not telling me sooner."

The skipper studied the tactical display on the ECDIS. With a couple of button pushes and a spin of the cursor, he drew a red circle around the spot where the Chinese submarines had just disappeared.

"If they slowed, one of two things happened. Either they are spooked by something and are going real quiet to be care-ful, or they are nearly to their destination and are going quiet to sneak in. Either way, we need to be extremely careful." He pointed at the circle he had just drawn. "That circle has a ten-thousand-yard radius. We won't go inside it without contact on them. The last thing we need is to go bumbling into their little party and get counter-detected. Or worse, have a fender-bender in the parking lot."

"Skipper," STı Hannon interrupted. "My guys just reported that the TAR board checked out fine. The twenty-nine is out of commission."

The TB-29 towed array sonar used hydrophones attached to a cable trailing behind the submarine and was over a mile long. The design allowed the sensors to be distant from the noise of the submarine to enhance its ability to detect and track very faint contacts, but the wiring was complex and delicate. An engineer once described it as the same as taking a cell phone apart, stuffing it in a garden hose, and then expecting it to work when towed behind a ski boat. TB-29A system did not enjoy a reputation for high reliability.

"Great!" Edwards said, frustrated. "Damn thing is great when it works. It only decides not to work when we really, really need it to." He turned to Wilson. "Mister Wilson, open out from our friends another ten thousand yards and come to periscope depth. We need to tell the boss the bad news."

Ψ

CDR Chet Allison was standing on the conn on USS *Boise*. He watched as Lieutenant Juan Esteban worked with his watch section. There really was not a lot going on, but Allison knew the value of being out and about, "walking the deck-plates." It was a practice he had learned from skippers under whom he had served. It was especially important right now. His inexperienced crew had been shot at, hurt, and then had successfully rescued the two pilots in a tense situation. Then they had been shot at and damaged again. It was important the crew saw that their commanding officer was not particu-

larly worried about things, and above all, that he was calm
and in charge. They needed to see that life was reasonably
normal aboard the submarine. And that their performance
during the whole episode had been completed successfully,
just as they had been trained to do it.

CTF-74 had been decidedly unhappy when Allison told
them that he took the time to pick up a couple of passengers.
Evidently putting a US nuclear submarine at risk in the midst
of someone else's shooting war was something a CO should
not do. That was especially egregious if that skipper had
already put some dents in that boat by steaming her into the
middle of that war.

His orders were curt and direct. He was to "immediately
and without further delay" make best speed for Guam. And
higher command would get to work trying to unscrew what
Allison and *Boise* had so wonderfully screwed up.

Henrietta Foster stepped into the control room, her
expression signaling what she was about to report.

"Skipper, we have a problem."

"You have to be more specific, XO. Which problem are you
talking about?" Allison shot back. "Problems, we got in abundant supply."

"It's those two pilots. Doc is in over his head," Foster told
him. "He has the Taiwanese pilot stabilized. He's sedated and
stable. Doc has him in stateroom one with one of the EMTs
watching him. It's the Chinese pilot that's the problem."

"Well, of course it is. Okay, let's go talk to Doc and see
what's going on."

The two made their way along the forward passageway
and then down the ladder to middle level before heading back
to the wardroom. When they got there, they saw that the space
had been completely transformed from its normal function as
a meeting room and dining area for the boat's officers. It was

now an emergency examination room, complete with powerful lights hanging over the wardroom table, transformed into an operating table. Medical supplies were lined up along the shelves while IV bags and tubes hung all about. A green oxygen bottle sat on the outboard lounge, its tube leading over to the injured pilot lying on the wardroom table.

Doc Hugh stood over his patient, a worried expression claiming his round, usually jovial face.

"Skipper, something's wrong here. Something's very wrong. He's just not exhibiting the responses that I would expect based on what I know to be his injuries. His respiration is irregular, shallow and short. He keeps slipping in and out of consciousness. And he is not responding to the treatments I have been trying."

Doc held up a tablet and swiped over to a particular screen.

"His symptoms keep pointing me here," he said, tapping the page. The paragraph he indicated started out: "The meninges are the three membranes that encase the brain and spinal cord, the pia mater, arachnoid, and the dura mater."

"I think he has either a subdural hematoma or a subarachnoid hemorrhage. Neither is good. This is a list of symptoms here. I discounted the headaches and nausea. After all, he did punch out of a jet at six hundred knots and swallowed a lot of seawater when he landed in it. But his motor responses are showing partial paralysis of the right arm. And to top it off, the language barrier isn't helping and I don't think he especially likes us."

"What's your best guess, Doc," the XO asked him.

"I can't tell from the symptoms which problem we have. I don't have the equipment or training to tell them apart. Now look at this." Doc Hugh pointed at the final paragraph of the explanation for subarachnoid hemorrhage. It said: "About one-third of all patients die from the initial hemorrhage, and a further fifteen to twenty percent die within the next month. It is therefore necessary to locate the area of bleeding as quickly as possible. Neurosurgery may repair the damage."

"Truth is, I need to talk to a neurosurgeon and find out what to do," Doc said as Foster finished reading the troubling words. "If there is even anything I can do."

Chet Allison was rubbing his chin, deep in thought.

"Lord knows we're deep enough in the middle of an international incident," he finally said. "Having the Chinese accuse us of murdering one of their brave warriors would be icing on the cake. Besides, this is a man in danger of losing his life here. We want to do the right thing. We'll have to talk with somebody."

As they discussed the situation, the Chinese pilot lay in delirium on the wardroom table. His left leg was splinted and a sizeable gash on his forehead had been closed with a neat row of sutures under a gauze bandage. But the young pilot repeatedly slipped in and out of consciousness. It was clear he was in trouble.

It took the better part of an hour to hook the communications patch up between Doc Hugh and Dr. Levi Yeargin, a neurosurgeon at US Naval Hospital, Yokosuka, Japan.

"Chief Hugh," the speaker on the wardroom bulkhead squawked. "I have reviewed the information that you relayed to us. Has there been any change in the patient since these last vitals?"

"He is currently unconscious," Doc Hugh answered. "Blood pressure has been one-six-zero over nine-five. The right pupil is dilated considerably larger than the left. The onset of cephalalgia, together with the other symptoms, points to a subarachnoid hemorrhage. The other possibility is subdural hematoma. Both are way beyond my capability to treat."

"Chief Hugh, it sounds like your diagnosis is on the spot," Dr. Yeargin responded. "You know your stuff. Is there any sign of opisthotonos?"

Without hesitation, the corpsman answered, "No, sir, the neck is stiff and he resists movement but no sign of opisthotonos." That would be spasms of the muscles in the neck, causing arching of the neck and spine.

After a brief pause, the 21MC again came alive as Dr. Yeargin answered, "Well, I think that we have a Grade IV subarachnoid hemorrhage. He needs to be moved to a neurological unit as fast as possible. The nearest one appears to be Kaohsiung Armed Forces General Hospital in Kaohsiung City, Taiwan. Can you get him there?"

"I'll have to talk with the skipper. I believe we are pretty close now," Doc replied. "What do I do in the meantime?"

"We've got to relieve the intracranial pressure, lessen the swelling. You have mannitol and dexamethasone in your AMAL." Dr. Yeargin's voice was now much more assured as it crackled over the circuit. "Administer an injection of mannitol and continuous dexamethasone through the IV. That'll reduce the swelling and maybe buy us a few hours. Place the patient in a cervical collar and catheterize him. Measure the urine output and give me the numbers every hour."

As they were completing their medical discussion and prognosis, Henrietta Foster interrupted. "Doctor Yeargin, we are about one hundred nautical miles south of Taiwan. Any problems you can think of with a helicopter medivac?"

"Those are always risky, and more so in this case," Yeargin slowly answered, obviously thinking through the possibilities. "But time is critical. As long as the helo stays below a thousand feet once the patient is onboard, I think it should be all right."

By the time all the logistics were arranged between CTF-74, the State Department, the government of Taiwan, and the Taiwanese Navy, the sun had set in the west. *Boise* was steaming on the surface just over one hundred nautical miles south of Taiwan.

Chet Allison stood on the bridge as Juan Esteban guided the submarine toward the rendezvous point. The skipper usually enjoyed the quiet and solitude of the night at sea. A million stars swept across from horizon to horizon with no haze or muck of civilization to obscure any of their brilliance. Still, on this night, he was uneasy, his boat out of its element on the surface for anyone to see.

He could barely make out a few ship masthead lights in the distance. The flashing amber submarine ID beacon played havoc with his night vision.

"Bridge, Control, XO." It was Henrietta Foster on the 21MC, disturbing his reverie. "In radio contact with the helo. Call sign Sierra Seven-Zero on channel sixteen. He's twenty miles out. Says he holds us on radar."

"Thanks, XO," Allison replied. "Tell him we're coming to course zero-one-five to head into the wind, speed three knots. We expect to do a main deck transfer."

He turned to Esteban to order the course change, but the young lieutenant was already passing the order to the helm.

"Skipper, request permission for the COB and helicopter transfer party to lay topside with the doc and the two pilots," Esteban said.

Allison smiled. It was encouraging to see youngsters thinking on their feet, anticipating what would need to be done. With a nod, the skipper told him, "Send the COB and helo transfer party topside with the doc. Allow the doc to control when the patients come topside."

The hatch swung open on the submarine's deck and several men spilled out topside. Each man had a ChemLight attached to his life vest. That would make it easier to find someone in the sea if they might somehow end up overboard. But the cluster of green-yellow lights gave the dark deck an almost festive feeling.

Soon Allison could make out the green and red helicopter anti-collision lights approaching from the north. He unclipped the marine band radio mike from his belt, put it to his lips, and engaged the push-to-talk button.

"Sierra Seven-Zero, this is US warship. I hold you visually, bearing north from me. Ready for personnel transfer."

"US warship, roger. I will approach you from astern. Verify all masts and antennas are lowered." Although Allison knew that the pilot was Taiwanese, the man had no discernible accent, as if he might have grown up in the American Midwest.

"Sierra Seven-Zero. All masts and antennas lowered. Deck is clear for transfer."

The S-70 Thunderhawk helicopter flashed on its brilliant white landing lights when it was still a mile out. Then he flipped on his cargo-handling light and smoothly came to a hover only a few feet to the starboard of *Boise* and about fifty feet above the deck. A cable dropped from a hoist at the port-side cargo door as the pilot slid the big bird over the submarine's deck. The COB reached up and grabbed the cable with his plexiglass grounding rod. The difference in the electrical potential between the helicopter and the submarine could be more than enough voltage to be lethal. The grounding rod fixed that.

Within a few minutes, the first patient was lifted up and into the bird. A minute later, the second one followed.

"US warship, Sierra Seven-Zero. On behalf of the Taiwan Navy, thank you for saving one of ours. Safe journeys."

The helicopter disappeared to the north, flying low and fast, with no mention of the second new passenger, the Chinese national, the man who had been bombing and strafing the chopper pilot's fellow warriors only a few hours earlier.

Chet Allison hardly noticed. That particular complication was no longer his problem.

But as he watched the chopper disappear into the curtain of stars, the skipper was thankful he, his crew, and the *Boise* had been able to possibly help save both young men's lives.

Even if that Chinese fighter pilot almost certainly would have sunk his submarine if he'd had the opportunity.

Ψ

Dr. Rex Smith watched the GPS display closely, its bright image reflected in the scientist's eyeglasses. They were almost back to the correct location, but precision was essential. That would make it much simpler to navigate the *Sea Raptor* UUV back to the desired fumarole if the submersible started its journey from the very same location. Merely a few seconds off in either latitude or longitude could mean missing their goal by several miles when the UUV had descended ten thousand meters to the pitch blackness at the bottom of the Tonga Trench.

Out on the broad afterdeck, the hot tropical sun bore down on the launch team as they worked furiously to complete final preparations to send the expensive submersible on its journey. Unsurprisingly, Mitch O'Donnell and Sandy

McDougal were heavily engaged in another of their interminable arguments about how to best prepare the *Sea Raptor*.
The brilliant sun shot diamonds from the sea's soft ripples,
causing the contentious pair to squint at each other as they
verbally sparred.

Bill Bix stuck his head through the bridge door, looked at
Smith, and shook his head.

"Doc, you better get down to the afterdeck," the ship's
captain suggested. "Those two hot-headed Irishmen are at
each other's throats again. If somebody doesn't go down and
referee, one of them'll end up in the water playing footsie with
the sharks."

"Nursemaiding a kindergarten playground is what it is,"
Smith muttered. "We picked those two because they were the
best in the world at what they do. Trouble is, they are simply
incapable of doing it together." The scientist pointed to the
GPS. "Bill, if you can get us on top of the dot and into auto-
station-keeping, I'll go take my turn at being the playground
monitor."

Smith stepped out of the pilothouse and climbed down
the ladder to the main deck, then headed aft. When he
arrived at the UUV, the two protagonists were still standing
on either side of the *Sea Raptor* and its cradle. Several other
crewmembers stood back, out of the line of fire, watching
the spat from a safe distance. A red-faced Sandy McDougal
was flailing her arms about, shouting at the top of her
lungs at Mitch O'Donnell. He stood there solidly, his feet
firmly planted and arms crossed, staring stone-faced at
McDougal.

"Damn stubborn Paddy," McDougal ranted. "Why won't
you listen to common sense for once?"

"You be 'a callin' me a Paddy, are ye?" O'Donnell shot back
in as thick an Irish brogue as he could muster. "Thick-headed

Ulsterman! I mean Ulsterwoman. Oh, I'll be PC an' ye be an Ulster-person!"

"Hey!" Smith shouted, interrupting the tirade. He stood at the bow of the UUV and gave a hard look to the two quarrelsome researchers. "Sandy, Mitch, can't you two ever work together peaceably? What set off World War III this time? Bushmills versus Jameson Irish whiskey again?"

Both answered loudly, each trying to out-shout the other. Rex Smith threw up his arms. "Okay then! Shut up, both of you!" The pair fell silent, mostly from the look on their angry boss's face. "We'll do this like the first grade. We'll take turns. Sandy, you go first."

The petite red-haired scientist started, "This dumb Irishman..." Smith held up a cautioning finger. "I mean Mister O'Donnell here wants to take off a bunch of sensors and add on some extra sample-stowage baskets. He prefers that we fly blind so he can scoop up and haul up more gold."

"Bullocks!" the Irishman exploded.

"Damn it, Mitch, you'll get your turn," Smith heatedly told him. "Sandy? Your input on the matter?"

"We need those sensors to even make this dive worthwhile," she finished her argument. "There's no telling what scientific discoveries we could be missing without those sensors. We need every camera and every single light to capture the most data we can while we can. Before weather, politics, or the environment way down there brings everything to a halt. The chem sensor package is vital to the fumarole study and the high freq side-scan is how we map them."

Smith shifted to face O'Donnell, whose belligerent posture had not softened one whit.

"Pragmatic," the Irishman started. "I'm just being pragmatic. Those sensors and their precious data won't be payin' the rent. At least not for a while. But with the boxes, we can be pullin' up over a hundred pounds of gold on every trip. That'd be over three million US dollars each run. After only a few trips down and up, we'd be paying our own way. Once we have the rent covered, then we can go back to playin' scientist, takin' pictures of hot water geysers and weird-ass animals."

Smith rubbed his chin for a few minutes as he weighed the arguments Solomon-like. Finally, he told them, "Here is what we'll do. We do need more samples to map the extent of the field, so we absolutely will need the side-scan. We'll forego the fumarole studies on this trip, so we can add that capacity. We can extend the bottom time to cover more research area. That should about divide the baby in half, maybe, and if we are lucky, without killing it. You two satisfied?"

The two frowned but then nodded reluctantly.

The rest of the launch sequence went without drama. The bright orange device lacked the sleek torpedo-like appearance of UUVs meant for open-water operations. More squat and boxy to help tolerate the unbelievable water pressure, with sensors and arms protruding from the vessel at odd angles. But they were all plug-ins, easily added or removed. Its electric drive propulsion systems were contained in small pods that could be rotated for easier maneuverability, but flexibility came at the expense of speed and range. Just for the *Sea Raptor* to travel from the sea surface to the bottom of the Tonga Trench would take ten hours.

The davit crane swung the UUV out and slowly lowered it into the water. After a few more checks were completed, divers released the *Sea Raptor* to slip smoothly below the surface. With nothing else to watch or argue about, and with the sun still brutally hot, the team repaired to the command center. From there, they could monitor the descent in air-conditioned comfort while enjoying cold drinks and a bite of dinner.

As the afternoon shifted to evening and then segued into

night, the novelty wore off. The bystanders began to thin out. By midnight, only Mitch O'Donnell and Sandy McDougal kept Rex Smith company.

The trio quickly perked up as they were finally able to watch the *Sea Raptor* slowly approach the sea bottom, so very far below their keel. Since they were floating in an out-of-the-way corner of a very large ocean, and concentrating on a view only a handful of people on the planet had ever had the occasion to see, they did not pay any particular attention to the waters around them.

It was the shattering noise of the radar proximity alarm that jolted them out of their fixation on the UUV control. Something had just approached within a mile of where they had the *Deep Ocean Explorer* keeping station.

Rex Smith jumped up and ran out the command center door. When he burst into the ship's pilothouse, he ran squarely into Bill Bix.

"We got company," the ship's captain informed him, then turned and pointed out the window. A fast-approaching patrol boat was clearly visible in the moonlight, making no effort to maintain stealth. The brightly illuminated boat had a spotlight pointed at the *Deep Ocean Explorer*'s bridge, all but blinding Smith and Bix.

But even in the bright light, they could make out a wicked-looking thirty-millimeter autocannon aimed directly at them.

"Pirates?" Smith asked.

"Not way out here, I wouldn't think. And not with that weapon."

Then, from the bridge of the approaching vessel, someone called out on a loud-hailer.

"Onboard the ship, you are conducting illegal activities in Tongan sovereign waters. Stand by to be boarded."

The patrol vessel slid to a stop a few hundred meters from

the *Deep Ocean Explorer*. The autocannon unerringly maintained its aim directly across the bow of the research ship. Smith and Bix watched anxiously as a team of heavily armed marines climbed from the vessel into a RHIB, obviously with the intent of making the short trip between ships.

Bix grabbed his own loud-hailer and stepped out onto the research ship's bridge wing.

"Tongan Patrol Vessel, we are an American-flagged research vessel conducting legitimate research in international waters. Interference with our activities is a violation of international law."

The autocannon on the patrol boat suddenly spat twice, sending angry rounds over the *Deep Ocean Explorer*'s bow and into the sea beyond.

"On the research vessel, you are in Tongan waters. Stand by to receive boarders. You are under arrest and your ship is impounded."

Smith and Bix looked at each other, mouths open, eyes wide. This was an eventuality for which they had not planned. Harassment? Sure. That happened periodically in some of the politically dicey waters where they sometimes found themselves. Maybe even being chased away. But the arrest of the crew and impoundment of the valuable and quite famous ship? This was a whole new level. Would they be held as prisoners, pawns to be bartered in a high-stakes game for control of the unbelievably rich gold field?

It appeared they were about to find out. The RHIB full of marines was rapidly approaching. There was not much time to do anything. And they lacked any weaponry to defend themselves. Just the righteousness of their research.

Smith bolted for the bridge door, shouting, "Get the word out to whoever you can, hopefully the Navy in Pago Pago. I'm going to take care of the *Sea Raptor*."

The marines were clambering up and onboard the *Deep Ocean Explorer* as Smith barged into the control room.

"Quick! Put the *Sea Raptor* in hibernation." Mitch O'Donnell opened his mouth to question. "Don't ask why, just do it."

Turning to McDougal, he asked, "All our data up on cloud storage?" When she nodded, he ordered, "Delete everything onboard. I don't want a single byte still here."

Someone pounded on the control room door.

"Open up! You are under arrest."

Smith waited to open the door as O'Donnell hit the hibernation button and then powered down his computer. At the same time, McDougal hit the button to wipe the servers. There was not enough time to power them down, but there was no way for their attackers to stop the deletion of all the data on the servers either.

The assault troops went compartment to compartment, herding the entire crew into the ship's small wardroom/dining room. The Tongans then stationed a pair of guards at the door while the rest went to work getting the research vessel under tow.

Smith sidled up to Bill Bix. "Did you get through to anyone?"

The ship's captain shook his head. "No. I left a voicemail with our Los Angeles office." He nodded toward the Tongans. "They grabbed my phone before I got through to the Navy."

Dawn found the two ships already twenty miles away, steadily moving toward Vava'u, the nearest Tongan island and an unknown fate.

19

ORCA One threaded its way past 'Eueiki Island and into the Ava Piha Channel. The channel was one of the passages through the scattering of coral islands that poked out of the water on the north side of Tongatapu, the main island of the Tongan kingdom. Tongatapu was also the last stop on the US Navy UUV's mission to sow sensors around the major clusters of land that formed the nation of Tonga. Niuatoputapu, Vava'u, Pangai, and Tongatapu lay in a rough array about four hundred miles long, aligned from north-northeast to south-southwest.

Spending a few hours placing sensors at each harbor entrance and avoiding the hundreds of tiny islands and coral heads, ORCA One had finally arrived off the main island. Planting sensors off Tongatapu would be a bit more complicated, though. There were really two harbors to monitor. Nuku'alofa was the main town and had been the traditional harbor for centuries. For all that time, the island's shipping had used the northern route—Lahi Channel—to get to the anchorages and wharves. But those anchorages were not well protected from the frequent storms in the region, so when the

Chinese came—with unlimited money and manpower—they decided to build an entirely new port with a protected deep-water anchorage at Niuatoputapu. After much dredging and blasting, the Ava Piha Channel was opened to the east for access to the Chinese seaport.

Only the narrow and treacherous Makaha'a Channel connected the two ports by water. As a result, Chinese ships came in from the east and all other vessels entered from the north. Now, as programmed, ORCA One planted a row of sensors across the Ava Piha Channel where it swung south and narrowed off Talafo'ou. Then, that task finished, the UUV turned around and headed for the Makaha'a Channel. At its narrowest, the ship passage between the Makaha'a reef to the south and the Monoafe reef to the north and east gave barely four hundred yards clearance between the jagged coral outcroppings.

At that narrowest point, ORCA One encountered a coral head not plotted into its electronic memory. As designed, its system smartly processed this new information and ordered a course and depth change around the obstacle. The little submersible boat came shallow and skirted around the coral head before dropping back down.

A Tongan fisherman working the reef caught a glimpse of the black object silently appear out of the depths and then, just as quietly, disappear again. In an instant, two centuries of Christianity were lost to the fisherman and the Pulotu 'Aka'aka —the spirit world—took its place.

The ORCA dutifully laid a line of sensors between Fafa Island and Alakipeau Island, thus completing the coverage to all entrances to Tongatapu. This part of her mission accomplished, the UUV next headed up the Lahi Channel. While transiting, the UUV came shallow and communicated back to the control center aboard the *Portland*. It reported the completion of the laying of the sensor fields and received a significant change in its mission profile.

After receipting for the traffic, it dropped down deep and promptly changed course to the northwest, heading out on its new assignment.

Ψ

Joe Glass was neck deep in a stack of forms and other bureaucratic paperwork, determined to find the bottom of the mess so he could get back to concentrating on the swirl of activity in the middle of which he had suddenly found himself. It took only a half-second of the annoying buzz of the secure telephone on his desk to wrench him back to the real world. He had left word with his aide to not disturb him unless it was of vital importance. He snatched the offending instrument from its cradle and growled, "Glass!"

He immediately recognized the chuckle at the other end. It was Jon Ward, his old boss when both men rode submarines. Before Glass became a CO of his own boat and then moved to his new command. And before Ward became head of Naval Intelligence.

"Joe, you need to work a bit on your people skills," the Navy's top spy suggested. "People will think your promotion made you a gruff old man."

"But, Jon, I was a gruff old man long before that," Glass retorted. "Even before sub school. And then I enhanced my gruffness skills by learning from the best, if we're handing out credit."

"Well, I got just the job for a gruff old man," Ward replied. And Glass could feel the call turn in a totally new direction. Pleasantries were over. This was a business call. "I just got off a call with the New Zealand naval attaché. The Kiwis are all in a dither. It seems that the New Zealand government has lost all contact with Niue. You may remember that little island is what they term 'associated with' New Zealand. It's complicated and really too much lawyer talk for a couple of old sub sailors, but basically, New Zealand is responsible for Niue's external security. Anyway, there has been no communication with the island for most of two days now. The weekly Air New Zealand flight was refused permission to land yesterday. The pilot reported seeing what looked like armed troops on the ground as he passed over and went looking for another freeway exit that had jet fuel."

"Wow!" Glass gasped. "Any idea what the hell is going on?"

"That's why I'm calling you," Ward answered. "We don't think it's internal. Not a coup or civil war or anything like that. We've seen plenty of aircraft and boat activity that suggests something different. Maybe even a small-scale invasion. Since you're already in the neighborhood working on your suntan, I figured you could get someone down there to take a look and see what the hell is going on. You got *Cheyenne* about ready to go, don't you?"

"Yep, she's finishing up fast cruise today. The plan was to do a final stores load and then send her out to chase those Chinese diesel boats that intel says are supposed to be heading our way."

"I suggest you revise that plan," Ward responded. "Send her down to do some recon work and then she can go out to chase Chinese subs."

"Will do, Boss."

"And Joe, one more thing. I recommend that you get your Marines ready to come off the bench for some action. I'm thinking we may need them in the game real soon."

Ψ

Vice Admiral Yon Hun Glo looked long and hard at the navigation plot on the table before him. The seemingly interminable transit from Hainan to Tonga was finally nearing its completion. By this time tomorrow, the wolf pack would be safely tied up in the new, protected Chinese base on the Tongan main island. Their sudden appearance at the dock on the American spy satellite images would come as a startling surprise to them. One that would ring alarm bells from their Pentagon to the Oval Office. But Yon had not time or will to contemplate the effect. He must now get to work on the true reason he had made this stealthy and thus far undetected voyage to a forgotten corner of the South Pacific. From here, he would take control of the gold field, and by doing so, assist his older brother, Yon Ba Deng, in employing that almost endless bounty of gold to secure the power and influence within the Party and their country's military hierarchy that they had so long deserved.

The admiral sat back and contemplated the next steps in the plan. Here he was, in his stateroom on the submarine *Changcheng Wushiwu*, idly stirring his tea as he pondered the future. He and his brother held all the cards. And the groundwork they had been laying for years—the people they had bribed, bullied, blackmailed, and bludgeoned—would finally be put to good use now that the mounds of precious metal on the sea floor had become their means to an end. They were in a strong position for success. However, as he analyzed the situation from all angles—as he always did with any prospective battle plan—he recognized two major obstacles that would have to be overcome to assure its accomplishment.

The first and foremost problem was the Americans. Of course. As always. But more than ever, that nation's leadership —business and government alike—had become weak, timid, lacking the will for such a contest as this one would be. They and their much-ballyhooed capitalistic system had become deeply dependent economically on China, on the entrenched business relationships, and on China's extensive investments in their country's private sector. They might bluster and complain, threaten and cajole, but ultimately, the US would not risk such an intertwined and complicated relationship. Nor could the Americans rely on the support from many more of the world's governments since they, too, had long since succumbed to China's economic addiction. Such hesitation should make it easy for Yon to shove them away with his submarines, just as his brother shunted them aside in the world of international politics and economics.

The other obstacle, though, was more problematic. And it was much closer to home. That was King Tofuwanga of Tonga. Yon knew he needed to come up with a way to deal with that pompous idiot, keeping him reasonably content with China's largess while at the same time curbing the greedy simpleton's more extravagant and dangerous proclivities. The fool had already demonstrated one of those inclinations, and he had almost wrecked their whole timetable, when he impetuously invaded Niue.

Fortunately, Yon Ba Deng had exercised the forethought to have a battalion of People's Liberation Army Marines at the ready on Guadalcanal. That had averted one potential catastrophe. But what would "King Two-for-One" come up with next to try to throw his considerable weight around and justify his existence as head of his government? Especially now that the man was aware of the strategic value of his islands because of the gold-spewing fumarole.

"Excuse me, Admiral?"

It was Yu Feng, *Wushiwu*'s political officer. Yet again, he had stuck his head through the stateroom doorway without bothering to knock or ask permission to enter. Yon decided not to make a fuss this time. There would be an opportunity later.

"Yes?"

"Captain Liu Zhang asked for me to report to you that they have completed a careful ASW search. No submarines have been detected. Captain Liu Zhang requests permission to secure the ASW search and continue the voyage."

Yon Hun Glo took a sip of his tea before nodding approval.

"Yes, please tell the captain to proceed. And please, see that I am not disturbed for the next couple of hours. I believe that I will take a nap now."

Yu Feng bobbed his head in a short bow and quietly shut the stateroom door.

The *lang qun* once again formed its familiar line astern and steered for Tongatapu. Or more precisely, for the narrow passage between the dreaded Dido Shoals and Kelefesia Island. From there it would be a relatively easy sail down to the Avi Piha passage and then into port.

However, no one in the Chinese wolf pack noticed that a fifth and uninvited member had joined the neat line of submarines a few miles east of Fiji. It was ORCA One, obediently following its recently downloaded commands. She fell in, unobserved, close astern of the *Changcheng Ershi,* the last of the Chinese boats. Then she followed along as if she belonged there just as much as they did.

Ψ

Jim Ward stared out the window of the Gulfstream G550 executive jet as it climbed out of Singapore's Changi Airport. The young SEAL lay reasonably comfortably on a small bed that had been specially fitted into the aircraft's otherwise luxurious interior. Although he had been weaning himself off the pain meds as quickly as he could tolerate, his wounds still left him sore and with a nagging ache in his left side where the Chinese bullets had done their damage.

The doctors at Changi General Hospital had been decidedly unhappy when Ward informed them that he would be checking out, with or without their approval. They had ultimately relented when Li Min Zhou, the Chinese spy lady, showed up with a world-renowned thoracic surgeon from Taipei University Hospital. The doctor carefully examined Ward and reviewed the diagnostic and treatment records, then his most recent CT images, before he pronounced him fit to travel, but only under medical supervision. Supervision by the doctor and his "assistant," Li Min Zhou.

The SEAL team leader certainly had no objections. And that was how he ended up on the Gulfstream, bound for Taiwan.

Though he assured everyone that he was able, Ward still could not walk without some pain, so they wheeled him out of his room to a waiting ambulance. It was a mercifully short ride from the hospital right up to the Gulfstream's ramp at the airport's JetQuay VIP terminal. By the time Ward was comfortably tucked in, the plane had begun its takeoff roll and he was starting to doze. It was the way of life for members of the Navy Sea, Air and Land Teams. Grab sleep whenever available. No telling when it might not be.

Once they reached their cruising altitude, Li Min Zhou unbuckled her seat belt, rose from her seat, and walked back to where Jim Ward lay, eyes closed and snoring quietly. Along the way, she secured two glasses of champagne from a small refrigerator and carried one in each hand. As she settled into the seat next to him, she gave him a gentle nudge. He instantly came fully awake, another valuable trait for one in his line of work.

Li smiled as she offered one of the glasses to Ward.

"Didn't realize I was booked into first class," he said as he pushed the button to raise the bed, almost to eye level with her.

She turned up the brightness on the smile. "Doctor's orders. You are allowed one glass, as long as it is properly chilled and at least a Dom Perignon 2002. Anything less might be too hard on your delicate system."

Ward assumed this lovely but mysterious woman was not serious, that she was only pulling his leg, but he was willing to take what she offered. He accepted the glass and took a sip.

"Delicious, but after my time in the Navy and associating with the characters I do, I'm not sure my palate could tell the difference between a 2002 Dom and a five-dollar Total Wine special."

"Barbarian," she said, but with a chuckle. "I should have expected as much. Your friend TJ Dillon is no better. At least you are giving it a try. He prefers Budweiser. Absolutely disgusting."

She leaned back in the overstuffed chair opposite his bed, carefully crossing her legs. He tried not to let her see that he was studying her. But as with most beautiful women, she was more than aware of how men saw her. And of the advantage that often gave her.

She took another small sip of the wine before placing the flute on the little fold-out tray. Again, the shifting of gears was obvious.

"Well, Mister Steely-eyed Trained Killer, I think it is time we talked a little. We did not spring you from that hospital room just to listen to you snore. As you might expect, not everything is as it seems in our most complicated world. That is especially true here in Asia. There are many players, and it is a very convoluted game in which we find ourselves. Some of the players you can easily see and can also quickly figure out what they are attempting to achieve. Others, not so much."

She picked up the flute and took another sip. She thought for a moment, as if deciding how to explain some dense math problem to him. Jim Ward was more than intrigued by this woman, by her beauty but also by her demeanor, her obvious smarts. But there was something else there he could not quite figure out. He hoped that he would have the opportunity to learn just what that might be.

Finally, she set the glass back down, looked hard at him, and went on.

"As you know, fighting has broken out between our Taiwanese Armed Forces and the People's Liberation Army Navy over the Dongsha Islands. It would appear that the Chinese were trying to stage some kind of nuisance raid that spooled out of control when one of our destroyers detected submarines and went out to investigate. There is nothing of any interest to anyone on that bit of coral and no reason for China to risk international scorn and retaliation over it. Of course, they have staged similar confrontations on the Indian border and, as you know only too well, on the Vietnamese border. As we always fear, such pushing and shoving can easily escalate into a serious knife fight, one in which people get hurt. This time, it happened. It cost PLAN a submarine or two and many men their lives. And another dozen of my countrymen died on the destroyer. Even one of your submarines was caught in the middle and suffered damage but, thankfully, no casualties. Now this event threatens even greater ramifications. There is a very real possibility that the current fighting could easily escalate and engulf the whole area in the major war over Taiwan that the world has dreaded for so long."

Ward nodded. He had studied naval engineering at the Naval Academy but had opted in for courses in Chinese history and politics. It had been obvious to him even then that China might possibly play a role in his military career someday. He had also read all of the intel reports that his father had sent him while he was flat on his back in the hospital. Nothing very enlightening about Dongsha, though. Mostly just reports of a lot of ordnance being expended over an insignificant little island since the initial fisticuffs between the submarines and destroyer.

"So where do we fit in? The US, the Navy, the SEALs?"

"Not so fast, my impetuous friend," Li Min Zhou cautioned, but again with a smile. "Please, allow me to continue. As I warned you, this is a very complicated game populated with many significant players. You should be aware that I have many contacts, some of them at the highest levels in the Party. As you are aware, these politicians are a very corrupt group. Maybe even more so than your own political elite. Both groups tend to posture and preen in public, but in their greed for ultimate power, they are deadly and dangerous in private, their blind ambition making them rotten to the very core."

The high-flying jet bounced a bit as it hit some minor turbulence. Jim Ward winced as it kicked off pain in his side. Li Min Zhou's champagne flute skittered across the little table and crashed on the carpeted deck. She did not seem to notice either his wince or the spilt wine. And her face held no trace of a smile now.

"My sources tell me that two rather minor functionaries are in a snit with each other as they both try to clamber up the ladder of power within the military. One is named Soo Be Xian, someone you have likely never heard of. Few in the US have. I am certain, though, that your father knows plenty about him. Your godfather, Tom Donnegan, too. Soo is the Vice Deputy to the Minister of National Defense. That would be roughly equivalent to your Secretary of Defense, though with much less public profile since he was not subject to Senate approval as your president's cabinet members are. He is strongly allied with the People's Liberation Army and is working to raise his level of influence by fomenting some kind of border conflict. You received your little boo-boo in one of his attempts to start another Vietnamese border war. He may be lacking in mental acuity, but he is utterly ruthless. That and his determination to gain power make him very, very dangerous."

Li Min Zhou shivered noticeably. Ward assumed it was in reaction to this Soo Be Xian's threat to peace. Only in part. As she described the man's position and goals, she was also remembering the man's clumsy attack on her at a National Day party only a couple of years ago. Now, for the first time, she shared her story with someone else.

She told Jim of how the fat little politician had positively slobbered over her as he drunkenly tried to force his hand up her dress when he caught her alone in a coat closet. She had managed to subdue him, put him on his back on the floor, and in a way that, in his drunkenness, would leave him to believe he had slipped and fallen. She could easily have killed the bastard. But she had since managed to never be alone anywhere with the vice deputy, despite his many attempts to corner her.

"However, be assured that Soo Be Xian is not the real threat. At least not regarding this situation," Li continued. "That honor belongs to the second functionary, Yon Ba Deng. He is the Assistant Vice Deputy to the Minister of National Defense for Naval Matters. Ostensibly, that makes him Soo Be Xian's underling. But again, all is not as it appears when it comes to Party politics. Yon is roughly the Secretary of the Navy for China, but he also holds the same title within the

Communist Party. Soo Be Xian does not have that advantage. Yon Ba Deng is every bit as ruthless, but he is far more intelligent and cunning. And that, my SEAL friend, makes him infinitely more dangerous."

"I assume he has never attacked you in a coat closet," Ward said.

"No. Though he has a wife and several mistresses, I know his primary appetite is for power. Infinite power. And now he believes he has a golden path to that very thing."

She looked out the window at the darkening sky for a long few minutes. Jim Ward wondered if that was all she intended to share with him for now. He was about to prompt her to go on when she turned from the window, again looking directly at him with those dark, intense eyes.

"This is where the plot thickens, Jim. The fighting on Dongsha bears the stamp of Soo Be Xian. It was not well planned and clumsily initiated. It points a dagger directly at Yon Ba Deng. However, that is just too obvious to be believed. Yon Ba Deng would never use submarines that can easily be traced right back to him. So, I am convinced that the dagger is actually a boomerang, and it is ultimately aimed at Soo Be Xian."

"So, Soo Be Xian is actually our target in this?" Ward asked, a questioning look on his face. The champagne, the pain meds, or the twists and turns she was taking him through were making Li's story even more difficult to follow.

Li Min Zhou chuckled dryly and reached for the glass of wine. Only then did she realize it had slid off the table. She went on anyway.

"Again, my wounded American friend, remember that in Asia very few things are as they appear. It is often difficult to explain to westerners the ways of our world so that they might better understand. That has created difficulties between our cultures for centuries, you know. Politically and personally. But that is why you, of all people, might be of such great value to us."

Jim Ward was not sure he heard the last statement correctly.

"Excuse me?"

"Your paper for the Naval Academy class in Chinese military history, senior year, Captain Caldwell's class. 'Politics and Military Promotions Within the Chinese People's Liberation Army and Navy Submarine Force Since World War II.' Some might not find it all that fascinating of a read, but I certainly did. And remarkably on target."

"I spent most of the term in the Nimitz Library researching that bad boy," Ward told her. "While my buddies were chasing girls. But the truth is, I found it fascinating, how China has built and maintained such a strong military after falling to the Japanese, even with such obvious and rampant corruption within. But how did you find...?"

"You had one particular source I assume you relied on heavily."

Ward looked hard at her. She had found his term paper. She had read it. She remembered it. Surely, this enigmatic spy lady did not know his top-secret source for some of the paper's best conclusions.

"I listed my sources. That's an academic requirement."

"But you neglected to credit one. Your godfather. Admiral Tom Donnegan. Who, at the time, just happened to be head of Naval Intelligence."

"But how would you know that?"

"He told me."

Jim Ward blinked, trying to clear his head. "You do, indeed, have some good sources, Miss Li. It is 'Miss Li,' right?"

She ignored his question.

"Indeed, I do. And some more of my very reliable sources assure me that Yon Ba Deng actually created this entire episode as a double-reverse trap, one set to catch Soo Be Xian. President Tan Yong actually bought this ploy and he is now setting up Soo for destruction. And when you are the President of China, that is easily accomplished. My sources also tell me that Tan Yong is planning to move Yon Ba Deng further up the ladder to power. He appreciates Yon's network and willingness to do whatever is necessary to accomplish his own goals. The president is perfectly happy to enable him to do so as long as they mesh with his own purposes."

"So, Yon Ba Deng is our target?"

"My, aren't you the eager one?" she chided him. "There is much to Yon Ba Deng's game that we don't know yet, and certainly far more to President Tan Yong's. But first we need to bring an end to this war being fought for nothing, the attack on Dongsha. And that, Lieutenant Commander, is where you..."

The Taiwanese doctor suddenly stood and stepped from his seat at the other end of the compartment, far enough away he could not have heard their conversation.

"Please excuse me, but the pilot has informed me that we are fifteen minutes out from landing at Taipei Songshan Airport. I need to make certain that our patient is ready for landing."

The physician was already pumping up the blood pressure cuff on Ward's arm.

Li once again showed Ward those intense eyes that the SEAL had already classified as mysteriously alluring.

"Get well quickly, Mr. Ward," she told him.

There was still not even a hint of another smile.

20

The moonless night had been especially dark as the USS *Cheyenne* glided silently past Breaker Point, which marked the mouth of Pago Pago Harbor. Even running on the surface, the submarine was all but invisible as it headed out to the open sea. She had quickly cleared the near-shore reefs before reaching deep water. There, *Cheyenne* had immediately dived and disappeared.

The short run over to Niue took eighteen hours. As was typical in this part of the world, the sun set very quickly just as *Cheyenne*'s periscope broke through the smooth surface of the sea. Bart Knox, *Cheyenne*'s skipper, looked around only long enough to make sure they were alone in this patch of ocean. A few minutes later, a tiny Black Wing Submarine Launched Unmanned Aerial System popped up and rose vertically into the darkening sky. The SLUAS's two X wings unfolded while the twin tails rotated upright and the device's tiny pusher propellor sent the bird high into the air above the submerged vessel.

Weighing barely four pounds and with a wingspan of just thirty inches, the drone was all but invisible against the night's canopy of stars. Nearly silent, too. The battery-powered electric motor hardly made a buzz. For all practical purposes, for anyone who might be watching, the Black Wing was not even there.

A fire control technician sitting in front of the command-and-control system module onboard the *Cheyenne* communicated with the Black Wing using a secure digital data link. The drone was directed toward the island of Niue's south shore.

The bird's sophisticated EO/IR system could see through the gathering gloom of night even better than an owl searching for prey. Images of the Chinese marines and their Tongan allies popped up on the submarine's large screens and were immediately relayed back to Naval Intelligence, to Jon Ward and his intel analysts in Washington, DC. The armored vehicles and the AAW missiles that had been brought ashore were also clearly visible, and those images were also sent at the speed of light to those in Washington who knew precisely what they were seeing.

The little bird made several passes over Hanan Niue Airport before starting a thorough recon of the rest of the island, using a pre-programmed grid-search pattern. Four hours later, Jon Ward had a thorough idea of what US Marines would encounter should the decision be made to send them in.

Since the Black Wing had completed its mission and its batteries were waning, the quiet little bird was headed back out to sea to crash in deep water where it would never be found.

And Jon Ward had already conferred with the necessary people and was on the phone to Joe Glass.

Ψ

The KH-11 Advanced Keyhole satellite passed two hundred and fifty miles above the Western Pacific Ocean, sending its imagery to a geostationary communications satellite hovering twenty-three-thousand miles higher up, over the equator. From there, the data was linked back to the National Reconnaissance Office in Fort Belvoir, Virginia. The NRO then fed their images, at near real time—and as they were being simultaneously archived to several server farms around the world—to the White House situation room, buried deeply beneath the familiar building located at 1600 Pennsylvania Avenue.

Inside that room, President Stanley Smitherman sat at the head of the table, intently watching the screen as the scene unfolded. It was from a small island in the South China Sea, eight thousand miles away from where the president watched and sipped his first whiskey sour of the day. There appeared to be nothing more than devastation. The buildings were all rubble, smoke still billowing from several of them. A burning truck sat in the middle of the runway on what he had been told was the island's lone airfield. A couple of mangled missile launcher emplacements—again identified for the president by others in the meeting—were scattered around what was little more than an amoeba-shaped pile of coral and sand.

Two of President Smitherman's cabinet were present. Secretary of State Sandra Dosetti sat on Smitherman's left, reading her notepad and ignoring the large-screen flat panel and its battle scenes. Secretary of Defense Harold Osterman sat on his left, closely watching every image that appeared on the screen.

Two other monitors flanked the intel display. On the left-hand one, General William "Winking Willie" Willoughby, Chairman of the Joint Chiefs of Staff, sat at his desk in the Pentagon. Willoughby got his nickname because of an eye spasm that caused him to appear to be winking, particularly when he was stressed or excited. Typically, he would have taken a quick car ride along the Potomac and attended the White House meeting in person. But the president was afraid the press might see military brass showing up at the White House and get all hot and bothered.

On the right-hand display, Admiral Rufus Clark, Commander Indo-Pacific Command, leaned back in his big leather chair in his office at Camp Smith, in the hills above Pearl Harbor, Hawaii.

"Admiral, I saw the briefing binder this morning, but I don't have time to read all that rigamarole they throw in there every day," President Smitherman said, abruptly beginning the meeting. "Sum it up for me, if you will. From your vantage point, more or less on-scene, what the hell is happening with this China dust-up? I assumed if we ignored it the whole thing would be settled by now. But it's still all we're seeing on CNN. I know it's serious stuff but it's startin' to affect my poll numbers. And we're only five months from the Iowa caucuses, you know."

"Mister President, we are fifty-five-hundred miles from Dongsha Island and they are eighteen hours ahead of us," Admiral Clark replied. "I really can't say that we're any closer to being 'on-scene' than you are back there in DC. We have a term for that out here. We call it the 'tyranny of distance.'"

Smitherman waved his hand. The geography lesson was over.

The admiral took the hint and shifted to briefly relating what he knew of the situation. He was aware from previous presidential briefings that it was best to keep it a simple list of bullet points.

"Firstly, the ROC troops, that is those from the Republic of China..."

"Just call them Taiwanese, so I don't get confused with all the 'Chinese this' and 'Chinese that,'" Smitherman told him.

"Yes, sir, Mister President," Clark acquiesced, then went on without missing a beat. "The Taiwanese troops on Dongsha Island appear to have eliminated or captured all of the Mainland Chinese troops that were put ashore from their submarines. The last time the satellites picked up any combat that was actually occurring on the island was the day before yesterday."

"So, Admiral, if the fighting is all finished, then what the hell are we doing here? And the media keep harping on it?"

Secretary of State Dosetti looked up for the first time and chimed in.

"Precisely! I have an important political function that I'm missing in order to attend this dog and pony show."

"No, Madam Secretary, Mr. President," Admiral Clark shot back. "That is definitely not the case. Ground combat appears to have been concluded. At least for the time being. But the Chinese air and naval forces are continuing to pound the island almost continuously. And the Taiwanese are giving as good as they get. Don't know how they are doing it, but the ground troops are being re-supplied with both surface-to-air and anti-ship missiles. They have been getting their licks in. We have intel that there will be a Chinese amphibious operation shortly, in an effort to capture and claim what's left of the island. However, so far our imagery hasn't detected any movement in that regard."

"I don't understand," Harold Osterman piped up. He was shaking his head, but his eyes had still not left the images on the display screen.

"Admittedly, we don't either," General Willoughby responded. "From a military perspective, it just doesn't make sense for the PLA...the Mainland Chinese military...to continue expending so many resources over that little speck of coral. There simply has to be some political reason they're putting on this show."

Smitherman glanced over at Dosetti, who had already lost interest and was once again reading her notebook.

"Sandra, this is why I requested State to attend this, to get the political aspect. You can plan your senatorial campaign when we come to some kind of conclusion here."

She shut her notebook in a huff.

"How am I supposed to know why boys so enjoy playing with their toys? Maybe they just get a thrill from watching things blow up."

Admiral Clark interrupted the tirade.

"Mister President, Madam Secretary, we do have perspective on this from a source that is feeding very interesting intel to the Office of Naval Intelligence. I was just read in on this operation a few hours ago. Sir, this source has access to the inner workings of the Chinese Politburo, something we have never been able to obtain before. And her information has been spot-on so far."

"Her?" the president blurted out, sitting up so quickly in his chair that he spilled a few drops of his drink on his tie. "This wonderful source of yours is a gal?"

"Hey, what do we know about this source?" Secretary Osterman asked, still watching the screen.

"Really about all we know is that she is native Chinese but eventually Taiwanese," Clark answered, "and that she is remarkably well-connected. And very motivated to see that her adopted country is never taken over by the Chinese communists. She has developed these links over the years and uncovered some kind of internal Chinese power struggle that is clearly the source of all this recent belligerent action. The border skirmishes. Deadly attacks on fishing fleets. The continued claims on seemingly useless specks of land in the region. The mutual defense agreements with poor nations in the region and across the globe. And now, this open attack on Taiwanese territory. The current read is that some hard-liners are making a play to go ahead and finally take Taiwan while some moderates are working against them, mostly for fear it will upset the economic momentum China has been enjoying in the last decade. Then there is the infighting within the Chinese military, angling for more power. Bottom line, it seems to be a very fluid situation and that is about all the info I have."

The president swirled the ice around his mostly empty glass.

"Why don't we bring this gal spy in and see how much we can learn about her little network in Beijing?" Smitherman asked.

Admiral Clark squashed that idea immediately.

"With all due respect, Mr. President, that would be a very bad idea. We do not want to risk this pipeline. And besides, she will not work with our normal intelligence agencies. Only the ONI. The Office of Naval Intelligence."

Osterman finally turned from the screen with a frown.

"Why the hell is that?" he sputtered.

"She hasn't exactly shared that with us. But I'd guess she doesn't necessarily trust some of them. Just ONI, and specifically Jon Ward. And a guy named Dillon who works with the CIA and, when needed, other agencies. We absolutely must—especially right now—let her do things her way."

Smitherman rubbed his chin for a few seconds as he thought. He was especially wary of anyone having the upper hand, regardless of the situation. But he had one other driving force that was even more powerful. Finally, he spoke.

"Harold, y'all have a major Asian voting bloc out there on

the West Coast. Chinese. Korean. Japanese. How does this mess play with them?"

Osterman, the previous governor of California, replied, "Stan, you should be aware that 'face' is of the utmost importance to the Chinese culture. To most Asians. You need to always appear to be strong in attempting to save face with them. Particularly after that *Tarbox* fiasco. I recommend we get the Navy over there as a show of strength. We don't necessarily need to go in with guns blazing. Just a bunch of ships and airplanes to look tough. It'll raise your favorability among the Asian demographic by ten points, guaranteed."

Smitherman turned to the left-hand monitor and looked hard at Winking Willie. The general's eye was blinking furiously.

"General, what is your advice?"

"I don't advise getting involved in a shooting war over there, Mr. President. Or doing anything that might provoke such. Especially with all the firepower China can rain down on anyone within the 'first island' chain. But I do believe that if we use a reasonable show of force, with some very specific rules of engagement for our guys, it could work to defuse the situation. And especially if the moderates within the Politburo are able to hold sway. They do not want war. Neither, I believe, does their president."

Osterman stood and waved his arms to emphasize his point.

"And it would give you a big boost in the polls, Mister President. Being tough when the cause is righteous. Always works with the voters when you can show some balls."

"Yes, balls are good," Secretary Dosetti interjected sarcastically. "Right up until the first body bag with a dead soldier arrives at Dover." But she was nodding approvingly. She was—as far as President Smitherman knew—planning to run for US

Senator from Washington state. Being the cabinet member that preserved the sovereignty of Taiwan would look good on her resume out there in a state she had hardly visited in twenty years. Or anywhere if she ran for some higher office instead.

Smitherman had a slight smile on his face. He always liked projecting the image of being a strong, decisive leader.

"General, Admiral, send everything you have that floats to the South China Sea," he ordered. "I want the Chinese to see that we stand for peace and freedom. But make damn sure that one of your swash-buckling commanders doesn't try to start a real shooting war. Understood?"

Willoughby and Clark both displayed a look of concern. And the same immediate thought. The Commander in Chief had just ordered them to send as much of the entire fleet as they could muster into dangerous, hostile waters, where ordnance was already flying. And to do so without clear guidance or a definitive objective. Throughout military history, many eventual disasters had started out with much better planning than this.

But they had their marching orders.

Ψ

As it turned out, Mitch O'Donnell and Bill Bix were sharing a cramped, dank jail cell. Rex Smith was alone in the equally depressing one next to them. The rest of the male crew and technicians from *Deep Ocean Explorer* were all housed in the same cell block. When a couple of local drunks joined them the first night, they not only learned where the best party on the island was being thrown but also that this was the town's only cell block and that they were all guests of the Neiafu Constabulary Police. There was no way to know where Sandy McDougall and the female crew were being held. That was a considerable concern, though O'Donnell offered that they should worry less about her and more about whoever her unfortunate jailer was.

The patrol boat had taken the best part of two days to tow *Deep Ocean Explorer* and the prisoners to the island of Vava'u. Bix had been there before and recognized the winding coral channels that led to Neiafu's public wharf. From there, the Tongan Marines had herded the crew on foot, marching them down the crushed-coral Kovana Road to the combined court-house and city jail. Since then, no one had even visited the prisoners, much less attempted to interrogate them. There was no offer of legal counsel or an opportunity to communicate with the US Embassy in Fiji. It was as if they were totally forgotten.

"I know it was like five a.m. on a Saturday in LA when I sent out the message about what was going on," Bix complained. "But you would think someone would have gotten the word by now."

Smith leaned on the bars separating the cells, mostly watching for the little man who brought them meals in the form of cold microwave dinners stacked on a little pushcart. And who refused to engage in any conversation whatsoever.

"Maybe they have, Bill," Smith said. "There's no way for us to know what might be going on out there. At least until the cavalry arrives to bust us out. That could take a bit. They have to find out where we are first. Jump through some diplomatic hoops, I imagine. Then put a plan together. We need to have patience."

Bix gave a half smile.

"I'd feel better if our hosts didn't know about that geyser of money down there. That kind of thing could make otherwise sane people..." Bix stopped and looked at the two drunks in the cell across the way. They both seemed lost in deep sleep, though, in an effort to outlast their hangovers. "Well, providing they leave our vessel tied up down on the wharf, finding us should be the easy part. I left the AIS energized so she will show up on any AIS receiver that is looking."

The AIS—or Automatic Identification System—consisted of automatic transceivers carried on ships that constantly broadcast their position, course, and speed. The information was captured by other AIS receivers to aid in collision avoidance or search-and-rescue at sea.

While the two were talking, they heard footsteps entering the cell block. Finally, undercooked Salisbury steaks and half-frozen mashed potatoes, but at least it was sustenance.

However, it was not the little jailer with dinner. It was a young man dressed in a dark blue *tupenu*, the Tongan knee-length wraparound sarong, and a light blue, button-down, short-sleeved shirt. He was obviously attired for business.

The man stopped in front of Rex Smith's cell and introduced himself. Clearly, he was aware of who their prisoners were, though no one had requested identification from them.

"Doctor Smith, I am Ahio Evaipomama. I am from His Majesty's Ministry of Justice and represent the Lord Chancellor's Office." The man's clipped British accent and official brusqueness screamed "bureaucrat," even if his demeanor was calm and cordial enough. "You and your crew have been charged under Tongan statutes with violation of Tongan sovereign territory, attempted theft of Tongan natural resources, violation of the Customs and Excise Management Act of 2020, violation of the Minerals Act of 1949, and possibly other statutes. We are still researching the extent of your numerous crimes against the people of our nation."

Smith frowned as he listened. This was obviously all a set-up, a ruse to take his ship. At best, they were going to hold the ship and crew for what amounted to a ransom. At worst, they would stop at nothing to stake their claim on what Smith and his crew had discovered in the deep water out there.

"I demand to see the US ambassador," Smith told him. "You can't hold us here like this on such trumped-up..."

"Oh, Dr. Smith, we most certainly can. And we will. We are a very long way from the US and in a very out-of-the-way part of the world. And we have long and painful experiences with colonialism perpetrated by the US and European powers. Our government, on behalf of our people, has vowed to no longer tolerate such." Ahio Evaipomama paused and smiled quite insincerely. "As you likely are aware, the US Embassy is on Fiji. It will take some time to notify them through the proper channels and then for a representative to journey here. In the meantime, I suggest that you make yourselves comfortable." He glanced around the cell block before adding, "Or at least as comfortable as the accommodations allow."

"And how about the female members of our crew?" Smith asked.

"Be assured they are being well cared for. Or at least as well as any other felons would be as they await justice."

With that, the Tongan bureaucrat turned on his heels and briskly left the cell block.

Ψ

Yon Hun Glo stood in the back corner of *Wushiwu*'s control room and watched as Captain Liu Zhang surfaced the submarine. It was only one of the things he missed about no longer being in direct command of such a wondrous vessel. Even now, proud as he was of his lofty position in PLAN's submarine service, he had to resist the impulse to take charge of the boat, to correct the captain when he did not do things precisely as Yon would have, to reprimand a crewmember who did not perform his duties as Yon believed he should.

The long trek from Hainan to Tongatapu was almost over. The *lang qun* now steamed in a slow circle a couple of miles to the north and east of 'Eueiki Island, waiting for darkness. Yon Hun Glo knew that transiting the narrow Avi Piha channel at night would be dangerous, but it was well worth the risk. He was convinced that they had managed to make the entire voyage without the American Navy being any the wiser. To risk being seen by one of their satellites during the last couple of miles of the transit would be foolish.

The sun was an hour below the western horizon when four black monsters slowly emerged from the watery deep. They formed a line astern with *Wushiwu* in the lead as they steamed past the coral bluffs of little 'Eueiki Island. Meanwhile, Yon Hun Glo climbed up to the bridge just as they slowed to rendezvous with the pilot launch at the entrance to Avi Piha Channel.

With the Tongan harbor pilot aboard *Wushiwu*, the submarines steamed on, bows pointed down the funnel-shaped channel. As the line turned to the south and headed past Talufu'ou, each of them, without ever being aware, tripped the sensor field that ORCA One had laid only three days before. The sensors' communication buoy up-linked the alerts to an overhead satellite. That meant Jon Ward's intel team knew of the Chinese wolf pack's arrival at Tonga even before the mooring lines were doubled.

The four submarines tied up alongside the Chinese container ship *Pearl Moon,* which was moored stern first to the quay. By midnight, camouflage had been constructed over the subs so that anyone looking down from overhead would only see a couple of broad, flat barges snuggled up next to the cargo ship.

An hour after the submarines disappeared under the camouflage nets, the Chinese research ship *Zhang Jian* motored into the port and tied up alongside the pier. The fully outfitted, deep-sea research ship was ostensibly cruising the South Pacific mapping migration patterns of pelagic fish as part of a Shanghai Ocean University project. The cover story did not really equate very well with the very-deep-water mineral recovery equipment that covered her ample and open main deck. That gear included the orange and white *Fendouji* manned submersible, one of only a few vessels in the world capable of reaching ocean depths as great as six miles.

Yon Hun Glo's first action was to send word to the palace that he desired to hold a meeting with King Tofuwanga at the earliest opportunity the following morning. Then, with his submarines safely moored at their destination and their presence adequately hidden from prying eyes, and with the meeting with the country's ruler arranged, Yon decided that his day's work was complete. It was now time for him to turn in so he would be well rested for the next day's important work.

Meanwhile, ORCA One had continued to follow the four submarines all the way to the moment when its command algorithm determined that the UUV was now within a restricted harbor. At that point, the submersible's brain ordered the mission aborted and instructed the UUV to retrace its path back to open water. Once safely out of the Avi Piha channel again, ORCA One communicated back to the command center on the *Portland*, detailing its completed mission.

In Pago Pago, Joe Glass, Commodore of US Navy Submarine Squadron Seven, had learned of the Chinese submarines' arrival at the port in Tonga at about the same time that Jon Ward had. Things were about to get very interesting in the backwaters of the Pacific, an ocean whose name literally meant peaceful and tranquil.

Ψ

The activity was massive, immediate, and very noticeable for any of the world's naval powers who might be watching. Four harbor tugs pulled the *George Washington* away from the pier at the Yokosuka Naval Base. By the time she had cleared Agatsuma Island, the rest of the Seventh Fleet ships—every one of the destroyers and cruisers stationed there—had left the pier and were underway. They steamed in a long, impressive line down Tokyo Wan toward open water. The *Blue Ridge*, the more-than-fifty-year-old Seventh Fleet command ship, was delayed by several hours in getting underway as her long-suffering engineering department struggled to make essential repairs to her boilers.

The carrier airwing flew out of Atsugi Naval Air Facility to join up with the *George Washington* as the battle group headed almost due south. Task Force Seventy, the Seventh Fleet Battle Force, was underway, bows pointing south and proceeding at full speed.

At the same time, Task Force Seventy-Six, Seventh Fleet's amphibious assault force, sortied out of Sasebo, Japan, steaming toward Okinawa. There, the Third Marine Expeditionary Unit was quickly making preparations to board the amphibs.

The ships of Destroyer Squadron Seven made an emergency sortie from Changi Naval Base in Singapore, northbound at full speed. Meanwhile, the *Vinson* Battle Group came from much farther away, from the Arabian Sea, across the Indian Ocean, then toward the Straits of Malacca.

The piers in San Diego, Pearl Harbor, and Bremerton,

Washington, were eerily empty and lonely places once the haze-gray ships disappeared over the horizon, heading west.

The Navy was simply carrying out President Smitherman's commands. But not even the top brass involved comprehended what was going on. Vice Admiral Stan Gray, Commander—Seventh Fleet, was totally confused by the vague orders. He was being asked to get underway with the greatest assembly of naval might put together since the end of World War Two. Then he was supposed to steam in tight little circles two hundred miles east of Taiwan. He was not to launch any aircraft sorties or take any actions that the Chinese or anyone else could even remotely construe as being offensive.

Just have all those warships steam in circles. There was no stated objective. And there was no end date.

Ψ

Joe Glass was well aware that he was on the wrong end of some damn serious problems. Even worse, they all seemed to have been dumped on him at once. As he stood in front of a large-screen display in the USS *Portland*'s Combat Information Center, he had to remind himself that problems were what he had signed up for in the first place. If things did not go sideways, there was little need for him. And he also reminded himself that he had the people and the machines available to address them. That was why he had gathered his small "command team" to review what they knew, what assets they had available, and to plan a course of action. Glass knew he had to get beyond how he conducted this process in his previous life, commanding a single submarine, and take advantage of everything else he had at his disposal to fix the issues piling up around him.

The *Portland*'s advanced Combat Information Center was the perfect place for this discussion with the team. Its state-of-the-art displays were fed by the ship's sensor system, but more importantly, her communications systems were fed by myriad outside sources. They could all be integrated and displayed here and would hopefully give them all the data they required to make correct decisions.

Glass and Marine Lt. Col. Stanton Readly, along with Mort Jones, the *Portland*'s CO, were intently watching the raw video footage from the Black Wing SLUAS that had been relayed to them by the *Cheyenne*. It proved quite informative.

"I counted at least a half dozen tracked armored vehicles," Readly noted as he intently watched the screen. "They sure look like Chinese ZBD-3s. Those are airborne fighting vehicles and typically pack a thirty mike-mike auto cannon and a seven-point-six-two machine gun. Real nasty stuff. These sure ain't Tongan Marines we're looking at either."

"Hey, Stanton, what are these wheeled vehicles under those palms?" Mort Jones asked, freezing the frame and pointing at two big trucks.

Readly stared at the image for a few seconds. He finally nodded, satisfied he knew what he was seeing.

"That looks like a pair of FB-6s. They are a Chinese anti-air surprise package. One of the vehicles has a pretty sophisticated phased-array radar while the other is the actual missile launcher. Those two make a deadly team. An airborne assault is going to be a real problem as long as those guys are serviceable. They hide out like that and can lock up on any target out to ten klicks or so. From this firepower, we have at least a battalion of Chinese Marines here."

"Can you and your guys handle this?" Glass asked. "And assuming you say you can, how in hell do we get you ashore?"

"Damn good question, Commodore. We only have two

Ospreys here. That's thirteen sorties to get all my shooters over there. Figure a two-hour round trip, so we are taking something like twelve hours of continuous flying. Not exactly conducive to your typical surprise assault."

"What about sending *Portland* out?" Jones asked. "We leave in the morning, we could be off Niue just after nightfall."

Glass shook his head. "Not with four Chinese diesel submarines out and about. Too big a risk there."

Jones piped up. "We need a new travel agent. I don't see that we can do much of anything with what we have to work with."

"What about their supply chain?" Readly chimed in. "Remember General Patton's old saw, 'An army travels on its stomach.' They're going to need groceries, some way of re-supply. Can't we hit that?"

Glass thought for a few seconds, then replied, "That's a good start. Only two ways to get supplies in. Either fly them in or haul them over by ship to Alofi." He punched buttons until he saw a chart of the island. "The place only has one small wharf. The rest of the island is surrounded by reefs and high coral cliffs. We could station ORCA One a few miles off Alofi to warn us of any approaching shipping. We could also use the Ospreys to chase them away. Interdicting air supply, though? That's going to be a problem until we can get some more assists in here."

"Excuse me, Commodore," Steve Weiss, the ORCA Team leader, interrupted. "We have Admiral Ward on the phone. He wants to talk to you."

Glass took the headset from the commander and spoke into the boom mike.

"Glass."

"Joe, as if you don't have enough on your plate, I got a hot one for you," Jon Ward started. "Seems that our friend King

Two-for-One has taken the *Deep Ocean Explorer* and the crew as hostage. We got a call from their Los Angeles agent. Looks like it happened a couple of days ago. Last satellite pass we could see the ship tied up at the port of Neiafu on Vava'u. That's the Tongan Island closest to you. The ship's AIS track confirms it."

Glass shook his head. This whole thing was spinning out of control. The Tongan monarch and his Chinese allies appeared to be hell bent on causing a dangerous dust-up way out here in this quiet corner of the Pacific.

"What about the crew?"

"We think they are being held in town. The only place big enough and the most likely spot is the city jail."

"Let me guess. You want me to stage a raid and get them out," Glass said.

"Good deduction. That would be the plan," Ward answered. "It's well within the range of your Ospreys and your CH-53s. I wouldn't expect a whole lot of kickback, especially if you hit them fast and hard."

Glass nodded, even though he knew Ward could not see it. He was already running scenarios—including minimum risk to the captives and the island's civilians.

"Okay, that one I can handle. I'm going to need some help with Niue, though. The Chinese didn't pick that particular spot for its lovely beaches and vistas."

"Get me a list of what you need," Jon Ward shot back. "I'll be working on it while you are noodling the *Deep Ocean Explorer* problem. But it's going to be tough getting much fire-power. Pretty much the whole Pacific fleet is heading toward the Philippine Sea, just in case that whole Dongsha Island thing spills over into a major war. It's tying up everything including most of our intelligence capabilities. All the intel and imagery that we have is on its way to you. Keep me posted. Holler if you need me."

Ward abruptly dropped offline.

Glass removed the headset and turned to the team.

"Guys, looks like we got ourselves a new knot to untangle."

21

It was not quite 0700 local time when the government car that had brought Yon Hun Glo from the docks pulled up to the gates of the Tongan Royal Palace on Vuna Road. Though Yon had seen little else that impressed him on the ride over, he was surprised by the enormous, white, wooden structure sitting at the water's edge. Its brilliant red roof was clearly visible from anywhere in the village of Nuku'alofa.

But it was also obvious that a business day at the palace did not typically begin so early in the morning. The king usually did not arise until noon. The guard was still rubbing sleep from his eyes as he jumped up and waved the vehicle through the gates with one hand while holding a big mug of coffee in the other. The driver steered the car into a large parking lot, climbed out, and opened Yon Hun Glo's door.

Two military officers, one wearing the insignia of a Tongan Army Brigadier General and the other of a Tongan Maritime Force Commodore, were lounging in the shade while waiting by the palace's main entrance. The pair snapped to attention and saluted as Yon Hun Glo emerged from his vehicle. He waved a perfunctory answering salute and charged past them, through the open door. The two officers rushed to catch up and guide the Chinese vice admiral to his meeting with their king.

After escorting Yon Hun Glo to King Tofuwanga's private office, the pair disappeared. The massively overweight potentate was waiting behind a huge desk. He appeared to have just crawled from bed, his thinning hair unkempt and his necktie a bit off center. The monarch waved the admiral to sit in one of the upholstered high-back chairs arranged in front of the impressive teakwood desk.

"Admiral, may I offer you a coffee? Something stronger? Perhaps a pastry?" Tofuwanga asked.

"No, thank you. I have long since completed breakfast."

"Very well. I trust that your journey was smooth and uneventful. I cannot imagine making such a long trip like that while stuffed into such a tiny submarine. I am afraid I am a bit..."

Yon Hun Glo waved aside the pleasantries. Instead, his already stern expression turned even darker.

"There is much for us to discuss and we have little time. First is the matter of the island of Niue. My government was most distressed when you took your ill-advised action there without even bothering to consult us. That is no way to treat allies." Yon glared at the king, who appeared to be taken aback by the admiral's sudden attack. "Fortunately for you, we had troops nearby. Otherwise, the Niue constabulary would likely have promptly expelled your puny force. And that does not even begin to consider the Americans and the New Zealand military and their potential response."

King Tofuwanga leaned forward as much as his large belly would allow and started to protest. Yon Hun Glo raised his hand, palm forward, stopping him before he could utter a word.

"To this point, Your Majesty, this has been your one major indiscretion. Trust me when I tell you that you will not commit another. If so, you will find yourself immediately deposed. And perhaps worse. I am certain that we could find someone on this godforsaken island who can follow our orders precisely and not be tempted to ad lib."

The king bristled at this obvious lese-majeste. No one was permitted to speak to him in this manner. Not without great peril.

"Admiral, my Tongan military, which I command myself, is quite adequate to defend our rights," he thundered back. "And our decision to reclaim territory taken from us. Niue is our territory by historic right, and we have bravely and success-fully protected what is Tongan. Only yesterday, we towed an American vessel into port that had dared to intrude into our sovereign waters. They were foolishly nosing around the gold fields, so we..."

The king stopped mid-sentence. It appeared the Chinese admiral was about to come over the teakwood table after him.

"You what?" Yon Hun Glo exploded. "You are a stupid, pompous fool! Were it not for the gold, we would simply leave you and your swampy islands to the Americans. And I assure you, you would be rotting in Guantanamo before the week was out." Yon sat back, took a deep breath, and tried to regain control of his temper. Tofuwanga appeared stunned. No one had ever spoken to him in such a way. "Now, where is this ship being held and where is her crew? Perhaps we can still salvage something from this disaster. And you best hope we do, or you may still be allowed to roast in your own juices."

King Tofuwanga, his voice now trembling, told the admiral that the *Deep Ocean Explorer* and her crew were being held on Vava'u, an island located two hundred miles to the north.

Yon Hun Glo listened, then stood, turned on his heels,

and, without another word, stormed out of the king's office in the Royal Palace. Once in his vehicle's back seat, before the car was even out of the palace's gate, he was on his cell phone, making arrangements for Chinese Marines to hasten to the out-of-the-way island of Vava'u. Once there, they were to guard the American research ship and take charge of the ship's crew.

And if anyone—anyone at all—came near either, he was to be eliminated as a possible threat to the Chinese people and the Party.

Ψ

Jim Ward decided that his wounds were now more annoying and uncomfortable than painful. He had recovered from enough injuries already in his line of work to be aware that this was a good sign, that he was on the mend. Shortly after the Gulfstream landed at Taipei's downtown Songshan Airport, an ambulance whisked him, Li Min Zhou, and his new personal physician to the swank Mandarin Oriental Hotel. Zhou quickly left, explaining she had work to do, and the doc departed shortly after getting Ward settled and hooked up to far more monitoring equipment than the SEAL felt he needed.

He found his suite to be an impressive cross between a hospital intensive care unit and Kubla Khan's Xanadu. Hospital medical equipment and blinking monitors vied with glossy lacquerware and polished marble. However, it was the views of the city and surrounding mountains from the big windows of his penthouse that really drew his attention. He asked one of his two personal male nurses to kindly move his bed a foot or so in order for him to gaze out the window. The way the sun lit the scene, the view could just as easily have been a fine Oriental frieze.

The SEAL had also been wounded and hospitalized enough in his career to realize that such luxurious and personalized treatment for a "grunt" like him was most unusual. For some reason, he was one highly valued patient. He decided to enjoy it while he could, before he learned what he would ultimately have to do to deserve such attention.

Ward was finishing up a fine pork chop with generous applesauce—almost the equal of the way his mom made it—when he heard a quiet knock at the door. The great teak double doors swung open and Li Min Zhou slipped in.

"How do you like your new digs?" she asked. "Better than Changi General?"

"Truth is, I'm worried about what somebody's going to expect in return for all this."

"You'll earn it." Li Min Zhou smiled. "You'll earn it, I'm sure."

She took a seat on the tufted leather couch, placing an attaché case on the chrome-and-glass coffee table, then waved the nurses out of the room. Jim Ward's sixth sense had already alerted him that those nurses likely had duties other than merely monitoring his blood pressure and O2 levels. They had not gotten those muscles slinging bedpans.

Once they were gone and had quietly closed the doors behind them, Li Min Zhou opened the case and extracted some files. Ward swallowed the last bite of pork chop, put down his knife and fork, and leaned back on his pillows. Clearly, a meeting had just begun.

"I brought you a little light reading to pass the time while you are lounging in the lap of luxury," she said as she handed the files over to Ward. "This will give you some background and details on what is happening in China. All facts have been verified by some very diligent, resourceful, highly placed...and loyal...people. This information may give you some grasp of what that might mean for our two countries."

Ward quickly scanned the first few pages.

"Interesting. This implies President Tan Yong is going to use the Dongsha incident as a ploy to keep our interest directed that way while he really makes a move to grab the gold in Tonga. Regardless of how that plays out, this is one hell of a dangerous game. The devious bastard could set the whole world on fire, you know."

Li Min Zhou nodded.

"Most really high-stakes games are dangerous. But not to belabor the point, this is Asia. There are layers upon layers here. Tan Yong is using Yon Ba Deng's plot to take down Soo Be Xian as a foil. But what the president is really doing is usurping Yon Ba Deng's move to grab the Tongan gold. This will have the effect of keeping the Americans busy doing their duty, keeping their promises, rushing to Taiwan's aid while the Chinese abscond with the gold. But where Tan Yong sees Dongsha as merely a diversion, the Taiwanese see it as a threat to their very existence. And they are going to fight all out to protect it. Tan Yong does not want a shooting war. He wants an economic war. He knows he has the best opportunity, the resources, and the groundwork it takes to win that kind of conflict. But now that the shooting has started, it is in danger of spinning into something the Chinese communists might not be able to stop. Primarily because there are those in positions of power who do not want it to stop, for many varying reasons."

"And we're going to be in the middle of it regardless."

"Yes. But I am convinced we are not too late. At least not yet. We need the Americans to continue to be diverted to Dongsha. To make the show of force way out there in the

Pacific, as is already underway. But to have other units come in and stop the shooting. To do so quickly and decisively. It is a matter of national survival for Taiwan. And it could well avert a horribly greater war."

Ward shook his head. The twists and turns were giving him a roaring headache. He stared out across the Keelung River toward Mount Qixing, standing blue-green and peaceful in the distance. For a moment, he wished he could get out of the bed, put on his running shoes, walk away from all the intrigue, and hike up that beautiful mountainside.

"So where do we fit into this little multiplayer game of three-dimensional chess?" the SEAL finally asked. Then he had another thought. "Zhou, tell me something. Are you asking me to keep all this secret from the US, including from my father? If that's the case, then why did you bring me here and share so much with me? Why did you not tell me that before you let me see all this?"

She sat there, looking at him for a long moment. Ward stared back, unable to ignore just how absolutely beautiful she was.

"Just the opposite, Jim," she finally told him. "We have you set up in this little pleasure palace so that we can feed you the straight, hot skinny, as you Americans so colorfully put it. Then you will be able to pass it along, backchannel, to your father. Some of it he will know already. We are not the only ones with big ears in key positions. Some of it will confirm what he suspects. Some of it can benefit from your perspective. All of it will be valuable in planning how he and the US can help unravel this tangle and possibly eliminate this particular threat. At least until the next one."

Ward rubbed his forehead. The headache had not subsided with her explanation. It had ratcheted up to a new level.

"But except for my genetic attachment to the head of US Naval Intelligence, I'm thinking I'm in no way qualified for relaying spy stuff. You spooks do that all the time. I mostly just shoot people and blow stuff up."

Li paused, seemingly looking for the right words. When she spoke again, she was pointedly deliberate.

"We've seen threats and bluster and even shots fired plenty of times before. But we've never been this close to open conflict between the world's top two superpowers. Plus, there are others—North Korea, Russia, Iran, and more terrorist organizations than you can imagine—just waiting to take advantage and rush in and fill the vacuum if this all escalates to full-scale war. Especially if it gets nuclear, which is a real possibility if some have their way. The gold. That's driving a lot of it this time. But this pot has been simmering for a long, long time, and it's finally about to boil over. Despite the monstrous potential events that could occur, subtle delivery of data, the nature of any armed response, and other aspects will be crucial in containing this whole thing. Your dad has the ears of the Joint Chiefs and they go directly to the president. You have a unique understanding of warfare and what the data from the field really means. We trust our people in the most important places in China and Taiwan. We trust TJ Dillon. We trust you. We trust your dad and anyone he trusts, and that obviously includes you. We don't trust much of anybody else. We know each of you will do the right and best thing to make this all a back-page story in *USA Today*. Not the end of the world as we know it. Even if there is several trillion dollars' worth of gold down there in that trench."

She sat back, as if exhausted. He looked at her for a long moment.

"Okay," Ward finally responded. "I hope I can justify that faith."

"You get healed up and read and take note of everything that you pass to your father. Don't hesitate to state your opinion or thoughts. TJ Dillon and I will do all the work while you lie here and relax and grow back together. We may well need to call on your other considerable and unique skills before this is all over."

Ward studied the big slice of chocolate cheesecake on his dinner tray.

"Something tells me you're not going to share any details on that part at this point," he told her.

"Hell, Frog Man, I don't even know yet how that's going to play out!" She smiled. The last of the day's sun streaming through the hotel window seemed dim in comparison. "And speaking of work, we're off to Beijing to be sure we benefit from Soo Be Xian's imminent fall from grace."

"Beijing?"

"Don't enjoy too much of that cheesecake, tough guy. You may need your wind before all this becomes nothing more than a thick classified file in a triple-locked cabinet drawer somewhere."

Ψ

Colonel Stanton Readly sat in a jump-seat in the back of the lead Osprey aircraft, call sign Mike Hotel One, and scanned the dark compartment. Twenty of his Marines were crammed into it. In the dim light, he could not see their eyes, but he knew they were nervous. Nervous but ready. Trained, briefed, and willing to do whatever was necessary to successfully complete their assigned mission.

Sergeant Major Fernando Ramirez, the battalion's senior enlisted Marine, saw the colonel sizing up his guys and gave him a thumbs-up. Ramirez was a grizzled, combat-hardened

Leatherneck. He knew the team was ready to rock and roll. They would do their best or die trying.

Readly looked through the small porthole in the starboard side access door. He could just make out the second Osprey, dubbed Mike Hotel Two. It was flying a hundred feet astern of his own aircraft with twenty-two more shooters aboard. Somewhere out there—somewhere below and behind them where he was unable to see—and if all went according to plan, there were two CH-53K "King Stallion" helicopters. They were Mike Hotel Three and Four and would be following them to their destination. However, they were mostly empty, carrying only a few passengers, a couple of corpsmen, just in case someone needed immediate medical care, and a pair of shooters, there to provide security. Their task would be to carry passengers out, once they were freed.

Readly ran through each step of the plan in his mind for the ten-thousandth time. But he knew only too well that so many things could and likely would alter the scheme on the fly. The Ospreys would split up, then simultaneously land and launch their teams on their respective attacks. One would hit the little island's public pier where the *Deep Ocean Explorer* was docked. The other would head to the courthouse and city jail, where they expected to find and safely extract the hostages. Or what the Tongans called "criminal prisoners." The intention was to strike fast, employing overwhelming force, to minimize casualties. The team at the exploration vessel was to board her, take out any guards, and guide the ship safely out of port. Meanwhile, the King Stallion choppers were to swoop in to transport the hostages off the island and back to Pago Pago.

Good plan. What might really happen was anybody's guess. But surprise and quickness were their primary advantages. That and what they expected to be a small, ill-equipped, and poorly trained group of defenders.

The colonel opened his laptop computer and made a final check of the latest intel updates. The plane's NOTM system (Network on the Move) gave him an onboard Wi-Fi that connected by SATCOM directly back to the *Portland*. That meant he had access to the latest updates right up to the second he stepped off the aircraft. Thankfully, there were no last-second changes so far.

"Colonel, ten minutes out." The pilot's voice crackled in his earbuds. The Wi-Fi also connected the plane's crew communication system seamlessly to his intra-squad combat radio's throat mike and earbuds. The pilot added, "Dropping down to the deck."

The two Ospreys zoomed down to just above the surface of the sea. Readly could see the wavetops through the small round window. Just then, the aircraft's crew chief lowered the rear cargo ramp and swung the GAU-21 .50 caliber machine gun into position. That would provide the Osprey a nasty little tail stinger. But one they hoped they would not have to employ.

The aircraft suddenly lurched upward to clear the high coral cliffs at the water's edge and then roared at near treetop level across the heavily forested tabletop plateau. They would fly past Lupepau'u Airport and then follow Tu'i Road down to the island's courthouse and jail building while their twin turned toward the pier and the research ship.

The pilot's voice was again on the intercom. "Colonel, some kind of military aircraft on the taxiway at the airport. I'm linking the FLIR image to your laptop. This bad boy must've just arrived. He wasn't on the pre-flight intel brief."

The picture popped up immediately on Readly's computer. He studied the screen intently. The FLIR—forward-looking infrared camera—provided him a surprisingly good, high-resolution image of an aircraft parked near the tiny airport's runway, a short distance from the small terminal building. He could not identify the exact model, but it was clearly a four-engine turboprop. Almost certainly a military transport. That was confirmed by the presence of half a dozen armed men guarding the plane. The Tongan military did not own such a plane. Nor any plane at all, for that matter.

Readly knew it had to be Chinese. That was the only possible answer. Especially with all those Chinese marines on Niue, only four hundred klicks to the east. Its presence and the likelihood of Chinese marines being on the island had just cranked up the difficulty level of this operation astronomically. The pilot was correct. The pre-mission intel imagery was only a couple of hours old. That plane did not appear anywhere on it.

But Readly's mission had not changed. Difficult or not, he would go ahead and try to free the hostages and secure the research vessel.

"Guys, listen up," he spoke into his throat mike. "It looks like we may have some Chinese party crashers down there. Based on a transport we are seeing on the runway, there could be as many as a hundred shooters on the ground. Stay alert and keep your heads on a swivel. If something shoots at you, kill it."

The colonel did briefly consider canceling the rescue mission or changing the plan to concentrate all four aircraft on the hostage rescue. He rejected the idea of aborting the mission out of hand. They were, by now, only seconds out from their destinations. It was far too late to change plans.

"Colonel!" There was urgency in the Osprey pilot's voice. "Troops on the road, one klick out from the LZ and heading that way. You're going to have company quick. I can try to keep 'em occupied while you grab the hostages."

As he spoke, his bird flared out, its two huge engines rotating upward, and shifted to hover mode. Then Mike Hotel Two roared past them, still flying horizontally, headed to the waterfront. As Readly watched the other aircraft zoom away, his Osprey kicked up a dust storm as it settled down smoothly into the dirt parking lot beside the courthouse. The bird's wheels had not even touched the ground yet when Ramirez yelled, "Follow me, world-beaters!" and jumped off the rear ramp.

The Marines roared "Hoorah!" in unison as they charged down the ramp and sprinted across the parking lot. Several set up a hasty perimeter while the rest crashed through the flimsy structure's wooden door. The bird was already starting to climb as Readly jumped off the ramp and ran toward the building. Just before he ducked into the wooden courthouse, he heard the unmistakable rumble of the Osprey's .50 caliber machine gun as it opened up on the Chinese parade headed his way.

Inside, Master Sergeant Ramirez stood guard over a pair of wide-eyed local constables. They were already disarmed and zip-tied to chairs.

Ramirez pointed down a narrow corridor. "Hostages are down there. We may have a diplomatic problem that requires your leadership, sir."

Readly could not tell if Ramirez was smiling or not. The colonel dashed down the hallway toward the cell blocks at the far end. Then he saw the released hostages hurrying back toward him, directed by several of the Marines. Behind them, two more Marines were frog-marching a rather well-dressed Tongan, someone who clearly was not one of the hostages.

And the gentleman did not appear to be cooperating with his escorts.

"Who's this dude?" Readly asked.

"He was interrogating the hostages when we showed up, sir," the squad leader answered. "And he didn't exactly appreciate it when we informed him we were here to bail them out of his little jail. He started spoutin' a lot of legal gibberish. We decided we'd introduce him to you, Colonel."

The Tongan struggled to get loose, to no avail.

"I demand to be released," he was ranting. "Do you know who I am? I am Ahio Evaipomama and I personally represent His Majesty's Ministry of Justice and the Office of the Lord Chancellor. I demand that I be released and that these prisoners be returned to my custody. They are under indictment for violating Tongan..."

Readly held up his hand.

"Shut the hell up! I really don't give a damn who the hell you are. You are going with us and will be charged with kidnapping and piracy once we get your ass to a proper international court." The colonel turned to the squad leader. "Restrain and gag him. Make sure he gets a VIP seat on the evac chopper."

The Marines dragged the struggling man away just as Sergeant Ramirez's voice popped into Readly's earbuds.

"Skipper, the 53s are five mikes out. Our Chinese friends are only about one. We'll need some shooters up here."

Readly ran to the front of the courthouse, joined by the rest of the squad. Ramirez and his fire team were crouched behind a low coral wall and, along with the men who had set up the initial perimeter, were already fully engaged in an active firefight with an unknown number of Chinese marines on the other side of the road. Readly's unit was clearly outgunned. Time was not on their side.

The situation was going sideways fast.

The colonel knew he needed more firepower and he needed it now. He shifted channels on his radio and reached out to both Osprey pilots. That was all the big guns he had at his beck and call until the 53s, the King Stallions, arrived with their door-mounted seven-point-six two-millimeter machine guns mounted on each door. Mike Hotel Two—the other Osprey—responded first. That team of Marines had quickly taken control of the boat with no opposition. So far, though, they had not figured out how to operate it since the Tongan captors had apparently done something to the boat's control room systems. They would need help and some time to get the engines going and the ship underway. But Mike Hotel Two was already in the air, heading back to the courthouse to help out Readly and his team.

Mike Hotel One chimed in next. He was still in the party but running low on ammo.

"Sarge, where are the hostages?" Readly yelled.

"In a ditch on the other side of the building. The female hostages are there now, too. I got two guys with them, but we need some help or..."

Then, just as the colonel could make out above the crack of rifle fire the welcome roar of the triple turbines of the approaching CH-53Ks, a rocket-propelled grenade arced over his head from the direction of the Chinese troops. It crashed through a window into the courthouse behind him. The explosion blew out several windows and started a fire in the building.

Osprey Mike Hotel Two showed up just in time to pepper the area where the round emanated with .50 caliber fire. The night sky above Neiafu was getting crowded.

Another enemy RPG flew overhead from a point to the right of the previous one. It, too, exploded into the building. The night was lit up by the rapidly spreading fire now roaring within the structure. As a sudden burst of fire from the just-arrived Mike Hotel Three concentrated on that patch of palms and brush, Readly and Martinez waved for their men to abandon their positions. They needed to pull back before the next RPG landed in their midst.

Readly knew that the parking lot was not going to work as the extract site, as planned. It was too open and exposed to the Chinese fire. The only option that he could see was to use the dirt road along the back side of the building. The hostages were already in the area and the burning courthouse offered a modicum of cover. He could only hope there was room for the helicopters to set down.

"Mike Hotel Three, extract site moved to backside of courthouse, on Pouono Road. Be aware LZ is hot," Readly informed the approaching helicopters. "Repeat, LZ is hot."

The chopper pilot curtly acknowledged.

"Sarge, confirm your guys with the hostages got the change of plans!" Readly yelled as they ran.

"Roger, Colonel."

Rifle fire from the Chinese troops had lessened a bit as the Ospreys and King Stallions continued to shoot at them from a reasonably safe distance. Ramirez and his men dashed around the raging flames of the old wooden courthouse, covering each other as they pulled back.

Readly and Ramirez started moving the civilians—and the lone Tongan legal official—from the vegetation cover around the ditch to the new extract site. But two of the civilians ran over and kneeled down next to Readly.

"Colonel, you aren't going to be able to get *Deep Ocean Explorer* out of here without help. We jimmied the drive system computer so they couldn't move her except by tow. I'm

Rex Smith. I own her. This is Bill Bix. He's the captain. We can help you run her."

Readly nodded and turned to Ramirez.

"Get me a fire team to make a run with us to the waterfront when we get everybody on their ride out of here."

The first King Stallion made another roaring pass over the courthouse as her door gunners unloaded on the Chinese marines. Then the bird flared out and somehow managed to squeeze into the little open lot and roadway behind the building as the second 53K took its place in the sky above the burning building. The landing aircraft's rotors were only inches from the fronds of nearby palm trees. Along with the two Ospreys, the bird above them continued to ferociously spit deadly fire at where the Chinese had last been shooting at them from the far side of the road.

Meanwhile, the civilians from the research ship piled onto the chopper as the marines helped them. A mere thirty seconds after setting down, the helicopter was airborne once again. Then the second 53K settled down in the same spot. The rest of the civilians—except Bix and Smith—and most of the Marines piled onboard.

As the second helicopter lifted off, Readly, Ramirez, the Marine fire team, Bix, and Smith sprinted down Pouono Road toward the waterfront. Mike Hotel One and Two kept the Chinese marines pinned down with their machine gun fire. Mike Hotel Three and Four and their passengers were well on their way back toward Pago Pago.

As the group charged down the coral road and then turned onto Fatafehi Road, they could hear almost continuous firing behind them, but no one seemed to be in pursuit. The Chinese must have assumed all the fighters had left onboard the King Stallions. The run to the dock was only eight hundred meters, but with the adrenaline and the exercise, all of them were winded when they finally piled onboard the research ship. Older and not in nearly as good a shape as the Marines, Bix and Smith were struggling, but the fighters helped them climb aboard their vessel.

"Colonel, Mike Hotel One." Readly paused to hear the update from the Osprey pilot. "We are out of ammo and bingo fuel. Two reports the same. We're heading back to refuel and re-arm in case you need us back here. Looks like those Chinese are heading your way on the double quick. Recommend you make yourself scarce. Good luck."

"Roger, thanks, Mike Hotel One. We'll let you..." The colonel was interrupted by the sound of Chinese marines running down Tu'i Road, shooting in the direction of the ship as they grew closer. "We'll update you. Thanks."

Bill Bix ran straight to the bridge, promising it would only take a minute to remove whatever hex he had put on the ship's controls. Meanwhile, Rex Smith, back in his element, took command. Pointing to two Marines, he ordered, "You two, use the fire axes to cut those lines!" He turned to Colonel Readly. "Bill will get her started and head us out of here while I get busy and bring up the nav systems. I think you guys need to play soldier while we drive the ship."

"We'll see if we can discourage these guys from shooting at us," Readly told him.

Ramirez and his team took whatever cover they could find and returned the fire, even as the ship suddenly came to life and began backing away from the pier. It was not a time to worry about scratching paint, damaging a wharf, or denting the hull as the research vessel needed to quickly head down the channel and away from the Chinese marines before they could set up and fire something more damaging and deadly than bullets from their rifles.

The forward camel groaned in protest as *Deep Ocean*

Explorer pivoted on it and backed away from the wharf. The bow was barely clear when Bill Bix slammed the starboard throttle to "Full Forward," port "Full Back," and the rudder to "Hard Left." The research vessel, not designed for speed or maneuverability, lurched forward a couple of yards before the bow started to swing around, even as bullets pinged off her hull.

The Chinese charged forward, taking cover in the farmers' market while now concentrating their fire on the bridge in an attempt to keep the ship from escaping. Ramirez's fire team shot back, spraying the area to convince the Chinese to keep their heads down.

The bow missed the wharf by mere inches as it swung around. Dodging breaking glass and ducking low, Bix jammed both throttles to "Full Ahead" and swung the rudder to fair up with the outbound channel. Just then, an RPG round arced up and over the ship, exploding harmlessly in the water beyond.

Deep Ocean Explorer was just starting to round Utules Point when the Chinese dared to come out of their cover and ran out onto the pier. But now all they could do was watch the ship disappear around the bend.

Bill Bix steered them around the point and headed down the center of the Teleki Channel, whistling happily. He had his ship back and beneath him. He would soon pick up his crew in Samoa.

Dr. Rex Smith stood at the rail on the vessel's upper deck, still catching his breath and allowing the cool night sea breeze to dry the sweat from the unexpected jog. He watched the stars above, especially bright with the lack of light pollution and smog in this part of the world. He could not wait until he could once again referee the clashes between his dedicated group of scientists and technicians as they all did their best to unravel the mysteries of the world's great oceans.

Colonel Stanton Readly, Sergeant Fernando Ramirez, and the rest of the US Marines ate energy bars and then settled onto mats on the open deck in an effort to catch a few winks. If the last few hours told them anything, it was that there would likely be more battles soon. They best be prepared. But with hostages safely on their way to American Samoa and with no casualties, despite a hot firefight, this mission had been a success.

The open water of the Pacific was still seven miles away and at least an hour's steaming through the tortuously narrow channel. However, they were safe now. Safe and on their way to whatever was next.

22

The big black Mercedes limousine elbowed its way through thick Beijing evening traffic so it could make a right turn from Wudaoying Hutong onto Yonghegong Street. It then pulled to a stop almost immediately, much to the displeasure of several other drivers who had to jump on their brakes after making the same turn. The driver ignored the honking horns and angry stares as he hopped out of the car and hurried around the limo to open the passenger door on the curb side.

The horn-blowing and shouting stopped as the miffed drivers watched Li Min Zhou step from the Mercedes limo. She dismissed the driver with a wave of her hand.

Min Zhou stood there for a moment, considering her surroundings, seemingly admiring the neighborhood but actually looking for anything that did not belong. Anything that would pose a threat. She glanced at the dun-colored, stone-walled exterior of the traditional *siheyuan* courtyard house where they had stopped. Satisfied, she stepped up to the ornately carved, wooden, red-and-gold-painted entrance portal. As prescribed by *feng shui,* the entrance was on the southeast corner of the house. A doorman, dressed in the gold-embroidered silk *bufu* surcoat of an Imperial Court functionary, stood by the *Guangliang* Gate, the entrance traditionally reserved for the comings and goings of high court officials. Only the *Wangfu*—or Emperor's—Gate would be considered superior.

As she walked his way, the doorman bowed deeply and swung open the massive bright red door. He greeted her in formal Court Mandarin.

"This lowly servant welcomes the respected madam to the King Joy Restaurant."

Li Min Zhou smiled at the restaurant's attempts to leverage the flavor of the Forbidden City, which was only a couple of blocks away, and to summon up a bit of ancient Chinese atmosphere. It would certainly impress visiting businessmen or foreign governmental officials visiting the Chinese capital. Its opulence was also favored by the many bureaucrats who worked in the area. But while the courtyard house was, indeed, a couple of centuries old, the high-class and very expensive King Joy Restaurant was, in reality, owned by a Taiwanese businessman. And it was highly unlikely that an Imperial Court official, no matter how minor his station, had ever served as a doorman at the place.

Min Zhou entered a small reception hall where the maître d' greeted her with another deep, formal bow. He was dressed in an apricot-colored *jifu* dragon robe, an outfit with even more gold embroidery than the one the doorman wore.

It was no longer unusual for an unescorted female to arrive at the King Joy. Many patrons met their mistresses here. And even officially sanctioned businesses as well as the communist government were now more populated with women than even a few years ago.

The maître d' escorted her through an outer courtyard heavy with the scent of potted shrubs and flowers. Next, he led her through the festooned gate to an impressive inner court-yard, an area that was entirely glassed over, creating a large, airy dining room.

As she walked across the cobblestones of the courtyard, Li Min Zhou was more than aware that every male eye in the large room watched her. Her deep-blue silk dress clung to just the right curves, and the stiletto heels, along with the skirt's high slit, accentuated her long, shapely legs. The effect was intended to draw attention.

However, she was looking for only one pair of eyes. And there he was.

TJ Dillon sat alone at a small table along the west wall, studying his menu as he tapped his ear. That gesture told Li Min Zhou that the microphone and tiny radio transmitter she was wearing were working fine.

Finally, the maître d' escorted Li Min Zhou toward a secluded table near the back of the room at the southeast corner of the courtyard, one mostly hidden behind an ornately carved screen. She could just make out through the screen that someone was sitting at the table. As she had antici-pated, the party she was to meet was already present and seated.

Li Min Zhou stepped around the screen and into the secluded alcove. The dimly lit corner was illuminated only by a pair of tapers. Their flickering light and shadow played on the red silk damask wall covering.

"Good evening. I suppose introductions are in order," the middle-aged gentleman told her as he rose and extended a hand. "I am Yon Ba Deng. I assume you are Wang Fang." She nodded, smiling, as she took the offered hand and shook it before sitting across the table from him. "I must say that I was a bit surprised when my assistant informed me that I had a dinner meeting scheduled for this evening. It is rare that the office of the Chairman of the Military Commission calls and requests that I attend a discreet, off-the-record dinner." He smiled, disarmingly. "And if I may be frank, I was expecting some elderly and overweight Party functionary who most likely wanted to discuss the merits of his son or nephew immediately assuming command of one of our aircraft carriers or some such."

Li Min Zhou allowed herself a half smile as she acknowledged his little joke. The man's curiosity was apparent.

"And I am Wang Fang. I hope I am not disappointing you, then. I have heard much about you and I wanted to meet you, personally and outside the office. I am afraid that I need to confess to calling in a favor with the chairman's office to arrange our dinner and conversation. I thought that would save some time and avoid a lot of unwanted questions if I used this particular route."

A waiter was there already. After ordering their drinks and meals, Yon Ba Deng placed his hands flat on the table and looked directly at Li Min Zhou.

"When the 'invitation' came, I, as you would expect, made some discreet inquiries. Normally, my sources are quite effective in finding whatever information I need, particularly within the Party." He flipped his hands up. "This time they mostly came up empty. Practically nothing. Could you explain why someone who clearly has the ear of the Chairman of the Military Commission has left so few footprints?"

Li Min Zhou looked directly into his eyes.

"I am not surprised. Let us simply say that my contacts are very discreet even though they extend to a very high level. Allow me to strongly suggest that you leave it at that. And that you make no further inquiries about me or my association with others. Be assured that it could prove, ah...let us say...embarrassing for you. At this point, that will have to satisfy your boundless curiosity."

Yon Ba Deng frowned but nodded. He understood that she had given him a warning. Whether or not he would heed it was a different matter. That would depend on the remainder of the conversation.

The waiter arrived with two glasses of wine. Li Min Zhou tasted hers while Yon watched her.

"Ah, an excellent vintage," she remarked. "Even the French cannot produce a better Bordeaux than the 2009 Yantai." She swirled the wine gently in its glass and sniffed the bouquet approvingly. "Now, let us attempt to make the conversation as pleasant as the wine."

He took a sip of his own drink. Li Min Zhou could tell from the man's expression that he had not appreciated it at all.

"To get to the heart of the matter," she continued, "we are well aware of your ambition for advancement, in the military bureaucracy and beyond. We are also quite aware of your ongoing conflict with Soo Be Xian." The man still held the wine glass, but his eyes had widened ever so slightly. She knew he was on highest alert now. "The people with whom I work have been impressed with the gains you have made in your position as well as the way you play the game. They are convinced that your intuition, your cunning, and the logical and committed pursuit of power melds well with their goals."

Yon Ba Deng set the glass down and leaned forward.

"And your people fit into all this how?" he asked, almost in a whisper.

"They are in a position to assist you in the matter regarding Soo Be Xian. And they are prepared and fully capable to pave the way for you to advance much, much further up within the Party." She took another sip of her wine. "Let me give you a little sample. Perhaps we should call it 'a tasting.' Tomorrow morning, just after sunrise, Soo Be Xian will be arrested on charges of corruption. The evidence will show that there is one hundred million yuan in a Swiss bank account in his name. There will also be other evidence of kickbacks within the army in areas over which he has direct control."

"Soo Be Xian is crafty. How is it possible for the government to know and confirm these things?"

Li had to work hard to avoid a knowing smile. She knew fully well what Yon was thinking. If they knew of corruption by Soo Be Xian, they might also know of his own lucrative side hustles. She imagined TJ Dillon having the same suspicions as he listened in from across the dining room, but she managed to keep a straight face.

"They know what they know because we—my associates and I—arranged it. We all know he is corrupt. We simply needed to be sure enough of the confirming evidence— whether it was valid or not—would fall into the right hands. By the end of the week, Soo Be Xian will be pleading for his life. And he will no longer be an obstacle to your own plans."

Yon Ba Deng sat back and stared at the beautiful woman sitting across the table from him. She was mesmerizing. But he forced himself to clear his head and consider what she was telling him. If she or her people could take down his worst nemesis, then they could well be the allies that he needed. Of course, they could also be an enemy he could not afford. This scheme of theirs could be his golden opportunity or the seeds of his destruction.

His first thought was to wait, to learn what he would be required to do in order to repay his new benefactors. Only then would he agree to the terms.

But even before their meals arrived, Yon had already made

up his mind. The risks of dealing with this mysterious, gorgeous lady were absolutely worth the potential rewards.

Ψ

Soo Be Xian was startled awake by the loud pounding on the door of his compound. He looked out his bedroom window to see a constellation of flashing blue and red lights from a covey of police vehicles pulled over at odd angles wherever he could see out the window. Armed men in combat gear were hidden behind the vehicles, but he could easily make out others, crouching as they moved across the grass and then scaling the compound walls.

This was not good. Something bad had happened. Where were the servants and the security guards? Why was the house so quiet despite all the clamor outside?

Soo grabbed his cell phone. The instant he touched the device it dinged with a new text message. Bien Sung, his factotum, was warning him that the secret police, the dreaded and much feared *Guoanbu*, were about to arrive at his apartment. They were coming to arrest him.

Clearly the text from his assistant had come too late to do Soo any good.

He was just donning his robe when a second text message arrived. Major General Shun was informing Soo that both he and Colonel General Xiang were being taken into custody. He also requested that Soo immediately clear up whatever misunderstanding was playing out and have them freed.

As he walked out of his bedroom suite and headed across the inner courtyard toward the outer one, the steel reinforced wooden outer door suddenly crashed open, left hanging loosely on its hinges. Half a dozen heavily armed troops stormed through and took up shooting positions around the suite's broad outer courtyard. All of their weapons were pointed squarely at Soo Be Xian, who stood stunned in the doorway to the inner courtyard.

A small, rotund, middle-aged man in a business suit stepped in from outside and walked to the center of the outer courtyard. He brushed some dust from his lapel, looked over the tops of his spectacles, and took something from his inside coat pocket.

"Soo Be Xian," he intoned in a squeaky voice, reading from the official-looking document. "You are being placed under arrest for violation of the Criminal Laws of the People's Republic of China. You will be charged with official corruption and bribery of high officials, both crimes having been committed against the People and the Party."

The disbelieving Soo Be Xian started to protest but the man held up a dismissive hand.

"There is nothing that you can say for yourself here," the little man told him. He waved toward the leader of the armed troops. The officer slammed Soo Be Xian against the wall and quickly bound his hands tightly behind his back. The now-former leader of the Chinese military was roughly marched out to a waiting prison van.

Qincheng High Security Prison would be his next stop.

Commander Geoffrey Smythe was still entranced by the scene playing out on the large-screen flat panel, even though he had been watching it for a couple of weeks now. The Sagem Series 30 Advanced Optronics Mast was delivering a crystal-clear picture of the mayhem happening only thirty feet above his head. Chinese attack jets were making repeated passes at Dongsha Island, raining down missiles and bombs on the few square yards of real estate that barely qualified as an "island."

From Smythe's position, in the control room of the Australian submarine HMAS *Audacious*, the skipper could not imagine how anyone could survive such a prolonged and vicious pounding. But tracer fire still came up from the smoke to meet the dodging and weaving Chinese jets. Sporadically, a surface-to-air missile would roar up as well. And sometimes flaming wreckage fell from the sky as a result.

It was mostly an awful sight, though, and Smythe was watching it from a front-row seat. He had his submarine cruising only a mile off of Dongsha Island, watching and recording the events for the rest of the free world. Every evening, he would slip out a few miles to report back to

Submarine Command in Perth, all the while snorkeling so he could recharge the batteries for a bit. Then he would snake his way back in, close to the island again. It had become mostly routine, and it was apparent the Chinese were more interested in annihilating Dongsha than in detecting any observers in their midst.

Now it was time to again head back out to make yet another report. They were each pretty much the same lately. The PLAN warplanes pounded the island all day while the Taiwanese defenders did their best to shoot back. The only variables were how many of those planes attacked and how many managed to get themselves shot down by the determined and heroic Taiwanese on Dongsha.

Smythe was just about to order the boat deep when he was interrupted.

"Captain, Signals, picking up a Dragon Eye AESA radar. High signal strength. Probably in visual range. That type is typically carried on newer PLAN destroyers and carriers."

With a swing of the scope, Smythe did a quick three-sixty scan. He did not see any ships at all.

"Well, Signals, but I don't see..."

"Captain, Sonar, new broadband contact, Sierra Four-Six, bearing one-two-six. High-speed screws. Correlated to a destroyer type."

Then, when Smythe wheeled around to the reported bearing, he saw it. The Chinese destroyer was coming fast, emerging out of a rain squall on the horizon. Looked like a Type Fifty-Two.

This was a definite threat. It was time to hide. Best course of action was to slink out of here quietly.

"Helm, come right to course two-one-zero. Ahead one-third." *Audacious* slowly came around and headed south, away from the island. Hopefully away from the destroyer.

The Chinese ship turned broad. Suddenly, a column of flame shot up from the warship's forward deck. A missile headed up high into the sky, then arced over and raced directly toward the tiny island. Four more missiles quickly joined the first one.

Then Smythe watched as the forward gun mount on the destroyer's deck slewed around and commenced blasting away at the island, too. Jesus, the Aussie captain thought, they're trying to wipe that bit of coral right off the map!

"Captain, Sonar, receiving active sonar. Equates to a Chinese Type Fifty-Two VDS. High signal strength. Better than fifty percent probability of detection."

This was not good at all. The destroyer seemed to be looking for something or somebody. Smythe had to expect that any foreign submarines detected loitering about in this particular area would not be welcomed. This class of destroyer carried a CY-5 ASW missile. They packed a punch. A couple of those, dropped close aboard, would ruin a perfectly good day for a submarine.

Smythe ran the table, trying to find a good tactic to try. He could not hope to outrun the destroyer. And certainly not the bastard's ASW missiles. He probably could not hide, either. There was precious little water beneath the keel. And based on the sonar signal strength, they would be easily tracked.

That left one option. Fight. And, at the moment, getting off the first shot made the most sense. Who owned these waters would be immaterial if what was left of the Australian boat and her crew were in the mud on the bottom.

Smythe turned to his XO. "First Officer, set up on the destroyer. Set your best solution. Surface tactics. Make tube one ready in all respects."

The XO turned pale but immediately set to work. Meanwhile, Smythe did a quick calculation in his head. With the destroyer five miles away, the Mark 48 ADCAP torpedo he was setting up to fire would take about five minutes to get to the Chinese vessel.

On the other hand, the destroyer's CY-5 ASW missile could make the distance in about seven seconds. The math was discouraging. It was way beyond a long shot that they would somehow get their asses out of this particular sling.

"Captain, Signals, receiving terminal homing radar, RIM-84A Harpoon missiles. Probably several."

Harpoons? The Chinese would not have Harpoons. Smythe looked at the flat panel just in time to see six of the big surface-to-surface missiles flash across the screen in the distance. It was like watching a video game screen as he saw the Chinese destroyer's close-in defense system perform as designed and splash three of the deadly weapons.

But the other three smashed into the ship's superstructure with stunning results. There was a split-second delay before great gouts of fire leapt up from the stricken vessel.

Smythe knew there was no time to stay and watch the show or try to determine who had just saved his bacon. With one of their ships badly damaged—likely done for—the Chinese would be mad as hell and looking for any other potential threat in the vicinity.

This was not a place for a slow diesel submarine to hang around and see what happened next.

"Dive, make your depth two-hundred feet. All ahead standard," Smythe ordered. "First Officer, let's clear datum for a couple of hours. That will put us twenty miles out. Draft up a message to Submarine Command with what we've seen today. Make it good. They're likely going to think we're crackers."

Ψ

Yon Ba Deng walked swiftly, leaving behind his office in one of the gray cement monstrosities that had been so unimaginatively named "the West Building Complex." But the name was actually quite descriptive of the buildings' reason for existing. They were nothing more than a compound of simple, utilitarian offices. Most of the buildings in Zhongnanhai—the true center of power for the People's Republic and the Party—had been built and named long ago, during the far more creative and colorful Imperial period. His destination, Qinzheng Hall, was a prime example. Originally constructed by the Kangxi emperor way back in the seventeenth century as the main hall of his palace complex, it now housed the office of the General Secretary of the Party, by far the most powerful man in all of China, a nation of almost a billion and a half people.

Yon Ba Deng had been sitting in his office, reviewing the reports from the Dongsha Island attacks, when the call came from the general secretary's office. The general secretary desired to speak with him privately at the Assistant Vice Deputy to the Minister of National Defense for Naval Matter's earliest convenience. Yon Ba Deng did not hesitate. He immediately closed the report, dropped it on his desk, and bounded out the door with only a quick word to his assistant about who he was going to see. It was understood by everyone who mattered that when Tan Yong requested the presence of someone "at your earliest convenience," it actually meant "at this instant" would not be soon enough to honor the summons.

Yon Ba Deng normally enjoyed—one of the very few things he truly enjoyed beyond work—the short walk along the Southern Sea Lake to the Qinzheng Hall. Today, however, there was no time to tarry in the Garden of Abundant Beneficence or pause and gaze over at the temple on Yingtai Island.

When he arrived at the general secretary's office, Yon was escorted into a small, darkened conference room. No one else was there. He sat in near-darkness, the silence only broken by the ticking of a clock somewhere in the room. Yon was beginning to worry that he had been forgotten when the lights abruptly flashed on. Tan Yong rushed in, unaccompanied by an advisor or bodyguard, and closed the door behind him. Yon Ba Deng jumped up and gave a quick bow toward the Chinese leader.

Tan Yong ignored him as he plopped down into a chair at the head of the small conference table. Only then did he motion for Yon Ba Deng to sit in the one to his right. Yon took that as a very positive sign.

"I am unhappy with the situation with Dongsha Island," Tan Yong began without any prelude or pleasantries. "The rebels have just upped the ante with this missile attack. Are we going to be able to save the *Qiqihar*?"

"Honorable General Secretary, the ship was treacherously attacked by the Taiwanese rebels on the island. They somehow managed to sneak in at least six American Harpoon missiles, of which we were not aware. Another breach in our military intelligence, I am afraid. It seems some, unaware of the potential ramifications, have paid little attention to this particular speck of territory. The *Qiqihar* was quite skillful in destroying three of the missiles before they could strike, but the other three, I regret to report, caused severe damage and great loss of life. The ship is now being towed back to Ngong Shuen Chau Naval Base for repairs, if feasible. The fires are almost extinguished at last report."

"Thank you, Assistant Vice Deputy to the Minister of National Defense for Naval Matters," Tan Yong said with formality, frowning and shaking his head sadly. "Thank you for your candor. A most regrettable tragedy and, even worse, a severe loss of face for all China, but especially PLAN." The president shifted gears with a wave of his hand. "After the shameful discovery of the indiscretions by Soo Be Xian, I find that we now need a reliable person to head our military organization. The Committee has decided to place great trust in you and immediately appoint you as Vice Deputy to the Minister of National Defense. You will also become the Party Assistant Secretary for National Defense. We will, of course, discuss the details of your new role later. Now, we have more urgent priorities that we will ask you to address immediately. We must determine how we are to deal with the rebels on Taiwan and the loss of respect that they have inflicted on us and our nation. And that will be your first duty."

Yon Ba Deng maintained a stoic face, but inside, he was ecstatic. Li Min Zhou had honored her promise. Yon had no idea how she had done it, but that woman had precisely predicted what was going to happen. Somehow, she had helped to point his career skyward, pushing him up another rung of the ladder, just as she told him she would.

The lovely lady was, indeed, proving to be a very valuable ally. Perhaps she could eventually assist him to become the one sitting at the head of this table.

"*Zongshuji*," Yon responded to the general secretary. "I have, of course, been studying this matter and have some ideas I can share with you. First, I am convinced that now is not the time to turn away and ignore the Taiwanese uprising. That would only signal to the rest of the world weakness and a lack of resolve, as well as give leverage to those insurgents on Formosa and within our own nation. Nor is it the time to answer with overwhelming force, of which we are certainly capable. We need to find a middle ground. One where we can regain face but also where we are most likely to not become involved in an all-out war with the Americans and their allies."

"Is there such a path?" Tan Yong asked doubtfully, leaning forward. "I agree that starting a war with the Americans is not in our interests at this time. It would be counterproductive since we already bleed their economy and will eventually surpass them as the world's top financial power. And we are also aware that they and especially their president have no will to employ their military. Against us or anyone else. Besides, we have already paid highly for significant influence with their most powerful politicians. So, what is this path of which you speak?"

Yon placed the fingertips of each hand together and slowly brought them to his chin. It was a well-practiced gesture, designed to make him appear even more astute.

"We simply declare a state of emergency," Yon Ba Deng responded. "We announce that because of the violent, murderous attacks on our sovereign ships and territory by the rebel terrorists, henceforth any military ships or planes within two hundred and fifty kilometers of Chinese territory will be treated as hostile and they will be attacked. But first, it will be necessary to deploy our submarines around Taiwan and Dongsha in order to back up our position should that become necessary. In the process, we totally isolate Taiwan until they come to their senses and abandon what is left of that worthless little island garrison. Then it is they who lose face, and we are a major step closer to finally claiming our rightful territory of Formosa Island."

Tan Yong smiled. He seemed pleased with Yon's answer.

"So, as justification, we will use the strategy that the Americans employed in the fiasco they called the 'Cuban Missile Crisis.' They claimed the right to embargo all military equipment from Cuba because the Russians had shipped missiles there. We will do the same for Taiwan because those were American missiles that killed our brave sailors." Tan Yong thought for a moment and then added, "The Americans have conveniently announced that they will not approach closer than four hundred kilometers. The American president, Smitherman, has personally assured me that this is only a political maneuver, a show of *gaowan* for his voters. Nothing for China to fear. Excellent. Put the plan in motion immediately...Mr. Vice Deputy."

Ψ

The alarm bells began ringing from multiple intelligence sources around the world. It appeared that every single Chinese PLAN submarine not previously deployed had begun to disappear from their mooring piers. Images from satellites maintained by several governments normally showed naval bases along the South China Sea and up into the East China Sea to be crowded with black hulls. They were suddenly empty. The analysts were at a loss to explain this unprecedented deployment of submersibles by the People's Liberation Army Navy.

Then Xinhua, the official Chinese News Agency, announced a military embargo around all sovereign Chinese territory, specifically including the "Province of Taiwan." This action was in direct response to the brutal assault on a Chinese vessel in territorial waters. An attack launched by a rebel force on Dongsha Island. An unprovoked attack in which American weapons were used.

A similar message went out through the usual diplomatic channels.

Almost simultaneously, sources maintained by Li Min Zhou—and relayed to Naval Intelligence via Jim Ward—

reported the approval by the Chinese president of the new stance, but with a bit more nuance than the official news report. Regardless of its delivery method, though, it was indeed a strong and dangerous message. The world had now been warned that all military traffic, whether ship or aircraft, that encroached within the embargoed area would be deemed hostile.

Appropriate action would be taken to protect the lives of Chinese citizens and the autonomy of its territory.

Ψ

Jon Ward steered the subcompact rental car out of Honolulu Airport and turned left onto Nimitz Highway toward the Pearl Harbor Naval Base. But rather than merging into the traffic heading toward the Nimitz Gate, he eased to the right onto Kamehameha Highway, toward Pearl City. As he passed the rusty steel monument of Aloha Stadium, he again merged right, this time onto the Aiea Access Road, and soon passed over H-1, one of Hawaii's three "interstate" highways. He glanced down at the bumper-to-bumper traffic heading out toward Ewa and the leeward communities. Rush hour in Paradise!

The Access Road ended at a T-intersection. Ward waited for the light to change and then turned left out Moanalua Road. He was out of the dense urban area surrounding the airport, commercial facilities, and military bases and now in a modest residential area. A couple of blocks farther, Ward turned right again onto Aiea Heights Drive. This was an area where the Ko'olau Mountains came down to meet Pearl Harbor. Aiea Drive snaked up a sharp, steep ridgeline, winding back and forth as it ascended the ridge toward the mountain heights beyond. Houses on the left clung to the steep slopes, the terrain dropping away to a green canyon. Those dwellings on the right were built up on terraces of black lava rock. Occasionally a street would drop off to the left and snake down to the canyon floor below or shoot off to the right to serve houses that had been built above.

Finally, the road made a sharp turn to the right, affording Ward a magnificent view of Pearl Harbor, now two thousand feet below. He made a turn onto another quiet residential street. Down at the end, at the very last driveway, he saw the house number: 99-1750. The blue-and-gold dolphin flag confirmed he had located the place he sought.

He had found Tom Donnegan's retirement roost.

When Ward pulled into the driveway, he recognized Tom's battered old Land Rover filling up the carport. He had barely parked the rental when Tom Donnegan came barreling out of the house with surprising speed for one so elderly and engulfed him in a huge bear hug.

"Jon, my boy," Donnegan growled. "Where the hell have you been keeping yourself? You been neglecting your old Papa Tom."

Tom Donnegan and Jon Ward had a long history. Donnegan had been the XO on a submarine skippered by Ward's father. That had been the case when Ward's dad was tragically killed while on a highly classified mission. Jon had been a very young boy at the time. But after that, Donnegan had been like a father for Ward as he was growing up. That had not changed after Ward was appointed to the US Naval Academy. He became young Ward's mentor and then his boss throughout his career before Donnegan retired from his job as the Navy's top spy.

It was only natural that when Donnegan stepped down, he made certain Jon Ward took over the job.

"You're right, Papa Tom. I'm going to blame it on the

requirements of the job, but I know that's a pretty shabby excuse."

"Yeah, the job," Donnegan said with a nod. "Seem to remember it chewed up and spit out a lot of my time and attention, too." He grabbed Ward's valise from his hand and motioned for him to follow him into the house. "But how's Jim-boy doing? I heard he got himself winged again. Just like his dad. Not smart or quick enough to duck when the shooting starts."

"The boy has a real knack for falling into a pile of it and then finding a rose," Ward said with a laugh. "Is that even a metaphor? Anyway, last time I talked with him, he was set up in some high roller's suite in Taipei. He has some Taiwanese muscle at his beck and call, involved in an operation with...well... I'll spare the old retired dude the details for the time being."

Besides, something smelled wonderful.

"Louise is fixing us a pupu platter and mai tais. Speaking of spouses, when the hell are you bringing Ellen out for a vacation? We got a whole suite set up for you downstairs."

"She's ready, believe me. But somebody who shall remain nameless quit his job and left me so much work to do that..."

Donnegan waved for him to stop his complaining and motioned for Ward to follow him out onto the lanai. Ward stepped through the sliding screen door onto a shaded stone deck.

"Wow! This is beautiful!" The deck was crowded with orchids of all varieties, and it seemed that they were all in bloom, covering every square inch in vivid purples, reds, yellows, and vibrant whites. The tropical perfume was intoxicating. And beyond the flowers, the view was spectacular. Pearl Harbor and the submarine base stretched out far below them. From here, Donnegan had an unobstructed view all the way past Hickam Air Force Base to the broad, blue Pacific Ocean beyond. And just to reinforce the myth that Donnegan still kept close tabs on his beloved SUBPAC submarines from his lofty perch, a large spotting telescope rested on a tripod at the lanai's edge.

Ward touched one of the orchids.

"Man, Ellen would be in heaven here."

Ward's wife—and Jim's mother—was a botany professor and specialized in the Orchidaceous family of flowers.

Donnegan waved Ward to a pair of wicker chairs sitting on either side of a small matching table. The old top spook pointedly put Ward's valise in the middle of the table. Though Ward had not told him the reason for his trip, Donnegan appeared to be fully aware this was not merely a social stopover.

Ward took a deep breath before resignedly opening his briefcase. He, too, would like to visit and tell sea stories a bit longer. He pulled out some files.

"Papa Tom, you told me if I ever needed some help, I'd know where to find you."

"So, I'm not just an excuse for a free trip to paradise, huh?"

Ward handed a thick file folder to Donnegan. He riffled through the papers. As always, the old top spy was a quick study.

"Yep, this is interesting, and not in a good way," he mumbled as he read. "This Taiwanese woman, Li Min Zhou, she came to visit me a few months ago. She was looking for some advice, too. She is one very well-connected woman. And not bad on the eyes, either."

Donnegan looked to the door quickly, making sure Louise, his wife of more than fifty years, had not heard his last comment.

Ward smiled. "Yeah, she told me about her visit with you.

I'm not sure that I can totally trust her, but she seems to have some spectacularly good resources in China. And it appears she is heading up this deal they have Jim working on. That, of course, involves me and my office on a number of levels."

Donnegan nodded. "One thing you can be sure of, she is on your side only as far as it helps Taiwan and confounds the military and government of the People's Republic of China. So, I'd say as long as our interests remain aligned with hers, we are good. But if they ever aren't, she is Taiwanese. And, I suspect, she's somebody we do not want to get crosswise with. Something tells me she could carve you up and have you filleted before you ever started bleeding. Anyway, from what I'm hearing, she's probably somebody who can help us, considering."

Ward nodded his agreement. He was not surprised Donnegan was still plugged in. "Yep. That's about the way I figured it. And with all the elephants dancing around on this Dongsha thing, I'm just trying to keep from getting trampled. We have been playing this 'Taiwan-Two Chinas' game for long enough. I think we can work it out. And you have confirmed my feelings on Li Min Zhou." He pulled another file out and offered it to Donnegan. "This is what I really want to talk to you about. It's way, way out of my field. But it has landed squarely in the middle of my desk."

Donnegan leafed through it as Louise brought out the mai tais. She gave Ward a long hug and asked him about Ellen, then told him the food was coming soon and disappeared back into the house. She, too, knew the drill, that business took precedence.

The old spy whistled softly as he read. "Is this estimate real? This guy, this Dr. Smith—I've heard of him—he's estimating that there's something like a million tons of gold down there. Jon, do you know what this means? There has only been something like two hundred thousand tons of gold mined in all of human history. This is five times that much. Even if he is off by a power of ten..."

Jon Ward was shaking his head, perplexed.

"I slept through all my economics classes, Papa Tom, but something tells me a discovery like this could have a negative impact besides just all the greedy shenanigans it would—and already has—set loose."

Tom Donnegan took a long sip of his Hawaiian mai tai—a variation of the cocktail known locally as mia tia—without tasting it. He frowned as he gazed out at the breathtaking view, not seeing it, thinking.

"If the world's markets were to get wind of this, and if there was a reasonable chance somebody has the technology to go way down there and get the stuff...Lord help us. That alone is more than enough to collapse the entire world economy."

Ψ

Jon Ward had another stop to make while he was on Oahu. This one was not going to involve pupus or mai tais. He needed to get over to Camp Smith, the headquarters for the US Indo-Pacific Command. There, he would meet with Admiral Rufus Clark, who ran that command.

Although he could easily see Admiral Clark's office building from Tom Donnegan's lanai, it was across a deep canyon. Ward had to retrace his route down from Aiea Heights and then climb back up Halawa Heights to Camp Smith, all while fighting traffic and the ill-handling subcompact rental car.

Admiral Clark met Jon Ward at the entrance to the head-quarters building and immediately ushered him down to the

SCIF, which was buried in the building's basement, safely away from prying eyes.

Ward well knew that Admiral Clark and his staff were extremely busy, frantically moving the fleet to counter the Chinese threat against Taiwan while also juggling all the other crises in an area of responsibility that covered half of the globe. Ward eschewed the normal pleasantries and got right down to business.

"Admiral, I asked to meet with you to discuss the current Chinese submarine deployment," he began, "and to brief you about a capability that you may not have been read in on." Ward went on to quickly explain how his Office of Naval Intelligence and a certain three-letter government agency had cooperated in developing and deploying a very sophisticated undersea tracking system. And how it had come about under the cover of being a seismic warning system for the Taiwanese Office of Earthquake Preparedness. They had the system operational and had recently successfully tested it. This had been accomplished without the Taiwanese and very few Americans being aware of its existence or its many capabilities.

Clark shook his head. "Jon, you sure this thing actually works? Sounds awful Buck Rogers sci-fi to me."

"It's what we used to detect and track the *Boise* and then warn her of that noisy screw problem she had. A real-world test, if you will. If we can detect and track one of our own boats that far away, I'm pretty confident that we can track the Chinese right there on top of the system."

Clark again shook his head and frowned. The frustration was heavy in his voice. "That's all fine and dandy, but as you know, the president has our hands firmly bound with the rules of engagement he required. Basically, we can't get within four hundred miles of Taiwan and we can't shoot at anything or anybody unless we have already been shot at. He's afraid we're going to get all trigger-happy and start World War III unless we are firmly hog-tied. And he's pretty sure such a thing might affect his chances for re-election or prevent him from getting the Nobel Peace Prize or something."

Ward scratched his chin but grinned. "I figured that might be the case. But I think I have the solution. We won't violate the president's orders and we won't shoot at anybody. The key here is we need to chase the Chinese subs back into their ports and blow the doors off this phony embargo. And the people who can do that are the Taiwanese. We simply vector them to the Chinese subs, based on the seismic warning system data we're collecting, and give them a way to ring the subs' chimes without sinking them."

"You got a way to do that? Cause if you do, I'm damned impressed."

"Actually, I think I do," Ward answered. "We give them the positions of the PLAN submarines without telling them where the information came from. Then we provide them with a planeload of our new very lightweight torpedoes. Something called a CRAW, a Compact Rapid Attack Weapon. Those babies are programmed to go after a boat's screw when we use them for ASW. They're not big enough to really do any serious or deadly damage to anybody's modern boats, but they will take out a screw. We just happen to have several pallets of them over at the torpedo facility at West Loch. If we get moving, we can have them loaded and ready to use by Taiwanese P-3s by tomorrow morning."

Admiral Clark gave Ward a long, hard look.

"Damn, Jon. Buck Rogers ain't got nothing on you!"

Ψ

Jim Ward looked up and then smiled broadly as his father

walked into his room unannounced. The young SEAL had been doing some calisthenics, trying to ease his sore body back into some level of fitness. The traffic he had been perusing as he passed it on to the ONI in the Pentagon suggested he might soon need to be agile, mobile, and hostile. His Taiwanese bodyguards had set up some gym equipment in the suite, but they still were not allowing him to roam around Taipei alone. That made it impossible for him to get back on his running regimen. Not that he was sure his body was up to it yet, anyway.

The younger Ward grabbed a towel and wiped some of the sweat from his hands and arms before grabbing his father in a bear hug.

"Dad, great to see you again, but I assumed you were back in DC..."

Jon Ward returned the hug, vigorously enough to shut off any questions.

"Great to see you, too, Jim-boy!" He pulled back and gave his son a look. "Hey, looks like you are getting back into fighting shape. You got a drink for an old, dehydrated sub sailor?"

The bodyguards, who had been working out with Jim, discreetly disappeared into the next room, almost as if they had been forewarned about the visit from the Navy's top spook. The SEAL stepped over to a small refrigerator and grabbed a couple of beers.

"I'm developing a real liking for these Taiwanese beers." He offered a bottle to his father. "Here, try this. It's called Formosa Bird Beer."

Jon frowned incredulously but took a swig anyway.

"Hey, not bad. Not bad at all."

The elder Ward glanced around the plush setting, then stepped over to the expansive plate glass door and out onto the small balcony. He took another big drink of the beer as he leaned against the rail and looked out over early-evening Taipei, stretched out below him like a carpet of blinking lights. Jim followed his father out onto the balcony and stood silently next to him for a bit.

"Very nice," Jon Ward finally said. "Certainly has a better view than any of the patient rooms at Walter Reed."

"Okay, Dad. This place is not bugged. It's swept every couple of days. Go ahead and tell me what you need to tell me."

Jon Ward reached into his pants pocket and handed his son a small slip of paper.

"Son, give this number and password to Li Min Zhou, then flush it. Tell her to call it, but only on a secure line. The people there will give her the URL address to a secure website. There she will find real-time location information for all of the Chinese submarines within five hundred miles of Taiwan, and that includes all those boats that have so suddenly been put to sea in the last couple of days. And tell her that several pallets are being unloaded at the Taoyuan Airport FEDEX air cargo terminal with her name on them. I suggest that she gets them to her navy."

Jim looked sharply at his father. "Dad, how in hell did...?"

"Don't ask. And tell Miss Li not to ask any questions about the source of the data either."

"Understood."

Jon Ward drained the last of his Formosa Bird Beer. He turned to his son, grabbed the SEAL's shoulder with his free hand, and looked him directly in the eyes.

"Jim, for the first time in my life, I'm thankful you didn't follow your old man into submarines."

Ψ

Forty miles south and east of the Tongan island of Niuatoputapu and ten miles below the ocean's surface, the Tonga Plate, under unimaginable geological stress, abruptly slid upward a few meters. In the process, it shoved the Pacific Plate down about the same distance. The movement occurred along a fault a few dozen miles long. The resulting tremor was enough to rattle windows in Hihifo, the small village that claimed to be the capital of Niuatoputapu. Few islanders even noticed. Such minor quakes were a regular occurrence there.

It was enough to register on seismographs in Sydney and Wellington. Even the Taiwanese seismic sensor, over five thousand miles away, detected the shock.

Geologists in those spots made notes after observing the tremble on their instruments—far from any significant human population and no threat to produce a tidal wave—but they had no way to see the other effects of the fracture at such depths. Not the new contour of the ocean floor along the plate. Nor the white-hot magma that began to ooze up through the crack in the sea floor like blood from a very nasty wound.

24

Joe Glass stepped out of his office onto the catwalk. Being up on the 05 level of the *Chesty Puller* gave him a real front-row seat to watch any ship coming into or departing Pago Pago. Today, he was watching the one piece of firepower that Big Navy could spare for his needs, if you could reasonably call it firepower. But the rest of the fleet, with the real ships, was flexing its muscles and churning up the waters off of Taiwan. This was all that was available unless he wanted an ocean-going tug.

The *Independence*-class littoral combat ship *Canberra* steamed past Breakers Point and into Pago Pago Harbor. The ship's twenty-five-hundred-mile trek from Pearl Harbor had taken nearly a week, but Glass at last had a ship that he could put to good use. The mottled-gray, all-aluminum trimaran attracted plenty of attention from pleasure boaters as it slowly made its way down the channel and moored alongside the *Chesty Puller*. The little ship's masts barely came level with the ESB's massive helo deck.

Glass gazed down at the warship and mentally began to inventory its capabilities. The little fifty-seven-millimeter cannon on the bow might be useful against King Two-for-One's ancient patrol boats but nothing any bigger. The Naval Strike Missiles she carried would be of very little use. There simply wouldn't be any targets for those bad boys.

Glass nodded. He decided that he might at least use the *Canberra* as a high-speed, sea-going pickup truck, just like a long-ago Chief of Naval Operations had described it.

Ψ

The P-3C Orion anti-submarine aircraft—tail number Three-Three-Zero—taxied out to take its place in line for takeoff. They were sixth in line, behind a flight of four F-16s, each of them fully armed and heading to the fight over Dongsha Island, and yet another P-3C. Six more aircraft were soon in line behind Three-Three-Zero, awaiting their turns to get airborne.

Pingtung Air Base was the closest airfield that Taiwan had to support the fight at Dongsha. That meant it was now serving as the temporary home to most of Taiwan's attack and fighter aircraft. Every revetment and tie-down space was crowded with planes and the equipment required to service them. Landings and takeoffs were nearly constant.

Finally, Three-Three-Zero swung onto runway two-six, spooled up the four big Allison turbos to full power, then roared down the runway and into the hazy morning air. While the F-16s climbed high into the atmosphere and headed southwest, Three-Three-Zero stayed down on the deck instead and headed east, toward the newly risen sun. It climbed just high enough to clear the Chungyang Mountains, the range that formed the island's rocky central spine. Once clear of those mountains, the lumbering bird dropped low again and thundered across the coastline, finally heading out to sea.

Three-Three-Zero's designated patrol box was a one-hundred-by-one-hundred-mile square that reached from the southern tip of Taiwan across the Luzon Strait to the Batanes Islands. Out to the east, it stretched across a hundred miles of what appeared to be an empty Philippine Sea. It was a huge piece of real estate to patrol, but Taiwan's air anti-submarine-warfare assets were very limited. There were only a dozen or so P-3s and about an equal number of MH-60 helicopters, all hand-me-downs from the US, and they were tasked with patrolling hundreds of thousands of square miles. It was a case of a few hunters looking for some very dangerous needles in a very large haystack. They simply did the best they could with what they had.

So far, that had been enough to keep them safe and free.

Three-Three-Zero had just entered its patrol box when a new target suddenly appeared on the data link. In their pre-flight mission brief, the crew had been told that they might receive targeting over this particular data link, based on intel reports. They were also instructed to immediately prosecute any target they received that way. This was very much out of the ordinary. Those particular intel reports were typically days old and useless.

The pilot followed orders. He flew the aircraft to the reported target coordinates and lined up to drop a row of sonobuoys across the area. ASW was a frustrating job. It was often called "Awfully Slow Warfare" for a reason. Especially in this part of the world. Submarines never surfaced and invited attention. And despite the emphasis on reacting to information from this data link, the pilot hardly expected to find anything down there. But he was bound to take a look, even if only to break the monotony.

"Madman! Madman! Madman!" the sensor operator hollered.

His magnetic anomaly detection meter swung wildly. Bingo! There was a big hunk of iron below the surface of the sea, just a couple of hundred feet below them. However, looking out the plane's window, they could see nothing but blue water and white wavetops.

The sonobuoys had only just dropped their sensitive hydrophones when the operator called out again. He announced that the sonobuoy data confirmed that they had themselves a submarine. And it had intruded well within the territorial waters claimed by Taiwan. Whoever was there was fair game.

As the P-3 swung around to line up again, the bomb-bay doors rolled open. A six-inch-diameter compact rapid attack weapon dropped out of the aircraft and splashed into the water two-hundred feet below. The sonobuoy operator listened as the submarine obviously heard the CRAW and began to frantically try to avoid the onrushing torpedo.

It was too late. The small weapon homed in on the sub's single screw, just as it was designed to do. The fish's two-kilo shape charge was not nearly large enough to do any significant damage if it hit anywhere else on its target. But it was more than powerful enough to knock a blade off the screw. The vibrations from the unbalanced spinning mass immediately began to violently shake the submarine, destroying the boat's electric drive train even before the crew could get the shaft stopped. The hydrophones heard and relayed every decibel of agonizing noise.

The black submarine suddenly shot to the surface. There it lay, dead in the water. The warship was not going to steam anywhere anytime soon.

Three-Three-Zero's mission commander was still in the

process of reporting they had successfully given one PLAN submarine a severe case of hemorrhoids when the same data link chirped once more, directing the P3 to a second contact.

By the time Three-Three-Zero's crew had finished their mission and were headed back to Pingtung with bomb bays empty, the comms channel was clogged with reports of similar successful attacks, all against subs in the waters near Taiwan. Thirty aircraft reported that they had gained positive contact on Chinese submarines and every one of them had carried out successful attacks.

Much of China's submarine force was adrift on the surface, in plain sight. And most of the world's military watched them with great interest on images sent down from various satellites.

Ψ

Yon Ba Deng was mystified and angry. But more than anything, he was fearful. Fearful his new promotion would now be yanked from him. Or worse.

His brilliant scheme to isolate Taiwan with his submarines—the plan he had sold to Tan Yong, China's president—had been underway for barely a day and it was already coming apart. Somehow, almost half of his navy's submarines had been delayed in departing by some mechanical problem or the other. Several others were reportedly limping back to port, broken before they ever reached their patrol area. And now the reports were flooding in from those boats that did make it to their patrol areas. Almost all of them had been located, attacked, and damaged. Several reported that they were barely able to make minimal speed and were heading for the nearest naval base, but necessarily on the surface. Most were requesting a tow home. Even more troubling were the three boats that had not yet reported in at all.

Yon Ba Deng ran his fingers through his thinning hair. He needed his brother to help him with the complexities of this most distressing submarine problem. But he was off creating diversions near Tonga. And, hopefully, figuring out a way to begin harvesting the gold near the Tonga Trench. Maybe Yon Hun Glo had some insight into whatever magic anti-submarine detection system and weaponry the Taiwanese seemed to suddenly have at their disposal.

Systems that appeared to have somehow made the ocean transparent. How else could they have located and successfully attacked so many of his invisible vessels?

But Yon Ba Deng feared his most serious problem was how to explain this failure to Tan Yong. He was not a man who tolerated failures.

Then something occurred to him. Maybe Li Min Zhou, with all her high-level connections, would have an answer that would satisfy the general secretary. Or at least an idea of how he might shift the blame to someone else.

He quickly reached for his phone, found her number in his contact list, and hit the "Call" icon.

Ψ

Yon Hun Glo stood watching the research ship *Zhang Jian* back away from the pier. The time had finally come to go after the gold at the bottom of the Tonga Trench. That fool, King Tofuwanga II, had only riled up the Americans when he launched the assault on Niue. Then again when he captured their research ship and held the crew captive on Neiafu. And to top it off, his total incompetence had allowed the Americans to raid the island, freeing the prisoners and stealing their ship back, all before Yon could get the bulk of his marines there to prevent it.

Fortunately, the Americans were finally occupied elsewhere, just as the submariner and his brother had intended all along. All their ships—a truly stunning number of vessels—were steaming to Taiwan's aid, token as it ultimately appeared to be. The *Deep Ocean Explorer* was probably back in Pago Pago by now. No other American ship had come out to bother him.

The sun was setting in the west and lights were blinking on in Nuku'alofa as the *Zhang Jian* steamed up the narrow channel and disappeared around Talafo'ou Point. Yon Hun Glo wearily walked down the pier and climbed up the brow to the main deck of the container ship *Pearl Moon*. This vessel would be his new home and office for the next few weeks.

At the end of that time, he fully expected him and his brother to be the wealthiest people on the planet.

Yon stepped over to one of the containers on the ship's deck. It was painted a rusty, sun-bleached red. The Japanese lettering on its side proclaimed that the big cargo box contained several tons of construction equipment. He gave the side of the container three hard raps, paused, then two more. A marine guard swung open a door for the admiral. A door that had been carefully hidden in the big freight box's side. He stepped into a brightly lit office space.

The containers on this level had been interconnected to form a hidden command center, complete with covert, secure data linkage back to Yon Hun Glo's headquarters on Hainan Island, and from there directly and securely to his brother in Beijing.

Yon Hun Glo quickly reviewed the printed reports a staff member handed to him. They were from his four submarines, verifying that they were each ready to sortie out of this tropical harbor. Satisfied, he wound his way through the labyrinth of containers. Along the way, he observed at least a dozen people busily at work. He followed directional signs until he reached a doorway that opened out onto the deck, right next to the ladder that led up to the *Pearl Moon*'s bridge.

He took a moment to look at all the other containers lined up and stacked on the ship's deck. Most were empty. And ready to fill with pure gold dust retrieved from the bottom of the sea.

Night had fallen and the harbor waters glistened blackly as Yon Hun Glo watched each of the submarines back away from the *Pearl Moon* and then head down the ship channel, around Talafo'ou Point. Finally, it was his turn. The *Pearl Moon* headed out toward the open sea after the boats.

The Chinese admiral smiled as he sipped from his cup of tea. Dawn's light would reveal that piers in the little harbor were now empty. The Americans and their satellites would almost certainly be able to soon spot the *Zhang Jian* and the *Pearl Moon*, but only after some frantic searching. There was nothing he could do to hide them, but there was nothing the Americans could do either. By noon tomorrow he would have an escort of Tongan patrol boats. And the Americans would have no idea that four PLAN submarines were steaming along on their mission several hundred feet below.

Then, unbeknownst to Yon or anyone else in the convoy, as the ship transited the channel, *Pearl Moon* passed directly over the bottom sensors that ORCA One had planted weeks ago. Just like the five other times already this evening, the sensors uplinked the detection to an orbiting communications satellite.

By the time the *Pearl Moon* had come around to steady up in the Avi Piha channel, Steve Weiss, who was sitting in the

Portland's Combat Information Center, had already ordered ORCA One to catch up with and intercept the vessels.

Then he placed a very interesting call over to Commodore Joe Glass.

Ψ

Joe Glass was already busy reviewing his resources and matching them up against what the Chinese were throwing at him. The call from Steve Weiss gave new urgency to his evaluation. The PLAN had four modern AIP conventional subs and a couple of civilian ships, plus a considerable number of well-trained marines close by on Niue. And for all intents and purposes, that king over on Tonga, being an enthusiastic and willing ally of the Chinese, could provide a few assets of his own if the shooting started.

Against that, Glass had two subs, the *Cheyenne*, which was already out on patrol, and the *George Mason*, which was now heading toward them. With those PLAN subs on the loose, and with the Chinese suddenly so willing to expend ordnance for whatever reason, he simply could not risk sending either the *Chesty Puller* or the *Portland* out to sea unless all-out war flared up. Additionally, Stanton Readly had a battalion of his battle-tested Marines ready to go, but his only means to deploy them were a couple of Ospreys and MH-53Ks. The newest arrival, *Canberra*, rounded out his available shooters. And he had very little chance of getting any backup from "Big Navy" with them all wrapped up around Taiwan. That left Glass with the problem of how to put these limited assets to work to head off whatever the Chinese intended to do.

But what were their intentions? Most everyone really in the know was certain they did not want war. That the attack on the Taiwanese island, the sudden scrambling of their submarine fleet, and the smoke and noise they were making around Tonga and Niue were clearly an attempt to distract the world's attention from something else.

It had to be the gold. Intel from some new and super-reliable source confirmed they knew about the find. It also made sense that whoever controlled that amount of glittery stuff had a stranglehold on the world's economy. But knowing where it was and managing to pull it up from over six miles down were two different things. Mining at depths like that would take some very specialized heavy equipment. The Chinese were certainly resourceful and might just have such equipment, but they still needed to get it out there and put it to use without anybody taking notice. Even if their buddies on Tonga did claim that shaft of seawater as their rightful territory.

That would explain the need for distraction.

Rex Smith, the head guy from the research ship *Deep Ocean Explorer*, had given Glass the *Geological Oceanography for Dummies* tutorial. Between all the discussions of fumaroles, plate tectonics, and acidic precipitates, the one thing that Glass took from the lesson was that getting enough of that gold to make it worthwhile was going to be damned hard and could take a long time.

The other thing that Smith had shared with Glass was the exact location of the gold. If the Chinese were headed there—and from what Weiss had told him, it appeared they likely were—then that was where he would send the *Canberra* to patrol. And considering how desperately somebody high up in the Chinese military and government wanted that gold, it would probably be smart to vector the *Cheyenne* over there to snoop around, keeping an eye out for the PLAN diesel boats.

At his orders, the *Canberra* completed refueling from the *Puller* and quickly topped off their groceries before heading right back out to sea. Almost as an after-thought, Colonel

Readly and a platoon of his Marines went along for the ride, equipped with one of his TOW missile units and a couple of heavy machine guns. That would give the little ship a bit more firepower.

Glass watched as the vessel pulled away and plowed out toward deep water. He thought again of his expectations when he first reported to his new position in Pearl. Sure, it was a tough gig. But he would learn and grow with the job. Get back in shape. Grab some beach time. Run a tight unit while relying on what he knew was a good staff. He figured the stress and hard decisions he would have to make could not be that much greater than what he experienced regularly as a submarine skipper.

Now, watching the phosphorescence playing in the wake of the *Canberra* as she, her crew, and the Marines headed off on a dangerous mission to which Glass had assigned them, he had to wonder just how naïve he could have been.

Ψ

Out there where *Canberra* was bound, in some of the deepest water on planet Earth, the Tonga Plate was once again shoved hard from below. Under the inexorable pressure of rock and magma, the mass of rock shifted several more meters.

This time, the grinding movement registered a relatively mild four-point-zero at the seismometer in Wellington, New Zealand. Given the dozens of tremors the world felt every day, this one did not cause any stirring of interest, only a minor entry in a database. But more importantly, this time the disturbance could be triangulated to an exact location on the globe: sixteen degrees, twenty-six minutes south latitude and one-hundred-seventy-four degrees, fifty-four minutes east longitude. But still, no instruments were capable of seeing the magma being squeezed up through the cracks. Molten rock that had begun to build a sizeable cone on the ocean floor.

Should this activity continue at the same rate for only a few hundred years, there would be a brand-new island in the South Pacific, centered on this very spot.

A brand-new island for the world's nations to claim and fight over.

25

The *Changcheng Shiba*, one of Yon Hun Glo's submarines, arrived in its newly assigned patrol area off the entrance to Pago Pago Harbor on the southeast side of the island of American Samoa. Once on-station, she came to periscope depth in order to watch for any interesting activity in the tropical harbor. Normally, they could expect to find the place to be little more than a quiet backwater, with only the occasional yacht sailing into or out of the harbor. The US Navy did have a presence there, but there was typically little of importance going on in this place, either. The high point of island activity was when the tuna fleet pulled in to dump their fishy load at the giant StarKist cannery on the north side of the harbor. Definitely nothing worth the submarine's attention, but, by order, *Shiba* was bound to take a look.

But this time, the PLAN submarine's first glimpse of the harbor showed things were quite different now. The giant, gray hulk of the *Chesty Puller* was plainly visible, anchored in the middle of the harbor. And the *Portland* was moored a few hundred yards further in. Yon Hun Glo had given the *Shiba*'s commander very explicit orders should he discover such warships this close to Tonga. First, he was to report any American naval vessels of this size that he might observe at anchor or leaving the harbor. Then, should it appear that any departing vessels might be headed toward the Tonga Trench area, he was to assume they were hostile, and he was to attack and sink them if he could.

But—and the orders were quite specific on this point—the most important thing was to make the report.

The submarine commander's first reaction to the orders was consternation. Sinking an American vessel would have ramifications the Chinese skipper did not want to contemplate. But he also knew that whatever Yon and the wolf pack were doing out here was of utmost importance. And the Americans clearly could not be allowed to crash the party, even to the point of starting a shooting war if they appeared bent on doing it.

He would follow the orders.

The *Shiba* was still setting up, acclimating to the new patrol area, determining just how safe it was to patrol even closer to the harbor mouth, when the commander spied a small, gray warship steaming out of the harbor. And the vessel —clearly US Navy—was heading very nearly straight at him, proceeding rapidly and on a collision course.

Was it possible that the Americans had already discovered the *Shiba*? Did they have remote bottom sensors that the submarine may have tripped? Of course, they did!

More importantly, and of greatest urgency for the commander to determine, was it possible that this warship planned to attack and sink his submarine?

The commander hurriedly lowered the periscope and ordered his submarine to go deep. They were to rapidly maneuver away from the on-rushing warship. But the oncoming vessel was already so close, the range was so short, that the commander knew it would be impossible to evade even the most primitive ASW ship. And the American ASW ships were anything but primitive. Plus, he was now convinced sensors had already revealed their presence and position.

He would have to act quickly. Even as they diverted and went deep, the approaching vessel made a turn to apparently follow his submarine. The captain could only assume that the Americans had him in their sights. That they were preparing to drop hell on him and his ship.

The only option now was to attack immediately and hope his torpedo destroyed the American warship before they had a chance to launch their own weapons. Let the politicians and diplomats sort out the mess later.

It took a little more than one minute for the *Shiba*'s fire control system to spit out a solution on the American warship. To upload the solution to the YU-6 torpedo in the Number One torpedo tube. To launch the torpedo.

The weapon whooshed out of its tube. Its otto-fuel-powered engine ignited and quickly came up to speed, racing in the general direction of the US vessel.

After the torpedo had traveled about five hundred meters from the submarine, its active acoustic sensors started searching for its quarry, finding it almost instantly.

Once located, it would take little time at all to reach the target and do its maximum damage, almost certainly before the American ship and its crew knew what hit them.

Ψ

The *Canberra* cleared Breakers Point and came around to a course that would point their bow directly for the gold fields. Their orders were to get there fast, and speed was one of this type of warship's primary advantages. The skipper ordered up a flank bell.

The two big General Electric 2500 gas turbines whined up to full speed, pushing thousands of gallons a minute of seawater through a pair of LJ150E Wartsila pump-jets while the two MTU diesels pushed the two LJ160E pump-jets. Crewmembers held onto whatever they could find as the LCS shot ahead, quickly coming up to her maximum speed of better than forty-five knots and doing so within a distance of only a couple of ship lengths.

The *Canberra* raced past where the *Shiba* lay without ever knowing the Chinese submarine was there. The US littoral combat ship was moving so fast that the PLAN YU-6 torpedo, even with a fifteen-knot speed advantage, could not catch up before it ran out of fuel.

The lethal torpedo soon slowed, then stopped, and immediately sank into the depths.

The LCS raced on, oblivious to anyone having just shot at her with the intention of sinking her.

Ψ

Yon Ba Deng was once again in a quandary. The reports from his brother, Yon Hun Glo, had so far been promising. He and his little armada were on their way out to the gold fields. There did not appear to be anything in his way. Nothing to hinder him from beginning to pull the stunning riches of Croesus from the ocean depths. And the world's attention was now focused on Taiwan, with no interest at all on the Tonga Trench. Yon Ba Deng allowed himself a smile as a weak but appropriate metaphor came to mind: all appeared golden on that front.

But on the home front, just as he was so close to unimaginable wealth and power, events were not proceeding so much in his favor. He had not even moved into his new, well-appointed office in the Forbidden City. He had not yet met his new staff or called his first meeting to establish his power. And already things were falling apart.

All of his submarines that had managed to get to their patrol stations, to begin the execution of his crafty embargo plan, as approved by the president, had been immediately detected and attacked. Even those boats that had been delayed by one excuse or another had been found. So far, he had been unable to blame this debacle on someone else.

He, of course, had someone in mind. The perfect foil. But he needed that foil to do important work at the moment, out there in the Pacific.

Right now, he needed to solve a couple of vexing riddles. The submarines had been detected—every one of them, including those that were way off schedule and plan—when such a breach of stealth was almost impossible. Even a spy could not have predicted the positions of the submarines that had suffered mechanical troubles, yet the Taiwanese had located every single one of them.

Then, once detected, every sub had been damaged, not destroyed. It seemed as if the Taiwanese were taunting him, showing him that they could just as easily have sunk much of his submarine fleet. But they did not want to waste the effort or the explosives.

Yon's brilliant submarine "embargo" had now become an international joke. Even the feeble effort to try to claim that this was all a complex exercise, a test of China's fleet preparedness, had been the subject of mocking coverage in the world's press. Especially when video of dozens of the PLAN boats being towed back into port with their screws shot off showed up everywhere from YouTube to most of the world's cable news channels. And, of course, in intelligence briefings in most world capitals.

Yon Ba Deng was sure that it was only a matter of time. He would likely have no chance to defend himself. Not even to place blame on his brother.

No, Tan Yong would soon demand his resignation. Or, worse, send the *Guoanbu*, the dreaded State Security secret police, to place him under arrest. There would be claims that he was a traitor, a saboteur, an enemy of the people. Then he would disappear into the same prison that held Soo Be Xian. That is, if he was allowed to live at all.

Just then, his private cell phone rang. He answered immediately. Few people had this number. He always responded to it when there was a call.

"*Wei, nin hao!*"

"Good! I got to you in time!" He recognized the deep, sultry voice. Li Min Zhou. "You must run. Now. The *Guoanbu* are already on their way to place you under arrest. The charges are treason against the people. You, of all people, know the punishment for such an offense."

Yon Ba Deng gasped. Yes, he did. A very nasty public trial, followed by execution.

"But, I..."

"There is time, but not for argument," she calmy interrupted. "And a way to save yourself. I have a jet waiting at Xijiao Airport, at the charter terminal. Leave right now. Do not go home. Do not try to pack a bag or take anything. Do not call anyone. Just drive yourself straight to the airport. With any luck, and with your adherence to my instructions, we may well get you to a safe place."

"But why are you..."

The line went dead. No time now for questions or answers.

Yon Ba Deng, the head of the Chinese military for less

than a week, was already heading out the door of his old office, never to return.

He left on his desk a half-finished cup of tea. And his favorite teacup. The one made for Emperor Shenzong of the Song Dynasty. A powerful monarch once considered to be the richest man in the world.

And thus, its most powerful.

Ψ

Night was upon them when Yon Hun Glo's ships arrived at their position over the Tonga Trench. The *Zhang Jian* and the *Pearl Moon* had departed Tonga the previous evening and steamed across three hundred and fifty miles of open ocean. Restrained by the speed of the submarines, the *Shijiu* and the *Ershi*, which were traveling submerged on their AIP systems, the journey had been much more leisurely than Yon Hun Glo would have preferred. However, it was important that his ships have some hidden protection from the Americans or anyone else who might bother them.

But especially the Americans.

Still, waiting for over three hours past their scheduled arrival for the three Tongan patrol boats to show up had tried the admiral's patience to its breaking point. When Yon found that the delay was caused by King Tofuwanga wanting to ride along on the gold hunt, he exploded. How could that obese, incompetent fool dare to risk everything for which he and his brother had worked so hard merely so he could go on a sightseeing cruise. There was one positive. Having the king along would give more credence to the pretense that this odd assemblage of vessels was, indeed, a Tongan-government-sanctioned mission. Even an air of legality. That realization was enough to keep the admiral from dispatching the bloated monarch right back to his miserable, mosquito-infested islands.

Now in darkness, the afterdeck of the research vessel *Zhang Jian* became a bustle of activity. Aided by brilliant, white, mercury vapor deck lights, the technicians scurried about, making last-minute checks and adjustments to the bright orange manned submersible, the *Fendouji*.

Alongside the *Fendouji* rested a squat, mist-gray, cylindrical vehicle that was joined to the manned submersible by a tow cable. The unmanned mineral recovery vehicle would be the means to haul the gold from the bottom on the six-mile vertical ascent back up to the *Zhang Jian*. The *Fendouji* had the tools that would be used to load the MRV, but because it was only a small research submersible, it had the capacity only for small samples on each trip.

The plan was for the *Fendouji* to tow the MRV down, load it up, and then guide it back up to the surface. The cargo bin on the MRV was not very large, only about a cubic meter. When Yon Hun Glo had questioned the engineers who built it, he was quickly informed that it would hold over twenty thousand kilograms of gold. A bit of quick math showed Yon that they were looking at an amount of gold equal to over one-point-one-billion dollars per trip at prevailing prices.

The full moon was high over the ship by the time all the preparations were complete. Yon Hun Glo donned a pair of deep blue coveralls and joined the *Fendouji*'s pilot and equipment operator in the little submarine's cramped inner capsule. He also carried a small pistol in his pocket, just in case the other two men became greedy at the sight of their haul. Nothing would keep him from making this first dive, or getting it back to the surface.

Once the men were inside, the technicians lowered the *Fendouji*'s fifteen-centimeter-thick titanium hatch in place and spun the locking dogs to seal it. The water pressure where this little vessel was going would be unbelievable, over ten thousand kilograms on each square centimeter.

Yon Hun Glo watched through one of the polycarbonate viewing portals as the mini-sub was lifted from the ship's deck and swung out over the relatively calm water. The sub settled into the dark sea and rested on the surface while divers disconnected the power umbilical and the lifting rig. As that was happening, the MRV was lowered alongside and the tow rig was connected between the two vessels.

Technicians and the crew completed a couple of last-minute equipment checks. Then the *Fendouji* and her tag-along companion, the MRV, slowly descended into the inky water. Yon Hun Glo sat back and tried as best he could to get comfortable in the cramped capsule. Even the veteran submariner was bothered by such close quarters.

It was over six miles to the bottom. Even with the four propulsors at maximum power, the trip would take the better part of three hours. Until then, there was nothing to do but relax.

Relax and think of over a billion dollars per roundtrip.

Yon Hun Glo had actually begun to doze off when the sub's high-speed acoustic communications system chirped. He read off the report that had originated with his command center, the one hidden in the cargo containers on the *Pearl Moon*. Their radar had detected a ship approaching at very high speed from the direction of the American port of Pago Pago on American Samoa. And it was not transmitting on its AIS transponder.

It was almost certainly an American warship. Nothing else would be traveling that fast, and only warships were exempt by the International Maritime Organization from using an AIS transponder. Yon's first question was how the Americans were able to get a ship out of Pago Pago without the PLAN submarine he had posted there seeing and reporting it.

The second was what was going to happen when the ship arrived. The meager Tongan patrol boats would be of no use against an actual warship, even if this area was supposed to be their territorial water and their responsibility to defend. He did have one surprise for intruders, but he could not be certain it would be enough, depending on the type of warship coming their way.

Yon Hun Glo decided he could not rely on the Tongans or his "surprise" to deflect the approaching vessel. Instead, he directed one of his submarines to attack the impertinent American ship.

But, unknown to Yon Hun Glo, there was other traffic in the area. The submarine *Cheyenne* cruised at periscope depth three thousand yards south of where the admiral's little group of ships slowly circled. The officer of the deck could easily see through his 'scope the brightly lit Chinese research vessel and a larger container ship a thousand yards further. Three little gunboats, flying the Tongan flag, wove in and out around the pair of bigger ships as if on joyrides.

The sub's sonar showed a little more complicated picture. In addition to the five surface ships, there were two submarines, one making wide, slow circles a couple of thousand yards to the west and a second doing the same a few thousand yards to the east. Both submarines were classified Chinese *Yuan*-class AIP boats. They were so quiet that they were only held on the TB-29A towed array. But they were definitely there. And not unexpected. The sensors in the ship channel had reported their passage, too.

Quieter still, barely a blank spot in the ocean, the American UUV, ORCA One, was a few hundred yards astern of the eastern *Yuan*.

And well off to the north, but closing fast, they held a broadband contact that sonar classified an LCS, the *Canberra.* It seemed to be rush hour in this typically empty part of the Pacific Ocean.

"Conn, Sonar, picking up acoustic comms from the research ship. Sounds like a data link of some kind."

Walt Smith, the *Cheyenne's* XO and currently standing watch as the command duty officer, grabbed the 21MC microphone and acknowledged the report.

"Sonar, Conn, aye. Can you make anything out of it?"

"No, not really. Not something we have heard before. Got it on tape, though. Maybe the ACINT brains can make sense of it when we can upload. Hold on a second." A brief pause. "Conn, Sonar, contact zig on the east *Yuan,* Sierra Five-Six. Looks like he has increased speed and changed course to the north."

"Sonar, Conn, aye." Smith turned to talk to the section tracking party manning the bank of computers on the starboard side of the control room. "Attention in the attack center. Confirmed target zig, Sierra Five-Six, turn away and speed increase. Set anchor range five-two-hundred yards. Continue tracking Sierra Five-Six."

Smith turned to the officer of the deck and ordered, "Make your depth three hundred feet and move over closer to Sierra Five-Six. Get yourself to three thousand yards behind him, deep in his baffles. I don't like where I think he's headed. I'm going to get the captain."

Smith had barely finished his orders when Bart Knox, the skipper, walked into the control room. "What you got now, XO? Sounds like things are picking up a bit."

"Skipper, Sierra Five-Six, the easternmost *Yuan,* just zigged, picking up speed and heading up toward where the *Canberra* is coming this way. I got a bad feeling about that. I figured we would get up in a position to make sure we can stop him if he is up to no good."

Knox looked at the sonar display for a few seconds and then at the fire control solutions for all the contacts.

"Okay, I agree. Let's get in this bastard's baffles and be ready to shoot, just in case. Man battle stations silently. But let's try to make sure we don't shoot the ORCA by mistake."

The *Cheyenne* slipped down into the depths and picked up speed as it closed on the Chinese submarine without being detected. Half an hour later, they were exactly where Commander Knox wanted them to be, thirty-five hundred yards astern of the Chinese diesel boat and off its starboard quarter. And in a position that was blind to the PLAN sub's sonar.

"Conn, Sonar, transient from Sierra Five-Six. He is opening his outer doors. He is making preps to shoot!"

Knox grabbed the 21MC and ordered, "Go active on Sierra Five-Six, steered beam, max power. I want him to know we're out here now!" Smith looked questioningly at Knox. "If he knows that we have the drop on him, maybe he'll think twice before shooting. Otherwise, the *Canberra* is about to be a sitting duck. They won't even know what hit them."

Knox and Smith watched the active sonar display as over two hundred and fifty decibels of acoustic energy pierced the water, heading toward the Chinese submarine.

"Positive return on Sierra Five-Six, range three-two-hundred yards, bearing three-four-seven."

Knox smiled. "I think he knows we're in town. Let's see if that makes him behave."

"Target zig, Sierra Five-Six!" Sonar reported. "Target sped up and changed course. Transient from the contact. Launch transients! Torpedo in the water!"

"Snapshot Sierra Five-Six!" Knox ordered. "Launch two evasion devices. Wait ten seconds and launch two more."

Smith looked at the fire control computer and sang out, "Solution ready!"

The weapons officer immediately followed with, "Weapon ready!"

Knox ordered, "Shoot on generated bearings! Right full rudder, ahead flank! Make your depth eight hundred feet."

In rapid succession, the ADCAP torpedo had been flushed out of Number One torpedo tube. Then, the ship jumped ahead and angled downward into the depths. Maybe, just maybe, amid all the confusion, they could outrun or get outside the Chinese torpedo's acquisition cone before it found and bore into them. All while *Cheyenne*'s own ADCAP torpedo kept the Chinese submarine equally busy trying to get away from it.

The sonar reports were a constant, pulsing litany, the voices remarkably calm, just like a thousand drills in the attack trainer.

"Own ship weapon running normal."

"Incoming torpedo bears three-five-five, zero bearing rate!"

"Hold own ship's weapon in active search!"

"Incoming torpedo still bears three-five-five, zero bearing rate. It blew through the evasion devices."

"Own ship weapon shifted to high speed, in attack."

"Incoming torpedo still bears three-five-five, zero bearing rate!"

"Incoming weapon shifting to close-in attack mode."

Then a loud explosion shook the *Cheyenne*. That was followed a few seconds later by a second loud blast.

But *Cheyenne* was still there.

When the reverberations died down, Sonar reported, "Loss of own ship's weapon, loss of incoming weapon."

Smith looked at Knox as the captain wiped the sweat from his brow.

"He shot at us instead of the *Canberra*," the skipper said. "But I think the ORCA ended up sacrificing itself for us. Thanks, little guy."

"And the Chinese boat?" Smith asked, knowing the answer already.

Knox looked sideways at his XO, his face solemn.

"I don't think that Sierra Five-Six and the submariners aboard the vessel were so lucky."

Ψ

The Gulfstream jet—tail number Golf Three-Seven-Two —entered the final approach landing pattern for Taoyuan International Airport near Taipei, Taiwan. The plane was cleared for final approach on runway two-three left. At the last minute, though, Golf Three-Seven-Two veered off and landed instead at the little used Taoyuan Air Base field, less than a mile to the east of the sprawling international airport.

The private jet touched down gently and then braked enough to quickly turn off from the runway onto a weed-strewn taxiway, all its lights already extinguished. It pulled to a stop on a cracked macadam apron at the south end of the field.

Two people waited in the darkness, standing beside a black Toyota Land Cruiser at the edge of the apron. Two more black cars sat a hundred yards back, near the fence.

Li Min Zhou silently watched the plane all the way from its approach, through the landing, and until it came to a halt only a few yards away. Only then did she turn to TJ Dillon and speak.

"So, partner, we are in agreement. The CIA takes custody

of our guest here and conducts the debriefings. But we share the intel equally."

TJ Dillon watched as the plane's doorway popped open and stairway dropped down.

"As usual, we are on the same page," Dillon confirmed. "Yep, that's the plan. And you and your people leak through your sources that he has defected and is cooperating with US Intelligence. That should keep him out of circulation for a very long time and irritate some folks mightily. So much for that famous Chinese obsession for saving face."

Li laughed out loud. It was the first time Dillon had heard her laugh.

"Yes. It is a beautiful thing! And he will have every incentive to be very forthcoming for your interrogators, too."

Yon Ba Deng stepped out onto the top step of the aircraft. He squinted into the darkness, obviously trying to figure out where in the world he had landed.

Dillon and Li looked at each other and smiled, imagining when the former high official learned he had arrived on the island of Taiwan.

Or, as the Taiwanese prefer, the Republic of China.

26

Oblivious to the nature of the battle that had just raged below it, making so much racket, or how close they had come to destruction, the *Canberra* charged right into the midst of the little fleet of Chinese and Tongan vessels. It slid to a halt less than a thousand yards astern of the *Zhang Jian*, pausing to take stock. The three Tongan patrol boats boldly sprang into action, urged on by their king, and commenced ominously circling the American warship, their forward-mounted machine guns manned and aimed directly at the newly arrived ship.

"American warship, this is Tongan Navy ship *Ngahau*." The transmission popped up on channel sixteen on the marine band radio. "You are trespassing in Royal Tongan sovereign waters. In the name of King Tofuwanga the Second, I order you to depart immediately. Please acknowledge your compliance."

Commander Louise Gadliano was the skipper of the *Canberra*. She suppressed a laugh as she glanced over at Marine Lieutenant Colonel Stanton Readly. He simply shook his head. The machine guns could do some damage, yes, but the outcome of a shootout between the patrol boats and the *Canberra* would not bode well for the Tongans and their king. This was precisely the kind of battle she was designed for.

Gadliano grabbed the microphone for her marine band radio.

"This is the USS *Canberra*. The United States recognizes these waters as international. Your claims are not valid. You are violating mineral rights legally registered by United States persons under the International Seabed Authority. You are hereby directed to leave these waters immediately."

As she dropped the mike, she signaled for the gunners to train their forward gun mount toward the patrol boats. A shot across a bow, though not likely necessary, would surely bring this dispute to a hasty close.

No one on *Canberra* was paying particular attention to the *Pearl Moon*. She was, after all, a freight vessel, her decks full of big containers. But then, the sides of one of the upper containers suddenly dropped down. From inside, a gunner fired an HJ-12 *Hongjian* missile directly at the American LCS. The missile arced up and raced toward the warship, leaving a bright, flaming trail across the starless night sky.

Admiral Yon's "surprise!" But there was more.

The sides of two more containers collapsed. A team of gunners slewed a Type 85 machine cannon around and opened fire on the *Canberra*. Twin streams of twenty-three-millimeter cannon fire spewed from the pair of guns and raced across the gap between the ships. The explosive shells reached the LCS even before the missile did, blowing away the fifty-seven-millimeter gun mount. The HJ-12 exploded into the wreckage, spraying the forward end of the lightly armored aluminum ship with shrapnel and destroying the vessel's Navy Strike Missile System box launchers.

The *Canberra*'s SeaRAM defense system sprang into

action, retaliating with a half dozen rolling airframe anti-air missiles zooming across the water at the Chinese ship. The rest followed in a second ripple launch.

Readly was lying flat on the deck, trying to avoid all the flying debris, when he realized Gadliano was down, injured. He pulled her from the wrecked bridge and delivered her to his Marine corpsman. His Marines had set up their TOW launcher on the ship's helo deck, along with their M2A1 fifty caliber machine guns. The pair of "ma deuces" were already launching deadly streams of fifty caliber bullets back at the container ship, spraying the decks with fire. And the TOW missile leapt from its launch tube and flew arrow straight toward the *Pearl Moon*. The projectile slammed into the containers just below the one holding the machine cannon and erupted into a fiery blast. The cannon tumbled into the blazing pit.

The *Pearl Moon's* stinger might have been pulled, but the *Canberra* was severely damaged.

Ψ

The *Fendouji* manned submersible glided down through total darkness broken only by the vessel's LED lights, illuminating the way directly in front of them. It showed nothing more than an occasional weirdly shaped denizen of these awesome depths, creatures that had almost certainly never experienced light before.

The pilot nudged Yon Hun Glo's foot to wake him.

"Admiral, bottom coming up. Another ten minutes, sir."

Yon Hun Glo shook himself awake. He rubbed his eyes and tried to stretch his aching muscles, but there was no room in the cramped capsule.

The *Fendouji* reached the ocean floor right on schedule.

The pilot smoothly brought the little submersible to a hover barely a meter above the featureless bottom. But then, the LEDs caught and reflected back a startlingly brilliant golden glow that appeared to stretch out in front of them as far as they could see. The little team stared, awestruck.

Yon Hun Glo could now finally see the culmination of all the planning and risk-taking, right out there in front of him on the other side of the submersible's twenty-centimeter-thick viewport. It was there for the taking.

He nudged the equipment operator with his foot.

"What are you waiting for? Get the MRV ready to receive the ore. It must be loaded, and we have to be headed back to the surface in one hour."

"But Admiral, it will be impossible at these depths to... okay, as you wish, sir."

The equipment operator knew better than to protest. It would take at least twenty minutes at these crushing depths to delicately maneuver the cumbersome MRV into place so that he could use the manipulator arms to load it. And twenty metric tons of gold would take some time to lift off the bottom and shovel over to the MRV's cargo bay.

He would not object. He would simply get to work. Then he would endure the old admiral's ire and impatience if it should become necessary. But the admiral would certainly be too enraptured by the gold to even remember his dictum.

Ψ

The *Cheyenne* came up to periscope depth to report sinking the Chinese submarine and the loss of ORCA One. They were greeted with the sight of tracer fire and missiles splitting the night sky, the loud and bright battle between the American LCS and what appeared to be a large container ship. The bow of the LCS exploded, a bright flame leaping up to illuminate the entire area. Another explosion erupted, this one on the container ship, and only a few seconds after the one on the *Canberra*, but with an even larger flash of light.

Then the night quieted. No more tracer fire. No more missiles racing overhead. It appeared *Cheyenne* was half a minute late for this particular party. And glad of it.

"Conn, Sonar, picking up transients from Sierra Five-Seven, the other *Yuan* sub. I think he's at periscope depth. He may be making an approach on the *Canberra*. Not getting any engine lines off the *Canberra*. I think she is DIW."

Not good. Not good at all. The stricken LCS was dead in the water and would make an easy target. And it would take *Cheyenne* far too long to get into position to stop the Chinese sub from doing its damage.

Bill Knox grabbed the 21MC mike.

"Sonar, Conn, aye. *Canberra* looks damaged, probable DIW." He turned to Walt Smith and mumbled, "XO, we're going to play this the same way as we did the last one. Get your team set to shoot, then I'm gonna light him up with active. Hopefully, we'll scare him off. If not, I want a weapon ready to go as soon as he shows hostile intent."

"Sonar, Conn, line up to go active on Sierra Five-Seven, sector search, max power."

"Sonar, aye. Captain, we'll be reverb limited if we use max power. High probability we won't get a return inside all the noise."

"Sonar, I understand. I want to ring his bell and advertise our presence."

"Sonar, aye. Max power at this range will certainly do that. Ready to go active, max power, sector search."

Walt Smith looked over at Bill Knox and gave him a nod. "Captain, ready when you are. Solution is set and the weapon is ready."

Knox gave him a thumbs-up. He keyed the 21MC mike. "Sonar, go active on Sierra Five-Seven."

The skipper could only imagine the looks on the Chinese crew's faces.

"Sonar, Conn, positive active contact on Sierra Five-Seven, bearing two-nine-six, range four-three-hundred yards."

A pause in the report.

Then, "Possible contact zig on Sierra Five-Seven. Looks like he turned away and is going deep."

Knox looked over at Smith with a broad grin.

"Well, XO, I'd say he got the message."

Ψ

Colonel Readly quickly assessed the situation. The *Canberra* was now essentially defenseless. Both the ship's lone gun and its surface-to-surface missiles were destroyed. The SeaRAM launcher was now empty, but he had already set a team of sailors to work reloading it. Until it was readied, his Marine unit was the only firepower that the LCS could muster.

To make matters worse, the ship's bridge was in shambles. Shrapnel from the exploding ordnance had shredded the ship's thin aluminum skin and heavily damaged the highly computerized ship control systems. Several sailors were now struggling to get back at least some control of the vessel's propulsion systems. Until they could do that, the *Canberra* would only sit there where she floated.

The Marine commander shook his head. He had read of so-called "Q-ships" back in World War II. They were enemy vessels disguised as merchant ships to try to lure surface warships and submarines into range. Then they would remove tarps or other coverings to reveal a deadly comple-ment of guns and launch a surprise assault. Readly was convinced he had seen his first Q-ship that night.

He hurried below decks and found Louise Gadliano in her cabin. His corpsman was still bandaging a particularly nasty laceration across her forehead. He had already splinted her broken arm and treated a leg wound.

"Looks like you had a bad night at the skating rink. How you doing, Louise?" the Marine asked as he stepped into her small cabin.

"I've had better days," the LCS's skipper answered, still managing a smile. "Question is, how's my ship?"

"Your crew is bringing her back best they can. The XO expects to have main propulsion back online in a couple of hours. Your weapons systems are out of commission. Your comms and electronic warfare systems all got shredded. We have limited comms back to the *Portland* on my team's comms package. I asked your XO to give me a list of all the things he needs. We'll see what they can fly out from Pago Pago in the morning."

"Could have been worse," she responded. "Casualties? Any update?"

"Could have been worse there, too. Several broken bones. They'll be out of commission for a while. Lots of scrapes and cuts. But no KIA."

Gadliano closed her eyes and let out a long sigh of relief.

Just then, Sergeant Major Ramirez stuck his head in the cabin door. "Excuse me, boss, but we got a problem. Those damn Tongan gunboats are getting uppity, screwing around out there a little too close for my comfort."

Readly followed his sergeant out to the flight deck. He

could easily see the three gunboats circling, as if they were taunting them. They had now moved their antics in to less than five hundred yards, clearly aware the littoral vessel was virtually toothless. As Readly watched, someone stepped out of the pilothouse of one of the boats. The man raised a loud hailer to his lips.

"On the American warship. Stand by to be boarded. You are in violation of Tongan sovereignty and are being placed under arrest. Your ship is being impounded."

Readly cupped his hands in front of his mouth and was about to yell across the open water for the speaker to perform an anatomically impossible sexual act. One of the ship's crew handed him a loud hailer. That gave the Marine an opportunity to reconsider what he was about to say.

"Go...to...hell!" was his significantly toned-down response.

Within five seconds, the patrol boat opened fire with its machine gun, spraying at the helo deck. Readly and Ramirez had already dived for cover. Within another few seconds, the other two boats also began shooting. That meant that the LCS was being attacked from three different vectors.

The Marines' fifty caliber M2A1s quickly answered, concentrating fire at the closest boat. Several other members of Readly's squad had sprawled on the deck and were firing with their M4 carbines.

Readly signaled his TOW crew and got their attention. He pointed at the lead patrol boat. Almost immediately, a missile jumped from the launch tube and lanced across the open water, pounding into the side of the patrol boat amidship. The resulting explosion left little more than a burning pile of debris. And that was quickly sinking below the surface.

The other two boats suddenly lost all interest in the fight or defending the sovereignty of their tiny nation. They spun about and headed for the horizon at full throttle.

Readly and Ramirez got to their feet and dusted themselves off as they watched the gunboats disappear into the night.

"So much for being defenseless," Ramirez said. "We'd better get a couple of teams over on those other two ships before they get any more ideas. Would be nice if we had some more firepower, though."

Readly nodded his agreement.

"Take a couple of RHIBs and head on over to that container ship. Take control of the son of a bitch. Arrest the ship's master and any combatants you find aboard. Last time I looked, using a commercial ship to launch an unprovoked attack like that is considered an act of piracy. Meantime, I'll call back home and see what we can do about getting some more shooters out here. I've lost my patience with these sons of bitches."

Ψ

The crust of planet Earth was showing its own impatience with the status quo. Ten miles below the surface of the Pacific Ocean, the Tonga Plate was still active, shrugging its massive shoulders. It yet again shifted the Pacific Plate down several more meters. The displacement of a colossal amount of rock, compressed by millions of tons more material and seawater above it, caused the earth to violently shake. The seismographs in Sydney and Wellington this time registered a seven-point-three tremor centered at sixteen degrees, twenty-six minutes south latitude and one-seventy-two degrees, fifty-four minutes east longitude.

Incredibly hot magma oozed up through the widening cracks in the rock, moving toward the seawater above. By the time it spewed out from the ocean floor and emerged as lava, the molten rock had cooled considerably, but only to a thousand degrees centigrade. This was still well above the boiling temperature of seawater at that depth. Massive amounts of water instantly flashed to steam, cooling the lava. The steam clouds produced by this process promptly collapsed in the ice-cold waters away from the lava. That caused loud explosions, like thunder, heard for thousands of miles through the water.

The lava began building a towering cone. In some places, it reached a height of more than five hundred feet above the sea floor in only a couple of hours. Even so, there was still over twenty-five thousand feet—almost five miles—for it to pile up before a new island popped up in the daylight at the surface.

The disruption was powerful enough to cause a massive ledge to break off the trench wall and begin a slide down into the abyss. Millions of tons of rock rolled down and fanned out over the abyssal deep. Mud and rock churned across the bottom, raising a thick cloud of silt that slowly sank back to the bottom and created an entirely new sea floor, burying the old one.

And that included covering the mounds of pure gold under hundreds of feet of mud and rock.

Ψ

The men on the DSV heard and felt the tremors and the rockslide. The wall of debris pushed the little submarine along its leading edge as the pilot tried desperately to lift the craft up and away from the roiling destruction on the sea bottom. He reached for the emergency disconnect from the MRV and its heavy load of gold dust, but Yon Hun Glo slapped his hand away from the switch. The admiral was not about to leave a billion dollars' worth of gold down here just because of a little earthquake and some mud. Even if this turned out to be their only trip down here, it would still be worthwhile.

"Take us up, now. Surface! Surface!" Yon shouted.

But then the heavily burdened MRV got caught up in the rockslide and tugged the *Fendouji* down toward what would certainly be its destruction. There was no driving away from this unbelievably powerful natural force. The men inside the little submersible braced themselves, but they were still thrown painfully against each other, against the bulkheads and instrument panels.

The wall of debris rolled on past, leaving the MRV and its glittery cargo covered by mud and boulders. The DSV lay on its side, partially buried. Rocks and debris jammed the disconnect link. The two craft remained permanently connected, stuck forever on the ocean bottom, ten kilometers below sunlight and salt air.

The *Fendouji*'s emergency distress pinger still managed to activate. That, at least and for what good it was, marked the location where the DSV lay on its side, miles below the surface of the ocean.

Ψ

The pair of Osprey aircraft arrived just as the sun was peeking over the eastern horizon, announcing a beautiful day in the tropics. The first odd-looking bird flew straight to the *Canberra,* where it unloaded twenty combat-ready Marines, a Navy doctor from the *Portland*, and a load of extra ammunition, supplies, and some of the parts needed to help get the ship underway again. Once unloaded, the plane was reloaded with wounded personnel. That included Louise Gadliano, who had argued forcefully, but unsuccessfully, with the doctor to be allowed to remain on her ship and help take her back to port.

As that Osprey lifted up and roared away from the LCS, headed back to Pago Pago, the second one came around to land. It delivered more stores and parts but also a couple of technicians from the *Chesty Puller*, there to help get the LCS back underway as quickly as possible. Before somebody else showed up to start another fight over this seemingly innocuous bit of deep ocean.

Colonel Readly had another mission for this bird once it was unloaded. Sergeant Major Ramirez and his team were already firmly in control of the *Pearl Moon* after only some minor skirmishing. But the other ship was still an unknown entity. For all Readly knew, there could be a whole boatload of shooters over there, waiting for their chance. He loaded up an assault team and promptly headed over to the *Zhang Jian*, the Chinese research vessel.

Since there had not yet been any hostile action from her, no one had paid a visit to the research ship. At least the vessel that was purported to be a research ship. The *Pearl Moon* had, after all, pretended to be a freighter before suddenly becoming something far different and more deadly. At any rate, Readly now had the team and the transportation to go over and take a look.

The Osprey did not even bother to transition to level flight on the short hop over after it took off from the LCS helo deck. It merely played helicopter for the thousand yards to the *Zhang Jian*. Readly was the first man to fast-rope out of the hovering bird to the ship's deck below. A dozen heavily armed Marines followed him down.

What they found was a research ship manned with mostly sailors, technicians, and engineers. No one offered any resistance. Most actually seemed relieved to see the Americans.

The research vessel's Stanford-trained chief research engineer, who introduced himself as Sun Ryn, hurriedly ushered Readly into the mission control module. There he explained that he had a serious problem. There was a DSV with three people aboard. As far as he could determine, it was on the bottom, but they had lost all communications with it. He had no idea of what might have happened to not allow the little submersible to return to the surface.

But there was one thing. They had heard an emergency pinger. It had been actuated ten thousand meters directly below them. The men down there needed help. Needed rescue.

The DSV only had enough life support for twenty-four hours submerged. As of now, they had already been down for almost twelve hours.

Readly thought for a half minute, then did the only thing he knew to do.

He made a call back to Joe Glass on the *Chesty Puller*.

27

The fog of unconsciousness in Yon Hun Glo's head slowly gave way to some semblance of lucidity. Groggy as he was, he was certainly aware of a pulsing pain at the back of his head. He reached back to feel.

It was sticky wet. Blood.

Then there was the blindness. The admiral was certain his eyes were open, but everything was completely dark. There was not the barest glimmer of light anywhere. Could it be that he really had been blinded in the tossing and turning they had just endured? Or maybe he was not even awake at all.

He groaned and tried to move from the awkward, painful position in which he seemed to be stuck. That was when he heard another dreadful growl from someone nearby. Then that someone moved. It was the pilot.

"I believe I am awake," the pilot said weakly. "Which of you is that?"

"It is I, Admiral Yon Hun Glo. What are you doing?"

He could feel the man fumbling about in the tight, dark space, looking for something. Then a small light clicked on.

When their eyes adjusted to the weak illumination, they

could see that the interior of the DSV was in shambles. It was now obvious that the mudslide—or whatever had slapped their vessel so hard—had tipped the *Fendouji* over onto its port side. The little view window on that side was useless, completely covered with silt.

The equipment operator lay still, jammed up against one of the control panels. A faint trickle of blood seeped down from his nose and dripped onto his coveralls. Yon Hun Glo reached over and searched for a pulse. If there was one, it was so weak that he could not feel it. At least not with his cold, numb fingers.

It did not really matter. There was nothing they could do for the operator. Not down here. Not until they got this machine back underway and to the surface. There they could see to him. But, more importantly, they could also determine how much of the load of gold they might have managed to hold onto in the turmoil.

The pilot was already fiddling with his controls, but he was also shaking his head and mumbling in frustration.

"Admiral, we do not have any propulsion at all. I am unable to make the vessel move. It does appear that the life support systems are working as designed. And the battery is showing about half charge." He suddenly hit the control panel in frustration. "But I am unable to get it to move. Not even a millimeter!"

Yon Hun Glo looked at the pilot and calmly told him, "You must remain calm. Do you understand me? You are the only one who knows how to drive this thing. We will simply tell the *Zhang Jian* of our problem. They will figure out something and get us back up to them at the surface. Remember, they, too, will have a share of the gold and ample motivation to rescue us. They will get us up once we inform them that we have run into difficulties."

The pilot offered only an ugly laugh. Then he snorted and laughed even louder, bordering on maniacal.

"That's the rest of our problem, Admiral," he finally said. "The data link and acoustic comms systems are both out of order. We do not have any communications with the surface. They likely have no idea of the seriousness of our situation. They only know they have lost communication with us." The pilot glanced at a gauge on his panel. "And here is the really depressing news. We have a bit less than twelve hours of air remaining."

"Twelve hours?"

"You are a submariner, Admiral. You know what happens when the air begins to run out. When it has become mostly expelled carbon dioxide. When the air you have left to breathe is so bad your lungs refuse to accept it, you gag, you cough. When you feel as if your head will explode and your fingers and toes turn blue and your lips..."

"Stop it! Stop that kind of talk." Yon resisted the impulse to slap the frantic pilot. Instead, he eased back down and tried to find a comfortable place to rest while he considered their situation.

"There is one bit of good news," the pilot said.

"Please share," Yon Hun Glo responded irritably.

The pilot pointed to the equipment operator, now clearly not breathing.

"We will have a third more air to breathe than we would have if Wang Wei had not just died."

The admiral gave the pilot a hard look. The man's insubordination would not go unpunished. Then he glanced at the air gauge on the instrument panel.

Peering sideways at the pilot, Yon asked, "So, what you are telling me is that we may not be able to get this first load of gold up to the ship right away?"

Ψ

Joe Glass eased the desk phone back down into its cradle. The call from Stanton Readly had left him with yet another major problem. At least the *Canberra* appeared to be under repair and would start limping back to Samoa shortly. The ramifications of one of his submarines sinking a Chinese sub had already been kicked upstairs to be handled by folks of a higher pay grade. He was also awaiting guidance on what to do with the two Chinese surface ships his people now held captive out there at the scene of the battle. He had also decided not to worry about the PLAN submarine that had tucked tail and fled.

The latest problem, though, had him in a quandary. Glass had no idea how he would solve it, but he certainly knew who to ask. Maybe the only person on the planet who might even possibly offer any hope. And Glass just happened to have on his desk the man's business card with his satellite phone number.

He punched in the numbers to reach Dr. Rex Smith. As the phone rang, Glass reassured himself that if anyone knew of a way to reach that damned Chinese DSV stuck on the sea floor, and if he just happened to be close enough to do anything, it would be the ocean geologist from the *Deep Ocean Explorer*.

Smith sounded almost chipper when he finally answered. And quite confident once Glass explained the situation. He was well aware of the potential result if they did not get the people off that little submersible.

"Yes, I know Sun Ryn well, by the way," Smith said. "His ship and crew, too. We did a project together off Wenzhou a couple of years ago. A good man despite it all, who tries to make the most of his situation."

"Well, we got three souls about to die a horrible death if we can't work some magic down there," Glass shot back.

The two quickly concluded that the *Deep Ocean Explorer* would not be of any use. There was no way to get the slow-moving ship out to the site until well after the clock would have run out on any possibility of mounting a rescue. But as Joe Glass had hoped, Rex Smith had an ace up his sleeve.

Back when Smith and his ship had been captured by King Two-for-One's henchmen, they had simply left the *Sea Raptor*, the scientist's unmanned research submersible vehicle, lying at rest on the ocean floor. And in a spot not that far from where the Chinese were stuck on the bottom. Now, if there was some way to re-activate it, they might just be able to do something with it to rescue the DSV.

Exactly what that "something" was had yet to be determined. But Smith was already talking with his people about it by the time the call from Glass ended.

It took only thirty more seconds for Smith's technicians to think of a major snag. To re-activate the *Sea Raptor*, they would have to disconnect the control and communications systems from the *Deep Ocean Explorer*, move them two hundred miles out to the site where the DSV was, set everything back up on the Chinese research vessel, wake up the UUV, and then, assuming the little gal responded to the wakeup call, put her to work rescuing the men stuck down there near the Tonga Trench. And all this would have to be done before the air ran out on the DSV.

Glass looked at his watch as if the instrument were a crafty adversary. If the chief research engineer on the Chinese ship was anywhere close to correct in his calculations, they now had only about eight hours left.

Rex Smith gathered up his team and set to work disconnecting all the electronic equipment that formed the remote-control system for the UUV. Everything had to be documented to be sure it went back together correctly. Other techs were tasked with assembling anything that they might possibly need, from manuals to patch cords to spare fuses. There would be no time to ask someone to bring out some part or gizmo they neglected to load.

Meanwhile, Joe Glass grabbed Lew Wooten, the skipper of the *Chesty Puller*, and worked to gather any parts or equipment that the massive Expeditionary Mobile Base ship might have to aid in the rescue. They would gather all the equipment onboard the big ship, mostly on the *Puller*'s expansive flight deck. The first load of electronics flew away on an Osprey, which quickly reached top speed of three hundred and fifty miles per hour, making it a relatively quick hop. Rex Smith, Mitch O'Donnell, and Sandy McDougal hitched a ride on that bird. Joe Glass and Bill Bix jumped onboard the CH-53K King Stallion helicopter for the ride out. The chopper carried several pallets loaded with heavier equipment. At a cruise speed of about two hundred miles per hour, it would take them a bit longer to get to their destination, but Glass figured the most important people and parts were on the Osprey.

Joe Glass checked his watch yet again as the two aircraft took to the air. The hands seemed to be spinning. The former submariner had had his own couple of experiences with too little and bad air while stuck beneath the sea. He did not wish that on anyone.

They now had about five hours left if there was to be any hope.

Ψ

It took two hours for the Osprey to reach the *Zhang Jian* and then hook up the *Sea Raptor*'s control and communications equipment to the research ship's power supply. Sun Ryn, the Chinese chief research engineer, walked them through the ship's hook-ups. Soon a rat's nest of wires and cables ran around the command center, but everything seemed to check out. Sandy McDougal sat down in front of the command console and promptly sent out the "wake-up" signal to the *Sea Raptor*.

The little UUV came to life on the very first ping. Everyone cheered as if the home team had just scored the first touchdown.

As the systems came online, Mitch O'Donnell ran through a quick diagnostic checklist to make sure the UUV was functional. All appeared nominal. All but one reading.

"Hey, Doc," the Irish roustabout yelled over to McDougal. "We only got twenty percent on the battery charge. We ain't got time for no lollygaggin' about, you know."

McDougal checked her watch. They had less than three hours.

"Well, we sure as hell don't have time to bring her up for a battery charge," she noted. "Reckon we go with what we have and not what we wish we had." She pointed at a Chinese screen monitoring the emergency pinger from the trapped submersible. "Feed those coordinates into the UUV. We need to tell the *Raptor* where to look."

It took almost half an hour for the well-rested UUV to travel from its former nesting place over to the coordinates coming from the emergency pinger. Once the *Sea Raptor* was in the area, it took another twenty minutes for it to dive deeper and locate the bottomed DSV.

Smith and O'Donnell huddled around McDougal's monitor. Sun Ryn stood off to one side. This was now Smith's show. Along with his crew and the American military. He would stand by to do whatever he needed to.

The compressed video being sent up from the *Sea Raptor* was noisy and barely in focus after traveling over six miles through saltwater. Still, they could make out the orange and white DSV, and could tell it was canted over onto its port side. As best they could determine, it appeared that at least two of the propulsors were badly mangled and the sub's steel outer hull had a number of scrapes and deep dents.

Something had slapped the vessel around pretty good. And that did not bode well for the condition of the three men aboard.

McDougal carefully maneuvered the UUV around to the bow of the DSV and nudged her a bit closer. They could all then see a dim light shining out from the front viewing port. The video was terribly fuzzy, making it almost impossible to see anything through the thick transparent material of the viewing port.

"I see movement!" McDougal yelled excitedly. "Some-body's still alive in there!"

O'Donnell, ever the contrarian where McDougal was concerned, piped up with, "Nothing but a bad picture. You're just seeing what you want to see. That's shifting silt is what that is."

"Shifting silt my ass! That's..."

Rex Smith interrupted her hot retort. "Children, we can duke this out later. Right now, we got an hour to get that thing sprung loose and on the way to the surface." The researcher squinted at the monitor. "And for what it's worth, I thought I saw movement, too. Maybe even somebody waving."

The little UUV slowly circumnavigated the downed DSV, looking from all angles. Sun Ryn finally stepped in closer so that he could see his trapped charge. The grainy video made it difficult, but to his eye, the damage looked minimal. That is, except for the lost propulsors.

Then Sun spied the tow link to the MRV, the attachment that had been hauling the load of gold. The shackle was badly mangled. The tow cable disappeared into the mound of debris.

Sun touched the screen, pointing to a spot on the video image. "Right there. That is at least one of the problems. The mineral recovery unit will be on the other end of that cable. It is almost certainly buried under all that rock and mud. And likely weighed down with a load of gold."

O'Donnell called out, "We got another problem, Doc. We're down to ten percent charge. Don't forget, at five percent, the emergency power protocols kick in and she'll start to shut down to preserve essential power."

Everyone in the room looked at O'Donnell. The Irishman had a deep frown on his face. "At that low power level, there would only be enough juice to get the *Sea Raptor* herself to the surface. Not a hitchhiker. And all the other sensors and auxiliary systems, like the video and the manipulator arms, would have automatically shut down to shunt every available amp to the propulsion system."

Despite O'Donnell's update, McDougal continued to maneuver the little UUV around until she could deploy an arm to reach out and grab the tow cable shackle. Then she could at least attempt to pull it free.

No. It was quickly apparent that the shackle was jammed shut and would not open.

"Hey, remember the lower port manipulator has a cable cutter attachment," O'Donnell reminded her. "In fact, you're the one who insisted it be added. Maybe you can finally get some use of that waste of time and money."

"Not a waste. That was added to be able to cut cable. Fishing line. Anything we might get snagged on," McDougal said. "I don't know if..."

Sun Ryn interrupted her. "Please be aware that is three-centimeter high-tensile-strength steel in that cable. Made to pull heavy loads. I am sorry. I do not believe you will be able to cut it."

McDougal grimaced but continued to manipulate the joystick controls on the console.

"Don't happen to have a cutting torch on me right now," she offered.

Then she swapped controls on manipulator arms and swung the lower port arm into position. Delicately, she began closing the grip of the cable cutter, biting down on the cable. The teeth of the device had just come into contact with the cable when a loud alarm bleated, startling them all as they quietly watched McDougal doing her delicate maneuvering.

The five-percent-power warning. Sensor screens went to their "failed system" outputs. The video screen went dark.

McDougal yelled, "Manual override the protocol!"

But O'Donnell was already flipping through control pull-down menus on the computer terminal. He clicked the mouse and the screech of the alarm stopped.

"Manual override in place," he reported. "Sandy, hurry up or we'll lose everything. I don't know how long we have before the battery cells go below minimum voltage. We've never abused her this way before."

McDougal closed the grip more on the cable cutter. She grasped the manipulator in a vise grip, as if her pressure on the controls would help the blades cut through the steel miles below them. "Mitch, I'm giving it all the close pressure I can muster. Let me know if the claw position is making any dent in it. And when it is fully closed."

"It's bit into the bastard just a tad. But still only at three centimeters."

Not a person in the room breathed. The research ship

rocked gently in the sea swells. O'Donnell fairly whispered the next reading.

"Two centimeters."

Either the cutter was making progress, or the blades were simply skewing against the hard cable, giving a false reading of its progress.

A red light flashed on the control panel and an especially loud alarm bell sounded. O'Donnell silenced the alarm bell with a slap of a switch.

"Low cell voltage warning on the starboard battery," he reported. "One centimeter on the cutter."

"One centimeter."

Brrrnnnggg! Another raucous warning.

"Low cell voltage alarm on the port battery now. She's spent. She's spent, Sandy."

Every screen went dark. McDougal looked up. Sweat poured from her forehead and down across her chin. There were tears in her eyes.

"Dammit, Mitch. We lost it. We were so very close." She glanced at her watch and wiped away drops of perspiration from its dial face. "And we still had fifteen minutes of air."

Sun Ryn stepped over to one of the *Fendouji* control panels on the other side of the compartment.

"We can only hope you got all the way through the cable when we lost power." He flipped a couple of switches. "The vessel has some natural buoyancy, but we can help her if she is free of the cable. Just in case. It is our only hope. And I doubt the men down there would begrudge our trying."

Sun opened a little cover and flipped a switch.

"Help?" McDougal and O'Donnell asked in unison.

"There, that shifts control of the *Fendouji* to us and simultaneously initiates an emergency surface." He checked a digital clock on the wall of the compartment. "From that depth, if my mental calculations are correct, it would take about ten minutes for the *Fendouji* to transit to the surface. Assuming, of course, that she is freed. And I choose to so assume. I suggest we all go out on the main deck to watch. It should be quite exciting."

Mitch and Sandy looked at each other. Slight as it was, there was still a chance.

The group moved outside onto the deck, stepping into the bright late-afternoon sunlight. It felt good. The control room had deliberately been kept cold. Everyone watched the sea around them, unsure where the DSV might surface. If it ever would.

But the deep, blue sea was empty and undisturbed. Nothing to the horizon in any direction except for the three ships, clustered together, as if holding hands for a homecoming.

Nothing. Eight minutes. Nine minutes. Ten minutes had passed and still nothing. McDougal and O'Donnell exchanged a mournful glance, no interest in sparring for the moment. It had been a long shot from the beginning. A literal shot in the dark.

McDougal fought to hold back tears. The worst thing was that she had seen movement inside the little stranded submersible. Somebody alive in there. Someone whose hopes were raised when *Sea Raptor* showed up, lights shining.

But it was not to be.

Then someone at the north rail let out a whoop.

"I see something! Look! Out there!"

A half mile to the north. It was an orange and white shape shooting impossibly high out of the water, and at an impossibly upward angle. Broaching like a freed whale. The thing splashed back down and bobbed on the surface. They could just make out its tiny sail.

A pair of RHIBs shot out from the *Zhang Jian* just as the MH-53 helicopter spooled up and pulled away, headed off to the little mini-sub. The King Stallion was there almost immediately and began hovering ten feet above the sub, its rotor wash kicking up a storm of sea spray. Four divers stepped off the back ramp of the helo and dropped into the water. They were still struggling to inflate a float collar around the sub when the RHIBs arrived on the scene. It took the divers several minutes to undog and open the damaged access hatch. They had just pulled out the two unconscious men when the hastily rigged float ring failed.

Without the buoyancy, the capsule, which was already flooding through the open hatch, quickly sank back into the sea like an unleashed boulder. As if the vessel really preferred being down there in the dark deep.

But the survivors were out and the divers clear. The two rescues—all two dead weight, not conscious—were quickly hoisted up to the helicopter for the flight back to Pago Pago and medical attention.

Back on the *Zhang Jian*, everyone cheered and slapped each other on the back. Mission accomplished.

Mitch O'Donnell and Sandy McDougal joined hands, looked into each other's grinning faces, and then danced an especially spirited Irish jig, even without the proper fiddle-and-pipe accompaniment. Then the two fell easily into each other's arms, held each other tightly for a long while, not really caring what anybody thought about the two usual adversaries embracing.

Then they kissed. Long and deeply.

When they finally pulled apart, Sandy looked up, staring deeply into Mitch's eyes.

"I told you all along the auto shutdown routine should cut power at two percent, not three," she scolded.

"And you know this battery technology can get awful nasty under load with insufficient voltage available!" he shot back.

They were still chirping at each other—but holding hands —as they went below with the others for a celebratory round of drinks.

EPILOGUE

President Stan Smitherman slammed the phone down with such force, it bounced right back off its cradle and to the Oval Office floor.

"Tan Yong is a conceited, overblown, two-faced ass," he growled, primarily at Secretary of State Sandra Dosetti. "The son of a bitch is demanding that we release those two ships down in Tonga and pay reparations for damaging the one and sinking their sub. And he wants me to make an apology at the United Nations! All because he and his henchmen got caught trying to steal my gold!"

Dosetti struggled to suppress a smile. Smitherman was doing a fine job of backing himself into a corner. One from which he could never escape without serious political damage. Meanwhile, her backchannel efforts to become the candidate to replace him on the ticket immediately after his poll data plummeted were looking better all the time.

"Stan, calm yourself before you have a stroke. Remember what the doctor said about your blood pressure. You sure don't want the voters to know those particular numbers." She waited a beat for him to stop ranting, close his eyes, tap his temples with his fingertips, and calm himself down. A tactic he had certainly learned from that Tibetan shaman he had employed and moved into his own quarters at Camp David, all to help the president relax. A bit of trivia Dosetti already had placed with key leakers, poised to share with the press. That quirky move alone would give her Texas and Iowa. "Now, why don't we just play hardball with Tan Yong. Voters love that shit. Remind the Chinese that we now have in custody the people in his regime who were trying to make off with the gold for themselves. Make sure they know that this whole affair was almost certainly a coup attempt, at least based on what they are telling us."

"Yeah, about that," Smitherman replied, the scarlet starting to return to his face. "He is demanding that we repatriate both of the Yon brothers. 'My most trusted military leaders,' he called them. Says he'll back off Taiwan if we do."

"And?"

"I'm going to agree to that. We can spin it that we stood up to the Chinese over Taiwan and they blinked. And we make a big deal out of having sent the Chinese packing without any shooting on our part. Nobody will have to know about that trigger-happy submarine jockey and the lost PLAN sub, right? If anyone complains about our giving back the brothers, they were just criminals that we extradited. That'll play pretty damn well in Peoria."

"No one cares about Peoria anymore. It has to play on Wall Street and in the media," Dosetti reminded him. "The gold?"

"We blame that all on King What's-his-name. Never could get that guy's name right. Anyway, it's all his fault. We could have gone in there and gotten a reasonable portion of it, provided thousands of jobs in the process, and shared the wealth with the world's emerging nations. You know, piping water to the Sahara. Building toilets in the Congo. Right? Hell, we'll get the press office to figure out the right angle."

Smitherman paused to take a big drink from the whiskey-and-water on his desk. Angling for leverage. He was back in his natural element. But Dosetti knew those same leakers to the press would soon share the fact that Smitherman was stone-cold drunk every night by the time he went to bed. "In the meantime, we need to figure out how we're going to pay for all the campaign airtime and social media crap we contracted for when we thought we could tap into all that gold. I've got calls in to a couple of PACs that…"

Dosetti settled back in her chair, hardly listening. Her conversations with her Wall Street backers and the party leadership were going to be even more interesting than she had previously hoped.

And to think, only a few months ago, she was angling only for the senate or vice-presidency. Now? Now the whole enchilada was hers to gobble up.

Ψ

Jon Ward slid from the driver's side seat of the rental car. His son, Jim, climbed out of the passenger side, stretching out the kinks from the short but cramped ride from the airport. But before either could complain any more about the dearth of full-size rental cars at Daniel K. Inouye International, they heard somebody yelling their names.

Tom Donnegan came bounding out the door of his house and charging toward them down the driveway. He grabbed both his visitors in a massive, three-way bear hug.

"Lord God a'mighty, it's about time you two war-horses showed up to pay homage!" He stepped back and looked the younger Ward up and down. "Jim-boy, you're looking a little peaked and underweight. How in hell you gonna save the world if you're so weak and scrawny? I figure you need some of Louise's cooking. Woman's been in the kitchen since she heard y'all were coming." He turned to Jon Ward. "Hey, where's the smartest and best-looking one in the family?"

"She's on the twenty-hundred United flight from SFO," Ward answered as they walked toward the front door. "I was hoping we would have time to sit out on your lanai, sip some mai tais, and swap stories until it's time to swing back down to the airport and collect her and her six suitcases of stuff." He pointed at his subcompact rental. "We'll need to borrow your Land Rover to haul it."

"Sounds like a plan. Papa Tom's Uber Service, open for business."

After a stop with more hugs with Louise Donnegan, the three made their way out onto the lanai and its spectacular view of Pearl Harbor. A submarine was making its way past Ford Island, outbound. Donnegan peered through his mounted telescope, told them the sub's hull number and name and its likely destination and mission. The man still clearly kept up with the comings and goings in his beloved US Navy.

They settled in with their drinks, a platter of pu-pus, and idle catch-up conversation until Tom Donnegan finally asked the question they all knew was coming.

"How did that whole China thing turn out?"

Jon Ward took the lead. Papa Tom may have retired, but he still held his clearance status and was often consulted, not just by Jon, his successor, but others throughout naval intelligence.

"Looks like the Chinese are pulling back, pretty much with their tails between their legs. The three remaining subs are steaming on the surface, northbound. They should be some-where off Luzon about now. Their research ship, the *Zhang*

Jian, is being released and heading back toward Shanghai. We are holding the *Pearl Moon*, pending charges in the International Court. From all the prancing around in DC, I expect that we will probably let them go, too. It's an election year coming up, you know, so I'd say the president and the appropriate cabinet members will do whatever it takes to look good on the nightly news. And make sure nobody knows the rest of the story."

Donnegan shook his head. "Damn politicians! They could screw up a one-car funeral. Then they convince you that they need a new government agency to fix the problem."

The old spy took a healthy swig of his mai tai. "But as you now know, Jon, you got to play the political game with them if you want them to spend a few billion dollars on all those toys you need."

"I don't remember you mentioning that in the orientation when I clocked in, Papa Tom, but I soon learned the lay of the land," Jon told him.

"Far cry from driving a submarine, ain't it?" Donnegan said with a laugh. "Decide you need to go right full rudder, ahead flank, you go right full rudder, ahead flank. No need to first run it by a bunch of guys with a chest full of ribbons, three Congressional committees, or any-damn-body else." Donnegan glanced over at the younger Ward, winked, and flashed a mischievous grin. "Now, tell me more about that Chinese girlfriend of yours, Jim-boy."

Jim Ward blushed.

"Well, I did just spend ten days in a hotel room in Taipei, sometimes with her there, but to tell you the truth, Papa Tom, it's mostly a very boring story."

"Damn, boy! Here's your daddy telling me what a hard-charger you are..."

The three warriors shared a laugh and a mai tai toast to beautiful spies, hotel rooms, and very boring stories.

Meanwhile, the departing submarine down below was moving past Iroquois Point, almost to the mouth of Pearl Harbor and the wide Pacific, on her way to do her part to try to maintain peace in a very unpeaceful world.

SILENT RUNNING

The fulcrum of global power is shifting.
Is it too late to restore the balance?

Biding its time for decades, China has patiently lain in wait for its chance at global dominance. Long content to needle the West while secretly amassing intelligence, technology, and resources, the war chest is now full and the gears of the colossus are grinding into motion.

New arenas of modern battle emerge as China wages an all-out cyber assault on the West. And the more familiar tactics of brute strength play out in its bold attacks against sovereign neighbors. The scope of the Chinese menace draws the US into the melee.

But then US Naval Intelligence learns the true reasons for, and the vulnerabilities of, the Middle Kingdom's aggression.

Will the men, women, and submarines of America's Silent Service be able to hang on to a tenuous world order...or have the scales already tipped too far?

Get your copy today at Wallace-Keith.com

JOIN THE READER LIST

Never miss a new release! Sign up to receive exclusive updates from authors Wallace and Keith.

Wallace-Keith.com/Newsletter

YOU MIGHT ALSO ENJOY...

The Hunter Killer Series

Final Bearing

Dangerous Grounds

Cuban Deep

Fast Attack

Arabian Storm

Warshot

Silent Running

Hunter Killer

By George Wallace

Operation Golden Dawn

By Don Keith

In the Course of Duty

Final Patrol

War Beneath the Waves

Undersea Warrior

The Ship that Wouldn't Die

Never miss a new release! Sign up to receive exclusive updates from authors Wallace and Keith.

Wallace-Keith.com/Newsletter

ABOUT THE AUTHORS

Commander George Wallace

Commander George Wallace retired to the civilian business world in 1995, after twenty-two years of service on nuclear submarines. He served on two of Admiral Rickover's famous "Forty One for Freedom", the USS John Adams SSBN 620 and the USS Woodrow Wilson SSBN 624, during which time he made nine one-hundred-day deterrent patrols through the height of the Cold War.

Commander Wallace served as Executive Officer on the Sturgeon class nuclear attack submarine USS Spadefish, SSN 668. Spadefish and all her sisters were decommissioned during the downsizings that occurred in the 1990's. The passing of that great ship served as the inspiration for "Final Bearing."

Commander Wallace commanded the Los Angeles class nuclear attack submarine USS Houston, SSN 713 from February 1990 to August 1992. During this tour of duty that he worked extensively with the SEAL community developing SEAL/submarine tactics. Under Commander Wallace, the Houston was awarded the CIA Meritorious Unit Citation.

Commander Wallace lives with his wife, Penny, in Alexandria, Virginia.

Ψ

Don Keith

Don Keith is a native Alabamian and attended the University of Alabama in Tuscaloosa where he received his degree in broadcast and film with a double major in literature. He has won numerous awards from the Associated Press and United Press International for news writing and reporting. He is also the only person to be named *Billboard Magazine* "Radio Personality of the Year" in two formats, country and contemporary. Keith was a broadcast personality for over twenty years and also owned his own consultancy, co-owned a Mobile, Alabama, radio station, and hosted and produced several nationally syndicated radio shows.

His first novel, "The Forever Season." was published in fall 1995 to commercial and critical success. It won the Alabama Library Association's "Fiction of the Year" award in 1997. His second novel, "Wizard of the Wind," was based on Keith's years in radio. Keith next released a series of young adult/men's adventure novels co-written with Kent Wright set in stock car racing, titled "The Rolling Thunder Stock Car Racing Series." Keith has most recently published several non-fiction historical works about World War II submarine history and co-authored "The Ice Diaries" with Captain William Anderson, the second skipper of USS *Nautilus*, the world's first nuclear submarine. Captain Anderson took the submarine on her historic trip across the top of the world and through the North Pole in August 1958.

Mr. Keith lives with his wife, Charlene, in Indian Springs Village, Alabama.

You can find Wallace and Keith at
Wallace-Keith.com

Ψ

Made in the USA
Coppell, TX
14 June 2022